SOMEONE ELSE'S PUDDIN'

SOMEONE ELSE'S PUDDIN'

A novel by

Samuel L. Hair

Q-Boro Books
WWW.QBOROBOOKS.COM

An Urban Entertainment Company

Published by Q-Boro Books

Urban Books
10 Brennan Place
Deer Park, NY 11729

ISBN 0-9776247-0-6
First Printing December 2006

Printed in the United States.

10 9 8 7 6 5 4 3 2

This is a work of fiction. It is not meant to depict, portray or represent any particular real persons. All the characters, incidents and dialogues are the products of the author's imagination and are not to be construed as real. Any references or similarities to actual events, entities, real people, living or dead, or to real locales are intended to give the novel a sense of reality. Any similarity in other names, characters, entities, places and incidents is entirely coincidental.

Cover Copyright © 2005 by Q-BORO BOOKS all rights reserved
Cover Layout & Design—Candace K. Cottrell
Editors—Melissa Forbes, Candace K. Cottrell, Pittershawn Palmer

Q-BORO BOOKS
Jamaica, Queens NY 11434
WWW.QBOROBOOKS.COM

PROLOGUE

Melody's loud snores were audible throughout the house, proving that she was sound asleep. Standing at the bedroom door, the shooter aimed, fired six times at Melody's naked body, and then speedily fled the scene, leaving the front door wide open.

Hearing the gunshots, several of Melody's neighbors ran outside and scanned the street. Suddenly Patty, a white lady from across the street, spotted Melody's front door open.

"Hey, look!" Patty yelled while pointing at Melody's house. "Melody's front door is wide open! Let's make sure everything is OK!"

Patty and her husband, along with several other neighbors, moved cautiously inside Melody's house. Melinda, another neighbor, entered the bedroom and saw Melody lying naked in a pool of blood. She screamed as loudly as she could. Her husband immediately grabbed the phone and dialed 911.

CHAPTER 1

2002

It was 10:52 AM when Melody Pullman finally responded to the loud beeping of her alarm clock. Byron, her thirteen-year-old son, had attempted three times to awaken her, but like always, she rolled over and fell back asleep. Seconds later, realizing she had an appointment with a customer, she jumped out of bed and began rushing. Hurriedly, she took a forty-five second shower, threw on a pair of skin-tight jeans and a Lakers jersey, and swiftly thumbed through her appointment book. Her first appointment, which she was already late for, was at eleven o'clock. All of her appointments afterward fell into forty-five minute intervals. She was never on time to meet her customers for appointments she'd made weeks in advance. Being late was normal to her.

"Byron, get up and make you a bowl of cereal, boy," Melody shouted while putting on her earrings and makeup. "And don't waste that damn milk all over the table like you do every morning!"

"I already ate, Mom," Byron shouted from his room where he was playing *NBA Live*.

"Do you want to go with me to the shop, or do you want to

stay at Bobby's until I get off?" Melody yelled as she slipped on a pair of her son's Jordan tennis shoes.

"It's boring at the shop, Mom. I don't like hanging around a bunch of women all day, so I'll stay at Bobby's." Suddenly the phone rang. Whenever she was running late, she made it a point not to answer her telephone. Instead she looked at her caller I.D.

"Don't answer that damn phone, boy! It isn't nobody but those damn Japs from the salon or my eleven o'clock customer!" She was now scrambling herself a couple of eggs. Once the phone stopped ringing she walked over and shot a glance at the caller ID. Just as she figured, it was her eleven o'clock customer. It being eleven fifteen didn't make her move any swifter. Seconds later her pager began beeping, and her cellular phone rang.

"Goddammit! I'm getting all these numbers changed Monday! Then I won't have to worry about people trying to track me down!" She was yelling, ignoring the rings and beeps. Eating her egg sandwich, she shouted again to Byron, who was still in his bedroom. "Hurry up, boy, so I can drop you off at Bobby's and get my butt to the shop!"

"Wait a minute, Mom. Michael Jordan is about to slam on Shaq."

"I'm gonna slam your ass if you don't hurry up, boy! Hell, I'm already twenty minutes late."

"It's not my fault, Mom. I tried to wake you up three times, and you—"

"Hush your mouth and hurry the hell up, boy."

Melody was a five-foot-five, cute hunk of sexy chocolate in her mid thirties. She had an attractive pair of 38Ds, a thin waistline, and a firm, rounded butt that several preachers—and supposedly married men of God—lustfully enjoyed looking at. She was born in Los Angeles, California, and raised in the city of Compton. Her mother, Stella Swift, was a retired nurse, and her late father, Anthony Swift, had been a contractor with his own business. Even though they were financially able to buy their children just about anything, they didn't. Instead, they lived a conservative, traditional lifestyle.

When Mr. Swift passed, Mrs. Swift assumed control of the business and sold the company.

Although Melody's parents tried to raise her right, she either lost or never gained the morals and respect her parents tried to instill in her. Melody got pregnant at the age of nineteen, but when she confronted Byron's biological father, Kenneth, about her pregnancy, he didn't believe the child was his.

"Yeah right," Kenneth said. "Hell nah. Unh unh! I don't think so! You've been with four different guys in the past four months and you think I'm falling for some bullshit like this? You've gotta be crazy!"

After Byron turned two, she decided to confront Kenneth again, telling him that she would pay for a blood test. Surprisingly, Kenneth agreed.

After taking the test, Kenneth discovered that he was Byron's natural father. The fact that he originally denied his son, and wasn't there for him in the beginning somewhat bothered him, but he had promised himself he'd make it up to Byron one way or another.

Melody graduated from cosmetology school at the age of eighteen, but barely managed to earn a living. It took a while for her to discover that making it on a beautician's salary limited her ability to do things like go on vacations, get medical and dental benefits, drive new vehicles, purchase expensive furniture, and wear the jewelry and clothing she desired. Her bills were always in final notice status. If her bill was two hundred dollars, she would only put twenty to twenty-five dollars on it, just enough for them not to shut off anything. Her older brother, Tony, and her younger sister, Antoinette, stopped by her home nearly every day after work and would see final notices scattered all over her dining room table.

"I've never seen any shit like this in my life," Tony would say. "Why do you wait until your bills become final notices before you pay on them?"

"That's my goddamn business!" Melody would respond heatedly. "If you're not gonna help pay them, then shut the fuck up!"

"Girl, you have only three days before they turn off your lights, two days before your phone gets turned off, and five days before they turn off your gas," Antoinette would say as she looked at the shut-off dates. "You still have a couple weeks before they turn off your water. Sis, you sure like living on the edge, and I don't know how you do it."

"I've been doing this since I was eighteen, and believe me, I know what the hell I'm doing. I'm used to it. Everyone has their own way of doing things, you know. And anyway, y'all quit discussing my damn bills unless you're planning to help pay them. As a matter of fact, why don't y'all go on home before the lights get shut off? Y'all just come over here to be nosey," Melody would reply.

As Melody stepped into the shop that Saturday, she noticed that Linda, her eleven o'clock customer, was seated in the booth chair looking disappointed.

Melody had been employed at Special Touch Hair and Nail Company for a little over nine months. She bounced around like a bad check from salon to salon throughout her career, but due to her talent and modest prices, she managed to keep her regular customers. Her customers were always more than satisfied, which was the reason why they never asked about her relocating every six months to a year.

"I try call you five times!" Sue, the most aggressive one of the Japanese owners said to Melody as she marched up to her, pointing her index finger in Melody's direction. "Your customer here ten thirty! You no answer! You no answer! Bad business! Bad business! No more chances for you! No more! You too many times late! Too many times!"

Melody didn't like being reprimanded in a salon full of customers, but she managed to maintain her composure, ignored Sue, and made her way over to Linda.

I wish that tight-eyed bitch would mind her business. I'll be glad when I get enough money to open up my own shop. Then I won't have to worry about nobody telling me a goddamn thing. I feel like knocking the hell out of her, Melody thought.

After greeting Linda with a few pleasantries, Melody began explaining why she was late.

"I'm so sorry, girl. My son kept me up until three sump'n this morning showing me how to work that damn Internet," she lied, while beginning the procedure on Linda's hair.

The real reason she didn't make it to bed until three forty-five AM was a pint of vodka, two twenty-four ounce bottles of Heineken, and three joints.

"Girl, that Internet is something else. Anything you want to buy, find out about, or do research on, you can do it on the Internet. Now that I'm learning how to use it, I'm gonna be searching for a new husband. You know what I'm saying, girlfriend?" Melody's explanation had calmed Linda down a little.

"You'd better be careful messing around on the Internet, girlfriend," Linda advised. "Just last week on *Eyewitness News* they were talking about a woman who met a man over the Internet and moved him into her house the following week. And a few days afterward girl, she married him. Now tell me, Melody, what kind of shit is that?" Linda was very emotional toward the matter.

Linda was a twenty-seven-year-old nurse who had a body like Toni Braxton and facial features and hair that resembled Halle Berry's. She owned a new Porsche and was single with no kids. Also, she owned a two-story, four bedroom home, which had cost her a little over two hundred thousand dollars. Several doctors she dated assisted her on paying for it. A favor for a favor. Her motto was plain and simple: Use what you got to get what you want.

"And the stupid bitch put his name on her grant deed, made him co-owner of her Mercedes, and even put his name on her goddamn bank account," Linda continued. "I figure she must be extremely ugly or fat, or just have a hard time getting a man."

"Damn," Melody responded.

"The police and the FBI are looking for the man now. Girl, he cleaned out her bank account, took her Mercedes, and even got a loan off her house. Melody, if you know like I know, you'd get yourself a couple of married men who make six figures or better, then you'll be set for life. You know what I'm talking about, girlfriend? That way, there's no strings attached. And the best thing about it is that he's gotta pay to lay. Give him what he wants, you get what you want, then send him back home to his wife. Hell, you might have a bill or house note that needs paying. Or you might want a credit card in your name. Take my advice, Melody, that's what you need to be doing rather than searching for a man on the damn Internet."

All the married women who'd overheard the conversation looked at Linda with hatred and envy. None of them were surprised at what they were hearing. They all had the same thought: *I wish I would catch that bitch with my husband. I'd blow both their fucking brains out!*

The single women who were listening to Linda actually wanted to hear more. Linda could sense that, so she continued.

"And just think about it, girlfriend. What if you had three or four of them? Humph. It's all good. Yep. It's all good," Linda said, smiling and revealing even, white teeth.

"Is that how you manage to drive a Porsche, live in a quarter-million dollar home, and dress like a million bucks every day?" Melody asked as she put the last roller in Linda's hair.

"Humph. What can I say? Hell, I sure couldn't manage those type of luxuries on a nurse's salary," Linda replied seriously, then added, "We all have choices in life, girlfriend. We could choose to be poor and live in ghettos where there's nothing but a bunch of broke niggas who wanna fuck all day, or we can live in fancy homes, drive expensive cars, and, as you put it, dress like a million bucks every day of the week. It's plain and simple, girlfriend. Use what you got to get what you want." Linda was very enthusiastic during her speech.

"Otis, I saw you lookin' at that woman," an elderly woman named Ruth, who'd been waiting to get a manicure and a pedicure, said to her husband. Ruth was referring to a fine, classy-looking woman who had just walked into the salon, sporting a pair of tight jeans and a blouse that revealed her cleavage.

"I wasn't lookin' at that woman, Ruth," Otis replied, smirking. "I was jus' admirin' how good those jeans fit her."

"I'll tell you what, man, if you look at her again, my fist is gonna fit inside your goddamn mouth. And I ain't playin' either, Otis." Ruth gave him a mean look.

The dime piece Otis was ogling was named Pat. Linda's beauty or class didn't compare to Pat's in any shape, form, or fashion. Pat had a complexion that was as smooth as peanut butter and easily defied her forty years. She was blessed with a body that was totally unbelievable—a brick house without a doubt. Her attractive, slanted eyes combined perfectly with her million-dollar smile. The tight jeans she wore revealed her widespread hips and soft, rounded butt, while her blouse revealed her delicate, delicious-looking breasts. Women envied her everywhere she went—hoping, wishing, and even praying for a figure like hers.

As Pat entered the salon, she bypassed the waiting area and the manicure and pedicure section and made her way to Melody's booth. A high-yellow complexioned man, who stood about six-one, walked in with Pat, but seated himself in the waiting area. His hair was styled in a short natural, and he was wearing a pair of well-fitting jeans that revealed the length and width of his penis. That instantly attracted Melody's attention.

Humph. He's packing meat. Damn, would I like to feel his big, fat dick inside me, Melody thought.

"Hey, girlfriend," Pat said, smiling. "Did you actually get here on time this morning?"

"Not quite, girl," Melody replied. "Byron's been showing me how to use the Internet lately, and girl, I swear, that computer stuff confuses the hell out of me. You're kind of early, aren't you?"

Melody was always glad to see and converse with one of her regular customers. They were the ones who kept money in her purse.

"Yeah, girl, I've been up since five this morning and figured I'd get an early start on my things to do. And besides, today is my day and my husband has to treat me all day long to anything and everything I desire," Pat stated.

Pat continued making small talk with Melody as Melody put the final touch on Linda's hair.

"Yeah, girlfriend, today is my day. After I get my hair, nails, and feet done, he's taking me to the mall shopping, then out to dinner, then to see a movie, and if it's not too late, I'm going to have him take me to test drive a Lexus. Humph. I'm getting all I can get out of my husband today. But hell, actually, I get what I want from him everyday," Pat boasted, but Melody's mind and eyes were elsewhere, checking out her husband. Melody's curiosity got the best of her.

"Who's that you brought with you, girl?"

"That's my husband, Larry. Haven't I introduced you to him before?"

"Nope, I don't think so. I guess you've been hiding him or something."

"Humph. Nah, girl, not at all. It's not that I be hiding him, it's just that I keep him at work where he's supposed to be, you know what I mean?"

"I heard that, girl." Melody envied the hell out of Pat.

"Now she's a woman who knows what's happening," Linda interjected. "There's no way in hell that we, as women, can drive fancy cars and dress like movies stars with an unemployed man."

"I've got my husband trained, girl," Pat boasted. "Why do you think he's waiting for me like he is?"

"I heard that. You've got it going on, girlfriend. I'm trying to hip Melody to a little game, you know, but for some reason she thinks she'll find Mr. Right on the Internet," Linda said sarcastically.

Melody shot repeated glances and smiles at Larry. He responded with eyewinks and tongue gestures.

After Melody finished with Linda's hair, Linda stood up and examined herself in the mirror.

"Perfect. I love it, I love it, I love it," Linda said, satisfied. She then handed Melody a fifty-dollar bill, made another appointment for two weeks later, and said, "Don't forget what I told you, girlfriend. The sky is the limit."

As Linda exited the salon, Otis's lustful eyes slowly followed her. Using his imagination, he undressed her, wishing for younger days. The fact that his wife was getting a pedicure didn't stop her from observing her husband. After reading the look on Ruth's face, Otis quickly picked up a magazine and began looking at pictures of boats and horses, anything other than looking at Ruth.

As Melody began doing Pat's hair, she shot a quick, fleeting look at Larry. It amazed her that each time she looked at him he was looking at her. He had even winked and smiled while making those circular movements with his tongue.

So, Melody thought, *he's the Superman she's been bragging about. Humph. She must not be giving it to him right, because he sure keeps checking me out. Knowing Pat, with her selfish ways, she probably doesn't give him any head. But I'll bet she makes him eat her out. She thinks she's all that and a bag of chips with dip. On the other hand, why would a man who has a wife as fine as she is be checking out a small-time, broke beautician like me? The only thing I can do for him is give him a whole lot of pleasure. And I mean, a whole lot.*

As Larry pretended to read an *Ebony* magazine, he checked out Melody.

Damn, he thought. *Not bad. Not bad at all. And she's checking me out, too. I wouldn't mind having a piece of her. I wonder will she give me some play, or is she just playing with me? I know damn well it's not just my imagination. Why would a woman as fine as she is be checking out an old scrap man like me? They say that the blacker the berry, the sweeter the juice, and believe me, I damn sure wouldn't mind a sip of her blackberry brandy. Umph.*

After Melody led Pat to the dryer she decided to play a little cat-chase-the-mouse game to find out whether or not her instincts were right. Quickly she scribbled her home, cell, and pager number on the front of an *Ebony* magazine, then using her sexiest walk she nonchalantly strolled toward Larry. As she passed Otis, he smiled. His eyes were following her butt, but Melody's focus was on Larry.

"Would you like to check out this special edition of *Ebony?*" Melody asked Larry as she deviously handed him the magazine.

She placed her finger inches away from her contact numbers. Her presence caused Otis to grin and flash the few teeth he still had. Ruth spotted him from afar and stared him down with a killer look, but he couldn't take his eyes off Melody's butt.

"Otis!" Ruth, yelled, "don't have me come over there and knock that goddamn grin off your face!"

Both Melody and Larry smirked at the jealous old lady, but quickly diverted their attention back to each other.

"I'd better get back to my booth before your wife looks up and tells you what that old lady just told her husband," Melody said as she realized that she was being observed by another hairstylist. "I wouldn't want to get you in any trouble."

"Yeah, right. I'm the one who wears the pants in my house, not my wife."

"Humph. That's not what she said a few minutes ago. Anyway, make sure you check the front page thoroughly, especially the small print. There might be something there for you," Melody said enticingly.

"Good. I'm really into special editions, if you know what I mean," Larry said, smiling.

"Time will tell." Melody purposely dropped a pencil in front of him and bent down slowly to pick it up.

Larry enjoyed her gesture, but when Ruth spotted Otis's eyes and mouth wide open, and his hand on his crotch, she wasn't too happy.

"I'll blow your goddamn brains out, man! I've jus' about had it with you! Get your ugly, no-good ass outta here and go wait inside the car!" she yelled.

"Hell, you should'nt've ever told me to come with you. Think I s'pose to jus' keep my eyes closed. You've gotta be crazy," Otis mumbled as he stood up and walked toward the door.

As Melody made her way back to her station, she decided that she could use someone like Larry in her life. If he did half the things for her that Pat bragged about him doing, she would be a much happier woman. Melody's husband and Byron's stepfather, Big Steve, could never seem to stay out of jail for more than two months at a time. As soon as they were on a good, stable, grooving pattern of everyday lovemaking, he'd go back to jail for one reason or the other. He spent more time in jail than on the streets. But through all of the ups and downs, Melody managed to always make ends meet by improvising. She was good at that.

The thought had crossed Melody's mind on a few occasions that she needed a side hustle to keep some extra cash on hand.

Her son was a growing teenager who had very expensive taste. She tried hard, because he was her only child, to give him the things he desired. Many times, she sacrificed paying a bill to buy him tennis shoes or designer clothing. She thought seriously about going back to school to get a degree to increase her knowledge and education, but she always dismissed the thought.

How in the hell can I go to school when my house payment is $850 a month, my bills total damn-near $200 a month, and that doesn't include paying my gardener or giving Byron lunch money every day? I do need to go back to school, but who's going to take care of these damn bills? she would wonder.

CHAPTER 2

Melody & Big Steve

1999

At the age of twenty-nine, Melody met a small-time street hustler from the hood who went by the name of Big Steve Pullman. The name definitely fit him. He wore his hair in a short, neat fade, and his vocabulary consisted of nothing but street slang. He weighed a little over four hundred pounds, stood six feet three and a half inches, and had a light brown complexion and a head that seemed too small for his huge body.

Big Steve was an only child and had been spoiled rotten his entire life. While he was growing up, his parents had provided him with the best that money could buy. Other kids envied him because of the things he had, but they would still come over to play with his toys, which their parents couldn't afford. For instance, the average kid had Hot Wheels sets, but little Stevie had Hot Wheels sets, electric train sets, remote control cars and airplanes, and huge, 4x4 remote controlled trucks. When the other kids in the neighborhood rode regular bikes, little Stevie had dirt bikes, ten-speeds, and mountain bikes, and once he was old enough, his father purchased him a go-cart and a mini-bike.

Stevie's shoes were purchased at malls—Foot Locker and other expensive shoe outlets—while the other kids in the neighborhood wore shoes bought at Payless, Wal-Mart, K-Mart, and swap meets. His parents felt that since he was their only child, they would provide him with all the things they didn't have as children.

The convertible Mustang Steve owned had been purchased for him as a high school graduation present when he made it to the tenth grade, although Steve never actually completed high school. Even though his parents had said to him several times, "You're not driving that car until you graduate, and don't ask us about it anymore," all it ever took was for Steve to throw an outrageous tantrum, a few pouts and cries, or a sad face, and he would get what he wanted.

One day Big Steve and a few of his homeboys set forth to do a big lick (criminal act), with intentions of having a big payday. They'd gone over their plan several times before actually deciding to go through with it. The plan was to break in to a computer warehouse.

Big Steve and his boys pulled off the robbery without a hitch. Big Steve's cut out of the deal was forty-two hundred dollars. He told himself he was going to invest his money in a legit business, but actually there was only one type of business investment he was familiar with—the dope business.

The following day after the robbery, Big Steve picked up Melody to take her out.

"Let's go to Las Vegas, baby," Steve suggested. "Let's go and do the damn thang, you know what I'm sayin', baby doll? Yeah, it's all good, you know what I'm sayin'. It's all to the good."

During that time, Melody and Byron were living with her parents while she was between apartments. She asked her sister, Antoinette, to watch Byron for her and told her parents she was going to Vegas for the weekend. She didn't dare tell them she was gong with Steve, but Tony, her older brother did. Mr. Swift was furious.

"Is that girl crazy or sump'n? She must be on drugs! It seems like the more I teach her, the dumber she gets! If I would've known she was going with that no-good street nigga, I would've told her to take her son with her! I don't know what she sees in that fat, funny looking muthafucka! Every time I see him his pants are hanging off his ass! I never saw him wearing anything but those goddamn khakis and that funky-ass T-shirt! What kind of man is that? He's good for nothing! All he's doing is taking up space on earth!"

"And every time I see him he's got a damn can of beer in his hand!" Mrs. Swift added. "He came over here last week, grinnin' and carryin' on when wasn't a damn thing funny. He'd probably been smoking some of that shit or sump'n. He was sittin' and laughin' like a goddamn hyena, lookin' like a goddamn Chinese person. I've told that girl I don't want him over here anymore, but he keeps comin' over here anyway. As far as I'm concerned, Melody can keep her ass in Vegas and never come back."

While cruising down the Las Vegas strip in the Mustang, Big Steve made a suggestion to Melody.

"Let's get married, baby. I love you, you know what I'm sayin'? And I think you're my soul mate, you know what I'm sayin'? I know that God made you for me, you know what I'm sayin'? And that's what I'm sayin'. And you know what else, sweetheart? I'll make a good stepfather for Byron, that's all I'm sayin'. You know what I'm sayin'? I can give a damn what people think about us bein' together, but I'm tellin' you how I feel from my heart, you know what I'm sayin'? I'm ready to settle down and do the damn thang and do it right, you know what I'm sayin'?"

While stopped at a traffic light, he looked her in the eyes and proposed.

"Melody, will you marry me?"

Without thinking or blinking she answered. "Yes, Teddy Bear, I'll marry you. I love you, Steve. Yes, I'll be your wife."

Bypassing the casinos, Big Steve and Melody headed straight to the wedding chapel downtown and got married. During that time, the price of a Las Vegas wedding was only fifty dollars.

Afterward, he rented a room at the Circus Circle Hotel and Casino, had a brief sex session with his wife, and then they made their way to the gambling floor.

After nine hours of playing wheel of fortune, video poker, and slot machines, they'd won a little over eleven thousand dollars. Steve handed Melody all of their winnings.

"Thank you for being my wife, Mel. I'll love you and cherish you till the day I die. And I promise never to cheat on you." He then gave her a big, wet kiss.

As they cruised down Interstate 15 southbound, headed home, out of the blue Melody reached over, unzipped Big Steve's pants, and leaned over, giving him a wedding present he'd never forget. While climaxing, he shut his eyes momentarily, which caused him to almost run into the back of a big rig.

"Damn, baby, that was good. Can I have this type of treatment every day of the week?"

"You're my husband, aren't you?"

"Yeah, I am, but you know how y'all women get sometimes. Y'all get in those sometimey moods, you know what I'm sayin'? Sometimes y'all act like bitches, and sometimes ya'll act real sweet. Especially when y'all want sump'n."

"As long as you honor your wedding vows, Teddy Bear, I'll always respect you and treat you like a king, giving you everything you want and more than you can handle," she replied, stroking his short erection.

A few hours later, still on Interstate 15, Big Steve came up with another suggestion.

"You know sump'n, baby? I think we need to do sump'n with this money, you know what I'm sayin'? It ain't everyday that people run across a lump sum like this, you know what I'm sayin'? And I don't want to have to go out and commit no crimes if we get broke, but you know I will if I have to, baby. But what I really think we need to do is buy us a house. That way we can raise Byron and do like the white folks do it, you know what I'm sayin'? Live happily ever after in harmony, you know what I'm sayin'?"

She lit a cigarette, inhaled, then exhaled.

"That sounds good, Teddy Bear, but how are we supposed to buy a house with fifteen thousand dollars? Keep in mind that I'm the only one working, and it's not like I'm on salary or receive a check every week or month. No customers, no money, bottom line. And besides, we don't have furniture, you don't have a job, and we only have one car. We need to prepare ourselves for a big move like that."

He wouldn't accept no for an answer.

"Check it out, Mel. I'll get a job and get my hustle on, you know what I'm sayin'? A few of my homeboys told me about a city in Riverside called Moreno Valley. They told me that a person could buy a house out there for little or nothing, you know what I'm sayin'? My homeboy Ant-Dog bought him a crib out there, and he only put three Gs down. And my homeboy, Crazy T bought him a pad out there with a swimmin' pool and only put down two Gs. We can do the damn thang, Mel; I know we can. We deserve it, baby doll, and we owe it to ourselves. All we gotta do is make that first move and everything else will fall in place."

"Of course we deserve it, Teddy Bear, but the question is, can we afford it?"

"I told you, baby, I'll do what I gotta do to make ends meet, you know what I'm sayin'? We're married now and we aren't boyfriend and girlfriend no more, so we got to make shit happen. Don't you see, Mel, this is our chance to show we capable of handlin' our business as responsible adults. If we don't do it now, we might not ever get the chance to do it again. So let's do the damn thang. You know I'm about the cabbage, baby, that mean green, you know what I'm sayin'? And trust me, Mel, we can do it, and we can damn sho' make it work, one way or the other."

He persuaded her to at least go and check things out. Instead of taking Highway 60 westbound to L.A., he took the 215 southbound turnoff to Highway 60, making his way to Moreno Valley. He exited at Fredricks Street, and continued going east onto Sunnymead Boulevard. He then turned into the Roadside Inn. Before getting out of the car, they had a brief conversation.

"Damn. I'm pooped and worn out from all that damn driving, baby. Let's go inside and get a good night's sleep, and first thing in the mornin', we can start checkin' things out, you know what I'm sayin'?"

"Oh, hell no, Steve. It's our wedding night and you're talking about going to sleep? Are you serious? This is supposed to be the biggest night of our life, Steve. And I'll tell you something else that you're not aware of. I'ma nympho, and I love to fuck, OK? And I'm not down with quickies. I'm an all-night woman, so you better get used to it."

"Well, baby, I guess you married the right man," Steve replied, surprised and impressed with his new wife, "'cause I'm a' all-night man, too, you know what I'm sayin'? Let's go ahead and pay for the room, then walk across the street to the liquor store. Then we'll come back and get our drink on, and get our groove on, you know what I'm sayin'? We're gonna see who the real all-night person is, 'cause personally, baby, I don't think you can hang with me. We're gonna do the damn thang all night long to the break of dawn, you know what I'm sayin'?"

The following morning at twenty of eleven, Big Steve rolled over and glanced at the clock. It had been a long night of getting loaded and having sex.

They'd celebrated with a fifth of Hennessey, a twelve pack of Heineken, a pint of Alize, and a fifty-dollar bag of chronic.

With Melody being a drinker and a nympho, their wedding night was all good to Steve.

"Damn!" he said. "We've messed around and overslept!" He began shaking Melody. "Get up, sweetheart. We gotta go. It's almost checkout time. We gotta go check out some houses. Get up!"

She rolled over and stared at him with reddened eyes.

"Five more minutes, Teddy Bear. I've got a migraine headache. Just five more minutes, please. Five more minutes."

"Get up, Mel, come on. We gotta go, baby. Let's go take care of our business, and then we'll get another room and kick back afterward, OK? Get up," he begged, which irritated the hell out of her.

"Damn!" she yelled. "I'm not a morning person, Steve. Shit! I don't usually get up until noon, so don't be waking me up this early anymore." She eased out of bed. "And hell, you don't even know where we're going."

Big Steve smiled, standing next to the door.

"I've got it all figured out, Mel, you know what I'm sayin'? A man like me be thinkin' 'bout things way ahead of time. You see, baby doll, some men do what they wanna do, while other men only do what they can. I'm one of those fortunate niggas who do what they wanna do, you know what I'm sayin'? I think you should be grateful to have a husband like me. First, we'll get a newspaper, then we'll go to a couple of those real estate places that will connect us with a little sump'n sump'n, you know what I'm sayin'? It ain't like we're broke and beggin'. I feel sump'n good is gonna happen for us today, Mel. Like James Brown said, 'I got the feeling.' Now hurry and get dressed before I jump back in bed and put this thang on you again."

After grabbing a couple of Breakfast Jacks from Jack-in-the-Box, the newlyweds cruised with the convertible top down through Moreno Valley. They both were sporting a pair of Ray-Ban sunglasses. Melody was enjoying the scenery and the ride, but she was not too enthused by the thought of relocating into a neighborhood of whites, Mexicans, and Asians. She'd watched movies like *Mississippi Burning* and *White Lie*, starring Gregory Hines, and she felt that white folks still had hatred toward blacks.

As Steve made a right turn onto Indian Boulevard, he and Melody observed with excitement and admiration the newly built tract-homes, modern looking shopping centers, and the many interracial couples. Melody enjoyed the fact that no thugs, bums, or drug dealers infested the streets—at least not so far. Big Steve enjoyed the thought of owning his own home without the help of his parents, and living in a decent, peaceful, middle-class environment. His father had told him periodically, "You'll never be your own man! You expect everything to be handed to you on a silver platter, and that's not how it goes, Son. I'm sorry, but I can't allow you to sit around here all day with a remote in your hand, eat up all my goddamn food, run my utility bills up, and provide you with gas money for a car that I bought for you. You've had your free ride, Steve, but this shit has got to come to an end."

Steve turned into the parking lot of a liquor store called Mel's and parked.

"It's not like Compton, South Central, Inglewood, or Watts out here, baby. It kinda reminds me of a baby heaven or sump'n, you know what I'm sayin'? This is us, Mel. We gotta be a part of this community. We belong here, and I'm gonna do everything in my power to see to it that we live out here," Big Steve said.

They walked in the store, grabbed a newspaper and a real estate guide, and then returned to the car. While Big Steve was checking out the people entering and exiting the store, Melody jotted down a few phone numbers to nearby realtors.

"Sweetheart," she said, "I'm about to call a couple of these real estate companies that are advertising homes for two to three thousand dollars down."

She stepped out of the car to use the pay phone. The receptionist who answered informed Melody that their company had many homes for sale. She also informed her about the numerous two-bedroom duplexes and apartments that were available. After that Melody wrote down the directions to the company's building and the name of the receptionist, then hung up. After getting back inside the car, she wasted no time relaying the information to her husband.

"You see, baby? I told you, I told you! We need to check out Ant Dog and Crazy T so they can show us around, you know what I'm sayin', and we can—"

"We're not checking out no damn Ant-Dog, Crazy T, or any of those so-called gangster, drug-dealer buddies of yours! I've had enough of those kinds of people in Compton. If we do decide to move out here, Steve, you're not going to be hanging on any corners with those lowlifes, and they're damn sure not coming to my house," she stated matter-of-factly. "Are we clear on that before we proceed any further, Steve?"

"Yeah, baby, I hear you. As jealous as I am, ain't no way in hell I'm gonna invite any man to my house. The next thing you know, those fools will be comin' over when I'm not home, tryin' to get in your panties, you know what I'm sayin', and then I'll have to kill a nigga over you, girl."

As they stepped into the company called Reality Executives, a blond, Caucasian receptionist, who appeared to be in her mid-twenties, greeted them.

"Hi," she said, smiling, and then walked from behind the counter and shook their hands.

"Hello," Melody said. "Glad to meet you. I'm Mrs. Pullman and this is my husband, Steve." Melody tried hard to be professional and intelligent. She was so used to being herself and dealing with ghetto people, she'd almost forgotten how to act classy.

"It's a pleasure meeting both of you, Mr. and Mrs. Pullman.

And thank you for choosing Reality Executives. My name is Nadine. How may I help you?"

Big Steve took over at that point.

"We got thirteen Gs, you know what I'm sayin', and—"

"Steve!" Melody interrupted. "Please excuse my husband, Nadine, but he's still kind of excited about us just getting married, and he's even more excited about trying to buy a home."

Nadine smiled. "That's OK, I totally understand. It happens every day of the week, so I'm used to it."

As Big Steve stared into Nadine's eyes, they appeared to change colors at least five times, causing him to stare even harder. He was hypnotized until Melody began talking.

"We're seriously thinking about buying a home if the down payment and monthly payments are reasonable and don't exceed our budget."

Amazed by the words coming from his wife's mouth, Big Steve glanced at her, shocked, but smiled proudly at her intelligence. Since they'd been together, he'd only heard her speak in Ebonics and street slang. He had never witnessed her holding an intellectual conversation or speaking in a business-like manner to anyone. Smiling, Nadine handed them applications.

"Please be seated, Mr. and Mrs. Pullman, and please complete these applications. By the time you've finished, someone will be with you. Oh, and by the way, congratulations and good luck on your marriage." She then returned to her desk.

Big Steve did not have the slightest idea of how to fill out an application. The only part he understood was where it asked him for his name and address. For five long minutes he studied the part that read "SS#," but he couldn't figure out what it meant. Frustrated, he asked Melody for help.

"Baby, what does this S.S.# bullshit mean?"

"Social Security number, honey," Melody calmly answered while continuing to fill out her application.

"Baby, what does this D.L.N. bullshit mean? Hell, I'm a hustler, you know what I'm sayin'? I ain't no goddamn rocket scientist. I'm jus' gonna let you fill this shit out, 'cause I ain't got time for all this spellin' and addin' and subtractin' and shit, you know what I'm sayin? Hell, we jus' tryin' to buy a goddamn house, not fill out papers to move into the fuckin' White House, you know what I'm sayin'?" He was extremely annoyed by not being able to spell or understand what was on the application.

"Driver's license number, honey," Melody coolly answered. "D.L.N. means driver's license number. Here, why don't you look at some of the homes inside this magazine while I fill out our applications, OK?"

"Check this out, baby. Ooh! Look! This one has a Jacuzzi!" Steve said excitedly after a couple minutes into turning the pages of the home guide magazine. He was more excited than a prisoner getting laid for the first time in thirty years. Melody took a quick glance at the home.

"Calm down before you give yourself a heart attack, Teddy Bear."

As she continued filling out the applications, Big Steve jumped up from his chair and rushed over to Nadine's desk.

"How much is this one? This one right here! We got thirteen Gs and—"

"Steve!" Melody shouted, embarrassed and perplexed. Regaining her composure, she said, "I apologize for yelling at you, honey, but you're getting out of control. The prices of the homes are advertised right underneath the pictures. Nadine has lots of work to do, Steve, which is why she called an agent to assist us. Now please, calm down, Teddy Bear. Please."

Mumbling like a kid who couldn't have his way, Big Steve made his way back to his seat and began thinking.

Hell, I've been wheelin' and dealin' on the streets since I was in the eighth grade. One thing I do know how to do is use my mouthpiece to get what I want. Hell, I remember when I talked that car salesman into givin' me that Pinto for five hundred when he was askin' seven-fifty for it at first. And I remember when I talked that dude down who was tryin' to sell me that VCR, from fifty dollars to twenty dollars. And to top it off, I remember when that fool on the corner was tryin' to sell me a Sony Walkman and a fan for twenty dollars, and I talked him down to fifteen. So basically, I consider myself a negotiator, you know what I'm sayin'? Hell, a nigga like me can talk the Pope out of his hat, Big Steve thought, sitting back with his finger on his chin in deep thought.

A tall, Caucasian man wearing a light blue suit appeared and introduced himself.

"Hi. I'm Stan Burrows," the man said, offering a handshake.

Big Steve and Melody stood up and introduced themselves, accepting his firm, professional handshake. After the pleasantries were complete, Mr. Burrows led them to his office.

His office was huge and furnished in attractive oak and soft leather. There were several types of licenses along with certificates and awards neatly hanging on his wall of fame. On Mr. Burrows's L-shaped desk sat an IBM computer, a fax machine, and a color printer. The oak parquet flooring shined like a mirror.

"Have a seat Mr. and Mrs. Pullman," Mr. Burrows said, smiling. He then seated himself and began studying their applications. Melody and Steve sat and waited impatiently for the realtor to speak. After a few seconds had passed, Big Steve couldn't hold his tongue any longer.

"Check it out, ah, Mr. Ah, Mr. Stan Burrows. Me and my wife got thirteen Gs, you know what I'm sayin', and we—"

"Excuse me, Mr. Burrows," Melody interrupted, "but if you will please excuse my husband. He's still kind of excited about us just getting married and he's even more thrilled about the idea of us trying to buy our first home."

"It's OK, Mrs. Pullman," Mr. Burrows smiled and replied. "This happens about ten times a week. Believe me, I'm used to it."

Big Steve interrupted again.

"Did one of my homeboys come here named Ant-Dog? Or maybe you remember Crazy T, 'cause he bought a house out here too. They told me that a cool white dude hooked 'em up with a cooool crib, and only charged 'em two Gs down, you know what I'm sayin'? Me and my baby lookin' for that same kind of action, Mr. Burrows, that's all I'm sayin'."

The realtor smiled at Big Steve. "I like you, Mr. Pullman. You appear to be a man who speaks his mind. I'll tell you what, how's your credit?"

The question caught Big Steve completely off guard, but he managed to answer. "Credit? Man, I pay cash money for what I want, you know what I'm sayin'? I don't like owin' nobody nothin'. But let me see, ah, I paid the homey, Bo-Bo, 'cause I owed him one fifty. And I paid the homey named Bullet, 'cause I owed him two hundred, but yeah, Mr. Burrows, I guess my credit is cool, 'cause I don't owe nobody, you know what I'm sayin'?"

Melody sat staring at him like he was from another planet. She was totally embarrassed but, after all, he was her husband and she loved him, even though he was uneducated and ghet-tofied.

Mr. Burrows spoke up. "No charge cards, huh?"

Big Steve shook his head. "Unh-unh."

"No outstanding phone or medical bills, huh?"

"Nah, man, I ain't got no medical bills. Hell, every time sump'n wrong with me, I go to the county hospital, you know what I'm sayin'? And man, that place be crowded as hell, you know what I mean? But it's free."

Melody shook her head in disgust. She was trying to keep her cool, but couldn't any longer.

"Mr. Burrows, like I said, please excuse my husband."

"It's quite all right, Mrs. Pullman. Your husband has a keen sense of humor."

When Mr. Burrows was done looking over their applications and interviewing them, Big Steve spoke up again.

"Show him the green, baby, show him the green. The man wants to see the green. Ain't you ever heard of the sayin', 'no money, no honey'? This is the same thing, Mel, but we jus' dealin' with houses instead of other shit, you know what I'm sayin'? Money makes the world go 'round and nobody can't do a damn thing without it. Hell, people need money to wipe their ass, 'cause you gotta buy toilet paper, right? You need money to pay your bills, to put gas in your car, to buy food and clothes and—"

"Steve! Please! Calm down and let Mr. Burrows finish saying what he has to say," Melody said, offended by her husband's behavior.

Mr. Burrows stood up, paced around his office, then stared at the newlyweds.

"I kind of like your style, Mr. Pullman, but actually, I think your wife's kind of fed up with you." Big Steve smiled.

"She'll be OK when you give us the keys to our new house, you know what I'm sayin'?"

"So much for the comedy," Mr. Burrows said. "Now let's get back to business. So, you guys are willing to put down thirteen K, right?"

"Ain't nobody said nothin' 'bout no thirteen K, man," Big Steve said as he stood up. "I said thirteen Gs, Mr. Real Estate Man." He was insulted by the realtor's statement.

"I take it that thirteen Gs is probably the same as thirteen thousand."

"Yeah, man, but what the hell are you talking 'bout, thirteen K?" Big Steve asked.

"Thirteen K, Mr. Pullman, is the same as thirteen thousand," the realtor replied.

"You gotta talk to me in ghetto terms, you know what I'm sayin'? Hell, I'm straight out of Compton, and I ain't never heard of no goddamn thirteen K."

"Steve!" Melody shouted, elbowing him in the side.

"Let me handle this, baby. This is a man's job, you know what I'm sayin'?" He turned to Mr. Burrows. "Check it out, man. You think we can put down twelve Gs instead of thirteen? 'Cause I jus' remembered that I got a little investment to make. I got to keep the cabbage flowin', you know what I'm sayin'?" The realtor smiled again.

"You're quite a character, Mr. Pullman. You're one of those Richard Pryor, Eddie Murphy type guys, you know? One day you might even consider having your own television show. I'm more than sure it will be a success."

"Just like you said a while ago, Mr. Real Estate Man. Let's get back to business." He didn't think the realtor's comment was funny at all.

After completing the necessary paperwork to get the deal started, Mr. Burrows took them to look at a few available homes. Big Steve was only interested in one. It was a huge, three-bedroom home on a corner lot, which had a barbecue area, a Jacuzzi, and a swimming pool. This was a dream home to Big Steve. It was also something that would make his parents proud of him.

After they were done, Mr. Burrows instructed them to call him at noon on Monday, and at that time he'd let them know whether or not their offer was accepted.

On Monday a little after noon, Melody made the call to the realtor. Mr. Burrows gave them the green light to bring in the money and to pick up the keys. The home was theirs. Big Steve felt like he was sitting on top of the world. He prided himself for coming up with the idea of purchasing a home, and gave himself all the credit.

Their new home was built on a cul-de-sac. There were only eight other homes on the block. They were all two-stories and recently built. The neighbors were working-class people who worked hard for what they had.

Due to Melody's expertise and experience in styling hair, it took no time for her to find employment. Big Steve's days were spent lounging around the house with a remote, watching talk shows, Court TV, and *SportsCenter*, but Melody would always come home after work, bitching.

"Steve!" she would shout, with her hands on her hips,

"you've been here all goddamn day and haven't done a damn thing around this house but make a damn mess! I work six long hours a day, and you don't even have the consideration to wash dishes, vacuum, take out the trash, or even water the damn lawn. Now tell me, Steve, what kind of shit is that?"

"Damn, Mel, I jus' woke up not too long ago. Don't start your bitchin' today, 'cause I ain't in the mood for that shit," Steve would answer while lying on the sofa eating snacks and an assortment of other junk foods.

"When we got married, Steve, we agreed to pay the house note and bills together, but all you're doing is making things harder and worse on me. I'm getting sick and tired of carrying the whole load by myself."

"Mel, you know goddamn well I've been looking for a job 'cause you're the one who fills out the applications for me, so it's not like I'm not tryin'. I can't make those white folks give me a damn job. What am I s'pose to do, call 'em and cuss 'em out 'cause they won't hire me?" Afterward he would shower her with hugs and kisses and one thing would lead to another.

Most days Melody left Steve ten dollars for gas money, but like most alcoholics and drug addicts, he would take the money and buy himself a cheap beer and a bag of marijuana. Then, once the effects of the alcohol and drugs kicked in, he would say out loud, "Fuck a job! Ain't no way in hell I'm gonna accept a fuckin' six- or seven-dollars-an-hour job! Hell, I'm Big Steve, and I'm worth way more than that. A company has to at least pay me ten, eleven, or twelve dollars an hour before I even think about workin'. Fuck that!" He would then go hang out with other jobless men.

The truth of the matter was, no education, no intelligence, no skills, no vocabulary, no determination, and on top of that, being a high school dropout, equaled zero. Zero plus zero leaves zero.

I ain't no nine to five man, Steve would think. I'm a 24/7 man. A man like me makes money all around the clock, you know what I'm sayin'? That's it and that's all. I was born to live large, to shine, to slam Cadillac doors, to wear and drive the best of the best, and to stand out among others. Yeah, that's right. I'm gonna be the man around this place in a little while. Everybody in Riverside County is gonna know who Big Steve is. Yeah.

Over the next few months things were still the same in the Pullman residence. With Big Steve's daily itinerary not changing, Melody initiated heated arguments each day she came home from work. His hugs, kisses, sex, and kind words did not work any longer.

"Steve, I need money to pay these damn bills and the house note, and an extra job to feed you! I love you true enough, but I can do bad all by myself, if you know what I mean. Besides, I'm tired of having sex with a broke ass man. I'm fed up, Steve, and I've been giving you the benefit of the doubt because you're my husband, but you haven't done a damn thing to make our living arrangements any better. I don't give a damn about how good you fuck or how good you eat pussy, because none of that is paying the bills around here." She was serious, direct, and firm.

"You wasn't sayin' all that shit when I was givin' you all my money and buyin' you everything you wanted," Big Steve would say defensively. "Hell no you wasn't, was you? But when I'm down on my luck and broke, you wanna talk that bullshit. What happened to for better or for worse, through thick and thin, and for rich or for poor? Don't those words mean anything to you, Mel?"

"Not when you're sitting on your ass and not even trying!"

"Goddammit, I'm tired of your bitchin'!"

"Oh, now you're calling me a bitch?"

"If I called you a bitch, you'd know it."

"You did call me a bitch! You said you were tired of me bitching, so you called me a bitch!"

"Shut the fuck up, Mel, and listen. You know goddamn well

that all I got to do is ask my parents for money and they'll give it to me, so quit trippin'. I've got everything covered."

"That's what's wrong with your spoiled ass! But it's not your fault, it's your mama and daddy's fault from spoiling you and always giving you what you wanted!"

"Yeah, and you didn't bother turning anything down they gave us, did you? Fuck you!" he shouted, and then stormed out the door, jumped in his the car, and sped off.

In every nice, middle-class city where citizens work hard to make a decent living and try to raise their children the right way, there are always those people who infest the neighborhood with drugs, alcohol, and the crimes that lifestyle creates. Big Steve met a few of these types of people. He drove to an area in Moreno Valley called Edgemont to meet a particular drug dealer who went by the name of Pork Chop.

Pork Chop was reputed to be "The Man" in Moreno Valley as far as drugs were concerned. His business consisted of selling large and small amounts of crack, heroin, marijuana, PCP, and crystal meth. Even though Pork Chop had the money to build shopping centers, expensive homes, and open a few car dealerships, he didn't have the intelligence, reasoning, or the education to operate or maintain such businesses. Basically, he was only capable of purchasing drugs in bulk for a good price and selling them in the ghettos for a large profit. He was satisfied with that.

Big Steve met Pork Chop at a car wash, but had seen him many times driving his Cadillac, his Corvette, his Benz, or his Suburban, and, on a few occasions, Pork Chop was cruising down the streets on his three-wheeler Harley. Pork Chop had offered Big Steve a job selling drugs, but Steve always turned him down.

"No thanks, man. I'm cool on that. I'm tryin' to go legit and find me a job so I can do things right and legal, you know what I'm sayin', 'cause I got a family and I don't need to be in nobody's jailhouse, you know what I'm sayin'? But if times ever get hard and those white folks won't give me a job, I'll look you up."

Big Steve's mind was now made up and he was ready to make some money—some real big money whether it was illegal or not. It was time for him to turn rags into riches and be "The Man."

If Pork Chop can be "The Man," I can too, Steve told himself.

He drove to the end of the block and spotted Pork Chop's Suburban. He parked, hopped out of his car, and approached the crowd of thugs that Pork Chop was among. At that moment, Pork Chop was kneeling down shooting dice.

"What's up, Pork Chop?" Big Steve asked while standing over the dice game.

Pork Chop shot a quick glance at him, threw the dice, and then replied.

"Chillin', homey, jus' chillin'. What's on your mind, big man?"

"I'm ready to do the damn thang, man, you know what I'm sayin'? Those white folks won't give me a job, and I'm tired of my wife bitchin' about bills and the house note. I need to get paid in a real way, you know what I'm sayin', Pork Chop?"

"You sure you wanna do this, homey?" Pork Chop asked, rolling the dice.

"I wanna be in it to win it, Pork Chop. My back is against the wall right now, and I gotta do what I gotta do," Big Steve explained.

"Follow me, homey," Pork Chop replied after scooping up his winnings. "I need to holler at you a minute." He then led Steve to an alley and stopped at a black Suburban with tinted windows and twenty-four-inch, gold-spoked rims.

Pork Chop stood five-five with a jet-black complexion and a pair of dark red eyes. He wore his hair in a long Jheri curl, and had a pair of big lips. The only thing that allowed him to get laid was his money. He wasn't just ghetto-rich, he was worth well over a million dollars—cash. He chose to hang out in the ghettos since that's where he'd made his fortune. His business was a 24/7 operation. He didn't believe in banks, so he kept his money buried in various spots in his mother's backyard. His everyday attire consisted of khakis, a T-shirt, and a pair of Chuck Taylor tennis shoes. He wore more gold than Mr. T, and even had three gold teeth. The money he made was unbelievable. After being in the dope game for eleven years, fortunately, he'd never been caught.

After lifting the hatchback of the Suburban, Pork Chop fired up a joint.

"You seem like a good dude, homey. Even though I don't know you, I'm gonna trust you with my products, which means I'm trustin' you with my money," Pork Chop said, and then pointed inside the Suburban. "See what's in there?" He was referring to artillery—a .44 Magnum, an Uzi, four 9 millimeters, and three AK-47s. "If you try to do me, homey, I'm gonna do you. I've got a rep for torturin' fools who try to do me. So don't get caught up in the mix and fuck yours off." He then passed Big Steve the joint.

"Man, you ain't gotta worry about me doing nothin' stupid, Pork Chop. I got a wife, a son, and a house, you know what I'm sayin'? And I got too much to lose to be going out backward. If anything, cuzz, I'm jus' tryin' to get ahead and have the finer things in life like you, you know what I'm sayin'? Trust me, Pork Chop, I won't let you down. If anything, I'll add to your riches and make your pockets fatter, you know what I'm sayin'?"

"I kinda like you, cuzz. You seem different than the rest of those niggas. Check it out, man, I could use a cold glass of water. Let's bounce over to your spot so I can check you out and see how we're gonna handle this business."

Pork Chop's main objective was to find out where Big Steve lived and to get an idea of what kind of person he was. He had heard the wife and kids story from others in the past. Unfortunately, the ones who'd used it were found in parks, at lakes, and on roadsides—dead. They had all been full of shit and had tried to diminish Pork Chop's riches. They were where they belonged as far as Pork Chop was concerned.

After checking out Big Steve's residence and seeing that he was a family man, Pork Chop fronted him an ounce of cocaine with a brief speech, then left.

A few months earlier when Big Steve was at the unemployment office, he met a streetwise dope fiend named Richard. During the short time they were there, they made small talk about the streets, whores, drugs, and bullshit, and afterward they exchanged phone numbers.

"I'll see you out there one day, homey," Richard said.

"For sure," Big Steve replied, and then added, "maybe we can make some money together, you know what I'm sayin'?"

"That's right up my alley, man. Jus' holler at me and let me know what's up. You got my digits, and I'm 24/7, and always ready to make sump'n happen," Richard said.

As Big Steve drove toward the 60 freeway, he began thinking. *I'm gonna be the man. Yep, Pork Chop ain't gonna have shit on me. Everybody is gonna know who I am. I'm gonna be bigger than life. Yeah, livin' large like movie stars, and drivin' Benzes, Beamers, or betta'. I'm 'bout to go pick up this dude, Richard, and we fixin' to make a whole lotta green. I'm gonna be the man.*

Twenty minutes after Steve made the call to Richard, he was parked in front of his house, honking. The house that Richard lived in was vacant. Sometimes the next-door neighbor allowed Richard to receive and make phone calls at his home.

Richard was tall and skinny and had a dark brown complexion. He stood six-one and was lacking most of his upper teeth, and the few he did have were rotten. When he spoke, his mouth resembled a walrus, or Bugs Bunny, but somehow he managed to eat apples all the time. He knew just how to bite them.

Richard had lived in Riverside County for twenty-four years, and he knew where all of the drug-infested areas were. He was in his late forties and had been a drug addict since high school. He enjoyed the life he lived, and would do almost anything to earn a nickel, dime, quarter, or any amount of money that would help him get a cheap can of beer or a hit of crack. Some days he panhandled at liquor stores and gas stations, and other days he stood by the freeway exits holding a sign reading: "Will work for food. U.S. Veteran. Homeless. Please help me. God will bless you forever. Give to the needy not the greedy."

Once Richard climbed inside the car, he greeted Big Steve.

"What's up, big homey?"

"What's up, my nigga? Jus' tryin' to make a dollar outta fifteen cents, you know what I'm sayin'? I got some product, man. Where's a good spot we can sell some?" Big Steve asked, flashing the ounce of crack. It was a huge rock wrapped in a plastic bag.

"You ain't sayin' nothin' but a word, Steve. We'll sell all this shit in a couple hours," Richard said excitedly. The panhandling business had been slow lately, and it had been a couple days since Richard had last taken a hit. His face glowed with eagerness as he instructed Big Steve.

"Go to the corner and make a right."

Fifteen minutes later they were on University Boulevard, which was one of the main streets in Downtown Riverside. It was known as "The U."

As Big Steve cruised down The U, he noticed it was populated by dope fiends, homeless people pushing carts, prostitutes flagging down johns, and crackheads walking up and down the street looking on the ground for whatever they could find. As he drove further, he observed people lying on bus stop benches, and wannabe-tough guys and gang bangers, strolling both sides of the street like they owned it.

"Cop a park in the Church's Chicken parkin' lot so we can break down the chunk to nickels, dimes, and twenty dollar pieces," Richard told Steve.

"Cool," Big Steve replied. "Damn, man, it looks like Downtown L.A. around here. This is some way out shit, man. Damn." Richard proudly defended his stomping ground. "But this is where the money is, man. Niggas have gotten rich down here overnight." After they broke down the huge chunk into smaller, more sellable pieces, Richard made another suggestion.

"Let me fire up a piece so I can check it out. I gotta make sure this shit is good. That way we don't have to worry about people tryin' to run games on us sayin' it's bunk." Richard then pulled a car antenna from his back pocket, which he'd made into a crack pipe, and held it, impatiently waiting for a test hit.

"Don't trip out on me, homey," Big Steve said. "We're s'pose to be makin' money, not smokin' it.

"Listen, man, I gotta check this shit out, 'cause what if—"

"Go ahead and handle your business, man, 'cause I'm ready to make some of that green out there, you know what I'm sayin'?" Big Steve said, eager to get business started.

After Richard took a hit he began looking around, paranoid. His eyes grew twice their normal size. He sat there completely frozen for a few moments, like he was under a spell. Big Steve got irritated.

"Snap out of it, man. Look at you, Richard, you can't even talk, man. Come on, homey, snap out of it." Richard continued looking around wild-eyed and paranoid.

"What's up, man?" Big Steve was now angry.

"Oh, all right. I'm cool, man. I'm straight," Richard replied, still paranoid. "I 'poligize, man, but this shit got me trippin'. Man, this is some bomb shit, man. I mean some bomb shit. We ain't gonna have no problem gettin' rid of this at all. Let me go put the word out, and I'll be right back." Richard got out of the car, looked around, and then made his way down the street.

"I'll be inside the chicken stand gettin' a bite to eat. Go handle your business, man, and bring me some sales." Big Steve watched Richard approach a group of dope fiends, and then he went inside Church's Chicken.

After entering, Big Steve glanced out the window at the stray dogs and cats prowling the street, the prostitutes, the cart push-ers transporting their life savings, and the bums eating out of garbage cans.

Damn. I don't ever wanna have to live like that, Big Steve thought. *That's a goddamn shame.* He ordered an eight-piece bucket of chicken and sat at an empty table.

Meanwhile, Richard was doing an outstanding job finding customers, decreasing the crack count, and making Big Steve's pockets fatter.

Later that night, Big Steve was down to one dime piece of crack. Eager to smoke it, Richard spoke up with a hint of des-peration.

"Let me have it, man. I need a hit bad. Come on, man, I wanna go get my freak on with one of those whores."

Thankful for Richards's salesmanship, Big Steve gave him the dime-piece, plus an additional thirty dollars.

"Here, man. Thanks for helpin' make this happen, you know what I'm sayin'? I appreciate what you did. I'll pick you up to-morrow morning about eight, all right? And hey, don't spend the money all in one place." Big Steve then left.

Although Big Steve wasn't capable of doing simple arith-metic and filling out applications, this didn't affect his ability to count money. He counted a total of eleven hundred ninety-nine dollars.

Damn. I wish all this money was mines, Steve thought, feeling good about his accomplishment, *but I got to go pay Pork Chop so I don't have to worry 'bout him puttin' a hit out on me. No tellin' what he's capable of doing.*

Later that day, just as Steve made it through the front door, Melody was already bitching.

"Where have you been? You still don't have a fucking job yet? Look at this goddamn house! Just look at! I'm sick and tired of the same old bullshit every damn day! I can do bad all by my-self! I don't need—"

"Here, baby. I love you, Mel. Thanks for stayin' by my side,"

Big Steve said, handing her $580. He then kissed her. "How you like me now, baby? I finally found me a good paying job. And guess what? I didn't even need you to fill out the application."

She stopped her bitching and wanted to ask a million questions, but decided not to ask any.

"Take it all, Mel, but I don't wanna hear your mouth about no goddamn house note, bills, food, or none of that bullshit, is that understood?"

"Yeah, baby, I hear you." She was smiling and felt at ease. "I think you deserve a treat," she said in a sexy bedroom voice. "Come on and let's take a shower together."

And that was the beginning of the rest of their relationship.

CHAPTER 3

Melody

2002

Surprisingly, a few days after she'd given Larry her contact numbers, he called her a little after midnight. He and his wife had been arguing, and like most times, she refused him sex.

One monkey don't stop no show. Where there's one who won't, there's plenty who will, he thought, then proceeded to make his booty call. He crept out of bed to the restroom, pretending to be sitting on the toilet, then quickly used his cell phone and pressed the mystery woman's buttons.

"Is this Melody?" Larry whispered while sitting on the toilet.

"Who's this?" Melody asked after taking a swallow of vodka.

"Larry."

"Heeey. I thought you'd forgot all about me." She was surprised but excited to hear his voice. Actually, she didn't think she stood a chance competing with the body and beauty Pat possessed. "What's up, sweetie? That beautiful wife of yours wouldn't give you any?"

"Sump'n like that. Are you asleep?" he whispered again.

"Nope. And the rate I'm going I probably won't make it to sleep until three, four o'clock in the morning."

"Is that right? Sounds like you're having some solo fun, huh? Where's your man?"

"In his second home, where he spends most of his time," she replied. "Why? What've you got up your sleeve? Oh, I almost forgot. You've got hang-ups so you couldn't possibly be up to anything too much." She exhaled.

"Things aren't always what they seem," he replied, trying to keep his voice to a whisper, but the conversation was getting good.

"How can I tell, 'cause you talk so swell?"

At that moment, Pat rolled over and didn't feel Larry's presence. She then called out for him.

"Larry! Laaary!"

It took him a few seconds to respond.

"Wait a minute!" he yelled to her as he covered the phone receiver, not wanting Melody to hear his conversation with his wife. "I'm on the toilet! I think I've got diarrhea from eating those damn collard greens. And Mike just called and said he was stranded in the middle of nowhere without a spare tire."

"Annnnd? Why doesn't he call his wife to come to his rescue?"

"He did, but he has the keys to both cars."

"Well," Pat said, "if you decide to go rescue him, and I know you will, be careful out there, you hear? I overheard a conversation at the salon about a bunch of gangsters from L.A. who recently moved out here and have been causing all sorts of trouble. I may be mad at you, but I wouldn't want anything to happen to you."

"Don't worry. I'll be careful," he answered. He then quickly flushed the toilet like he'd been using it. Minutes later he left.

He had stored Melody's address and directions in his memory bank, just in case he accidentally misplaced it around his house.

When he arrived at her home it was almost one thirty in the morning. She'd been waiting impatiently for him.

"Heeeey." She greeted him like she had not seen him in twenty years. After giving him a kiss on the cheek and a hug that caused her huge breasts to rub against his chest, she then led him to her bedroom. She was dressed in a white see-through negligee. She had on no panties or bra. She was excited, hot, and ready. He trailed behind her watching her butt shake like Jell-O, and wiggle like pudding.

"Damn, girl," he said, holding his crotch. "What are you gonna do with all that?"

"That depends," she replied, walking through her bedroom door. She then seated herself on the edge of the bed and fired up a joint.

"Do you smoke?" she asked.

"Do I? Baby, I put the 's' in smoke. As a matter of fact, I was about to ask you the same thing," he replied with a smile that said, *I'm gonna tear this ass up.*

After hitting the joint a few times, Melody passed it to him.

"Would you like something to drink?" she asked.

"Damn, girl, ump. The question is whether or not I want something to eat," he replied, staring at her breasts and holding his crotch.

"You're talking my kind of language, baby," Melody responded, smiling. "Make yourself at home, and I'll be right back." She went to the kitchen.

His erection had not gone down since he'd walked through her front door. While looking around and observing her bedroom, he'd come to the conclusion that a beautician's salary sucked. The bed had no frame, and the mattresses sat on the floor. The old wood grain dresser opposite the bed was missing three drawers, and the thirteen-inch color television, sitting on top of the dresser, had a clothes hanger for an antenna. The television was missing several buttons, and an old VCR sat on top of the television. Next to it, in a shoebox, were a few X-rated movies.

While fixing drinks in her kitchen, Melody thought, *Just*

what I thought. He's a dog just like the rest of 'em. This man got out of bed with his wife and told a big, boldface lie to be with me. Knowing Pat, she probably wouldn't give him any pussy. She probably told him to get off on her looks. But hell, I haven't had a dick in my bed in so long, I probably wouldn't know how to act. I know he's not mine, but hell, I need me a piece and he looks like he knows how to fuck, so I've gotta take advantage of this opportunity.

She returned minutes later carrying two glasses of vodka. While handing him one of the glasses, she seated herself next to him.

"So, what brings you to my bedroom?"

"Curiosity, baby. Simple curiosity," he replied, and then took a swallow of his vodka.

"Curiosity, huh? Well I guess that makes two of us," she responded, then lit another joint.

After a brief, "lets-get-a-little-acquainted" session, she inserted an X-rated movie into the VCR. As they lay back relaxing, the movie seemed to have their undivided attention. There was a tall, black man with a long snake-like penis being sucked and licked by two women who seemed to be enjoying their roles. Their body temperatures increased right away, reaching maximum levels.

"Ump, ump, ump. Damn," Larry said, grabbing his crotch, watching the porn stars suck the man's penis head nicely, slowly, and skillfully. The other woman was licking up and down the length of his shaft and his balls.

"Ump, ump, ump," he said again, and then took a long drag from the joint.

Melody's nipples looked hard and strong like a newly-sharpened pencil. Her pussy was flaming like hot lava. She felt like a volcano ready to erupt. She then got up and locked her bedroom door, stripped out of the negligee, approached Larry, and shamelessly unzipped his pants.

"Damn!" she said, after pulling it out and holding it in her hand. "It's so big and strong, and—"

"Isn't that how you like it, baby?" he asked after exhaling. He took another swallow of vodka.

"This thing looks like it belongs to a horse. Damn, this is the biggest dick I've ever seen in my life."

"Don't worry, sweetheart, I use it gently and easy."

He then began playing with her breasts and kissing her wildly, causing her to moan and purr. As his penis pointed in the air like a rocket ship about to take off, she leaned over and slowly began kissing it, rubbing it, slurping it, and then sucking it like she had a degree in suckology.

"Yes, uummee, oh, yes mama, ooh yes, ooh suck it, baby, damn, yes, uummee, yes," he moaned, wishing this feeling could last forever.

"Do you like that, baby?"

"Ummee, yes, ooh, damn girl, oh, hell yeah, I like it," he responded.

"How does it feel?" She talked to him while sucking.

"Good. Damn good."

"Does Pat give you head?" she asked, licking up and down his shaft and stroking it.

"Nope, ummee, yes, ooh, yes."

"Why?"

"Uummee, ooh, yes, yes. She says it's too gross and she couldn't imagine herself doing it." He continued moaning.

"She wouldn't give you any pussy tonight either, huh? Is that why you're in my bedroom, Larry?" she asked, continuing her rhythm.

"I didn't say that, you did. Ooh yes, suck it baby, suck it," he responded. His eyes were closed.

"Well, is it true?"

"Ump, ump, ump, damn. Ooh, wooo, yes, wooo, ah, ooh," Larry moaned, then yelled like a bear coming out of hibernation. "Ahwww, ooh, ahww, damn, oh, mama, woo-weee!" His thick white juice squirted all over her face, but she loved it.

After a couple minutes of recuperation, he eased up and began kissing her while twirling a couple fingers inside her wet, juicy tunnel and playing with her breasts. Her body trembled, causing her to move as if she were being electrocuted. It had been a long time since she'd felt this type of pleasure. She wished the feeling could last forever.

"Sit at the edge of the bed, lie down, relax, and put your legs over my shoulders," Larry commanded.

Melody wasted no time following his instructions. There was nothing she loved more than a man in control.

"Wait," she said, then took a quick sip of vodka, followed by a pull off the joint, and then lay back down and enjoyed the pleasures of his tongue licking and slurping her clitoris. "Uummee, ooh, oh, ooh, yes, daddy, yes, yes," she moaned in ecstasy.

No man had ever made her feel this way before. Big Steve had been an amateur pussy-licker and all the other guys she'd been with had only wanted to fuck. But this man, even though he was someone else's, knew how to make a woman scream, have multiple orgasms, and feel like a woman wanted to feel.

"Oh, God, yes, ummm, lick it, baby. Lick it, daddy, lick it. Ump, ump, ump. Lord Jesus!" Melody moaned with pleasure.

As soon as he sensed Melody was about to have another orgasm, he stopped. He then flipped her like a pancake, grabbed her butt, positioned it upward, and inserted himself inside her. He eased his fat, long penis slowly into the depths of her womb.

"Damn. Ooh, damn. God, wooo, wooo, ah, ah, ah, ah, oohh," she moaned. He eased himself in and out of her, making sure she felt the thickness and the length of it.

"Ooh, yes, yes, damn, mmm, ooh yes, fuck me. I want it all, yes." She moaned, feeling joy and pain simultaneously, and never wanting it to end. He then sped up his rhythm and began pounding, pounding, and pounding, harder and harder and deeper, developing a crazed, serious look on his face. Her screams caused him to pump even harder and faster. Suddenly, they both exploded with shouts and relief. Afterward, they lay together, making small talk while finishing their vodka and smoking a joint.

"Damn. Where did you learn that?" Melody smiled and asked.

"Self-taught, baby. Self-taught."

After they made plans to meet the following day at two PM, Larry reached into his pocket and handed her a hundred-dollar bill.

"Here, baby. It's not much, but you can pay a bill or sump'n with it. I know it's probably hard on you being a single parent and all, but I hope this'll help you out a little. Thank you for showing me a good time and I hope this won't be our last encounter."

"There's no way in this world I'll let you just walk out of my life that easy, so don't even think about it," Melody said as she accepted the money. "I want you in my bed, Larry, every day of the week, whether or not you're with Pat. Thanks for stopping by and thanks for the money." She smiled. "You must've spotted one of my final notices on the table, huh?"

"Nope, actually I didn't. It's just that I'm a considerate man."

She walked him to the door, kissed him goodnight, and then returned back to her bedroom, closing the door behind her. She lay across the bed and closed her eyes.

Damn. That man knows how to make a woman feel good, she thought. *I mean real good. Hell, I'm gonna see if I can get him in my bed every goddamn day of the week. I'm glad Byron didn't hear us carrying on.*

Melody then smiled and fell into a peaceful sleep.

The following morning Melody entered Special Touch—late as usual; her eleven o'clock customer had been impatiently waiting for over twenty minutes. Sue, the owner, wasted no time marching up to her.

"Your customer here eleven o'clock!" Sue shouted. "You no here! Bad business! Bad business! Too much liquor! You too much liquor! You need A.A.!"

Melody ignored her and continued walking to her chair.

Melody approached her customer, greeted her with a few pleasantries, and began explaining why she was late.

"Girl, I'm so sorry I'm late. Please forgive me, but me and my son stayed up all night, and he was—"

"Yeah, yeah, yeah," interrupted the gay beautician, who went by the name of Tosha. "We already know, girlfriend. You stayed up all night watching movies and on the Internet with your son, right?" Melody glared at Tosha.

Ooh, damn, I can't stand that gay muthafucka! she thought. *He makes me sick!*

"That's right, Tosha. I spend lots of time with my son doing things that you probably wouldn't know anything about," Melody responded withoutn revealing her true feelings. "We watch movies together, play Nintendo, discuss different issues, and lately, yes, he's been teaching me how to work the computer. Is that all right with you, Tosha, or are you jealous because you can't have a son?"

She then began the procedure on her customer's hair. Tosha snapped his fingers like he was performing magic.

"Humph. My man got a son, and what's his is mine. So you can back that shit up, girlfriend, and talk what you know," Tosha said as he put the finishing touches on his customer's hair.

Tosha had worked side-by-side with Melody for a few months, but they hated each other with a passion. His real name was Timothy, but each time someone referred to him by Timothy instead of Tosha, he got extremely angry.

He was a six-foot-one, thirty-one-year-old, dark complexioned black man. He wore his hair short and neat, and always wore skintight jeans that revealed his penis. He was skinny, and had a pair of huge Bart Simpson eyes. He was the only boy in his family, and had six older sisters growing up. When Timothy was a kid, he would parade around the house wearing his sister's panties and bras, and put on his mother's lipstick and high-heels, then stand in the mirror admiring himself. Soon, he began liking the feeling of imitating a woman, and as years went by, he began loving it. It became a way of life for him. Deep inside, he felt he was born to be a woman, regardless of the piece of meat hanging between his legs.

But Melody could care less about Tosha and his issues, as long as he didn't bother her. Unfortunately, they got on each other's nerves all the time. Deciding to ignore Tosha for the time-being, Melody quickly got to work on her client. Before she knew it, she was putting the final touches on her customer's hair. She glanced at her watch. It was fifteen minutes until two.

Damn! she thought. *I've got to hurry up and get out of here. I can't be late on my date with Larry. Hell no. I need some more of him.*

Melody sped up the process, and five minutes later she was done.

When she pulled into her driveway, Larry was parked, waiting inside his white Ford pick-up, smoking a joint. Upon seeing her, he climbed out, approached her, and then greeted her with a kiss and a hug. They then made their way inside the house and into the bedroom.

From that day on, they made it a ritual to meet each day at two PM Larry had made it a point to always leave no later than six. Sex, chronic, alcohol, and lunch became a daily formal procedure for them. He had become Melody's knight in shining armor, her Captain-Save-A-Whore, and her personal bail bondsman. Each time Melody's bills piled up, Larry would come through, scoop them up, and religiously pay them. If she was short with her house note money, he'd take pleasure in making up the difference. If she was short on cash during a holiday, or needed money to buy someone a birthday present, he would give her what she needed, or whatever she asked for without question. To Melody, Larry was everything any woman could ever want. The only thing that discomforted her was that she could not call him hers. Due to the circumstances, she was forced to share him with her longtime customer.

Half of him is better than none of him at all, she thought.

CHAPTER 4

Larry

Larry and Pat Myers first met when they were teenagers. It was love at first sight. Each day he carried her books to and from school. The fact that Pat's mother was very fond of Larry made things even easier for them to be together.

"Larry is gonna make someone a good husband one day," Pat's mother told her on several occasions. "He's a fine boy, and he enjoys working. Do you plan on marrying him someday, Pat?".

Pat would always blush and answer the same way. "Mama, I'm not thinking about marriage. The only thing I'm thinking about is graduating, going to college, and making something out of myself."

That turned out to be a lie. Actually, Pat went to sleep every night, and awakened every day, thinking about Larry. She dreamed about him every night. She knew that one day he would be her husband and they would have a house full of kids. They had already discussed it. And so it came to be.

When Larry was fifteen his Uncle Leroy picked him up each weekend to work. Larry's duties were to remove the metals from the bins and place them on his uncle's truck. No brains were required, only muscle. During that time, which was 1968, Uncle Leroy owned a couple of one-ton Chevy trucks, which had reinforced rear ends and powerful engines, which he used to get his work completed. Larry, being curious and eager to learn, learned the business quickly and had it down to a science in no time.

During the summer, Larry worked with Uncle Leroy six days a week. On the seventh day, which was Sunday, he did chores at his parents' house. He would cut their lawn, work in the flowerbeds, or whatever other chores needed to be done. He proved to be more helpful, dependable, and honest than his two older brothers, Leonard and Eddie.

"One day, Larry, this business is gonna be yours," his uncle had told him, "and you're gonna make lots of money with it. You can provide for your kids with it and make sure they have a decent living. And one day when you finally have a son, you can train him the way I trained you, and someday he can take over the business and take care of his family with it. Every man needs his own business, nephew, so you won't have to take mess from the white man and ain't got to punch no time clock."

By the time Larry turned sixteen, he knew all aspects of operating and maintaining the business without assistance from Uncle Leroy. As time passed, he'd proven to be a razor-sharp businessman.

Uncle Leroy had contracts with businesses such as transmission shops, places that rebuilt engines, machine shops, auto body and fender shops, and companies that dealt in sheet metal. He would pick up their scraps once or twice a month, depending on how fast their bins were filled. To the advantage of the company owners, Uncle Leroy paid them twenty to fifty dollars each time he picked up. He had bins at businesses in Riverside, Los Angeles, San Bernardino, Santa Barbara, and San Diego, and even had accounts in Las Vegas, Nevada. The business owners benefited by being paid for junk that was actually in their way, while Uncle Leroy benefited by collecting four hundred to a thousand dollars a day recycling the scrap.

When Larry had taken over the business at the age of eighteen, Uncle Leroy already had twenty-seven well-established accounts. In less than a year after taking over the business, Larry picked up twenty-two additional accounts. More than thirty years later, Larry was putting two of his children through college, had bought a couple of homes and a new truck, and took long vacations each year. Thank God for Uncle Leroy.

Larry had spoken to his son, Randy, several times about taking over the business, but Randy would always say, "I'm not ready yet, Dad." Larry would leave it at that. The truth was that Randy's wife, Paulette, had said, "Hell no! Your daddy thinks he's slick! He's just saying the business will be yours, but the truth is that he wants you to do the goddamn work, while he sits back like a fat rat and collects all the money. He'll have you out there from sunup to sundown, riding all over the goddamn world! Unh unh! I'm not having it, Randy!"

And that would be the end of the discussion.

Paulette made decisions for Randy. He had no say in any matter. Even though he had a burning desire to take over his father's business, marriage made him a henpecked man.

Larry claimed he loved his children equally, but his youngest daughter, Monique, was essentially his favorite. He would do things secretly for her and would tell her, "Don't tell your brother and sister what I've done for you. If you do, you won't have anything coming from me again."

"Thank you, Daddy," Monique would always smile and reply. "Don't worry, I won't tell them." She would then give him a kiss and run off smiling, knowing that she was Daddy's girl. He gave her money to buy new outfits and shoes, basically whatever she wanted.

He did things for Randy as well. On a few occasions, Randy had asked, "Hey Dad, can you help me out? I'm short on this month's rent, and I need to borrow a couple hundred dollars. I promise to pay you back as soon as I get my check."

"I'm gonna help you this time, son, but don't tell your sisters.

If you do, you're going to burn your bridge with me. Do you understand?"

Angela was too proud to ask her parents for anything, simply because she was practicing independence. Pat and Larry would brag about her to Monique and Randy.

"Why can't you two be like Angela, and save your money instead of spending it quicker than you get it?" Larry would ask Randy and Monique. "You two spend money like it grows on trees. Your sister has a bank account, pays her own car note and insurance, and even bought her own schoolbooks."

Larry loved Pat. She was his first wife, and as far as he was concerned, she would be his last. They had planned to grow old together. But for some unknown reason, Pat just couldn't seem to give Larry that sense of happiness, contentedness, or pleasure that he received from Melody. Melody talked to him about any and everything—his business, how his day went, his plans for tomorrow, his wife and kids, his brothers and sisters, and general life issues and problems.

Melody and Larry would converse over vodka and a few joints, and would constantly laugh and giggle like little kids. They made each other feel happy and wanted, needed, and at ease.

Unfortunately, for Larry, when he was at home, it was a totally different ball game. Since Randy had been born, Pat had transformed from a loving, caring, and sensuous woman, into a controlling, boastful, arrogant, and outspoken bitch. There was no sitting down to talk things over, no socializing over a glass of wine, no sex by candlelight, no champagne, roses, or bubble baths, and no watching television together. Even though she accepted roses and chocolates from him, Pat showed no appreciation or smiles when receiving them. Due to these circumstances, Larry felt that he had to do what he had to do in order to stay mentally strong and focused throughout each day. Leading two lives wasn't an easy task, but he made it seem like a piece of cake.

CHAPTER 5

Melody

One gloomy Sunday morning, not long after she had begun seeing Larry, Melody awakened and decided to go to church. The guilt of her affair, excessive drug and alcohol abuse, cursing, lying, and manipulating people on a daily basis gave her the thought of confessing at the altar and possibly repenting. She wasn't in denial of any of her sins.

It was ten minutes after nine when the thought popped in her mind. She looked at the clock, and then took a few moments to think.

"Byron! Wake up, Byron! Get up and wash your face and fix you a bowl of cereal, boy! I want you to get your butt ready for church! Do you hear me?"

"Yeah, Mom, I hear you, but I don't understand you," Byron answered.

"What are you talking about, boy? What in the hell do you mean when you say you don't understand me?"

On his way to the restroom, Byron stopped at her bedroom door and stood there wiping the sleep from his eyes.

"Because, Mom."

"Because what, boy?

"Because every night you drink vodka and curse up a storm, but now you want to rush off to church like God is going to be there personally handing out free round-trip tickets to heaven. I don't understand you, Mom," Byron explained.

Momentarily lost for words, Melody stared at her teenage son, realizing he wasn't naïve or stupid. Soon he would be a man. She wanted him to be a wise, smart, intelligent, and prudent, but damn, he was just growing up too fast.

How am I gonna get my groove on if my son pays attention to every damn thing I do? Hell, I guess I've got to be more careful, she thought.

"Bring your ass here, boy." She eased up, sat at the edge of the bed, and looked him in the eyes. "Don't you ever, as long as you're black and living, tell me what you don't understand about things that I say or do! I'm the one who pays the bills around here, boy, and I'm the one who lets bills turn into final notices to buy you all those expensive, name brand tennis shoes and jerseys you be wanting. Now do you understand me, boy?" She gave him a hard, serious look.

"Whatever, Mom," Byron turned around and attempted to walk away, but her powerful shout of authority stopped him in his tracks.

"Don't you walk away from me, boy! I'm the one who brought you into this world, and I'll damn sure take you out if you give me reason to! Don't you ever say 'whatever' to me! I'll break you a new asshole, boy! The next time you say some shit like that to me, I'm gonna put my foot knee-deep in your ass!" she threatened, holding him by both his arms and shaking him with force and aggression.

He tried remaining calm like the shakes weren't fazing him, but he couldn't take it any longer.

"That's what I'm talking about, Mom! You're hurting me. Stop, Mom! You drink too much, and you curse too much, but now you wanna go to church. God sees what you're doing, Mom. He's watching you right now!" Byron yelled as he began to cry. He then pulled away from her, ran to the restroom, and slammed the door behind him.

She got up, ran after him, and stood at the restroom door, crying. "I'm sorry, Byron. Please forgive me. Mama didn't mean to do you like that. I was just upset, that's all. After church, I'll take you to the mall, OK? I'll buy you those jerseys you've been asking me for, and I'll buy you some matching hats too. Please forgive me. Please," she pleaded. Seconds later, Byron opened the door and gave her a big hug.

Melody and Byron were seated in the second row from the pulpit. Their Bibles and ears were open. The good Reverend Joe Black was a few minutes into his sermon.

"God doesn't like double-minded people, and he surely won't bless them. You can't have one foot inside the church and the other foot in the world. You see, the Bible says that a double-minded person is unstable in all his ways, and in everything he does. He's like a wave in the ocean tossed to and fro. I know there are a lot of you in here who fit that description. Oh yes, I know there is. You see, I know there are a lot of you in here that partied last night and indulged in various kinds of sins," Reverend Joe Black preached. He then got louder and more emotional.

"There's a lot of you in here, who had the nerve to call somebody, or tell somebody that you're coming to church today! And I know that there are a lot of you here who have the habit of using the phrase, 'I'm blessed,' when people ask you how you're doing. Quit lying! Quit lying to make yourself look good! I know there are a lot of you in here who entertain evil thoughts, but run to the Lord's house to cover them up! You can run, my people, but Lord knows, you can't hide! The eyes of the Lord are everywhere! God is always watching you! There are a lot of you in here who commit fornication, adultery, and can curse enough to start an earthquake, but you still run around town saying 'I'm blessed!' I'm here to tell you, people, that you're not fooling anybody but yourselves! You better try to get right with the Lord! You can fool some of the people some of the time, but you can't fool all of the people all of the time! And you can't fool God at no time."

Melody felt as if the Reverend Joe Black was directing his sermon directly toward her. Guilt tore through her like a machete tearing through flesh.

Tosha, Melody thought. *That goddamn Tosha must've told the Reverend about me.*

She quickly scanned the faces of the congregation, the choir, and the men sitting in the pulpit, but didn't see anyone she recognized. Then she grabbed Byron's hand.

"Come on, Byron. Let's go. Something fishy is going on in this church, and I'm ready to get the hell out of here."

"But Mom, the Good Reverend Joe Black isn't finished, and he's talking some good stuff."

"You heard what I said, boy. Get up, and don't let me have to tell you again," Melody said, giving him a hard look.

Once she pulled away from the church, she felt relieved, but Byron wasted no time voicing his thoughts and opinions.

"You know what, Mom?"

"What now, boy?"

"In a way, church reminds me of a bank account."

"Why in the hell you wanna say some stupid shit like that, boy? Churches take money out of your bank account, not add to it," she explained.

"But that's not what I'm talking about, Mom."

"Well go ahead and say what you gotta say, boy. Hell, you take all day just to say one goddamn sentence."

"What I'm trying to say is that a church is like a bank account to me, because if you don't put anything into your spiritual account, you can't expect to get anything out of it, right? And if you don't put any money into your bank account, you can't get anything out of it, right?" Byron stated seriously.

"Boy, I don't know where you be coming up with all this

stuff, but you sure ask a lot of damn questions, and you come up with some of the weirdest shit." She still had not responded to his philosophy.

"Mom, I watch Reverend Price and Creflo Dollar on television every Sunday, and I'm trying to put something into my spiritual account, you know?" Byron said as they pulled into the driveway. "Because when it's time for me to die, I wanna make sure I go to heaven, and not to hell. Granny says that people who go to hell burn all day and all night, just burn, burn, and burn. She says they never actually die, they just burn 24/7. I couldn't imagine that, Mom. Could you?"

She had no answer for him. She shook her head back and forth.

CHAPTER 6

Big Steve

2000

Big Steve had been on the streets for six months and had finally accomplished his desire to become a big baller. He was known as "The Man," not only on The U, but also in Moreno Valley, Perris, Banning, and throughout San Bernardino County. His operation had gone so large he had to hire eight underlings. He made it to the point where he did not have to touch any of his products. He paid someone else to do it. His transformation from rags to riches seemed like it had happened overnight.

Melody treated him like he was her king. She loved him now more than ever. Even though he was big and fat, and had a tiny penis, she felt good about the recognition she received from being his wife. Practically everywhere she went people would notice her, and say, "That's Big Steve's ole lady," or, "Damn, man, Big Steve got a fine woman, man. She's the bomb!"

His profits allowed Melody to drive a black Audi, and permitted him to cruise around in a brand new Continental Town Car. He purchased Melody a new piece of jewelry every other week, and had even opened a bank account for her.

Steve made sure that Byron dressed in the best and latest

name brand clothing, while his own daily attire consisted of expensive tennis shoes, matching jerseys and hats, and name-brand jeans. He was finally living out his dreams. He took pleasure in receiving compliments, and he loved the attention and recognition he received from being The Man. Sex was thrown at him like raindrops falling from the sky, but he honored his wedding vows and had never been unfaithful to Melody, at least not yet. She was the queen of his heart, and not a day went by when he didn't show her how he felt.

On a gloomy day in December, Big Steve was on The U, in the process of making a cash pick-up from a few of his workers. While leaning on the hood of his Town Car, sipping a pint of Hennessy and admiring his achievements, a whore named Peaches approached him.

"When are you gonna give me som'a that dick, Big Daddy?" Peaches asked.

The question caught him off guard, but after taking a long swallow of Hennessy, he replied, "What makes you think you can handle this, shorty?"

Peaches had been a University whore for close to twenty years. She was very attractive, neat, and petite, and had a big, round butt shaped like a basketball. Even though she smoked crack on a daily basis, somehow she managed to still possess a firm pair of 34Ds. Her complexion resembled a Creole with a slight dash of Asian brown. While giving her a quick look over, Steve wondered if she was as good as she looked.

"Big Daddy will put you across his knees and spank you, shorty," Big Steve said as the chronic and Hennessy took effect. "You're just too damn little to be talking all that big shit, you know what I'm sayin'?"

Boldly, she pulled out her breasts. "Good things come in small packages, Big Daddy. And believe me, things aren't always what they seem."

She eased her soft hands down his pants, giving him an instant erection. She paid no attention to the passersby. One thing she was capable of was using what she had to get what she wanted. The combination of an erection and curiosity got the best of Big Steve. He turned up the bottle of Hennessey until it was empty.

"Let's go to the liquor store, then get a room so I can see what you're working with. You got Big Daddy curious, Li'l Bit, and I'm ready to see if good things really come in small packages, you know what I'm sayin'."

"You got some smoke, Big Daddy?" she asked.

"Don't worry about nothin', you know what I'm sayin'. Big Daddy got you covered on that."

After purchasing liquor and getting some crack from one of his workers, they went to a cheap motel room. Peaches wasted no time stripping naked, and neither did he.

"Lie down, Big Daddy, so I can show you what you've been missing all those days you passed me up." She took a quick hit of crack, and then went to work licking and sucking on his short erection. Her lips and tongue were in magical rhythm as they expertly worked his short shaft and baby-sized balls. Minutes later, she paused to take another hit, then blew the smoke onto the head of Steve's penis, and continued doing her thing like she was trying to win first place in a penis slurping contest.

"Ooh, baby, yes. Uh-huh, yes, suck it, baby, suck it, Li'l Bit. Uummee, yeah," Big Steve moaned, lying back receiving his first blowjob from a whore.

She sped up her rhythm.

"Ahwww, oh, ahwww, damn," he whimpered, sounding like a grizzly bear in the wilderness. She didn't stop her rhythm until she sucked him dry. She then smiled.

"So, what do you say about small things now, Big Daddy?" She popped open a can of Old English 800, and then fixed herself another hit.

"Damn, Li'l Bit, that head was good, you know what I'm sayin'. That's the kind of head that has men leaving their wives," he emphasized, then he took another swallow of Hennessy and lay back like a king, watching her parade around the room naked, dancing to rap music. The effects of the drugs and alcohol erased any feelings of guilt about his actions. He felt that he deserved to be entertained by this whore. After all, he was "The Man."

Suddenly, Peaches jumped on the bed and began playing with her pussy and breasts while watching Steve massage his limp penis.

"Lie down, Big Daddy. Let me hook you up with some more of this good head."

Once again it was on. When he felt himself about to climax, he pulled away.

"Lie on your back, Li'l Bit. I jus' want to stare at your pretty pussy, you know what I'm sayin'?" He then began playing with her pearl while stroking himself. Then he climbed on top of her, looking like a polar bear on top of a kitten, and inserted his penis inside her. He pumped fast, like a sewing machine, for thirty seconds, and then he was done.

Big Steve fed Peaches crack for the next few hours, allowing her to smoke all she wanted, and then she made a sudden suggestion.

"Let me blow you a charge, Big Daddy. I'll bet then you can fuck me all night long." She was stroking his penis.

"You know I don't mess around with this stuff, Li'l Bit. I jus' sell it, you know what I'm sayin'? This shit could take a king off his throne, and I don't need that to happen," Big Steve replied, rubbing her hardened nipples.

"But, Big Daddy, you're not weak, and you're not a wimp, so it's kind of impossible for a strong man like you to get hooked from receiving a charge. Only weak people fall prey to this stuff, and you're not anywhere in that category. You're a big, strong man, Big Daddy, just how I like 'em." She was now licking him.

"Yeah, you got a point, Li'l Bit. All right, I'll let you jus' blow me a charge, but under one condition," Big Steve said after exhaling.

"And what condition is that, Big Daddy?" she asked, giving him a few licks and sucks.

"That you sit on it and ride the hell out it afterward."

"But I want you to fuck me doggy-style, Big Daddy. I want you to knock the lining out of this pussy."

"OK, Li'l Bit, I'll tell you what. We're gonna fuck all night, and when I get through with you, girl, your pussy is gonna be so damn sore that you won't want to fuck for a month."

After she blew the crack smoke into his mouth, he exhaled and a strange look began developing on his face. His eyes grew larger and he stared around the room in complete silence, paranoid as hell.

"Are you all right, Big Daddy?" Peaches asked. She then positioned herself to ride his penis, but it was lifeless.

"Blow me another charge, Li'l Bit," he said, and she wasted no time in doing so. One thing led to another, and minutes later he was hitting the pipe. For the next six hours they smoked crack and consumed alcohol like there was no tomorrow. He was no longer interested in sex.

"I hear sump'n. Somebody's comin', Li'l Bit," he would whisper each time he took a hit. "The motel owner probably called the police and told them we're smoking crack." And minutes later he would say, "Fix me another hit, baby. I need another hit."

Peaches showed no change in behavior from smoking the crack. It was like it didn't faze her at all, but she continued to smoke. She remained naked and played with herself, hoping he would soon mellow out and want some pussy. One thing she enjoyed was sex while smoking crack. His eyes remained focused on the windows and the door, thinking that at any given moment someone was going to burst in. He'd put on his clothes hours earlier, and was ready to jet out of the room when necessary. He paced back and forth, from the restroom to the window, peeping out the door and window repeatedly.

"I hear sump'n," Big Steve whispered. "Somebody's standin' on the other side of the door. I think the police are gonna kick down the door. Listen. Did you hear that? Somebody's callin' me, and it sounds like my wife. Maybe somebody saw us come in here and told her. Turn off the lights, turn off the lights, hurry, they're comin'!"

He attempted to hide underneath the bed, but couldn't fit. Peaches tried to calm him down by putting her breasts and pussy in his face, but he shooed her away each time.

The crack was plentiful and free, so Peaches took advantage of the situation and continued smoking all she wanted. After taking another hit, Big Steve began sweating and moving uncontrollably fast.

"Get dressed! Hurry up!" he said suddenly. "We gotta get outta here before they come. They're comin', they're comin'! I can sense it. Come on! Let's get the fuck outta here."

He was standing next to the door. Peaches didn't bother asking questions. She simply carried out his demands. He eased open the door slowly, hoping nobody would kick it in, and worriedly peeped out, making sure the coast was clear. Without thinking about turning in the key to the room, he trotted to his Town Car, fired it up, and before Peaches could close her door, he was driving off.

Heading toward the freeway, he was completely silent. Peaches attempted to turn on the radio, but he turned it off.

"I can't concentrate hearing that shit," he said.

As he entered northbound on the 215 freeway, he finally spoke.

"Hey, Li'l Bit, I know you're mad at me, you know what I'm sayin'? But I 'pologize for actin' the way I did. But like I said, baby, I got you covered as far as drink and smoke is concerned, so don't trip. Oh, and by the way, you proved that good things do come in small packages."

"Told you so," Peaches replied, smiling. She then knelt over and took a hit.

After stopping at a liquor store to grab a couple six-packs of beer and a fifth of Hennessy, Big Steve made his way to the City of Colton, where he checked into a nice hotel called the Red Tile Inn.

For the next three weeks, Big Steve was so turned out on crack that he did not think about going home. The only time he left the room was to go to his underlings to get back from them what he'd given them to sell, and to purchase more liquor. His wife and parents had not heard from him since the day he took that fatal first hit. The only thing he thought about was smoking more crack, drinking, and having sex with Peaches.

A month and a half later he finally decided to call his parents and wife, and inform them of his drug problem.

"Come on home, son, so we can get you some help," his father told him.

"Baby," Melody said, "please come home. We need you, sweetheart. Your son asks me about you everyday, and I-I-I, just want you to come home, Steve. We can work it out. We'll get you into N.A. and—"

Big Steve hung up, feeling ashamed and guilty. He was too embarrassed to face his parents and wife. He was at the lowest point in his life, and he regretted ever taking that first hit. The crack stripped him of his self-esteem and 99 percent of his common sense.

It took Steve three months for him to hit rock bottom. During his downfall Peaches remained by his side, and because of her guilty conscience, she tried to help him back up, but it was no use. He was hooked. Out of compassion and pity she felt obligated to help get him back on his feet, but from the looks of things, it was going to be hopeless. He was gone with the wind. Lost and turned out.

Steve's daily attire had deteriorated to a stale pair of jeans, a filthy T-shirt, and a worn out pair of Nikes. His drawers were so dirty and smelly that Peaches suggested he throw them in the trash. He went without washing his face or brushing his teeth for days at a time. Several times, Peaches tried to encourage him by reminding him of his past.

"You weren't like this when I met you, Big Daddy. I wish you'd at least try to slow down a little so you can get yourself back on the right track. Just because you smoke crack doesn't mean you have to stop taking care of yourself. Look at me, honey, I've been smoking crack for twenty years, and the average person probably couldn't even tell. It's not what you do, it's how you do it, Big Daddy." Her speeches would go in one ear and out the other.

Four months later Big Steve finally decided to go home. It was 11:30 AM on a Thursday morning. He figured Byron would be at school and Melody would be working.

I'm going to make this quick. I'll stick and move, Big Steve thought.

He made his way to the front door and tried to insert his key, but discovered the locks had been changed.

"Damn!" he shouted. He then made his way to the back door. "Bitch! You fuckin' low down bitch! After all the shit I did for you! Fuck you!" he shouted, discovering that those locks had been changed as well. "Sorry, baby, but I'm gonna kick this muthafucka down! I'm the one who bought everything in this damn house! Now I'm 'bout to do like Robin Hood, and take from the rich and give to the poor, which is me."

Big Steve stood back ten feet, and then charged the door full-force, knocking it down like a cannonball going through paper. He then sped through the house, gathering all the valuables he could. He took two nineteen-inch color televisions, two VCRs, a microwave oven, two dual cassette players, and a snub nose .38 he'd bought for Melody for her protection. He also took Byron's Nintendo, fourteen game cartridges, and Melody's jewelry box containing three-thousand-dollars worth of jewelry. Once he'd piled the valuables inside his Town Car, he hurried back inside, grabbed a pillowcase, filled it with food and snacks, and then left. Mission accomplished.

His next stop was Pork Chop's. He planned to talk up some crack on credit. Since he was in the clear and didn't owe Pork Chop for any fronted drugs, Pork Chop didn't have a problem fronting him an ounce, but there was a speech that went along with the generosity.

"All right, homey, don't fuck with my money, and don't come back with no excuses about why you're short. Bring me seven hundred in five days. And please don't get on my shit list, cuzz, 'cause if you do, you know you're a dead man." Steve knew the deal and agreed with Pork Chop's terms.

"Have you been smoking this shit, man?" Pork Chop asked before Steve walked away. "You lookin' kinda shabby, homey, and you didn't look like this when I first met you." He was giving Steve the once over.

"What are you talking 'bout, man? Hell nah, I ain't been smokin' this shit. I'm about the money, homey, you know what I'm sayin'? I'm layin' low, keeping an eye on thangs; that's why I'm dressed like this," Big Steve replied, and then shook Pork Chop's hand and left.

After selling the merchandise he had stolen to a Mexican who owned a taco truck, Big Steve cashed out with a little over nine hundred dollars. Possessing an ounce of crack and the money from the Mexican, Big Steve felt that he was somewhat on the right track back to riches.

He then returned to the cheap motel on The U and began chopping up the chunk of cocaine into sellable five, ten, and twenty-dollar pieces. Afterward, he stood on the street corners and began selling it.

As usual, crackheads, drug dealers, gang-bangers, prostitutes, and derelicts flooded The U. Due to the lifestyle Big Steve was living he easily blended in with them. Rather than hire someone to assist him in making sales, he decided to sell it himself to eliminate the expense of having to pay a middle man.

Damn, things jus' don't change around here, Steve thought as he stood on the street corner, scanning his surroundings for as far as his eyes could see. *The same niggas are still hangin' on the same corners, talking the same ole shit. But hell, I can't talk about them, 'cause I'm right out here with 'em.*

At that moment a crackhead named Billy approached Big Steve.

"What's up, Big Steve? Where you been, man?" Billy was missing all his teeth. He had gotten a pair of dentures, but they were knocked out a couple months earlier when he attempted to steal someone's car radio.

"Chillin', man, jus' chillin', you know what I'm sayin'. What's been going on around here, man?" Big Steve asked, darting his eyes in all directions.

"Same old shit, man. Ain't nothin' changed but the date. Man, I'm hungry as hell, but I'm broke, man. You got a dollar I can borrow until I get my welfare check?" Billy asked.

"Nah, man, I'm short with money. Hell, I'm out here tryin' to make a dollar out of fifteen cents, you know what I'm sayin'. But check with me later, and maybe I can do a li'l sump'n for you."

Billy had been a certified crackhead for over twenty years. He spent the majority of his time begging at liquor stores, gas stations, and freeway exits. He was dark complexioned, six-feet tall, and extremely unattractive. Like others on The U, he dressed in shabby clothes, slept at bus stops, and ate leftovers from hamburger and chicken stands.

"Hey Big Steve, you know what, man? I forgot I got close to five dollars, man, but I was tryin' to hold on to it so I could get me sump'n to eat. But damn, man, I need a hit," Billy said, half lying and half telling the truth.

"I ain't out here tryin' to cater to your needs, man, so make up your mind, homey. Do you want a nickel, or are you gonna buy you sump'n to eat?" Big Steve asked, checking out a couple of whores strolling down The U.

"Fuck it, man, go ahead and break me sump'n proper for a nickel," Billy said, not paying any attention to the passersby or the traffic, but keeping a close eye on what Big Steve was serving him.

"Bring me a few sales, and I'll take care of you, man," Big Steve said after serving Billy. "I'm tryin' to do big things out here, you know what I'm sayin'?"

"Yeah, OK, Big Steve," Billy replied, hurrying away to go get high with no plans to help Steve.

Meanwhile, there were three prostitutes on the opposite side of the street, huddled together, having a conversation regarding Big Steve.

"Girl, Peaches told me she blew big man a charge, and he's been hooked ever since," Tastee, the first whore, said.

Tastee was five-nine, wore a long wig, and had a mouth full of false teeth. Her complexion was dark brown, and she possessed a big butt and a pair of big, droopy breasts.

The second whore, Candy, was a high-yellow complexioned woman. She was blessed with a nice body and long, straight, black hair. She stood five foot six, and was fine as all outdoors. The fact that she had a pussy as wide as the Pacific Ocean was irrelevant. She gave the best head on the West Coast, and possibly in America.

"Yeah, girl, that's what I heard too," Candy interjected. "Shit, it's been kind of slow out here lately, so I might just try to push up on ole Fat Daddy, you know what I mean?"

The third whore, who went by the name of Special, was not attractive at all. She weighed no more than ninety pounds soaking wet, had a medium-brown complexion, and wore her hair in a short natural.

"It looks to me like he's gone down since last time I bought from him," Special said. "He used to be a baller, but now he's just a tore up looking smoker. That's a damn shame, girl. I'll tell you, they weren't lying when they said crack ain't for every-body. But what the hell, fat-daddy might just want to work a lit-tle sump'n with us. And I don't have a problem at all with a favor for a favor." She then flagged down a potential customer, but unfortunately, he kept going.

While pacing up and down The U, the whores kept a watch-ful eye on Big Steve, waiting for the right time to make their ap-proach. By midnight, Big Steve had sold out of product. He was kicking back in his Town Car counting his cash.

After I give Pork Chop his money, he thought, *I'll still have seven-hundred left, plus the money I got from the Mexican. Yeah, I'll be back on top of things again in no time. Yeah, I'm fixin' to pick myself up off the curb and be the man again.* His thoughts were interrupted as Special approached the driver's side of his vehicle.

After Big Steve rolled down his window, Special stuck her head inside. "What's up, Big Daddy? Long time no see." She was twirling her tongue around like a snake.

"Ain't nothin' happenin', baby. What's up with you?" Big Steve asked, getting an erection by watching the movements of her tongue and imagining her giving him a blow job. She then reached inside the car and rubbed on his crotch.

"Damn, Big Daddy, I want to suck it. It's so big!" she lied, hoping he would bite. "Do you think you can handle three of us, Big Daddy, or would you prefer a one-on-one?" Then she unzipped his pants. Fully erect, Big Steve stuck his hand out the window and rubbed her pussy. It had a distinctive foul odor to it, but he ignored it.

"Ump, ump, ump. Damn, girl, ain't nothin' I like better than a hairy pussy."

At that moment, Candy and Tastee appeared and wasted no time flashing their breasts, sensing that would speed up their plan. Seconds later the whores were inside the Town Car, en route to the liquor store and to buy some crack.

So far, so good, Special thought.

The motel room was shabby like all the others on The U, but

affordable. The rates were twenty dollars a day, and five dollars an hour.

As soon as they stepped inside, the whores immediately got naked, and Big Steve followed suit. Tastee quickly prepared herself by taking out her upper and lower dentures. Steve was ready to take part in his first threesome. He'd heard talk of threesomes, and had seen them performed on X-rated movies, but now he was about to actually be in one.

Damn. I wish there was a camera in here, he thought. *Because it's some freaky shit about to go down up in here, and the movie could go worldwide.* He smiled to himself.

"I'll be right back, y'all. I got to clean myself up right quick," Special said as she made her way to the restroom. After removing her panties, she finally smelled the foul odor lingering below. It came from having sex with her last five customers without washing up between tricks.

"Have you ever had a gum job?" Tastee asked with a toothless smile.

"Nope," Big Steve answered. "But I bet it feels good as hell, huh?"

"That depends on who's gummin' you, Big Daddy. I'm one of those experienced whores who knows what a man wants, and exactly how he wants it," Tastee bragged, stroking his small erection.

"Well show me then, baby," Big Steve said. At once, Tastee began handling her business. She had no problem deep-throating his small penis. "Ump, ump, ump," he muttered as the pro gummed, licked, and sucked him like a lollipop.

"Oh, yes, baby, ump, damn that feels good," Big Steve said, lying back and receiving and enjoying his first gum job. After taking a hit of crack, Candy joined in. She ran her tongue up and down his huge stomach, then took turns with Tastee slurping his penis. When Special reappeared out the restroom, she grabbed her bottle of Cisco, and then sat on Big Steve's face. Even though the odor had disappeared, the thought of the smell caused him to frown as he licked her pussy. He was having the time of his life until he took a hit.

Bingo. Mission accomplished, the whores thought, giving each other a thumbs up. When the crack ran out he began sending Special back and forth to drug dealers, spending a hundred dollars each trip. Of course she was pocketing money each time. Instead of giving the dope man the full hundred dollars, she'd give him eighty dollars and keep twenty for herself.

Two days later the party was still going strong, but Big Steve's cash count had decreased tremendously. He was down to his last fifty dollars, and once again the crack was gone.

He sat at the edge of the bed, thinking while the whores were in a crack coma.

Damn! I fucked up and took this shit a little too far. I got my freak on, and my smoke on, but I've fucked up Pork Chop's money! Now I've got to worry 'bout him puttin' a hit out on me. I should've taken his damn money to him before I started messin' around with these bitches! It's too late to be thinkin' 'bout that now. I got to make a quick move so I can pay him.

Big Steve then attempted to wake the whores up, but they wouldn't budge. They had been up for three days, drinking and smoking dope, and now they were dead to the world.

As he eased off the bed and headed for the door, the movement of the bed finally awakened Tastee. She turned over and took a quick look at him.

"Where you going, Big Daddy?" Tastee asked. "Are you about to cop some more smoke?"

"Nope, not right now. I gotta take care of some business, you know what I'm sayin'. But the room is paid up till tomorrow, so y'all can stay here, do y'all thing, and make y'all some money," Big Steve said as he held the door open. "Thanks for showing mc a good time, and I want you to know that you made me feel good as hell. That gum job was the bomb, girl!" he emphasized.

"I'm glad you liked it, Big Daddy. If you ever want it again you know where to find me," Tastee replied as she twirled her tongue around inside her mouth.

After leaving the room, Steve went a few doors down and spent his last fifty dollars with the dope man. His intentions were to double his money. He then sat in his Town Car, pulled out his pipe, and took a test hit. It was nine thirty AM. After exhaling, the drug began taking its effect on him. His mind began playing tricks on him, making him think people were after him and watching him. He sat there turning his head from left to right, aware of every sound—birds, passing vehicles, pedestrians, airplanes, and the wannabe gang-bangers/crackheads.

Big Steve then saw two bums pushing shopping carts and walking toward him, both dressed shabbily with long, unkempt hair and nasty beards. He stared at them, not knowing who they were or what they wanted. He was nervous. As they approached, he realized he'd seen them digging in trashcans and begging for change on The U on several occasions. As they neared, he shooed them off, but they continued their stride toward him.

"I need a twenty rock, man. You got a twenty, man?" the taller bum asked.

Before answering, Big Steve tried thinking, but couldn't. It was the effect of the crack. He realized he couldn't sit there with the windows up and say nothing, so he responded.

"Who are you, man? Do I know y'all?" His window was still up.

"I'm Pete, and this is Fred, man. We usually cop from Big Black, but he ain't around, so we was hopin' you had sump'n," Pete replied.

After being ignored for a few minutes, the bums turned and began walking away.

Big Steve didn't want to pass up the opportunity to make his first twenty dollars, so he rolled down his window before they were out of sight.

"Hey! Wait a minute! Come back, y'all. I got a twenty!" They turned around and approached the Town Car, accepted the dope from him, then drew their guns.

"Freeze! Police!"

Big Steve was arrested and transported to Riverside County Jail, where he was then fingerprinted, booked, and charged with selling drugs, possession with intent to sell, and possession of drug paraphernalia. He was sentenced to one year in the county jail for his first offense.

He called his parents to inform them of what happened, but was too ashamed to call Melody. He didn't even know if he still had a wife.

CHAPTER 7

Melody

Big Steve was in and out of jail, and his absence provided an open window for Melody to have a relationship with whatever man she chose. And indeed she took advantage of it.

Larry and Melody clicked together like a happily married couple. They would always be on the same page, as if they'd known each other since childhood. Like the majority of men in the world, Larry had a problem being faithful to his wife, but he expected to be treated with loyalty, honor, and devotion. He was accustomed to having things his way.

Faithfully, every two weeks Pat kept her appointment with Melody, which gave her another opportunity to brag while getting her hair done. Even though Melody put up with it, deep down inside she envied Pat. Each time Pat visited the hair salon she made sure she was seen and heard, whether or not people knew her. Melody played it off like she liked Pat, but secretly she envied and hated the hell out of her, although Melody had never turned down an invitation to Pat's home. They would have a sociable drink and gossip about friends, family members, or customers. Mainly, Melody wanted to be nosey and see how Pat really treated the man who was paying her bills and sexing her daily.

The fact that Melody was playing on deadly ground did not

bother her at all. She had no conscience whatsoever about what she was doing. Financially, she needed Larry, and sexually, he needed her. It was a perfect connection.

As time went on, Melody made it a habit to place her due bills on her dining room table, making sure Larry saw them once he entered her home. Like a faithful provider, he'd scoop up the bills and pay them. There was no other man she knew who would pay her house note, all of her bills, buy her son whatever he wanted, make her have multiple orgasms, and on top of that, give her a few hundred dollars a week in pocket money. *What a man, what a man, what a mighty good man,* she thought.

Byron knew not to knock on his mother's door whenever Larry was over. That was a no-no. Actually, Byron never caught his mother having sex, but he had told his Uncle Tony about times he passed his mother's bedroom and heard noises like, "Ah, ooh, yes, yes, fuck me, Big Daddy, yes, yes, ooh, ahww."

"They're just handling their business, nephew," his uncle laughed and told him. "You'll understand when you get older." And he left it at that.

One day, when Byron passed his mother's bedroom and heard her making those noises again, to him, it sounded like his mother was in pain and screaming for her life. He couldn't make up his mind whether to ignore the sounds, like he normally did, or to kick down the door and rescue her. Wisdom told him to stand by the door and listen carefully before he did anything stupid.

"Mom!" he yelled. "Are you OK?"

Larry continued his rhythm, stroking her doggy-style, but she managed to respond.

"Mama's OK, baby. Mama's back and neck are just hurting a little bit, and Larry's rubbing some of that burning solution on me. It's burning like hell, but Mama's all right," she lied, trying hard to hold back her grunts and moans.

"OK, Mom. Just checking," Byron answered. Afterward, he

went outside and began shooting hoops. After dribbling a few times then going in for a lay-up, a car approached the area where he was playing, causing him to momentarily stop shooting. As he stared at the vehicle and its driver, he realized he'd seen the car before. He couldn't quite remember where, but he knew he'd seen it before. The car stopped, and a black man wearing a baseball cap and dark sunglasses began scribbling something down while looking at Larry's license plate. Byron could have sworn on a stack of Bibles that he'd not only seen the vehicle before, but he had also seen the driver before as well. He just couldn't remember where. Suddenly, the man burned rubber and made a sharp right turn at the end of the block. Dismissing the scenario, Byron went back to shooting hoops.

After Larry left that day, Melody had a seat at her dining room table and began thinking while sipping a glass of vodka.

Damn, I might have to start meeting him at a motel. Byron is getting older now and he's not going to keep believing these lies I'm feeding him. But hell, I can't help moaning and hollering because that man knows how to fuck. His wife has to be the craziest bitch in the world not to give him what he wants when he wants it. But personally, I don't have a problem with that. Humph, the pleasure is all mine. But tomorrow, I've got to try be quieter.

She then smiled to herself and took another sip of her drink.

"Byron! Don't answer that phone, boy! It ain't anybody but those damn Japs from the shop and my ten thirty customer!"

"OK, Mom, I won't answer it," he shouted from his bedroom, and then asked, "Can I stay home today until you get off, Mom?"

"Boy! You've gone crazy if you think I'm leaving you here by yourself. Don't start asking me all those damn questions. It's too early in the morning for that shit, and I'm already late. You can either stay at Bobby's, or you can go to the shop with me."

"Ah, Mom, please?"

"Don't please me, boy, you heard what I said." She then slipped her feet into a pair of his tennis shoes and threw on a Lakers hat over her weave. "Hurry up, boy. You know I'm running late."

"It's not my fault you stayed up all night drinking, Mom," Byron said. He then looked at her feet and noticed she had on his Jordans. He had asked her several times not to wear his shoes or jerseys, but she figured that, since it was Larry's money that bought them, she had the right.

"Take off my shoes, Mom. I've asked you not to wear my shoes several times, because your feet are big and you always stretch them all out of shape," Byron said, frowning.

She approached him and grabbed him by his collar.

"Number one, little smart ass boy, don't you worry about how long I stayed up last night, what I drank last night, or what the hell I did. I'ma grown ass woman, and I'm the one who pays the bills around here, not you. And number two, hell no, I'm not taking off these shoes," she stated. "Who do think bought the damn shoes, boy?"

"You didn't buy them. Larry did," Byron replied, still frowning.

"Well, who you think—I don't have to explain nothing to you, Byron. And I sure as hell don't have time to go through this shit, so you might as well shut the hell up."

"I planned on wearing my Jordans today, Mom. They match perfect with my Karl Kani pants," Byron explained with an attitude.

"Boy, if you don't hurry up I'm going to be wearing my foot knee deep up your frail ass. Now shut up and let's go!" she demanded.

As she entered the salon—late, as always—both Japanese owners rushed up to her pointing at the clock and shouting.

"Your customer here ten thirty! You late! You late! Bad business! Bad business! No good! Bad business Melody! You late one more time, you fired! Too much drinking liquor! You need A.A.!"

Tosha, the gay beautician, laughed while observing the altercation. Ignoring the owners, Melody continued walking toward her customer, who was already seated in the styling chair.

If I had a gun, I'd shoot the shit out of both those tight eyed bitches! Damn, I can't wait until I have enough money to open my own shop, she thought.

Tosha wanted to bring up witnessing Melody's long term customer's husband's truck parked in front of her house, but he wasn't sure if he was making repairs around her house, there on business for Pat, or there for a booty call. But Tosha was going to make it his business to find out.

After greeting her customer, Melody began explaining why she was late.

"Girl, I'm sorry, but I stayed up all night long with my son, and—"

"Girlfriend, that lie is so damn tired I don't even see why you keep using it," Tosha interrupted with a serious look on his face. "Humph, you must don't need a job, Melody, 'cause you're never here on time. Apparently someone must be taking care of you, and I know it isn't your institutionalized husband. With all those bills you have and those two-hundred-dollar shoes your son be wearing, I know damn well you can't manage that only doing three to six heads a week." Tosha grinned sarcastically.

Melody wanted to ignore him, but figured she had to say something in her defense.

"You know more about my business than I do, huh? Hell, you need to be trying to keep your own backyard clean instead of being all in mines all the time. And since we're on an open discussion, Tosha, why don't you tell us a little bit about you? I'm sure the audience, since you're into talking today, would love to hear whether you've gotten your sex change yet, or are you still hanging?" Melody laughed derisively.

In a huff, and caught off guard by Melody's quick comeback, Tosha yelled back at her. "Don't you worry about what's between my legs, bitch!"

"Well, don't you be worrying about my finances, my son's expensive shoes, my husband, or who I'm fucking!" Melody said defensively. "And by the way, girlfriend, how are your hemorrhoids doing?" Melody asked Tosha.

Tosha gave her a constipated look. "You bitch! You're gonna get yours! Just wait and see. And don't think I'm joking."

"Yeah, yeah, yeah, whatever," Melody responded, holding up her hand. "Talk to the hand, fag. Talk to the hand."

Melody's eyes were bloodshot red and her head was throbbing from last night's activities, but her empty wallet, combined with her depleted bank account, motivated her to go on.

After Tosha began working on his next customer, curiosity and hatred caused him to run his big mouth.

"I see you bought a new truck, huh? Humph, I bet you're a call girl on the side, huh? Yep. You've got to be doing sump'n else other than hair, Melody. I'm not anywhere near stupid, girlfriend, and come to think of it I could swear on my mama's grave that I saw that truck that has been parked in front of your house about the same time everyday, parked in front of this salon before. Yep. And instinct tells me that the owner of that truck is probably the husband of one of your customers." Tosha had everyone's attention now. "I know you're not messing around with someone else's puddin', are you? Or could this just be a coincidence?"

Knowing she had to keep her cool, Melody played it off.

"There's no way in hell I could afford a truck like that, and as much as you know about my finances, it seems like you would've known that, girlfriend. But anyway, I wasn't doing too much of anything yesterday. You could've stopped by and chatted with me for a little while. And for your information, as far as me messing around with someone else's puddin', you've got me twisted. That truck belonged to my cousin who's now living with me, and since you know everything else, I'm surprised you didn't know that." She hoped Tosha would leave it at that and change the subject.

"You can't fool me, Melody. You've got to wake up early in the morning to fool a bitch like me, and you damn sure don't wake up early. You see, bitch," Tosha said, moving closer to Melody and pointing his index finger in her face, "you think you're slick, but I've got your number, and that's not the only number I got. Your card has been pulled, bitch, and you're going down. Your husband stealing days are over. You see, I was watching you that day when you wrote down your number on that magazine and handed it to your customer's husband. That's when I knew you were a snake. How can you do some shit like that, Melody? Tell me? How in the hell can you fuck your customer's husband, and then turn around and do her hair every two weeks? You're a snake bitch and the truth isn't in you. But I'll tell you what, girlfriend, if I ever catch you with my man, I'll shoot you first and ask questions later."

The customers waiting to get serviced waited impatiently to hear Melody's response. It was like watching a movie to them. The owners sensed something was about to take place.

Knowing she had to use nasty words or aggressive action, Melody stood face to face with Tosha, giving him a hard, mean look, then suddenly she grabbed a pair of hot curlers and threw them at him, striking him in the face, charged him like a bull, and rushed him to the floor.

"Stop! Stop! Stop! I call the police!" one of the owners yelled in a state of shock.

"Oh my God, Lord Jesus, please stop them!" Tosha's customer screamed.

"Stop! Stop! Go outside! Please, get out!" the other owner screamed.

To Melody's surprise, Tosha eased out of the hold and

flipped her over, then struck her with a series of punches, slaps, and bites. As Melody lay on the floor out of breath, Tosha then grabbed her and put a chokehold on her.

"Bitch!" he yelled. "You don't know who you're fucking with! Don't let the smooth taste fool you! Like I said, if I ever catch you fucking with my man, I'll kill you! Do you understand me?"

Melody nodded, managing to let out a whisper.

"Yes, I understand."

Just then two security officers who were walking by on their way to lunch stormed in and broke up the fight. Their backup arrived minutes later and arrested Tosha and Melody, and then transported them to Riverside County Jail, where they were fingerprinted, booked, and placed in separate holding cells. They were given two phone calls, and neither of them wasted time before taking advantage of the privilege. Melody called Larry's cell first and spoke with him. Then she called Bobby's mother, informing her that she would be home a little late and to watch and feed Byron until she showed up.

Tosha called Darrell, his lover, who he referred to as his husband, and informed him of what had happened. Darrell was there in less than twenty minutes to bail Tosha out. Larry got the bail and showed up little later

A few hours later, Melody was released on bail. She was handed papers instructing her to report to the Riverside Municipal Court in two weeks. As she walked outside the county jail, a free woman, she spotted Larry leaning against his truck, smoking a cigar. She approached him, and like they had not seen each other in years, they began kissing, hugging, and whispering sweet nothings to each other.

As Larry drove eastbound on Highway 60 to pick up Melody's vehicle from the salon, Melody unzipped his pants, leaned over, pulled out his penis, and began showing him her appreciation by giving him an enthusiastic blow job.

Larry smiled and thought, *Heaven must be like this.*

* * *

The following day Melody began calling beauty salons in the Riverside area, inquiring about booth rent and availabilities. Being a licensed cosmetologist, and having a large clientele of her own ensured that just about any beauty salon would accept her. The customers she had gathered throughout the years would more than likely follow her, due to the satisfaction they received, her affordable prices, and the flexibility she offered. Out of the seven salons she phoned, each of them agreed to rent her a booth. She decided to make her decision as to which one she would choose on Monday. She then called each of her customers and informed them that she was, once again, relocating. She diverted the customers who had upcoming appointments to her home.

I hope I don't have to work around any more damn homosexuals, because they're worse than women. Another thing I'm glad about is that the schoolteacher, whose hair I was doing when the fight broke out, wasn't one of my regular customers. Hopefully everything will work itself out, and things will soon be back to normal. The thought of having to walk around with two black eyes irks me. I hope Tony and Antoinette don't bring their asses over here and see me, because the first thing they'll think is that Larry or his wife kicked my ass. I damn sure can't tell them I got my ass kicked by a fag. I hope this swelling goes down by tomorrow, because I look like a damn monster.

CHAPTER 8

Melody

Melody received several letters from Steve while he was in jail, but she was not planning on answering any of them. She still had love for the man, but he just wasn't fulfilling any of her needs. As far as she was concerned, their relationship was over. Terminated.

The most important thing in her life was Larry. He kept her mind off Steve. The fact that he was not hers, and belonged to another woman, did not matter to her. He meant the world to her, and always came through for her, like when the court held Melody accountable for her actions at Special Touch, and punished her by imposing a fine of twenty-five hundred dollars. Larry paid her fine.

The name of the new salon she worked for, which was also owned by Asians, was Creativity. Not only was it a beauty salon, but it was a barbershop as well. The business had been established in 1990. It was filled with customers seven days a week, from opening to closing. Its reputation for professionalism was known throughout Riverside County, and even customers from San Diego and Los Angeles County didn't mind driving the necessary miles it took to get complete satisfaction. The prices were not cheap, but people would pay to get what they wanted.

She had been at her new location for a little over two

months. As usual, she barely made enough to pay her bills—nothing at all to brag about and very little to be thankful for. Fortunately, her long-term customers had faithfully followed her. That made life a little easier for her, but still it wasn't quite the way she desired it to be.

There was only one thing about working at Creativity that irritated Melody—having to work side by side with another homosexual. This gay beautician's name was Hubert, but he went by the name of Happy. Happy derived joy from attention. Not only did Happy have the skills and expertise to be a hairstylist, he was also a manicurist, a pedicurist, and a barber. This allowed him to earn more money than the other employees. He was an asset to the owners, and they loved and respected him, regardless of him.

Happy was six foot one and weighed 189 pounds. He was dark brown complexioned and kept up his appearance better than the average woman. He also made a point of doing his own pedicure and manicure once a week. Like Tosha, Happy felt that he was born to be a woman, and there was nothing, or no one, who could make him feel any different. For the past two years he'd been saving to have a sex change operation. The way business was going, he would soon have enough to pay for his dream.

One day, Larry was about to drop Pat off at Creativity, but after discovering the salon was also a barbershop, he decided to wait in line for a haircut. Both he and Melody felt uncomfortable being inside the same room as Pat, but Pat, being naïve, contently carried on like she always did, gossiping and boasting about who she was, what she had, and what she was going to do.

"Girl, I looked at a house last week in Perris that was so immaculate and extraordinary, it's unbelievable. It had four huge bedrooms, each with its own bathroom, his and her closets in the master bedroom, a swimming pool, a wraparound balcony, a three-car garage, and it even had a built-in barbecue pit and a Jacuzzi. My husband said that if he could talk them down a little, then he'd go ahead and get it for me. Humph, but I told him, girlfriend, I didn't care if he had to work 24/7, I want that house. Actually, I've already claimed it. All he has to do is a little negotiating," Pat said as she examined her fingernails, determining whether or not she should have them done.

Spoiled bitch! Melody thought. *Ooh, I can't stand this big mouth ho!*

"I heard that, girl, go for it," Melody said while remaining poised. "Everybody isn't able."

Larry was pretending not to be listening, but he could not help hearing his wife boast. He and Melody tried hard not to acknowledge each other's presence, but it was almost impossible. Every now and then they threw sneak-peeks and smiles at each other, trying to keep things on the down low.

After Happy finished doing his weave customer and collected for his services, he strolled over to the waiting area using his sexiest walk. He approached the five men waiting for haircuts, then scanned their faces.

"Who's next?" Happy asked. He was wearing a pair of skin-tight jeans, a pink tank top, and a matching pair of pink woman's sandals.

Among the waiting men was the good Reverend Joe Black, who was reading scripture. Happy's presence caused the Reverend to pause momentarily and shake his head in disgust.

"God made Adam and Eve, not Adam and Steve, young man."

Happy ignored the Reverend and looked at the remaining four customers, but the men looked at each other with dumbfounded expressions. None of them were down with the "gay" thing, and they didn't want the homo to put his hands on them. They had heard too many frightening stories about homosexuals.

Instinct told Larry that none of the gentlemen desired the attention of a gay hair stylist, so he stood up.

"Well, what the hell? I'll be next."

As Happy led the way to the styling chair, switching like he was modeling a thousand-dollar dress, Larry turned his head in disgust. All the waiting men thought Happy was obscene, but the women smirked, thinking he was rather funny.

As Pat sat in the styling chair watching her husband get prepped by Happy, she commented to Melody.

"I swear, girlfriend, if that fucking faggot touches my husband in places he doesn't have any business, I'll get up from this chair and beat the hell out of him."

Melody smiled.

Yeah, bitch, that's what you think, Melody thought. *A fag isn't nothing but a man, and believe me, he'll make you regret you ever fucked with him. I wish you would, bitch, 'cause I'll be laughing my ass off while he's beating your ass.*

"I heard that, girlfriend, but if I were you, I'd just shoot him, 'cause I heard they're strong as hell, and know how to fight," Melody responded.

"Let him touch my husband in the wrong place, and I'll put some hot lead in his ass," Pat said as she touched the gun she carried in her purse.

"You carry a gun, girl?" Melody asked.

"Damn right I do. I don't leave home without it. Ever since those gang-bangers began migrating from L.A., I make it a point to carry some protection. "

Once Happy finished with Larry's hair, Larry went outside and waited in his truck, simply because each time he looked at Melody, he got aroused. So under the circumstances, his truck was the safest place to be.

While appraising herself in the mirror, Pat smiled.

"Yes. I love it, I love it, I love it. How do I look, girlfriend?"

"Marvelous, sweetheart. Better yet, outstanding. You look like a million bucks and a queen," Melody answered.

Pat paid her for her services and gave her a twenty-five dollar tip. "Thanks, Mel. You're the best."

Yeah, bitch, your husband thinks so too.

Pat had taken a couple steps toward the front door, and then turned around like she'd forgotten something.

"Why don't you and Byron stop by later this evening for some barbecue, Melody?" Pat asked.

"Sounds good to me, girl. And hell, that's right up my alley. You know I don't like to cook anyway. Byron calls me the microwave queen."

As Melody was about to walk Pat outside, Reverend Black paused momentarily from reading scripture to a few customers.

"Loooord, have mercy. Ump, ump, ump. Father God in Heaven, I can say that you've blessed those women in all the right places. Please forgive me, Lord, but I know you don't mind me looking. 'cause, Lord, all that you created is good, and believe me, Lord, that's all good. Lordy, Lordy, Lordy."

The men he was ministering to agreed, saying, "Amen!"

Melody rushed back inside and began thumbing through her appointment book.

Damn, I'm behind schedule. It's one fifteen, and if I hang around and wait for my next customer, I'll be late for my two o'clock date with Larry. So she hurriedly put away her supplies and left.

At three-thirty, Larry walked through Melody's front door. As usual, Melody led him to her bedroom. She had been arguing with Byron for the past twenty-five minutes because of his laziness.

"Boy, me and Larry give you ten dollars a week for allowance, but you don't do a goddamn thing around this house but watch BET, ESPN, and play that damn Nintendo all day. But that shit is gonna stop!"

Melody made it a point to make sure Larry heard her chew out Byron if he was over. She didn't want him to think she was soft or too easy on her son. Standing at his bedroom door, Byron was upset, but wisely he did not say a word, realizing his mother was showing off in front of Larry. She continued scolding him.

"You don't take out the trash when I ask you, you don't clean up your room, you half wash the dishes, you half vacuum the floor, and boy, from the way you're performing, when you grow up, you're going to be just like your Uncle Charlie, who hasn't worked a day in his goddamn life."

"She's right, Byron," Larry interjected. "Your mother is only trying to mold you because one day she knows you'll be a man. But it all starts when you're young," Larry explained, proud to be stepping up and schooling the youngster.

"You're not my father, and you don't tell me what to do!" Byron shouted, annoyed that someone other than his father was giving him advice.

"Watch your mouth, boy!" Melody said. "You don't talk to grown folks like that! After all the things Larry has done for you, you'd better show him some respect! Now I want you to apologize to him right this minute!"

Byron stood there frowning.

"Why do I have to apologize to him? He's not my father! I'm about to call my father and tell him Larry's bossing me around!" He took off running.

"You're not going to call nobody, boy! You're going to apologize like I told you to do!" Melody yelled.

Byron slammed the door to his room and stood behind it.

Larry tried to calm down Melody. "He'll be all right, sweetheart. Let him cool off a bit and he'll be all right." He then closed her bedroom door, got undressed, fired up a joint, and took a seat at the edge of the bed. Like an ant crawling to food, Melody eased up to him and began stroking his penis, then began sucking it. He was fully erect, just the way she liked it. Her lips moved up and down his shaft, giving him the pleasure he had never received from his wife. After fifteen minutes of oral sex, Melody was overheated with passion and was close to melting.

"Put it in. Hurry and stick it in," Melody said desperately. Like a professional wrestler, he flipped her over, positioned himself on top of her, and rammed his penis deep into her hot, wet womb, pumping like a madman. Her sex cries caused him to plunge even harder and rougher, but that's how she liked it. Then suddenly, the door was kicked down and Byron came charging in like Superman, holding a butcher knife.

"Get off my mama before I kill you!" Byron yelled.

"Get that boy out of here, Melody. What the hell is wrong with him?" Larry shouted on the down-stroke.

"Get out of here, Byron!" Melody said, embarrassed that Byron had caught her in the act. "And put that goddamn knife back in the kitchen, boy! I told you to stay in your room!" She was lying underneath Larry.

Byron stood there in shock until he witnessed Larry pulling his long penis out of his mother. Byron turned around and ran back to his room, screaming, "I wanna call my father! I wanna call my father right now!"

Melody jumped out of bed, hurriedly got dressed, and went to the kitchen. She had no idea what she was going to tell Byron, but she knew she had to come up with one quick. Confused, embarrassed, and not knowing what to do, she decided a glass of vodka might calm her and help her figure out what to do next.

When she returned to her bedroom with drinks, Larry was already dressed and kicking back, watching the *Montel Williams Show* while smoking a joint.

"I apologize for this, honey. But from now on when you come over, I'll send him to his friend's house, or tell him to go to the park and play basketball."

"Yeah, that'll be a good idea," Larry said, and then took a long swallow of vodka.

After finishing their drinks, Melody walked Larry to his truck and gave him a kiss.

"By the way, your wife invited me and Byron over for barbecue later this evening, and I wouldn't want to disappoint her, so we'll be over about six."

"I hope I can control myself, sweetheart. Hell, if I think

about what you just laid on me, I'll probably be trying to sneak you inside my bathroom for a quickie."

Melody smiled, leaned inside his truck, gave him another kiss, and then said goodbye.

Once inside, she fixed herself another drink and lit a cigarette, now trying to figure out what she was going to tell Byron.

Damn. What lie am I going to tell that boy that would make any sense to him? He's not stupid, so I can't tell him just anything. Damn!

Two glasses of vodka and a joint later, she came up with what she thought was a bright idea. She figured for now a new outfit and a new pair of tennis shoes would erase what he had seen.

First, we'll go by Pat's for barbecue, and then I'll take him to the mall. And on the way home, I'll stop by Blockbuster to rent him a few games and a movie. By then he should be all right. Tomorrow is another day.

"Byron!" she yelled from the dining room table. "Come out and wash yourself up so I can take you to the mall with this money Larry gave me for you. But first, we're going to stop by Pat's for barbecue."

"Yes!" he shouted, forgetting he was ever angry.

It was six-fifteen PM when Melody and Byron arrived at the Myers residence. There were several cars parked in the driveway and lots of cars parked on the street. Melody rang the doorbell and stood there, smiling. Seconds later, Pat appeared, looking as beautiful and flawless as ever.

"Hey girl," Pat greeted, smiling. "Glad you guys could make it." She then looked at Byron. "Hey, Byron, how you doing, man? Boy, you're growing by the minute, aren't you?"

"Yep. I'm going to be a basketball player, Auntie Pat." Byron grinned.

"Good, Byron. That means Auntie will get free tickets to come see you play all over the world, right?" He stood there grinning. Pat continued. "I told my nephews you were coming over, and they're in the room waiting for you."

"Yes!" Byron shouted excitedly, and then disappeared down the hallway.

"Come on, girl," Pat said, leading the way. "Let me introduce you to a few of my friends and relatives. And hey, girlfriend, you might find a prospective husband, you know what I mean? Availability is plentiful here."

Like always, Pat was dressed perfectly for the occasion. She had on a pair of cut-off jean shorts, revealing her nice, thick, smooth, peanut butter-complexioned legs and rounded butt. The rainbow colored halter-top she was wearing exposed her enticing cleavage and nipples. On her feet she wore a pair of sandals that matched the gold bracelets and chains she had on.

Proudly, Pat walked with Melody to the den to meet the others. Larry, at that moment, was acting as the DJ and had just put on the James Brown hit "This is a Man's World."

As Melody walked side-by-side with Pat, she prayed that Pat didn't smell Larry's odor on her. She hadn't taken a bath since her sexual encounter with him. Once Melody had spotted Larry, she tried her best to keep her eyes off him, but thoughts of the hot sex they had earlier kept haunting her mind. After Pat introduced her to a few family members and friends, Melody made it a point to separate herself from Larry by mingling with others, but still she couldn't seem to keep her mind off him. It was no use. She was in love with him and was more than willing to accept being the other woman.

After fixing her and Byron two plates of food to go, Melody then said goodnight to everyone and left.

At the mall, Byron picked out an outfit that cost a little over $125, and without complaining, Melody paid for it. After all, he had not only caught her with her pants down, but he'd caught her fucking. She felt she owed him at least that much. And besides, it prevented her from having to explain. After scooping up video games and movies from Blockbuster, they made their way home.

"Mom, are we going to church tomorrow?" Byron asked before he even said thank you for the new outfit. "I want to hear Reverend Black preach. Please, Mom, please?"

"No telling how I'll feel tomorrow, boy, but we'll see," Melody answered while continuing to walk to her bedroom. Once she got inside her room, she took off her clothes and got ready for bed.

The following morning she awakened with the good intentions of going to church, but dismissed the thought after drinking the remains of a half-full bottle of Heineken.

Damn, I sure wish Larry was my husband, Melody thought as she sat at her dining room table. *He makes a lot of money, knows how to fuck good, knows how to make woman feel good ,and he's good looking. What more could a woman ask for? I guess for now, I've got to accept being the other woman.*

Later that evening, Larry dropped by unexpectedly. It was unusual for a Sunday. He picked up Melody and took her for a ride.

"I've got a surprise for you, baby," he said to her.

"Oooh, I love surprises. Especially yours," she replied. Forty-five minutes later they were entering the doors of Levitz furniture store.

"Baby, I know you've been talking about that worn-out, old furniture for the past six months or so, and since you've made me a happy man in more than one way, I've decided to let you choose whatever you want out of here to furnish your home," Larry announced as he smiled at her. "I'll arrange for someone to pick up your old furniture tomorrow morning and deliver your new furniture. Thanks for being so considerate and loving, sweetheart."

Melody grabbed him and held him tightly. "I love you, baby. Thank you for being a part of my life," Melody gushed.

Four days later, Larry arranged for a CD player, two brand-new twenty-seven-inch color televisions, two VCRs, and a house full of beautiful plants to be delivered to Melody's home. She was grateful that her home, thanks to Larry, now looked complete and attractive. Later that night she showed him her appreciation.

One day while relaxing inside in her brand new recliner, sipping vodka, Melody decided to call her mother, who had relocated back to her native Mississippi after Mr. Swift's passing.

"Hey, Mama, how you doing?" Melody was in great spirits.

"I'm jus' fine, chile. We been having thunderstorms here lately, and it's been pretty cold down here too, but Mama's all right," Stella said.

"Mama, I've told you time after time, you need to move back to California where the weather is always great, but you're too much in love with the country life," Melody said, then took another sip of vodka.

"Chile, it's too many damn people in California for me. It's too fast, and there's too much goddamn crime out there for me. And besides, those damn gang-bangers have taken over y'all cities. So, I'm jus' fine where I'm at, chile," Stella said. "So how are things going with you?" She was waiting for Melody to begin lying, which she had a habit of doing.

"Everything's OK, Mama. Complaining ain't going to do me any good, so I've learned to accept things the way they are, you know?"

"Have you divorced him yet?"

"Mama, lately I've barely had enough time to wash my own face, and I—"

"Quit makin' all those damn excuses, chile. If you know like I know, you'd quit makin' excuses and let that heavy baggage go, so you can move on with your life."

"Where am I going to get money for a divorce, Mama? Hell, after I pay these bills around here, I hardly have anything left for myself. It isn't easy being a single parent, you know," Melody said, and then took another sip of vodka.

"If you quit buyin' Byron all those expensive clothes and shoes, then maybe you'll be able to pay your damn bills," Stella stated. She then paused. "Are you still foolin' around with that married man?"

The question caught Melody off guard. She was a little shocked that her mother knew so much, but she was more annoyed than anything.

"Mama! Why are you always asking me about my personal life?"

"I guess that means you're still foolin' around with him, huh? Chile, I don't know where you got that shit from, 'cause you damn sure didn't get it from me or your daddy. Tell me sump'n, chile, how would you feel if he was your husband and he was foolin' around with one of your friends?"

"If he was my husband, Mama, I'd know how to keep him in my bed," Melody replied, and then took a long swallow of vodka.

"You sure talk stupid, chile, but I'll tell you what, when your customer finds out you're sleepin' with her husband and still doing her hair every two weeks, she'll have every right to blow your goddamn brains out."

"Where are you getting your information from, Mama?"

"Don't worry about it, chile. Like I said, when that woman finds out, your ass is gonna be ten feet under."

"Yeah, yeah, yeah, whatever, Mama. It wasn't nobody but big-mouth Tony who told you that stuff."

"I didn't say that, chile, you did."

"Whatever. But anyway, if I wanted to hear a sermon, I'd go to church."

"Church!" Stella shouted. "Chile, how in the hell could you sit in a church, doing the kinda shit you be doing? You need to get right with God, chile, that's what you need to be tryin' to do. Ain't no way in hell you can sit in the Lord's house with all that smut on you. You need to repent and ask for forgiveness, chile, 'cause the way you're livin', you're going straight to hell. Your daddy and me didn't raise you that way, Melody. Hell, you should be tryin' to find yourself a real husband, that's what you need to be tryin' to do."

"What makes you think I want a new husband? And how you know I haven't already found somebody?"

"Quit talking crazy, chile. If you had somebody new, you would've told me by now. That's how I know you're still foolin' around with that married man," Stella explained.

"Are you done preaching, Mama?"

"Yeah, chile, I'm finished. Hell, I ain't doing nothin' but wastin' my breath anyway. But you need to straighten out your life for your own good, and for the well-being of your son."

"OK, Mama. Take care and I'll talk to you later," Melody said.

Initially she had called her mother to inform her about her new furniture and electronics, but after receiving a long sermon, she decided not to bring it up.

She then made her way to the new CD player and put on a bootleg CD by Shirley Brown entitled *Woman to Woman*. She begin singing along with the lyrics.

"Woman to woman, if you were in my shoes, wouldn't you have done the same thing too…"

The effect of the vodka kicked in, causing Melody to talk out loud.

"Why me? Why me? Why do I have to share a dick with another woman? Mama's right! I need my own damn husband! But what in the hell am I supposed to do in the meantime about these goddamn bills?"

She then began crying. "I need a man to sleep with at night, so he can hold me and tell me everything's gonna be all right. I need a man to wake up to, to kiss me in the mornings, and fuck me all night. I need a man to take me on vacations once a year like normal people do. I need a man to sit next to me in church, and to watch movies with me. I need someone to love me, for me, not because of how good my sex is. Why me? Why? Why do I have to share a goddamn man? Why in the fuck can't I have my own? Fuck it!" she wailed.

* * *

The following Sunday, Melody and Byron sat among the congregation in church. The Good Reverend Joe Black was preaching up a storm.

"I'm here to tell you what you need to hear. Can I get an Amen?"

"Amen!" the congregation shouted in unison.

"You see, there's a lot of you in here that has some nerve!" The Reverend continues. "There's a lot of you in here who committed fornication and adultery last night! And there are lots of you in here that lusted for someone who isn't yours! There are a lot of you in here that had alcohol last night and smoked weed! But I'm here to tell you, people, that as long as you're full of sin, you won't be blessed! And there are some of you in here that are so full of sin, you're confused and don't know which sin to eliminate first! But you'd better start somewhere! Yes, you definitely better start somewhere, because God is watching you! Get right with the Lord, my people! Then someday you can look forward to joining our God in heaven."

At that moment Melody grabbed Byron's hand.

"Come on, baby, let's get out of here. Mama doesn't feel too good."

During the ride home, Byron began asking questions.

"Mom, why does Reverend Joe Black be screaming like he's mad or something?"

"That's his way of expressing himself and hoping to get a message across to the congregation," Melody answered, turning into her driveway.

"Did God tell him to scream at people in the church?"

"No, he didn't, Byron, but the Reverend is an emotional and energetic man. God uses people like him to spread his word in hopes that they'll get a true understanding out of it, and they'll live right, according to the way God wants them to live."

"Oh," Byron replied thoughtfully. "Mom, why is it that when Reverend Joe Black starts preaching, you always want to leave?"

He stared into his mother's eyes. The question caught her off guard.

"Mama be tired, Byron," she replied. "My feet and my head be hurting most times, but today, my stomach hurts," she lied.

"Why did you even bother going to church today then, Mom?"

"Byron, you're giving me a damn headache from asking all these unnecessary questions. Now I've told you I don't feel good, boy, so rest your tongue and save the rest of your questions for later. Better yet, for tomorrow. Maybe by then I'll feel a little better."

She then made her way to her bedroom, took off her church clothes, and sat on the edge of her bed.

Damn, that boy asks too many questions. Maybe he'll be a lawyer one day. Humph, I sure hope so.

After getting comfortable, Melody went downstairs, put on Al Green's "Love and Happiness," fixed herself a glass of vodka, and began talking out loud to herself.

"I'll bet that goddamn Reverend Joe Black ain't no saint! I'll bet he's fucked every one of those women in the church. I'll bet he has! I know he was looking at my and Pat's asses that day he was in the shop. He hides behind that Bible like he doesn't do any wrong, but he ain't fooling me. It takes one to know one." She then turned up her glass of vodka and finished it.

Around four thirty the phone began ringing. Melody quickly checked her caller ID, but couldn't figure out who the caller was. She hadn't recalled ever seeing the number before.

"Fuck it!" she said out loud, and then lifted the receiver. "Hello?" Melody answered.

"Hey, baby, how you doing?" the caller asked.

"Who is this?" Melody asked, not recognizing the voice.

"This is your junior high and high school sweetheart, baby."

"Maurice?"

"Yep, it's me, baby. What's up?"

"Hey love, what's going on with you? And why haven't you called me lately?"

"Well, number one, I just got back from the Middle East last night. And number two, I had to make over twenty calls to find out your number."

"I'm sorry, baby, I didn't mean to make it so hard for you. But anyway, how have you been, and are you still traveling?"

"I've been all right, Melody, but what I'm not too enthused about is leaving for Japan in two weeks."

She was intrigued. "Where's your wife?"

"Where's your husband?" He shot the question back at her.

"That's not fair, Maurice. I asked first."

"OK, you win. She's in Texas, but we're in the process of getting a divorce. Now, where's your husband?"

"In jail like always," Melody answered, massaging her clitoris. The sound of his voice aroused her. She visualized his huge penis.

"Well, baby cakes, since neither of us are tied up by our spouses, let's get together for old times' sake."

"I'd probably enjoy that, Maurice," she answered. After giving him her address, she hung up and took a hot bath.

Maurice had joined the military after high school. Fortunately, he made a career out of it and had become a Lieutenant Commander in the Navy. He stood six-one, and had a hard, military build. He wore his hair in a neat, short fade, and was of a medium-brown complexion. He smiled when he spoke, and he had excellent manners. However, his personality had changed once he'd gotten promoted from sergeant to lieutenant. He went from a polite gentleman to becoming demanding and speaking with more authority.

He had taken Melody's virginity when they were in the eighth grade. By the time they made it to the twelfth grade he dropped her like a hot potato, and went for a girl who he felt was more attractive and more of a freak than Melody.

Melody sensed it was going to be a long night, so she hurriedly microwaved a couple potpies for Byron, and then rushed them to him, along with cookies, chips, and a glass of fruit punch.

It was almost nine when Maurice arrived in his Mercedes Coupe. The military had served him extremely well, both mentally and physically. As he stepped into Melody's home, she wished like hell that they would've remained together after high school, gotten married, and had kids. During their phone conversation she remembered him more by the size of his huge penis than by his good looks.

Damn, he's still fine and built good too, Melody thought as she led Maurice into the den.

While seated side by side on her new sofa they began talking about old times and drinking Hennessy.

"So, what's been going on in your life?" Maurice asked, running his hands up and down her legs. She showed no sign of resistance. Deep down inside she yearned for what she had not had in close to twenty years. She then put on a few tunes that took them back to their junior high and high school days. They reminisced about the times they had sex in her father's garage, in the backseat of her father's car, and in parks. Afterward she returned to the den, grabbed Maurice by the hand, and led him to her bedroom.

Damn. Humph, he's hard already, and it feels like it's gotten bigger, Melody thought as the slow danced in her bedroom. *Damn, does he look good in his uniform. I wish he was mine, but like all the others, he had to be married. Maybe we could have a couple more kids, and maybe I could travel overseas with him, and maybe...*

Maurice's tongue sliding in and out her ear and up and down her neck interrupted her thoughts. She welcomed his tongue by opening her mouth, and began kissing him in the same way they kissed in school. Instantly, she wanted him to fuck her, but decided to hold off. She wanted it to be worthwhile and memorable. It might be another twenty years before she would get the opportunity to get a piece of him again. She definitely wanted to savor the memory.

I wonder if he knows how to eat pussy? He has to know how, because he's been all over the world. Hell, I hope he doesn't have any of those damn diseases those people be carrying overseas.

They then began discussing school days, people they went to school with, and people they had known who were now either dead, on drugs, or doing life in prison.

At one thirty AM the party was still going on. The Hennessy had taken its toll on the both of them. They were sloppy drunk, heated with passion and curiosity, and desperately wanted each other, not just for old times' sake, but also for the moment.

Melody was about to erupt. Her pussy was as hot as the forth of July and as wet as the Pacific Ocean. They wasted no time getting undressed or indulging in foreplay. Instead, they got right down to the nitty-gritty.

"Damn, that thing doesn't look human," Melody said while staring in disbelief at Maurice's penis. She had forgotten just *how* big it was.

"And I know how to use it too, baby," Maurice replied roughly, pinning her down like a wrestler. With no mercy, he rammed his rock hard penis inside her and began plunging into her quickly and deeply.

"Ahwwooo! Oooh, ahww, ohhh, ahww, oh, ah," she cried with pain. It was sweet music to his ears. He loved it when they screamed.

"Ahwoo, Ohhhoooo, ah, shit," she screamed, unable to hold back the yells. Twenty minutes later, Maurice still had not climaxed and was still plunging hard and deep. Then suddenly he grabbed her like he hated her and positioned her at the edge of the bed, doggy-style, ramming himself inside her, again, and plunged in and out like a piston. He was sweating like a madman.

Damn, I hope Larry can't tell I've been fucking, Melody thought while holding her face into a pillow, trying to conceal her yells of pain. *My pussy hurts. He's going to open it too wide. I'd better put some vinegar on it to tighten it up. Damn!*

Finally, he climaxed. When he pulled out his penis there was blood everywhere.

"Look! You may have caused me to have female problems," Melody said hysterically. She then rushed to the restroom. He followed behind.

"That's the way you liked it back in the day, remember?" He grabbed a towel and cleaned the blood off his still erect penis.

"I'm scared of you, Maurice. You acted like a wild man out in the jungle. Do you fuck all women that way?" She climbed in the shower.

"That's the way they like it, baby. And like I said, the last time me and you had sex, you liked it rough." He was smiling, adoring his penis.

"I like to be caressed, kissed, and talked to, Maurice. I wanted you to make love to me, not try to kill my pussy. Damn, how many kids do you have?"

"Just one; after my wife had Jay Quan, she wasn't able to have any more due to female problems," he replied.

"Hell, I can tell why."

He then got in the shower with her, still fully erect, and attempted to put his penis inside her, but she refused.

"Nope. Sorry, baby, but I've had enough for one night," she answered.

When Melody woke up the following morning, it was almost eleven. Maurice was still sleeping, but she noticed he still possessed an erection. She stared at his penis like it was an alien. She didn't want it back inside her, thinking he may cause her severe damage, so she attempted to take it in her mouth, but it was too big. She could only lick it up and down the shaft and stroke it, but it felt good in her hand. He awakened and was immediately ready to go another round, but as she began thinking about Larry, she refused to let him stick it in.

"I'm sorry, honey, but you've worn me out. My pussy is sore as hell. Maybe next time, but right now, I just can't," she explained.

At that moment, Byron pounded on the door.

"Mom! I'm hungry, Mom!" he shouted.

"Fix you a bowl of cereal, boy."

"I can't, Mom, 'cause we're all out of milk!"

"Wait a minute, boy. I'll be out in a minute."

After they had gotten dressed, she led Maurice to the dining room. Byron approached them and stared at Maurice curiously, wondering why this stranger was coming out of his mother's bedroom.

"Byron, this is an old friend of my mine I've known for years," Melody explained. "We went to school together and now he's about to go to Japan."

Standing proudly in his uniform, Maurice extended his hand. "Hey, Byron, how you doing, guy? Your mother's told me lots about you and how well you're doing in school." Without accepting the handshake, or saying a word, Byron took off running to his room and slammed the door behind him.

"What's the matter with him?" Maurice asked. "He acted like he saw a ghost or something."

"He's just acting like that because he doesn't know you, and saw you coming out of my bedroom."

"Protecting Mommy, huh?"

"Yeah, I guess."

After breakfast Melody walked Maurice to his Mercedes, and gave him a kiss and a hug and watched him drive off.

After fixing Byron breakfast, and promising to take him shopping, Melody fixed herself a glass of vodka and sat at her dining room table.

I've never seen a dick that big in my life, Melody thought. *Damn, my pussy is sore as hell. I better take my ass to the doctor to see if I'm all right. Yeah, I'll tell Larry I'm sick. That'll be my reason for not giving Larry any for a few days. Or a week. I wonder if I can go a week without fucking.*

CHAPTER 9

Pat hit the city in her brand-new Lexus, driving slowly, and making sure people noticed her while she moved her head to the beat of Michael Jackson's "I'm Bad." Her Lexus made her feel rich and arrogant. She felt like she owned the world.

After visiting a few friends and relatives, she stopped by Melody's to show off and boast. Luckily for Melody, it was before two o'clock. Otherwise, Pat and Larry would've run into each other. Pat pulled up in front of Melody's house, parking in the wrong direction, and began honking the horn like a New York cabbie. Melody walked outside and approached the Lexus.

"Hey, girl. You got it, huh?" Melody asked, acting as if she were excited.

"Yep," Pat answered. "I picked it up yesterday after I moved into my new house."

"You go, girl, with your bad self," Melody said. "When are you going to take me for a ride? Maybe then I can find me a real husband, and one with money."

"Whenever you're ready, girl. First, I'm about to treat myself to lunch at Sizzler. Would you and Byron like to join me? Treat's on me," Pat offered.

"Thanks, girlfriend. I appreciate the offer, but I have a lot of things to do today, and besides, I promised my sick aunt I'd pay her a visit today," Melody lied. "But will you take a rain check?"

"Anything for my favorite beautician. Oh, and by the way, do you think you can hook me up with a new hairstyle to go with my new house and car?" Pat asked, smiling.

"Just let me know a couple days in advance so I can squeeze you in, girl. Better yet, hon, let's make it for eleven o'clock Wednesday."

"Perfect. I'll see you then."

Before leaving, Pat changed CDs and was now jamming to "Shining Star" by Earth, Wind, and Fire. She eased off, sticking her hand out of her moon roof and waving goodbye.

"Bitch! I hate that bitch!" Melody yelled as she stepped back inside her house. "She's always bragging about this and about that! Ooh, I can't stand her! It's a damn shame that heffa is so spoiled! What if Larry would've been over here? What if we would've been fucking? I've got to have a talk with him, anyway, about his wife! Hell, I'm the one sucking his goddamn dick, not her, but he goes and buys her Lexuses, new homes, and no telling what else! Fuck that!" She then took a long swallow of vodka and lit a joint.

The Sizzler was not as crowded as it normally was during lunch hours. Pat ate lightly—a chef salad, shrimp, and a glass of raspberry iced tea. While eating, she began thinking about her new home and her Lexus.

Whatever the current year is, will always be the year car I drive, Pat decided.

Suddenly Pat heard a voice she recognized from somewhere. The voice was talking loudly and gossiping as it approached the dining area. *Where do I know that voice from?* she wondered. Pat then turned her head toward the direction of the oncoming chatter to see Tosha, the gay beautician from Special Touch. Two other homosexuals, who were also yakking up a storm, accompanied him. After being seated, Tosha spotted Pat and knew right away who she was.

"Unbelievable!" Tosha said, staring wide-eyed at Pat. His companions turned their heads to see what, or whom he was talking about. "That's Melody's client. I swear, today must be my lucky day," Tosha said excitedly. "Remember the bitch I told you I went to jail over? Well anyway, to make a long story short, she's been fucking that woman's husband, and today is my opportunity to spill the beans. Excuse me for a minute while I go put a bug in her ear." As he was about to get up and walk away, annoyed, his lover stopped him.

"Why can't we ever spend time together, Tosha? Every time I look around, an issue, an obstacle, or a person interferes with our quality time, and I've had just about enough of it."

Calmly, Tosha leaned over and whispered something in his lover's ear, and then kissed him on the cheek.

"I'm sorry, baby, but this is something I have to do while I have the chance. I'll make it up to you. I promise."

As usual, Tosha was dressed in skin-tight jeans, a feminine top, and a pair of unisex slippers. Pat had spotted him and his gay friends scrutinizing her, and she hoped they didn't come her way. But her prayers were not answered.

"Hey, girlfriend," Tosha greeted. "It's a small world, isn't it?"

"Uh, yes. Tosha, right?" Pat asked.

"Yep. You remember me, huh?"

"How can I forget you? It's been a while since I last saw you, but one thing I never forget, Tosha, is a face and a name."

"Humph, I see. Anyway, I'm glad to see you, and boy have I got some news for you," Tosha said, batting his eyelashes like a woman.

"Thanks, Tosha, it's a pleasure seeing you again, too," Pat said. "I just left Melody's house a few minutes before I came here. I had to show her my new Lexus, you know," Pat bragged.

"Was your husband there?"

"No, he wasn't. Why, was he supposed to be?" Pat stopped eating and locked her eyes on Tosha.

"You know, girlfriend," Tosha said, and then seated himself, "I hate to be the deliverer of bad news, but I'm not one who beats around the bush, so I'm going to come right out with it."

"What are you talking about?"

Bingo, Tosha thought. *Just what I thought. She might be pretty, but she's stupid as hell.*

"Everyone knows but you, girlfriend."

"Knows what?"

"Knows that Melody has been fucking your husband, and that he's at her house every goddamn day of the week between two and six," Tosha said.

"What makes you say something like that?" Pat asked, stunned.

"I don't see how you didn't know. Hell, it's so damn obvious, girlfriend. I mean, if my man came home late every goddamn day, I would at least suspect something and question him about it," Tosha elucidated.

"But my husband is a working man, and sometimes he works long hours," Pat stammered.

"Yeah, that's what he wants you to think, girlfriend. You see, I remember his truck when he brought you to the shop a few times. And when I kept seeing that same truck parked at Melody's house every day, I put one and one together, added it up, and bingo, my answer was there all the time. Yep, that bitch isn't nothing but a slut, girlfriend, and she's sneaky as hell. Boy, does she have a lot of nerve. I'd kill the bitch if I were you. I thought back to the first time I saw you and your husband at Special Touch. I remembered seeing her write something on a magazine then walk over to your husband and hand it to him while you were underneath the dryer. Yep, I was watching that bitch, because I knew she was up to no good."

"Why didn't you tell me before?" Pat stuttered, wiping tears from her eyes.

"Because at the time, girlfriend, I wasn't sure. I didn't want to jump to conclusions, you know. But now I'm more than sure. You see, my man stays around the corner from Melody, and I'm at his house every day at the same time, just like your husband is at Melody's every day at the same time. And I even got the license plate number from his truck, for proof, so he can't lie about it."

Pat was in a state of shock.

"I bet he's there right now, and you can see it for yourself. I'll tell you what, let's meet outside and we'll go in my car so they won't notice yours," Tosha suggested.

Pat got up from the table, and as if she were hypnotized, walked out the door without paying for her meal.

"Miss! Miss! If you don't pay, I'm calling the police!" the cashier yelled. Satisfied that he'd gotten revenge against Melody, Tosha stepped up and paid Pat's bill.

While waiting for Tosha outside, Pat vomited. Her mind was flooded with thousands of thoughts. She didn't know whether to believe Tosha or not. She actually did not want to believe him.

He just might know what he's talking about, because he has the license plate number to the truck that I cosigned for. And as a matter of fact, Larry doesn't come home until six every day.

Pat got into her Lexus and started it up her, but before she could back up, Tosha pulled up next to her and began honking his horn. Forgetting to lock her new ride, Pat climbed out of her car and got into Tosha's.

It was three thirty when they parked down the street from Melody's. After seeing the license plate number of the white Ford pickup, Pat identified it as Larry's. They waited impatiently for him to come out. Suddenly, Melody and Larry appeared on the doorstep, holding hands and kissing, then she walked him to his truck. She then put her arms around him, pulled him toward her, and gave him a long, wet tongue kiss. Pat watched, bewildered, as tears fell from her eyes like a rainy day in April.

"How could he? How fucking could he! I gave him everything he wanted. I had three kids for him! Gave him so many years of my life! Gave him love, and—" She cried, observing her husband kissing her beautician.

Larry then climbed in his truck and sped off. Immediately, Tosha fired up his Celica, attempting to catch Melody before she made it back inside her house. He stopped in front of her house and hurriedly jumped out the car.

"You bitch!" he shouted. "You're busted, bitch! Your husband-stealing days are over!" Tosha then opened his trunk, grabbed a bumper jack, and handed Pat a crowbar. They rushed at Melody with quickness, but Melody was too swift for them and ran in the house, slamming the door behind her and hurriedly locking the deadbolts. Furiously, Pat and Tosha stood pounding at the door.

"I'll kill you, bitch! You've been doing my hair and fucking my husband at the same time! You dirty, low-down, no good bitch! I'll kill you! I'll fucking kill you!" Pat yelled. Several neighbors came out of their homes and witnessed the scene.

"You phony bitch! I knew it, I knew it, I knew it!" Tosha yelled. The pair then began breaking the windows to Melody's house with their weapons. Minutes later, they climbed back into the Celica and left.

"Well, I felt that you should know, girlfriend," Tosha said once they made it back to Pat's car. "I knew she was up to no good when I saw her approaching your husband and shaking her ass when she handed him that magazine. But now, you're not blind to the fact anymore, and you can handle things the way you see fit. Anyway, you take care, and if you're ever in need of a good beautician, you know where to find me."

After dropping Pat off, Tosha congratulated himself on a mission accomplished, but he left Pat feeling rejected, depressed, and totally confused.

Fortunately, Pat's car was still there when she returned. She sat in her car dealing with a mix of emotions—hate, love, and hurt. She was eager to hear what lie her husband would tell. She fired up her car and accelerated out of the parking lot. She did not look to see what was behind her, and did not care about what was in front of her. She sped southbound on Heacock, repeatedly running red lights.

"Why! Why! I gave my life to him! Why did he do this to me?" she yelled. She reached speeds of eighty miles an hour and didn't care about red lights or the vehicles and pedestrians she almost hit. "Why! I gave him three kids! Three fucking kids! I took care of him when he was sick. Why did he do this?" she cried hysterically.

Pat thought about going to question Melody, but she wanted to interrogate her husband first. Then suddenly she put the pedal to the metal and drove in a fury of rage. The vehicles beside her slowed down to let her have the road, and the oncoming traffic pulled over as she swerved from one side of the street to the other.

As she approached an intersection, the horn from a big rig blared out, but Pat was deaf to all the sounds around her. The two vehicles collided, the Lexus no match for the huge tractor trailer. Pat's car flipped over several times and rolled into a vacant field.

CHAPTER 10

Pat had been in a coma for twenty-eight days. By the looks of things, she wasn't coming out any time soon. Her son, Randy, who was twenty-four, her twenty-three-year-old daughter, Angela, and her twenty-year-old daughter, Monique, had all put aside their schooling and jobs to be at their mother's bedside. For the first week, half of Larry's time was devoted to being at the hospital, 20 percent went to Melody, and the other 30 percent was spent dutifully working on his scrap accounts. Even though he loved his wife, he told himself that life went on.

During the second week of her hospitalization, Larry and Melody began seeing each other more often than before, which enhanced their relationship and allowed them to be more open. They began going to restaurants, liquor stores and grocery stores, video outlets, and even local fast food stands together. No longer did they try to conceal their relationship.

The third week Pat was in the hospital, Larry took Melody back to Levitz furniture, but this time, he purchased completely new bedroom sets for her and Byron's rooms. The total cost was twenty-two hundred dollars. Later that night, she loyally showed him her appreciation.

Each day Larry was with Melody, his children, who were at

the hospital with their mother, naturally assumed he was out working. That was what he told them.

One Thursday morning while at the hospital, Angela and Monique decided to leave for a few hours to go to a beauty salon to restore their attractiveness. They were much overdue.

"Daddy, Monique and I are about to find a beauty salon to get replenished. Do you mind staying with Mom and Randy until we get back?" Angela asked.

"Of course not, angels. And, hey, I want both of you to know I really admire what you've been doing. Leaving school to come see about your mother and showing your concern means a lot to the both of us," Larry said. He then grabbed his daughters and hugged them. "You two go ahead and take care of your business, OK? I'll pull a bed out alongside your mother and look at her while I reminisce about the good times we've had together. Hell, as tired as Randy looks, he'll be out like a light before I know it. So what salon are you going to?"

"Nowhere too far, Dad." Angela answered. She was the more talkative of the two. "We don't know too much about this city, so we'll probably just drive around until we find somewhere we think is appropriate."

"Hey, you know what? There's a lady named Melody who's been doing your mother's hair for a long time. Supposedly, she's talented and affordable. I think they do manicures and pedicures there too."

"Excellent," Monique replied. "How far is it, Dad? We don't want to be gone too long, you know?"

"Ask for Melody," Larry said after giving them directions.

"Good. Thanks, Dad," Angela said, and then walked over to her mother and kissed her on her forehead. Monique followed suit, and then they left.

A few minutes later Randy fell asleep in the chair watching an old rerun of *L.A. Law*. Larry left the room and made his way to a telephone to call Melody.

"Hey, baby, what's up?" he asked, sitting in the waiting room.

"Heeeey. I was just thinking about you, honey. What's on your mind?"

"You, baby, as usual. I just called to let you know I'm still at this damn hospital, and I miss you, need you, and want you right now."

"I'm here for you, baby. Always."

"That's good to know, sweets. Believe me, about right now, I really need a shoulder to lean on, you know. One of those soft, juicy, delicious titties to lick on would be right on time, too."

"Sounds good to me, honey, but later sounds even better." She was styling a customer's hair at the moment.

"Just to let you know, babe, I've sent you my daughters as customers. Fix them up for me, OK? They're taking this kind of hard. I hate that they left college and all, but they chose to be at their mother's bedside. Anyway, I gave them directions and they should be there within the next twenty to thirty minutes. Their names are Angela and Monique. You won't have a problem telling which one Angela is, because she's the outspoken one. Monique is the shy one."

"For you, the world, sweetheart. Don't worry, I'll take care of them. Oh, and by the way, how's your wife doing?"

"She's still in a coma right now."

"Oh, I'm sorry to hear that. You sound depressed. Are you all right?"

"Yeah, I'm fine. It's just this hospital thing is burning me out, you know?"

"Well hopefully everything will be back to normal soon and you can go on with your life. In the meantime, don't worry; I've got your back. I don't need you stressing yourself out and getting a heart attack, so try to stay calm," she said vigilantly.

"Thanks, I needed that."

Larry made his way to the cafeteria, grabbed a couple of burritos, and then went back to the room and began watching television. A few hours later, a doctor appeared at Pat's bedside and began studying her medical chart while monitoring the machines that were connected to her.

"Hi, I'm Dr. Smith. Are you Mr. Myers?"

"Yes, I am," Larry answered. He then offered a handshake. The voices awakened Randy. He discreetly began listening.

"Well, I have some news for you. It doesn't look too good at this point," the doctor explained. Randy jumped up from his chair.

"Is my mother going to be all right?"

"Wait a minute, son, and let the doctor give us his evaluation."

"I'm going to make this as brief and to the point as possible," Dr. Smith elucidated. "Mrs. Myers is paralyzed from the waist down. The neurology staff doesn't hold out much hope for any improvement."

"No! You're wrong! You're dead fucking wrong! My mother's going to be all right! No!" Randy yelled. He then went into a rage and began pulling down curtains, throwing objects around the room, and crying. "No! This can't be! Not my mother! No!"

Larry grabbed his son and embraced him. He then glanced at Dr. Smith.

"Oh, my God! Please tell me I'm not hearing this, Doc," Larry yelled. Larry led Randy to Pat's bedside. After allowing them a few minutes to calm down, Dr. Smith spoke up again.

"Thank God she's still living," Dr. Smith said. "You both need to count your blessings. It could have been a lot worse. There's not many people who'll survive going eighty miles an hour and getting struck by a big rig. So actually, Mrs. Myers is a very fortunate woman, and hopefully, within the next few days, she'll be out of the coma. I'll leave it up to you to break the news to her. You guys stay strong and may God bless you. I'll see you tomorrow," Dr. Smith said, and then he left the room.

Holding hands, Larry and Randy began praying. Since Larry wasn't a godly man and didn't know how to pray, Randy led the prayer.

* * *

As Angela and Monique entered Creativity, they observed the professionals at work, then approached the receptionist. Angela, who was the more arrogant and aggressive of the two, spoke up first.

"Excuse me, ma'am. We're here to see a beautician named Melody."

Even though it was ninety-two degrees outside, Angela was wearing a beige pantsuit and a pair of matching low pumps, as if she were on her way to a business meeting. She was five-seven and had a caramel colored complexion. Her hair was long, wavy, and jet-black like her mother's, and also like her mother, she possessed an extremely high dose of self-assurance, arrogance, and egotism. Both sisters wore glasses, and had small breasts and flat butts, but they were very smart, clever, and intelligent. Next year would be Angela's first year at Harvard Law School. Through sheer determination and persistence she was already ahead of the average Harvard Law student. By working part-time for a prestigious law firm, she was able to learn many different aspects of law.

Monique had two years left at Florida State University before she could join her sister at Harvard. She was shorter than Angela, standing five foot five, and weighed 115 pounds. She'd inherited her father's high-yellow complexion and her mother's good looks.

Melody shot a glance at the sisters when they entered the salon. *That must be those stuck-up bitches. Just look at them, coming in here like they own the goddamn world or sump'n,* Melody thought while continuing to work on her current customer's hair.

As Angela and Monique stood at the counter waiting for the cashier to finish ringing up a sale, the Asian owner, who owned a chain of salons, looked toward Melody.

"Melody! You got customer! Come!" Melody acknowledged them by holding up her hand, displaying a forced smile, and saying, "One moment, please. I'll be right with you." The Myers sisters glanced around the salon, admiring the skillful professionals at work.

"How convenient," Angela commented.

"Yes," Monique replied. "Very convenient."

"Hi ladies. Can I help you?" Melody asked as she approached the sisters with a pleasant smile.

"I'm hoping you can," Angela replied. "We're overdue as you can see. My dad recommended us to you, and said you've been my mom's beautician for quite some time now. He also told us that you're said to be Moreno Valley's finest."

I wish this spoiled bitch would cut her speech short and have a damn seat. Hell, I've got a two o'clock appointment with your daddy, Ms. Wannabe Lawyer, Melody thought.

Melody's animosity toward Monique and Angela could be traced to a phone call Larry received some time before when Melody and Larry were lying in bed together. The girls called to tell him they needed laptop computers for school.

"I'll check around to see if I can find a couple on sale, and if I find them, I'll Fed Ex them to you right away," Larry told his daughters.

"But, Dad," Angela said, "we need them like yesterday. What if you can't find a sale?" Monique, who had always been Daddy's little girl, interrupted.

"Dad, come on! We really need the laptops to do our work more efficiently, and we need them by next week. Besides, the other students all have them."

"OK, OK. I'll stop by Circuit City and Sam's Club to see who'll give me the best deal," Larry answered. "Why can't you girls get them on the credit cards I gave you?"

"The cards only had a five thousand dollar limit, Dad, and we're already over that," Angela said. "Anyway, give my love to Mom, and make sure you let the salesman know that both laptops need to be Internet ready. He'll know what that means."

"OK, Internet ready, got it," Larry had said, getting aroused by Melody rubbing his penis.

Once the connection was broken, Larry explained to Melody what his daughters had requested. Thoughtfully, she gave him a few reasonable suggestions.

"There's two swap meets in Moreno Valley that sell laptops, Larry, and I've even seen them in pawnshops. Maybe we should look in the recycler, you know, that way we could save you some money."

"Sweetheart," Larry said, "if my daughters knew I bought their computers from a swap meet, a pawnshop, or out of a recycler newspaper, they'd probably send them back to me quicker than they received them."

"A computer is a computer, Larry," Melody said, raising her voice a few decibels.

"Not to my daughters, honey. They're not the secondhand, swap-meet type, you know."

"Yeah, whatever. Everybody isn't able," Melody said, pissed off at him for giving his daughters what they wanted.

Now, as Melody was finally face to face with the Myers sisters, she did her best not to reveal her animosity toward them.

"You must be Pat and Larry's daughters, huh?" she asked with a phony smile plastered on her face.

"Yes, we are," Angela said. "I have a new hairstyle in mind, like a short, conservative cut, sort of like Halle Berry's. And while we're here we may as well get a pedicure and manicure. Oh, and by the way, how soon could you finish, because my mother's in the hospital and we desperately need to be at her bedside."

"Is she all right? What happened?" Melody asked, pretending to be concerned about Pat and unaware of the accident.

"She was involved in an accident, and, I—never mind. I

don't feel like discussing it. If you'd like to visit her she's at Riverside General on the sixth floor."

"Oh, God. I hope she's all right. I'm sorry to hear that, girls, but please give her my love, and tell your father to hang in there. Now, as far as the hairstyle is concerned, it won't be a problem at all." Melody then forced another fake smile. "They don't call me Moreno Valley's finest for nothing. A beautician has to be flexible, you know, and—"

"I'd like mine curled at the top, and I would like the back to hang down my shoulders and curled at the ends. Can you handle that, Melody?" Monique interrupted.

"Not a problem," Melody replied. "One of you can come with me, while the other sees our manicurist and pedicurist."

These two sure are some rude bitches. Hell, I thought they're s'pose to be smart. Humph, so smart but yet so dumb, Melody thought as she began the procedure on Angela's hair.

CHAPTER 11

Big Steve had written Melody three times a week, but she didn't have the courtesy to respond to any of his letters. She had a collect call block put on her phone to prevent him from calling, but on a couple of occasions he traded his food with an inmate in exchange for a three-way call. Upon hearing his voice she would slam down the receiver, saying out loud, "Fuck him" before he caught the dial tone.

If it weren't for his parents putting money on his account, he would have been doing without. After all, he was still their son, no matter what he had done. There wasn't anything in the world they wouldn't do for their only child.

His mother was infuriated with how Melody treated her son, and she hated her with a passion. She had only put up with Melody because her son loved her, but she had told him many times, "She isn't any good, Steve. If she loved and cared anything about you, she would write you, or she would at least take the block off her phone so she could talk to you. She doesn't care about you, son, and she's probably seeing someone else."

But love, hope, devotion, and loneliness had fueled Steve to continue writing her.

After a year of being in jail, he sent Melody a letter and informed her that he would be released. Although she knew Big Steve would never be all the man she needed, she thought he at least deserved to think he was. She wasted no time springing the news to Larry.

"I have something to tell you, baby," she said to Larry.

"What is it, sweetheart?"

"I received a letter from Steve a couple days ago, and he's about to get out."

"Well, I hope he doesn't mind sharing you, because there's no way in hell I'm going letting you go. I have too much time, money, and feelings invested in you to give you up like that. Unh-unh, no way in hell."

"I wouldn't call it giving me up, sweetheart. Actually, from the way I feel about you, giving you up would be impossible. But sweetheart, don't you think I should at least play it off like I still have feelings for him? After all he is still my husband and he deserves another chance. And that doesn't mean we can't connect on the down low, you know what I mean? We'll just have to be more secretive, you know?"

"You don't have to explain, Mel. I understand. Hell, I'm married too. Both of us are committed to someone else, but we're devoted to each other, so I guess we'll, like you say, be secret lovers and deal with it. We've come too far, sweetheart, to end this now, and believe me, as hooked as I am on you, there's no way in hell I'll let you walk out my life. Not in this lifetime," Larry said sincerely.

"I promise you, honey, we'll make it work," Melody said. She then gave him a long, wet, emotional kiss.

When Melody picked up Big Steve at the county jail, he appeared to have gained twenty-five to thirty pounds. His hair was short and neat, and he had a solemn, calm look on his face. He was dressed in Tommy Hilfiger and a pair of Nikes his parents had sent him. His disposition was different. He was carrying a plastic bag with the accumulated items he'd bought or collected in prison. Melody was leaning against the fender of her car as he neared her. Glad to see his wife, he dropped his bags and showered her with wet, long, emotional kisses.

"I love you, Steve, and I missed you so much. I apologize for not answering your…"

"Shhhh," Big Steve said, embracing her tightly and wiping the flow of tears from her eyes, "You don't have to explain, sweetheart. As long as we mend our relationship, we can forget the past and start on a new future together. From this day on, baby, let's be newlyweds again, OK?" As he looked into her eyes, tears began running from his. "As long as I have you, Melody, I feel like I own the world, but without you, baby, I wouldn't want to go on living. I love you and I forgive you, and hopefully, you'll forgive me for my stupidity and weakness."

"I love you, too, Teddy Bear. And yes, I'm willing to start over fresh and give it another shot," she replied, hiding her true thoughts.

They went home and made love until the sun came up. Every sex act Larry had taught her, she performed with perfection on Steve. Even though he enjoyed the pleasures and new positions, deep down inside, he thought, *She wasn't doing this kind of stuff before I left. I wonder where she learned it.*

"Where'd you learn how to give head like this, Mel?" Big Steve asked out of curiosity.

"Watching X-rated movies and using my imagination. I wanted to have a big surprise for you when you came home, honey, and I was just trying to—"

"Don't get me wrong, baby, it feels hella good, but shit be running through my mind, you know what I'm sayin'?"

"Like what?"

"You know, like you've been—"

"I know goddamn well you're not accusing me of cheating, Steve. I've been faithful to you ever since we've been married, and the only reason I didn't write you was because I've been too busy working and trying to pay these damn bills and keep food on the table! I love you, and I've been faithful to you since you left," she lied.

Silence then filled the bedroom, and minutes later they were sound asleep.

The alarm clock went off the following morning at ten o'clock sharp. Melody wanted to lie there, but thinking about the final notices, and the new gear she'd promised Byron caused her to get up. While she showered, Big Steve fixed himself a bowl of Frosted Flakes until the scrambled eggs, grits, hot-links, french toast, and fried catfish finished cooking. Byron awakened to the smell of breakfast. Knowing his mother didn't cook, he quickly washed his face, brushed his teeth, and then made his way to the kitchen. Upon seeing his stepfather, his eyes brightened with joy.

"Hey Pops, when did you get home?" Byron asked, and then ran to embrace his stepfather with a welcoming hug. Steve picked him up.

"Your mother picked me up last night, son. I want you to know that I love you, and I'm sorry I left without giving you notice. But I promise you, son, that I'll never leave you again." Steve was very sincere. Tears ran from their eyes.

"I love you too, Pops."

It took no time for Byron and Big Steve to restore their father and son relationship. They got along extremely well and began spending lots of quality time together. Byron enjoyed having not only a father, but a friend as well. They went to the movies, to Lakers and Raiders games, and to each of Byron's soccer games. Big Steve would always be standing on the field like he was a coach, cheering for his son. Melody had gotten money from Larry to pay for Byron's uniforms, but neither of them had shown up at any of his games, even though Byron was the best forward in the league. They also enjoyed watching all types of television—ESPN, BET, and both NFL and NBA games—and often played Nintendo games against each other. Out of all the things they had in common, the greatest thing was their love for Melody.

One day after breakfast, Big Steve and Byron walked to the store to grab a newspaper and some sweets. So far, Steve had no luck in finding a job, but he made it a daily ritual to check the classifieds for jobs that did not require any experience. It felt good to be a free man and to walk the streets, observe people, cars, and drama, check out all the hamburger stands, and just to inhale the fresh, clean air.

After entering the store called Fastrip, Big Steve grabbed a paper while Byron helped himself to sweets and snacks.

"Where's my money, nigga?" a voice suddenly yelled from behind Big Steve. "I warned you, cuzz, not to try and do me, but I guess you said, 'fuck me,' so now, homey, I'm about to fuck you in a real way, nigga!" Pork Chop clobbered Big Steve with a baseball bat, while his homeboys knocked him to the floor and stomped him.

"Stop! Stop! Get outta here! I'm calling the police! Stop it!" the store employee shouted.

Byron ran over to see what was going on and he saw his stepdad being stomped and beaten with a baseball bat. He hurriedly grabbed canned goods, bottled sodas, and whatever else was in his reach, and threw them at his father's attackers.

"Leave him alone!" Byron yelled. "Leave him alone!" At the sight of the young man's presence, Pork Chop yelled to his comrades.

"All right, that's enough!" He then directed his words to Big Steve. "Listen, cuzz, this ass kickin' don't mean you ain't gotta pay me. I still want my muthafuckin' money, homeboy! That's it and that's all!" Pork Chop then ran out of the store, climbed into his Suburban, and peeled off.

Byron knelt down at his stepfather's side.

"Call an ambulance! Call the police! Hurry, he's hurt!" Byron yelled. The store employee speedily locked both doors, and then hurried back to the counter and dialed 911. Byron called the salon to inform his mother of what had happened.

The police and ambulance were there within minutes, and Big Steve was transported to Riverside General Hospital. Byron rode in the ambulance with his stepfather.

CHAPTER 12

Melody phoned Larry and informed him of what had taken place at Fastrip.

"I figured this kind of shit was going to happen. I knew it, I knew it, I fucking knew it! I don't wish any bad luck on nobody, but I wish he would go back to jail. Just think, my son had to witness that bullshit."

"Calm down, sweetheart, and chill out for a minute. Like I told you, people like your husband, who are used to living wrong and indulging in all types of illegal activities, sooner or later make their way back to their second home. But anyway, meet me at the Travelodge in an hour, OK. I'll be waiting," Larry said.

When Big Steve regained consciousness, it was three forty-five PM. His parents were sitting at his bedside along with Byron. Melody had called the hospital several times to see if he recovered, but to her advantage, he hadn't. She didn't want to break her promise to Larry, and she had lied to Byron and Steve's parents, telling them that due to her upcoming bills, she needed to stay at work and make some extra money. Big Mama, Steve's mother, did not believe a word Melody said.

"Hey, Pops. How're you feeling?" Byron asked excitedly, happy to see that his pops was doing all right.

"OK, son," Big Steve answered as he looked around the room. "I'm all right, I guess." Steve then surveyed the room more closely. Instinct told him that the picture wasn't complete. Someone was missing. Someone important was missing.

"Where's Melody?" he asked.

Steve's head was pounding in agony. He heard the steady beeping first, a comforting rhythm he latched onto, and then he observed a needle stuck in his right arm attached to an IV. Finally, he noticed the wires attached to his chest and forehead. He couldn't muster the strength to move, so instead he listened and observed. While holding Steve's hand, Woody spoke up.

"She's working late, son. She says she'll be here when she's done with her last customer. She mentioned something about a couple of final notices and insurance payments. But she's called several times to see how you were doing.

Before leaving the Travelodge, Melody made another call to the hospital. Steve was still in a deep sleep, and like a good son, Byron pulled an empty bed so it was beside his father, and he was sleeping as well. Before leaving the hotel room, Melody made a suggestion to Larry.

"Follow me home for a minute, sweetheart, so we can have a quick drink together. Steve probably won't be home for a couple days, and Byron's stuck to him like glue, so we have the house to ourselves. Besides, it's been a good while since I had you in my bed." She then gave him a long, wet kiss.

When they arrived at Melody's they went straight to the bedroom. After sex, they made small talk and plans over vodka and a joint.

"Don't you think you should call the hospital and check on your hubby?" Larry asked after exhaling.

"Yeah, I guess so." She then made the call.

Byron answered and told her that Big Steve was still in a deep sleep, but he had occasionally opened his eyes for a few seconds, and then dozed back off.

"I'm finishing with my last customer now, Byron, but I'll be there shortly."

Melody finally made it to the hospital around eight-thirty. Now that everyone was present, Byron began telling his grandparents and mother what he had witnessed.

"After me and Pops walked in the store, a real ugly man with three gangster looking friends walked over and started hitting Pops with a baseball bat and stomping him. Then I ran over, 'cause that's my pops, and I started throwing sodas, canned dog food, and anything I could get my hands on, so they'd leave Pops alone. Actually, Grandpa Woody, I think I did a bomb job, because after I hit a couple of them with the cans, they ran away, jumped in a black truck, and took off."

"Good job, Byron. And I'm sure your father is very proud of you," Woody said.

"I've got a bold and courageous grandson, huh?" Big Mama said. "I'm proud of you, Byron, but you could've gotten yourself hurt messing around with those gangsters. You know they're probably from L.A., and pretty dangerous."

"I learned karate, kung-fu, jujitsu, and even wrestling watching TV, Big Mama. If those gangsters would've kept stomping and beating my pops, they would've been in trouble. I stay ready for people like them, you know," Byron said seriously.

"You'd better try to stay in those books and back off that TV, boy. That TV can't teach you anything except how to get into a whole lot of trouble," Melody interjected.

"She's right, Byron," Woody said. "Whatever you do, stay in your books so you can get yourself a good education and be somebody someday."

Big Mama walked over to Steve, who was still in a deep sleep, and kissed him. She then began crying.

"We'll be back tomorrow, baby. Mama's going on home for now, so I can call the police station to find out if they've caught those idiots who did this to you." Next Woody knelt over his son.

"Don't worry, son, you'll be all right. We'll see you tomorrow, OK?" He then diverted his attention to Byron. "Watch over your father, OK? God will bless you for that."

"Don't worry, Grandpa Woody, I will," Byron said proudly.

Knowing her mother-in-law didn't care much for her, Melody stood back and listened until after they left. She then relaxed in a chair, grabbed the remote, and scrolled through channels, stopping at the *Jerry Springer Show*. Actually, she wasn't interested in Jerry Springer, Steve, or anything else around her. Her mind was on Larry.

Byron knelt over his stepfather and said a prayer.

"Dear God, please heal my pops and make sure he'll be all right. Forgive him for what he's done, dear God, and please set him back on the right path. He's a good man, God, and to me, he's the best pops in the world. Please answer my prayers, dear God, and please see to it that my pops comes home sooner rather than later. Thank You, Father God, and please watch over my mom too."

Melody observed him and was very surprised at hearing him pray. After Byron finished, Melody told him that it was time to go. After stopping and purchasing a pack of zigzags, a pint of vodka, and two packs of double mint gum, Melody and Byron finally made their way home.

When she entered Creativity the next morning, Happy was running his mouth while styling a customer's hair.

"Girl, did you hear about what happened yesterday at Fastrip?" His words were not directed to anyone in particular. "I heard some gangsters from L.A. raided and robbed Fastrip, beat the hell out of a four-hundred-pound man, and left him lying there for dead. Rumor was that the fat man owed the dope man some money when he lived in L.A., so he moved out here trying to get away from them, but you know how that saying goes, girl. You can run but you can't hide." Happy was sporting a pair of tight, white shorts. His T-shirt exposed his lower stomach and navel, which appeared feminine since he had removed all the hair. The T-shirt read, "Satisfaction Guaranteed."

Melody's ten thirty customer was already seated in the styling chair waiting. Her name was Lisa. She had driven from Oceanside, which she did every two weeks, to get a touch of Melody's perfection.

After placing her customer underneath the dryer, Melody put in a quick call to the hospital. Big Steve was finally fully conscious, and at his bedside, faithfully, were Byron and his parents.

"How's my Teddy Bear doing today?" Melody asked.

"Hey, sweetheart, what's up? I'm fine, but I'd feel much better if you were here," Steve replied, forcing a smile to his beat-up face.

"Well, unfortunately, I had to work, baby. The house note is due, my insurance is due, and—"

"Chill out, Mel. I don't feel like hearin' about bills right now, OK? Anyway, when will I see you?"

"More than likely it'll be after six due to my five o'clock customer," she lied. She then asked, "Do you think you'll be able to whip that thing on me when you come home, because last night, and the night before, you left me using my vibrator and dildo."

"Well, if I can't, baby, I'll sure have fun tryin'. Hey, I really want to thank you for being supportive of me through all this, and believe it or not, I think Byron has a lot to do with me being conscious."

"The agreement we made when we got married was to love one another till death do us part, through thick and thin, for better or for worse, and through sickness and good health. I promised to love you and be faithful to you, Steve, and I'm only doing what I'm obligated to do. I'll see you a little after six, but until then, take care, and get your joy stick ready for me. I'm in need."

"For sure," Steve replied, getting aroused.

When Melody hung up, she dialed Larry's cell number.

"Hi, baaaaby," she said, glad to hear the voice of her secret lover.

"Hey, sweetheart. I miss you like crazy, babe. Where are you?"

"Still at the shop, hon. Where are you?"

"In room 222 of the Travelodge, butt naked and waiting for you," he replied, and then took a swallow of vodka.

"Just the way I like you. I can hardly wait. Give me thirty minutes and I'll be there to take care of your desires."

"Hurry, baby. I'm so hard, I'm throbbing," Larry said, stroking his erection.

After finishing her client's hair and paying booth rent to the owners, Melody then made her way to room 222. She smiled upon entering the room, and then wasted no time getting undressed. The room was filled with chronic smoke and huge, heart-shaped balloons, which read: "I love you." Also there were three boxes of chocolates and a huge, two-foot love card, which read: "You're the best thing that's ever happened to me."

After having sex for close to fifty minutes, they then began discussing the new carpet and tile Larry was about to have put in her home.

"I priced the tile earlier today, baby, and it's going to cost me close to a thousand dollars, and that's at a discounted price," Larry said.

"Isn't that kind of expensive?" she asked, caressing his penis.

"Considering it's marble," Larry said, as if he were a salesman, "actually, that's a damn good price."

"What about the carpet, sweetheart?"

"I bought the carpet already from a wholesale warehouse, and fortunately it only cost me $450. All I have to do now is hire a couple of Mexicans to do the work. Don't worry, baby, I've got all bases covered. What do you think your husband will think when he sees new carpet and marble tile in the house, knowing that you can't really afford it on your salary?"

"Fuck him!" Melody responded. "He can think whatever he wants to think. Hell, he can't afford to do anything for me, Byron, or the house, so what he thinks really doesn't matter to me. And if he doesn't soon find a job he's going to be out on the streets or back at his Mama's house. I don't have time for a broke, jobless man."

"We have to keep things on the down low, Mel, because actually, we both belong to someone else, you know, and things could get real ugly if either of our spouses found out about us."

"Let's not think that way, sweetheart. We can have each other forever if we play our cards right," Melody said. She then gave him a long, wet kiss while stroking his erection.

They departed room 222 a few minutes later and went back to their spouses.

Once Melody and Big Steve made it home and into the bedroom, the freaky show began. Steve had done everything possible to satisfy Melody, but due to her high sex drive, he failed to make her climax. She was furious. She'd gotten used to bigger and better things, and had only gotten irked at not being satisfied.

"Damn, Steve, I haven't cum yet!" she replied. She acted as if she was mad at the world.

"I'm sorry, Mel, but I'm not a hundred percent right now, baby. But in the morning, you know what I'm sayin', I should be able to handle my business."

"I can give a damn about in the morning, I'm talking about now! Hell, I might not wake up in the morning!" she yelled angrily. "Fuck it, I'll get myself off! You've got to understand, Steve, that I'm a woman, and I have a strong appetite for sex. Hell, I told you that when we first got married!"

"I know, Mel, but I—"

"Fuck it, it's cool," she said. Then she got her sex toys out and went to work on herself.

She gave herself six orgasms all by herself while Steve sulked next to her.

"I know you've been fuckin' somebody else, Mel, 'cause your pussy just ain't the same. It's bigger, and I can't feel the walls anymore!" Big Steve yelled.

"Maybe your dick got smaller. Have you ever thought about that?"

"Bullshit! You're lyin'! I know you're lyin'! Before I left, you didn't know how to give head, but now, you seem like you been to college for dick sucking, 'cause you suck like a goddamn pro! What's up with that, Mel?"

"Think what you wanna think! I don't give a fuck!"

"Why don't you admit it, Mel? Confess, goddammit! Tell the fuckin' truth for once in your life!"

"Fuck you! Why don't you go back to jail!" she yelled. She then stormed out of the room and went to the dining room table. Big Steve lay across the bed until he fell asleep. Melody made an effort to calm herself by drinking and smoking a joint.

Hell, I don't think I said anything wrong, because basically, I just don't need him anymore. He can't buy me the things I need or want, and he damn sure can't sexually satisfy me. I'm giving him one month to get his shit together, and if he doesn't start bringing anything to the table, he's got to live with his mama and daddy. I'm not having this bullshit! It's simple. If a man can't help me, eat me, and fuck me the way Larry does, then fuck him, she thought. Two hours later, she went to the den and fell asleep.

The following morning at six forty-five, Steve called his parents. The words Melody had said to him cut through him like a sword, and prevented him from sleeping the previous night. He didn't understand how this could be. Thinking about the past year, he came up with several possibilities.

I know she's been fuckin' somebody else, but maybe I was the cause of it. It seems to me that someone has turned her into a stone cold freak, because she wasn't like this before I left. I wonder if she has a sugar daddy.

I'm still in love with her, but damn, somebody's been beatin' up her pussy. It wasn't wide open like this when I left. I wonder if it's really the bills that are irritating her? Maybe she just doesn't love me anymore. I'm willing to help out, 'cause I'm the man of the house, but she could at least give me a goddamn chance. I wish those damn police would'nt've impounded my car, 'cause now I can't even look for a job. Bottom line is, I need some wheels so I can find a job, then maybe she'll chill out and show me some love, Steve thought as the phone continued to ring.

Woody turned over and glanced at the clock before answering the phone.

"Hello?"

"Hey, Dad, it's me."

"What are you doing up so early, boy? The doctor told you—"

"I know what the doctor told me, Dad, but sump'n's come up. Me and Melody had an argument last night. I don't understand why she's trippin', Dad, because hell, I've been in the hospital, you know," Big Steve said sadly.

"That's probably the problem, son. Your wife has had a heavy load on her since you've been gone, and she's probably under a lot of mental stress. Give her time to get used to you again, and things will soon fall back in place," Woody explained.

"Dad," Big Steve said, "bottom line is, I need to find a job, and I need some wheels to make things happen for me."

"You haven't even healed yet, boy, and you're already talking about a damn job! How are you s'pose to work and your health isn't up to par?" Woody asked.

Overhearing Woody's conversation, Big Mama awakened.

"I told you that woman ain't no good!" Big Mama interrupted. "How in the hell does she expect him to work and he just got out the damn hospital? I'll tell y'all what it is. Her boyfriend probably told her to get rid of him, and that's what she's doing. She's jus' actin' like it's the job thing. That woman is full of snake shit, Woody."

"All right, Steve," Woody said, ignoring Big Mama. "I'll help you this time, but if you do sump'n stupid again, I'm sorry, son, but you're on your own. Be ready at nine."

Steve's soreness was erased from his mind and body. At the moment, he felt no pain. He had to do what he had to do, even if it meant working with dark shades to conceal his swollen eyes and working while on medication. It was time for him to step up. He had wasted an entire year in jail, and somehow he had to make up for it.

After breakfast at Denny's, Steve and Woody grabbed a newspaper and drove to a car lot in Riverside called A-1 Motors. A huge, white man, wearing a pair of suspenders to hold up a dingy pair of black pants approached them and began his sales pitch in a strong Southern accent.

"How're you good folks doing today?"

"Fine, and you?" Woody scanned the car lot.

"Well, to tell you the truth, I've had better days, you know. Complaining isn't gonna do a damn bit of good, so's we jus' gotta make the best of it," the salesman said.

"How much for the black Bronco?" Big Steve asked.

"She's a beauty, huh?" the salesman replied. "Just got her in yesterday, and already had three offers on her. Well, let me see here. Since you people seem like nice, easygoing, hardworking citizens who're tryin' to save a buck, I'll give you this Bronco, tax and license included, for, ah, let say, ah—"

"Give us a good deal, man, and we'll buy it right now," Big Steve interjected excitedly.

"I'll tell you what, make me an offer I can't refuse," the salesman said, standing back and holding his hands on his suspenders.

"I'm not here to play *Let's Make a Deal*, sir. I'm here to purchase a vehicle," Woody explained.

"OK, OK, I'll tell you what. Why don't you good folks take her for a test drive, and if you like it, I'm sure I can give it to you for a price you'll like."

"Let's do it," Steve said, and then swiftly headed to the Bronco. Woody and the salesman followed behind.

After returning from the test drive, woody agreed to purchase the Bronco. He signed the necessary documents and made out a check for the total price. Woody then handed Steve two hundred dollars as pocket money, and watched his son drive off.

During the time the Bronco was being purchased, Melody was conversing with Larry over the telephone.

"Hey, babe, can you talk?" Larry asked, cruising down the 60 freeway.

"Yes, sweetheart, I can talk. Where are you?" Melody asked, stretching and yawning.

"On the 60, headed to El Monte. I just called to say I love you, and to remind you that the carpet and tile crew will be there in less than an hour."

"Thanks for reminding me, babe. I had forgotten all about it. Well, so much for that. When and where are we meeting today?"

"I've got that covered too, babe," Larry assured her. "Before I hopped on the freeway, I paid in advance for two weeks at the Travelodge. Room number 222. There's a key waiting for you at the office. I'll see you about two."

"I can hardly wait." Melody blew him a kiss through the telephone and hung up.

CHAPTER 13

Pat finally came out of her coma, but she was severely suffering from a combination of post-traumatic amnesia. She recognized neither Larry nor Randy. Her speech was slow and uncertain. Because she was so disoriented, Larry saw no use in informing her of the severity of her injuries. As he stared at his wife, who appeared to have aged twenty years in the past four days, he shook his head in disbelief and then walked over and began talking with Dr. Smith.

"She's not going to be like this for the rest of her life, is she, doc?" Larry asked.

"By the looks of the CAT scan, Mr. Myers, I'm sorry to say that your wife's condition will more than likely get worse before it gets any better," Dr. Smith explained. Randy stood beside his mother's bed crying.

"Why! Why!" Randy shouted. "Why did this happen to my mother! Why!"

"Well, goddamn, doc," Larry yelled. "I need you to run some more tests or sump'n, man. This shit is—fuck!"

"I'm sorry, Mr. Myers. I know how you feel and I really sympathize with you, but you have to realize that I'm not God and I can't perform miracles."

"Fuck!" Larry screamed. He then began pacing the length of the room in a rage.

While standing over the woman who'd given him life, Randy tried to make sense out of her mumbling, muttered words, but it was a waste of time. He stood there for a couple hours waiting for her to recognize him, but her condition did not change.

She lay there staring at the ceiling as if God was up there and about to snap her out of it. She showed no emotions and appeared to have no pain. She just lay there spellbound. No cries, no smiles.

"Give it all to me, daddy. I want it all, and I want it now!" she said desperately, like there was no tomorrow. As the headboard banged against the wall, Larry made loud groans and grunts, sounding like a wild animal in the woods. As he plunged, and plunged, and plunged, deeper and harder, he then let out a loud, "Aaarrrhh! ahh, shit! Aaarrrrh!" and slowed down his pace.

"Yes! Ooh, yes, damn! I'm cumming, ooh yes," she yelled, and then they both exploded with excitement and relief. After regaining their strength, they relaxed on the bed, turned on the television, and watched the *Montel Williams Show*. Satisfied, Melody went to the minibar to fix them both a glass of vodka while Larry rolled a couple joints.

"So, how's Pat?" she asked as if she were concerned.

"She's paralyzed from the waist down and has a case of amnesia. Her head was banged up pretty bad. The doctor said things will probably get worse before they get any better. The good news is that she came out of the coma, but mentally she's still not with us."

"I'm sorry to hear that, baby," Melody said, smiling to herself.

"You know, baby, deep down inside, I love my wife. After all, she's the mother of my kids and helped me raise them, and for their sake, I hope she recovers," Larry said. He took a long swallow of vodka.

"Oh, and by the way, your daughters are beautiful. The younger one looks just like you. And Angela, wow, I think she's going to make a hell of an attorney. I feel sorry for criminals if she's going to be a district attorney, because she'll send them all to prison. I find her to be bright, clever, and also controlling, just like her father," Melody replied, then gave him a big kiss.

"Yeah, Angela's the smart one. She's the one who orchestrates all of the family negotiations and planning, and lately, she's been trying to run my finances. Hell, you saw how quick she made me come out of my pocket with three grand for those two laptops."

Melody grunted and rolled her eyes.

Larry sensed her animosity and jealousy toward his daughters, but he remained cool, calm, and collected. Instead of making a stink about it, he suggested they go to Red Lobster for dinner.

CHAPTER 14

Big Steve felt good about himself while cruising in his new Bronco. He knew that in order to repair his relationship with Melody, he needed more than a new vehicle; he needed a job. He circled several job openings from the classifieds and decided to call them for directions. Later he would pick up a few applications and take them to Melody to fill out.

The first ad he circled read: Will Train. *No experience necessary. Sales/Manager positions available. (909) 645-9124. Ask for Jerry.* After phoning Jerry and speaking with him for less than a minute, Steve was on his way to SLH Wholesale and Warehousing Company in the city of Fontana. The owner himself, whose name was Jerry Ball, hired Big Steve immediately after the interview. He wasn't too impressed by Steve's dark sunglasses, but it didn't prevent Jerry from hiring him. Little did Steve know that nineteen employees had recently quit, and Jerry Ball desperately needed help.

"I feel you're going to be a great success with our company, Steve. You've got a keen sense of humor, you're ambitious, and with your attitude, you'll be a district manager in less than a year," Jerry promised. "Just bring your paperwork back tomorrow and be ready for work."

"Cool. I've always wanted to be a manager, Mr. Ball, and I really 'preciate you givin' me this job."

As Big Steve departed SLH he felt like a new man.

It's all good, you know. Damn, I can't believe I got a new truck and a job in the same day. Life is good. Mel shouldn't be trippin' now, he thought.

As Big Steve exited the freeway, he entertained the thought of taking his wife out for lunch, and minutes later he was pulling up in front of Creativity. He took a quick look in the mirror, adjusted his shades, and then climbed out and went inside. Melody was with a customer, but that didn't prevent him from approaching her booth and grinning as if he'd won the lottery.

"Hey, Mel, how you doing, baby?" he asked, feeling like a million bucks.

"Hi," she answered dryly. "What's up?" She didn't ask how he was feeling, where he'd been, and showed no signs of love or concern.

"I didn't mean to interfere with your work, but I got some good news for you, baby,"

Damn, she thought. *Why did he have to bring his fat ass to the shop? Ooh, I could kill him. He needs to take off those stupid looking shades and go find a damn job. I wish he'd leave. I've got to meet Larry in a little while. Damn!*

"Can you step outside for a minute, baby? I want to share this news with you in private," Big Steve asked humbly.

"Excuse me a second, Beverly," Melody said to her customer. "Let me see what he wants."

After stepping outside, he grabbed her, held her tight, and then began kissing her like they were behind closed doors. Passersby observed them, but they continued kissing like they were in high school. Then suddenly, Melody resisted.

"I love you, Mel. Please don't be mad at me anymore, OK? I don't want us to argue, baby. All I want to do is love you, and try my best to keep you happy," he said sincerely.

"I love you, too, Teddy Bear, and I apologize for those bad things I said to you last night. Please forgive me, OK?" she asked, looking into his eyes with tears of guilt

"I forgive you, baby. Like I said, all I want is for us to be happy and to finish what we started, you know what I'm sayin'? We can't go halfway. We gotta go all the way with this, Mel. I married you for life, sweetheart, I didn't rent you for a couple years, you know what I'm sayin'? I'm gonna love you forever no matter what. But please, Mel, if you're messin' around with another man, please let him go for the sake of our marriage."

"Whoops, you almost made me forget I have a customer in my chair," she said as she wiped her tears and ignored Big Steve's plea. "I'll tell you what, I've got three more customers. I should be home in a couple hours, OK, then we can finish this discussion. And if you act right, I might even have a nice treat for you."

"Girl, I like it when you talk like that," he replied. He pointed at his new Bronco. "Look, see that black Bronco over there? It's ours, sweetheart. My Dad just bought it for us. I wanted to take you to lunch, but I see you're pretty tied up. Oh, and that's not all. I got a job today, too. I'll tell you all about it when you get home, OK?"

He then climbed into his Bronco, feeling as though he'd conquered the world, and left.

As he approached his residence, the sight of a group of Mexicans in his yard drinking beer filled him with curiosity. He parked on the opposite side of the street, climbed out of the Bronco, and approached them.

"What's up?" Big Steve asked, holding both his hands up. The Mexicans looked at each other, astonished. They then looked back at Steve and began speaking in Spanish, while pointing at him like he had committed a crime. Steve quickly got irritated.

"What's up? English? English? English?" The Mexicans shook their heads.

"No Ingles! No Ingles! No Ingles!" they shouted.

"Well, I'll be goddamn!" Big Steve yelled. "How in the fuck do you people come to a country and can't even fuckin' communicate with nobody! Do y'all know how stupid y'all are?"

The Mexicans nodded yes, not realizing what they were agreeing to.

At the sound of his stepfather's voice, Byron put down his controllers and ran to the front door.

"What's up, Pops?" Byron asked, excitedly.

"That's what I'm tryin' to find out," Big Steve replied, observing the materials and equipment.

"Pops, Mom said those Mexicans are pulling up the old carpet and tile and putting down some brand-new stuff," Byron said, hoping to clarify the situation. "And, Pops, our house is going to look better than everybody's on the whole street." Big Steve thought for a minute.

"No wonder she's been complainin' about the bills and the house note. Hell, I know this shit must cost a lot of damn money. That doesn't make any sense! How in the hell can she afford to—" He paused and regrouped. "Come on, son, let's go for a ride in my new truck."

"Yes!" Byron yelled excitedly. "Yes! New carpet, new tile, and a new truck, yes! We're rich! Wait until I tell Bobby. Come on, Pops, let's roll."

Byron had a craving for a Quarter Pounder with cheese, which resulted in a quick stop at McDonald's. Afterward, Byron made another suggestion.

"Pops," Byron said.

"What's up, son?"

"Let's check out a soccer game, all right? My ex-team is playing against the Riverside Giants, and I bet Bobby a dollar that we'd win."

"Why not," Steve answered. "I guess that's better than watching a bunch of non-English speaking Mexicans work on our house."

"Yes!" Byron shouted.

They made it home at a little after seven. Melody was seated at the dining room table, sipping vodka and listening to Barry White.

"Hey, baby," Steve greeted, walking through the door. He then gave her a kiss.

"Oooh. Nasty, nasty, nasty," Byron said. "Why don't you guys save that stuff for behind closed doors?"

"What do you know about behind closed doors, boy?" Melody asked.

"More than you think, Mom," Byron answered sarcastically. "Anyway, Pops and me went everywhere, Mom. We went to McDonald's and we just left the park watching my ex-team whip the Giants. And Pops' truck is the bomb, Mom, I mean, *the bomb,*" Byron emphasized.

"Humph," Melody said after taking a swallow of vodka. "I see. Well, I'm glad to hear that you two had such a good time. Maybe—"

After observing the new carpet and tile, Big Steve interrupted her.

"I love the new carpet and tile, sweetheart. It must've cost close to two grand, huh?" Then giving it more thought, he added, "You've been bitchin' about bills, but yet and still, you go out and spend God knows how much on some goddamn carpet and tile. What kind of shit is that, Mel?" She took another swallow of vodka.

"Wait one goddamn minute! How in the hell can you tell me what I can't afford, or about my fucking bills! When you start contributing to this household, then you can have some say so, but until then, you're in no position to give opinions, thoughts, or comments about a goddamn thing around here!" She was now heated and ready to argue. Noticing Byron was still present, Melody ordered him to his room. Byron ran upstairs and slammed the door.

Mom doesn't talk to Larry like that, and she didn't talk to the man in the uniform like that when he spent the night, Byron thought. *I*

wonder why she's talking to Pops like that? Maybe she's drunk again. I
wonder if she will get mad if I tell Pops about the man in the uniform
and Larry?

Byron had to blast his music in order to drown out his parents' voices. Meanwhile in the dining room, things had gotten ugly.

"Who in the hell do you think you are? I'm the queen of this goddamn castle, and as far as I'm concerned, I'm the fucking king, too!"

After thinking a few moments, Steve realized he'd taken things a little too far. He didn't want to argue anymore. He suddenly had the desire to kiss her, caress her, and make sweet love to her.

"Baby, I don't want us to argue no more, OK?" He then stood up and tried to hug her, but she rejected him.

"I ain't your goddamn baby!"

"Listen, Mel, please. Let's take a shower and calm ourselves down, OK?"

"I told you, Steve, I'm not your baby, so quit calling me that."

"I'm sorry, baby. I was wrong for mentioning anything about the carpet and tile. Now would you please just calm down? Please?"

"You must be some kind of goddamn fool! Now that I think about it, why in the hell did you ask your daddy to buy you a goddamn truck when I'm buried in bills up to my fucking head? What kind of sense did that make? Why didn't you ask him to pay some of these damn bills, instead of buying you a damn truck, huh? Wouldn't that have made more sense?"

"Listen, Mel, if you need a couple hundred on the bills, that's not a problem. I'll get it from my parents tomorrow. But, please, let's bring this dispute to an end, OK? I apologize for getting you upset. Now please forgive me," Big Steve pleaded solemnly.

"Apologize, apologize, apologize! You're full of shit and full of fucking apologies! Last night, you apologized for not being able to fuck, do you remember? You apologized for going to jail, do you remember that? You apologized for leaving me for a year with all these goddamn bills, do you remember that? And now you're apologizing for saying something stupid? Ain't that a bitch! Let me tell you what I've told you before, I can do bad all by my goddamn self." She was staring at him with reddened eyes and an attitude.

"Will you calm down, Mel? I've been trying to be cool with you, but you're pushing me to the fuckin' edge! Don't make me do sump'n I don't wanna do!"

"Oh, is that right? I've been waiting on this. I guess you're going to hit me, huh? Hit me, come on bitch, hit me!"

He stormed toward her in a rage and stood face to face with her.

"You know what, bitch? Fuck you! Just like my mama said, you ain't nothin' but a goddamn slut! Yeah! Part-time beautician, full-time slut! I'm outta here! Fuck you!" He then stormed out of the house without closing the door.

"Take your fat ass back to your mama, and stay over there!" Melody yelled as Big Steve was getting into his truck. "Don't you come back here, and I'm dead serious! And fuck you too, you little dicked muthafucka!"

CHAPTER 15

Big Steve cruised The U for two hours fighting the feeling of getting high, but he finally ended up in the twilight zone. He was caught like a fly in a spider's web and there was no way out.

He pulled into the Church's Chicken parking lot and exited his Bronco. As usual, the University whores flooded the Boulevard and drug dealers were making sales. It was a 24/7 thing.

Big Steve scanned the area, but the only faces he recognized were the same old drug users, drug dealers, and whores. He wouldn't have been able to spot an undercover cop, even if it was one of the two who had arrested him, simply because they had thousands of disguises and could present themselves as a bum, a dope fiend trying to buy drugs, an old lady begging for money, a lost tourist, etc, which kept him on his Ps and Qs.

At that moment, Tastee approached him.

"Hey, Big Daddy, what's up?" she asked. She then gave him a quick kiss and hug, and continued talking. "I heard what happened to you, and I think that was pretty fucked up." While conversing she kept her eyes on passing vehicles, not wanting to miss a potential customer.

"Yeah, it was pretty fucked up, you know what I'm sayin'? But Big Daddy's back, baby. That shit is history now, you know what

I'm sayin'? But anyway, you got a room, babygirl?" he asked, darting his eyes up and down the streets. Thoughts of his last sexual encounter with her caused him to grab his crotch.

"Yep," Tastee replied, smiling and revealing her false teeth. "Why? Would you like a repeat of last year or sump'n?"

Big Steve grinned.

"Hell, yeah. That'll definitely work, you know what I'm sayin'? I need a quick release to relieve some of this tension, you know what I'm sayin'?"

"Damn right, I know what you're saying, Big Daddy. And I know just what you need and how you need it," she replied. She then eased up to him and rubbed his crotch.

Tastee led Steve a block or so to her motel room.

"You got some smoke, or do you want me to run upstairs to cop some?" she asked before they entered the room.

"Nah, I ain't got none, baby girl," he responded. "But here's forty dollars. Go ahead and run upstairs and cop us sump'n so we can get our groove on, you know what I'm sayin'?" He then walked into the small, shabby room and waited impatiently at the edge of the bed, rubbing his small erection.

He began reminiscing about how good she had made him feel a year ago. She'd removed her dentures and gummed him like a porno pro, something he'd never forget.

"Ump, ump, ump. Damn, does she know how to give good head," he shouted out loud.

With that thought he quickly undressed. A few seconds later, Tastee returned. After showing him what she'd bought, she removed her dentures and sat them on the ragged old dresser.

"Do you still give some bomb head, baby girl?" Steve asked as he lay naked across the bed.

"Like they say, Big Daddy, it just gets better with time, you know what I mean?" She then glanced at his penis and congratulated him. "Damn, it looks like you've grown since the last time I saw it," she lied, hoping to boost his ego a few notches.

"Yeah, I know. I noticed that the other day," he replied while caressing his penis.

The party ended quicker than it began. In less than thirty minutes the crack was gone. He wasted no time giving her additional money to buy more.

Damn! I fucked up again! Big Steve thought. *I'm supposed to start my new job tomorrow, but my goddamn wife didn't fill out my paperwork! But either way, I'm fucked, because they're gonna drug test me. I wonder if Tastee knows how to fill out paperwork? Probably not, but I guess I'll have to wait till this shit gets out of my system.*

When Tastee returned, she undressed in a hurry and went to work on Big Steve's limp penis. Fortunately for her, after taking a hit, Steve was no longer interested in sex. The only thing he wanted to do now was peep out windows, listen for the police or noises, and smoke more crack. An hour later, the crack had once again gone up in smoke. He didn't hesitate to give her his last twenty dollars to cop some more.

When she exited the room, he got dressed, sat at the edge of the bed, and began talking out loud in frustration.

"Damn! I only got twennie-seven cent left to my fuckin' name! If Melody would've just been cool and not talked all that bullshit, everything would've been aright! I would've been cuddled up in the bed with her right now. But the bitch had to act like a damn fool, and here I am, out here smokin' this shit, knowing I'm supposed to go to work tomorrow. Damn, I can't win for losing. I wonder what my parents are thinking."

When Tastee returned to the room she began to take off her clothes again, but Big Steve held up his hand up and told her to stop.

"You don't have take them off, baby girl. My dick can't get hard from smoking too much of this shit." He picked up a piece of crack and took a hit.

"Bullshit, Big Daddy," Tastee replied. She pulled out her dentures and unzipped his pants. "Don't forget that I do what I do for survival, and I consider myself the best in the business, Big Daddy. Just lie back and imagine what I'm about to do to you." She began massaging his balls. "I'm gonna suck it, lick it, slurp it, and gum the hell out of your big dick." She then acted out her words.

He tried following her instructions, but the effect of the crack took its toll and caused his mind to change channels. As he lay there, his first thought was about Melody. He then thought about peeping out the window because he thought he heard something. Then he thought about the undercovers who'd busted him a year ago. Then his mind switched to the possibility of his Bronco being broken into. His final thought was the door being kicked in at any given moment. He became completely paranoid, and there was no way could he concentrate on the pleasure he was receiving from the whore. It was no use. His penis just wouldn't respond to her professionalism. He had twenty-seven cents left, had cum only once, and he felt like a damn fool.

A couple of hours later, after he'd come down off his high, he left the room and made his way to his Bronco.

What the hell am I gonna do? he wondered as he sat inside his truck. *I don't even have enough to buy me a goddamn forty-ounce! Guess I gotta get my hustle on and panhandle, you know what I'm sayin'.* He then exited the Bronco and began walking The U.

The first person he ran across was a man dressed in business attire waiting at a bus stop. Steve approached the man.

"Excuse me, sir, but can you spare some change? I ain't ate in three days, you know what I'm sayin', and—"

"Get a job asshole, and quit smoking crack! Then maybe you can keep some fucking money in your pocket like a grown man should!" The stranger gave Big Steve a hard, stern look. *Bitch made muthafucka'! I should've fucked him up,* Steve thought. But instead of carrying out his thoughts, he walked away and made his way to a gas station a few blocks up the street. He didn't hesitate to approach another man, who appeared to have just gotten off work. The man was pumping gasoline into his work truck. This time, Steve used a different approach.

"I ran out of gas down the street, and I was hoping that—" he began.

"So fuckin' what? Get a life, you piece of shit!" the white man replied angrily while continuing to pump his gasoline. Big Steve walked away.

"Damn! These muthafucka's make a nigga wanna knock the shit outta 'em! They act like a nickel or a dollar is gonna break 'em or sump'n. Fuck all these muthafuckas!" Big Steve shouted.

He then contemplated his next move. Glancing down the street he noticed the familiar faces of people he'd smoked crack with in the past.

Maybe they got a little sump'n sump'n for me, you know what I'm sayin'? Hell, I've got both of those fools high before, so maybe they'll look out for me. Steve then made his way across the street and approached them.

"What's up, homies?"

"Hey, what's up, big man?" the shabbily dressed man asked. The two men were sitting at a bus stop fumbling around with drug paraphernalia. The one man shot a quick glance at Steve. "Where you been, man?"

"Locked up, homey. I got busted by some undercovers right here on The U a while back," Big Steve replied, staring at the man's paraphernalia.

"No shit?"

"No shit, homey. Seems like everything been going fucked up for me, you know what I'm sayin'?" Big Steve then seated himself between the crackheads.

"Yeah, I heard about you, man. Ah, ah, yeah, you got busted by those undercovers named Starsky and Hutch, huh?" the other man asked, taking a long swallow of his cheap beer. Big

Steve's throat was dry as the desert as he watched the man down the thirst-quenching beer. All he wanted was one good swallow of the man's beer. Just one good swallow.

"Hey, homey, let me get a swallow?" Big Steve asked.

"This is all I got, man, and I ain't givin' you my last. Nope. Shit, I wouldn't even give my own mama my last swallow of beer," the man replied.

"I didn't say that shit when I gave you a hit of my dope, nigga, so why you trippin' off a swallow of beer?"

"Man, you bringin' up some old shit that you gave me a year ago. I don't wanna hear that bullshit, man." The man then mumbled, "Brangin' up some shit he gave me a goddamn year ago. What the hell wrong with this fool? Fuck him."

"Give him a swallow, nigga!" the other man interjected. "It ain't gonna make you, or break you, man. And he's right, 'cause I remember when he gave us a hit when we was in the vacant apartments."

"Fuck you, man. You don't tell me what to do with mines. Fuck both y'all niggas!" The man then turned up the can of beer and finished it.

Before he could throw the can away, Big Steve stood up and knocked the hell out of him, causing him to hit the ground and roll off the curb. The other man applauded.

"Good for that muthafucka'!" the other man said. "I'll bet next time he won't be so damn stingy."

"Hey man, you got some change I could borrow so I can get me a beer?" Big Steve asked the nicer man before walking away.

"Man, I'm doing bad, homey. All I got is three pennies, and I was tryin' to hold on to that until I get some more. But if you need 'em, here, you can have 'em."

Big Steve was more than happy to accept them. "Anything is better than nothin', you know what I'm sayin'? Thanks." He then shook the man's hand and walked away. He now had thirty cents, but he was still a dollar fifty short of buying a forty-ounce.

As Big Steve strolled down The U searching for familiar faces, he spotted a whore he'd partied with on a few occasions on the opposite side of the street, flagging down potential customers.

"Peaches! Peaches!" Big Steve shouted, trying to get her attention.

Not realizing from where the voice was coming, Peaches looked around until she spotted Steve in the middle of the street, stopping traffic as he tried to get across.

"Fucking crackhead!" a driver who was forced to stop in order to avoid hitting Big Steve yelled.

"Your mama, punk!" Big Steve responded, proceeding toward Peaches. He was sure that she had some money, at least enough for him to buy a can of beer.

"What's up, baby?" he greeted, giving her a hug and a kiss on the lips.

"Hey, Big Daddy, what's up? When did you get out? Are we about to have some butt-naked fun for old times' sake, or what?" she asked, not taking her eyes off the passing vehicles.

"I wish," Big Steve answered. "I'm broke as hell, you know what I'm sayin'? Shit, I was hoping you could help me out with some change."

Damn! Peaches thought. *Why did I have to be the one who turned him out on crack?*

"Nope, I'm broke too," Peaches responded. "Why don't you go hustle up some cans like Mike and Eddie, or pump people's gas for them?" She then gave him a quick kiss and trotted over to a vehicle that was approaching the curb.

Angered by her suggestion and with everyone else, Big Steve made his way back to his Bronco and began talking out loud.

"Why did you do it, Melody? Why? Look what you've done to me, goddammit!" He did not care who heard him.

As he neared his Bronco, a known drug dealer, who went by the name of C-Crazy, approached him.

"Are you all right, homey?" C-Crazy was scanning both sides of the street for undercover cops and crack seekers.

"Yeah, I'm cool," Big Steve replied, frustrated by his condition and angry at his wife for supposedly putting him in this situation.

"I saw you an hour ago, man. I was tryin' to holler at you, but it looked like you was on a mission or sump'n, so I left you alone. But anyway, homey, I need a favor," C-Crazy said. "You wanna make some money?" Those were magical words to Big Steve.

"Hell yeah, I wanna make some money," Big Steve replied. "What's up? What I gotta do?"

"I need you to take me to recoup some dope, and then to the liquor store and the hamburger stand," C-Crazy replied while darting his eyes around and checking out his surroundings. "I'll give you five dollars cash and a five dollar hit if you do that for me, cuzz."

"You ain't sayin' nothin' but a word, homey. Let's do the damn thang," Big Steve replied. He then led the way to his Bronco.

C-Crazy was well known by the drug users on The U, as well as by the police. During the past twenty-five years, he'd been arrested seventeen times for possession with intent to sell. The streets were the only life he knew. He was a Crip gang member and was originally from the City of Compton. After robbing one of his homeboy's dope houses, getting away with over eighteen thousand dollars and a kilo of cocaine, he realized his days were numbered so he moved to Riverside. A long streak of bad luck caused him to come out on the losing end of life, leading him to sell nickel and dime pieces of crack.

He stood five-five and had a pair of huge arms, which he'd built up in prison. His skin was jet black and he always wore a mean look. He kept his hair in long braids and had a swift, aggressive stroll. He was considered scandalous to some, and ruthless to others. Recently, he'd been released from prison and had already robbed five people and was an accomplice in two home invasions. Now both the police and the Compton Crips were looking for him.

As they cruised the streets in Big Steve's truck, Big Steve inquired about his earnings.

"Let me get the five dollars so I can buy me a forty-ounce right quick." Steve desperately craved a beer.

"Wait, nigga! Don't be rushin' me, cuzz. I said I'm gonna take care of you, so quit trippin'!" C-Crazy responded angrily. "Make a right at the light and cop a park."

Once the Bronco came to a halt, C-Crazy hopped out without saying a word and slammed the door behind him.

While waiting, Big Steve observed several gang-bangers hanging out shooting dice, smoking weed, and drinking forty-ounces of beer. They were talking loudly and blasting music by Tupac. C-Crazy had disappeared into the crowd of thugs, stayed a couple minutes, then trotted back to the Bronco carrying a nine-millimeter in his right hand.

"Pull off," C-Crazy demanded after getting back inside the Bronco. "Go to the end of the block and make a left!" After examining his products, he put the bag of dope underneath his seat. Big Steve noticed this gesture, but he was too afraid to say anything.

"Make a right, cuzz," C-Crazy ordered while adjusting the radio stations to what he wanted to hear. Fed up with C-Crazy's bullshit, Big Steve finally found the courage to speak up.

"I thought we were going to the liquor store and to the burger stand?"

"Jus' chill, nigga! We gotta pick up a couple of my bitches, first," C-Crazy replied with a mean look, toying around with his 9mm. "Cuzz, you ask more questions than a fuckin' lawyer! Are you practicin' to be a D.A. or sump'n?" C-Crazy yelled.

"Nah, man, it ain't that, you know what I'm sayin'?I It's just that, we agreed on—"

"I ain't agreed to a muthafuckin' thing, fool!" And I 'preciate if you quit trippin', nigga! I don't agree with nobody on nothin', so don't get that fucked up! If you say one more thing to me, I'm going ballistic on your ass! Now pull over and park, fool!"

After hearing the tone of C-Crazy's voice, Big Steve had no problem obeying.

Once the Bronco came to a halt, C-Crazy hopped out, slammed the door behind him, and walked down the street. While waiting impatiently, Big Steve began thinking.

I should pull off and leave this muthafucka. I'm doing this fool a favor, but he wanna talk crazy to me. He's got a gun and dope in my truck, and he didn't even ask me if it was all right. Yeah, I should pull off and say fuck him. But he might start shooting at me.

Big Steve sat still in his truck, constantly checking his mirrors and watching for police and other people like C-Crazy. He grew more nervous by the second and felt uneasy about C-Crazy. He wanted to get rid of him in a hurry. This was the first time they actually had any dealings together, and hopefully it would be the last.

At that moment C-Crazy, accompanied by two under-aged females, approached the Bronco and hurriedly climbed inside.

"Go to the corner and make a right," C-Crazy demanded while rummaging through Big Steve's cassettes. Big Steve was getting irked by C-Crazy's commands.

"Where are we going?" Big Steve asked. "I thought that—"

"Shut up, punk! Didn't I tell you not to ask any more fuckin' questions? I should bust you in your goddamn mouth, nigga! I told you to shut the fuck up! You're interfering with my thinkin', so jus' shut the fuck up and drive! That's what I hate about y'all fuckin' crackheads, y'all some stupid muthafuckas!" C-Crazy then reached over the seat and kissed one of the girls. Big Steve kept his cool and didn't say a word. He wanted answers for at least five questions, but decided not to ask any. After all, soon he would dispose of this rude asshole.

After going to the liquor store and hamburger stand, C-Crazy then ordered Big Steve to take the young ladies to buy some chronic, and to then take them back to their apartment.

"Wait here a minute!" C-Crazy demanded once they arrived back at the apartments. "And don't leave, nigga!" He climbed out of the Bronco and escorted the young ladies back to their apartment.

Five minutes passed. Then ten minutes. Then twenty minutes. *What the fuck is wrong with this nigga? Why is he trippin'? I should leave him and go hang out in L.A. for a while. Yeah, fuck him,* Big Steve thought. He then reached underneath the seat to make sure the bag of dope was still there. Hurriedly, he fired up the Bronco, but then he spotted C-Crazy in his rearview mirror carrying a forty-ounce in one hand and a joint in his other. *Damn!*

"Now take me back to where you picked me up, fool!" C-Crazy demanded once again. "And no fuckin' questions!" He then took a long swallow of beer. Big Steve wanted to ask for some, but dismissed the thought.

When they arrived at Church's Chicken, C-Crazy grabbed his bag of dope and climbed out.

"Later, fool!" he said, then walked away.

"Damn!" Big Steve yelled. "I should've left 'em and took off with his fuckin' dope! Damn! Damn! Damn! Fuck this! I know what I'm about to do!" He then fired up the Bronco and took off.

After making a few lefts and rights, Big Steve pulled up in front of a fenced-in house and parked. Cautiously, he approached the fence. Two Rottweilers, who were guarding the premises, charged at him and began barking viciously. Seconds later, a thug appeared on the steps.

"What's up, Big Steve?" the thug asked, standing with a forty-ounce of Old English 800 in his hand.

"What's up, Spank?" Big Steve greeted while remaining a few feet from the fence due to the bad-tempered dogs. "I need to holler at you a minute, homey!"

"King! Queenie! Get the fuck outta here!" Spank suddenly yelled. And like amenable animals, they obeyed and went inside the house. After shaking hands and making small talk, Big Steve stated the real reason for his presence.

"Check it out, Spank, I need to hold two twenty-dollar rocks and ten dollars in cash until tomorrow night. You can keep my Bronco for collateral. Normally, cuzz, you know I wouldn't come at you like this, but I'm kind of down, you know what I'm sayin'," Big Steve explained.

"Damn, Big Steve. You know I don't be doin' no shit like that, man." Spank took a long gulp of beer.

"Come on, Spank," Big Steve begged. "I need you to do me this favor. Fuck it, homey. I'll tell you what. You can keep the Bronco for two days. Now how does that sound?"

"Is it yours? 'cause I had a fool who pawned me his mama's car and another fool pawned me his little brother's car. And the worst thing about it, homey, is that neither of those fools ever came back to get the cars. A couple days later the police came with a goddamn tow truck and towed 'em both away. I took a big loss, homey, and I don't wanna go through the same bullshit with you." He took another long gulp.

"Man, this truck is mine. And besides, Spank, you know I wouldn't do no bullshit like that. I've got the papers inside the glove compartment. Let me show them to you right quick so you can see that everything's legit."

After seeing the paperwork, Spank accepted the offer.

"Thanks, man," Big Steve said. He then shook Spank's hand and happily left. As he strolled down the street he felt like jumping in the air and kicking his feet together. Instead, he walked at a fast pace back toward The U.

Not too many vehicles and very few whores were out at three AM. Each bus stop was occupied either by a sleeping derelict, a group of dope fiends getting high, or a tired whore.

As Big Steve strolled down the street with a smile and a new attitude, the first familiar face he saw was Tastee. Instantly, he developed an erection thinking about their sexual encounter a few hours ago.

"Tastee!" he yelled. "Come here, girl!"

She was on the opposite side of the street about forty yards away, but as she turned around and recognized him, she began a slow trot in his direction.

"I thought you were gone, Big Daddy. I've been asking around for you, but everybody said they hadn't seen you. What's up?" She smiled, hoping to hear the magic words: Let's have some fun.

"You know me, baby," Big Steve said. "Jus' tryin' to get my groove on, you know what I'm sayin'." While talking to Tastee he quickly scanned the area for cops.

"Well, let's do the damn thang, Big Daddy," Tastee responded. She then led him to her room. During the first thirty minutes of their stay, they had sex, smoked crack, and like always, Big Steve got paranoid and began tripping out, assuming someone was after him and about to burst into the room. He couldn't figure out why he spent so much money getting high when the results would always end in him being terrified.

Why do I smoke this shit? he wondered. *It makes me think people are after me who don't even know me. It makes me think people are plotting against me. It makes me think everybody's watching me. It makes me dysfunctional and nervous, and my dick won't even get hard. Why do I keep spending my money on this shit? Fuck that. I'd better check into a drug program before it's too late.*

Big Steve sat miserably at the edge of the bed. Once his money was gone, Tastee left.

At six AM he had two dollars left. This time he made sure to save enough to buy a forty-ounce. His time had expired on the shabby motel room, so he decided to go to the liquor store.

As he strolled down the street he began thinking about past episodes and his present life. He thought about how C-Crazy did him and cursed himself for being so naive and stupid. After all, he was from the streets of Compton and should have seen through C-Crazy's scam But unfortunately, the only thing he was thinking about was a hit of crack and a swallow of beer.

As morning light crept through the clouds, and stray dogs sniffed through the trash that bums had already beat them to, Big Steve strolled down University Boulevard with a forty-ounce in his hand. He made his way to an alley filled with junk, a couple of crackheads getting high, shopping carts filled with cans, bottles, and cardboard to be recycled, and a couple of abandoned vehicles. He sat on a milk crate, took a long swallow of beer, and began talking out loud to himself, not caring who heard him.

"I think she's fuckin' somebody else! Her pussy wasn't that wide before I left, and now it's larger than the goddamn Pacific Ocean! But she thinks I'm stupid! I'll bet she has a sugar daddy or sump'n! How in the hell can she afford to buy a thousand dollars worth of goddamn carpet and tile and pay those damn Mexicans to do the work? The bitch only do six to seven fuckin' heads a week, but she thinks I'm crazy enough to believe she's making that kind of money! But I'ma long ways from being stupid, bitch!" Everyone paused and looked at Big Steve as they passed by.

After finishing his beer, Big Steve got up and strolled back down The U, not knowing where he was going or what he was about to get into. A few familiar whores were flagging down potential customers, and there were bums pushing shopping carts containing their life savings. These were everyday scenes on The U.

He strolled at a slow pace with no actual destination in mind, until a drug dealer named Cyco spotted him.

"Hey! Big Steve! Let me holler at you a minute, Blood!"

Ah, damn! Big Steve thought. *Another one of those C-Crazy type niggas! Damn! I wonder what the hell he wants.*

Steve then approached Cyco, who was leaning against the brick wall in back of Church's Chicken. Big Steve noticed that

Cyco couldn't keep still. He constantly twitched, twisted around, darted his eyes from left to right, and moved uncontrollably.

That nigga must've just took a hit, Big Steve thought.

During the days when Big Steve was known on The U for selling drugs instead of using them, Cyco had purchased crack from him on a few occasions. He was always short with money. Instead of having the full ten dollars, Cyco would have seven or eight dollars. Or if he wanted to buy a twenty-dollar rock, he would always be three or four dollars short. He was originally from a Blood gang in Compton. Like C-Crazy, he was on the run from a few of his homeboys and couldn't return back to Compton.

He was dark complexioned, short, ugly, and resembled an ant. He had a tiny pair of beady eyes, which caused him to have a suspicious look even when he wasn't up to anything. Cyco had the type of look that, if he entered your place of business you'd keep one finger on the alarm button and the other finger on a trigger. If you had twenty other paying customers surrounding you, your focus would still remain on Cyco.

"What's up, Blood?" Cyco asked without ever looking Big Steve in the eye. His point of focus was elsewhere.

"Ain't nothin', homey," Big Steve replied. "What's up with you?"

"Jus' tryin' to make a dollar outta fifteen cents," Cyco replied while continuing to twitch and move uncontrollably. "I jus' got out yesterday, Blood, and already had to knock out a couple of fools, you know what I'm sayin'. I served 'em swell, too, Blood. Those fools stepped up to get knocked the fuck out. But they gonna remember Big Cyco, always and forever, you know what I'm sayin'. Yeah, they gonna remember me for the rest of their lives, homey, you can believe that. But anyway, I'm jus' treatin' myself to a little sump'n, sump'n." He then turned around, pulled out his pipe, and took a hit of crack.

Big Steve wondered where this conversation was going, but what the hell, he had nothing to do anyway.

After Cyco exhaled the crack smoke, he began moving around even more.

"Niggas around here know me! Yeah, I'ma O.G, Blood. I'm the one who started this gangsta shit around here! And these niggas wonder why I be beatin' their ass and takin' their money and dope. I do it 'cause they're pussies, Blood! They ain't got no respect for an O.G. like me." Then suddenly Cyco pulled off his shirt, threw it on the ground, and began walking around flexing his huge, twenty-four inch arms. "I had to knock two fools out a little while ago, Blood. If they would've just loaned me the two dollars I asked them for, everything would've been cool. But they lied to me and told me they was broke, so I socked both of them in the head and took they money and they dope."

As Big Steve stared at Cyco's gigantic arms and solid chest, he imagined someone getting hit by him. When Cyco spoke, strong emotions began building, and his facial expressions changed depending on what he was talking about.

"I wish those fools would come back and test Big Cyco again!"

"Yep, I know what you mean," Big Steve agreed.

"I've been waiting on those fools, Blood!" He had a mean look, hitting his hand with his fist. "But anyway, Blood, that's the kinda shit I'm talking about. But anyway, if you wanna make some money, bring me a few sales and I'll take care of you."

"Cool," Big Steve replied. "Let me get on it right away and I should be seein' you in a few tics."

Big Steve then strolled down The U seeking out potential customers. *I hope Cyco don't send me through the same bullshit C-Crazy sent me through. Nah, I don't think he's like that. Matter of fact, I should tell him to beat the shit out of C-Crazy.* Knowing he was about to earn himself a hit, gave Big Steve a tingly feeling.

During the next four hours his efforts paid off. Thanks to the hustling and soliciting of Big Steve, Cyco had completely sold out of crack. So far, there were no problems with police. It was all good.

After counting a total of $587, Cyco handed Big Steve fifty dollars.

"I gotta go handle my business and recoup, Blood. I'll be back in 'bout twenty, thirty minutes."

"I'll be inside gettin' a little sump'n to eat, you know what I'm sayin'?"

"Cool," Cyco replied, then left.

The following day, Big Steve retrieved his Bronco from Spank and made his way home. He had spent all his money and once again was broke and frustrated. He still blamed Melody for his current troubles. When he entered the house, the screaming began.

"Stop it! Stop before I call the police!" Melody screamed.

"Call the fuckin' police, bitch! And tell them that you been fuckin' another man in my goddamn bed, bitch! Yeah, that's what you can do!"

Byron had heard all the yelling, and at that moment he kicked in his mother's bedroom door like he was Superman.

"Byron! Stop Byron! Stop!" Melody yelled. Suddenly everyone froze. Seconds later, Big Steve stood up and led Byron into the living room. After having a few words with his stepson, Big Steve grabbed his paperwork off the table and went to his parents' house.

"I told you she wasn't no goddamn good! I hate to say it, but she's nothing but an undercover slut, Steve. And while we're on the subject, just last week, a friend of mine told me she heard some talk about Melody having a fight with a homosexual in the shop she worked at. From what I gather, the homosexual saw Melody fooling around with her customer's husband in front of a shop full of people. They said that Melody was so embarrassed and upset that she threw some hot curlers at the homosexual, but the homosexual ended up beating the shit out of her. Steve, I don't want that bitch at my house anymore. Do you understand?"

"Why didn't you tell me, Mama?"

"Well, I didn't wanna be the bearer of bad news, son. And besides, what if it was a lie, and you would've left her because of what I told you? How do you think I would've felt?"

Steve had heard enough. He called it a night, walked upstairs to his old bedroom, and tossed and turned.

The following morning at ten AM, Big Steve went to Special Touch and had a chat with Tosha. He found out more than he planned to, and more than his mind could bear. After relaying what he'd learned to his parents, he officially moved in with them.

Four months later, Big Steve was doing an outstanding job of maintaining his sobriety. He had established himself well in the community and affiliated himself with several positive organizations. To add to his accomplishments, he earned a promotion on his job, which came with a raise. In addition, he joined a local church and participated faithfully in N.A. and A.A. meetings. He felt proud of himself, but deep down inside he missed Melody. He tried dismissing her from his mind, but that only worked for an hour or two, then thoughts of her would return.

One day after work at the warehouse, he spoke at an N.A. meeting about his prior experiences with drugs and alcohol. The listeners were drug addicts, who were participating only because their parole or probation officers gave then the ultimatum of going to jail, or attending a drug rehabilitation program. Naturally, they chose to attend the program. When Steve finished speaking, the audience craved to ask him questions.

"What made you stop using crack?" one of the people asked.

"Well, actually, I felt as though I was killing myself. Sometimes, I felt like a walking dead man taking up space on earth, and serving no purpose at all. I also felt that I was not only letting down God, but letting down my parents as well. My parents raised me better than that."

"Have you ever stolen from your parents, kids, wife, or family members to buy crack?" another listener asked.

"Nope," Big Steve replied. He then thought about the time he broke into his own home, but decided not to bring it up. "I guess I wasn't that far gone yet."

When time expired for asking questions, Big Steve decided to make a brief speech.

"By the grace of God and by following the twelve steps, I've been sober for 121 days. These medals I'm wearing weren't just given to me. I'm proud to say I earned them." He paused, took a drink of water, and continued. "Being sober for 121 days might not mean anything to some of you, but to me, considering the condition I was in, it means an awful lot. Today I can say that I feel like a million bucks. My sobriety is very important to me. If you have goals and aspirations and want to do something positive and worthwhile with your life, sobriety should be a main factor. Set high goals and take whatever steps are necessary to accomplish them. Reach for the sky, and if you end up on a mountain, you'll be in good shape. But if you only set your goals as far as a mountaintop, you might end up on a hill or in a valley, lost. Stay focused while maintaining your sobriety, and put God first in all that you do.

"There's a scripture that reads: 'I can do all things through Christ who strengthens me.' Another important verse to keep in mind is 'My God shall supply all my needs according to his riches.' Don't let the devil steal your pride, future, godliness, love, or your life. Thank you all for coming, and please keep coming back."

Later several people approached Big Steve, shook his hand, and congratulated him on his speech and accomplishments. He felt good about himself and wished that Melody were there to see him. He wished she could hear him speak. He wished she could see him fill out his own job application. He wished she could . . .

Three nights a week Steve attended a tutoring class and was in the process of obtaining his G.E.D. Even though he had come a long way, he figured the best was yet to come.

He was in charge of the shipping and receiving department at S.L.H. Electronics. His duties were to check in freight being delivered by trucks, and to make sure the count was accurate and matched the invoice. He was also in charge of the company's inventory control. The owners, managers, and supervisors took a liking to him right away.

Every weekend Big Steve picked up Byron and spent some father and son quality time with him. They went to Lakers and Clippers games, U.S.C. football and basketball games, soccer games, and out to breakfast, lunch, and dinner. They enjoyed each other's company and took pleasure in wearing the same types of clothes and tennis shoes.

Big Steve's hopes and prayers were that one day he and Melody would reunite and start over for the sake of Byron, for the sake of love, and for the sake of their marriage. He wanted that more than anything in the world. Even though the cards had begun to fall in his favor, what was success if you had no one to share your life with? He wanted to hold his wife and tell her how much he loved her. He wanted to make love to her early in the morning and late at night. He wanted to sit in church with her. He wanted to . . .

Every man needs a woman, he thought. And every woman needs a man. But I won't be satisfied with anyone but Melody. She was my first, and I want her to be my last. She's my everything and I'll love her until I die.

CHAPTER 16

Pat

It was six months since Pat had come home from the hospital. Larry treated her like a queen. But between the hours of two and six PM, he still belonged to Melody.

Pat's amnesia had not improved. She still remembered nothing. Her speech consisted of mumbles, grunts, and weird sounds. This was excellent as far as Larry was concerned, especially after Melody told him that Pat had witnessed him kissing Melody on the day of her accident.

Pat spent her days lying in her three thousand dollar recliner bed and watching the news, *Judge Joe Brown, Judge Hatchett,* and *Divorce Court.* Her evenings were spent watching reruns of *Matlock, The Streets of San Francisco,* and *In the Heat of the Night.*

When Larry arrived home he fed her and bathed her. It became a daily ritual for Larry to fix her coffee, make her breakfast, and dress her, even though she never left home. Also, he took her to Creativity every two weeks to keep her beauty appointments. Her appearance at the salon was far from what it had been in the beginning. She appeared to have aged ten years. No longer did she possess beautiful looks, a mouth full of gossip, or self-satisfaction. Before, whenever she was in public or even in church, her beauty always seemed to attract people, but now, everyone that saw her felt sorry for her— everyone except Melody. Pat had been completely stripped of her self-sufficiency and haughtiness. She was so embarrassed by her condition that she didn't look people in the eye. When Larry wheeled her to grocery stores, malls, parks, or the salon, she would always hold her head down.

Pat felt bad about not being able to sexually please the man that she was told was her husband. She figured, sooner or later, he might turn to another woman, and she had grown fond of this man who was taking such good care of her.

As time passed, her medication began doing its job. Although Pat had no feelings in her lower body, she began wanting to have sex just to please her husband. She'd ordered several books such as *How Paraplegic Women Satisfy Their Mates* and *Sex and the Paraplegic Woman*. She'd even read a book entitled, *Paraplegics Do it Better.*

Her goal was to satisfy Larry and keep him in her bed. Little did she know, it was too late.

One day, she decided to put into action what she'd read in all three books. When Larry walked into the bedroom at six twenty, she was primed and ready. The nurse Larry hired to help look after her had bathed her, lotioned her body with Victoria's Secret body lotion, and dressed her in a see-through sexy gown. She felt sexy.

Using her remote, she turned off the television, dimmed the lights, and turned on the CD player. She selected a song by Luther Vandross entitled, "Always and Forever." She'd never been more ready in her life.

As Larry stepped into the bedroom, he barely could see her.

"Hey, baby. What's going on with you today?" he asked, puzzled by the low lighting and romantic music. He then began removing his clothes.

"Just trying to be sexy for the man of my life," Pat replied, smiling.

"Well, you're doing a damn good job of it, honey. You're looking sexy and hot, girl. And you're wearing my favorite gown, too. Hell, I remember the first time we made love at my brother's house, and you had that gown on, remember? I told you to never get rid of it," Larry said, smiling and playing her game.

"For you, the world, baby," Pat replied. "This bed is large enough for the both of us, sweetheart. I want you to lie down and make love to me all night long." To his surprise, she pulled him next to her and began kissing him wildly. She suggested he stand next to the bed, and for the first time in twenty-six years, she took his hard, long penis in her mouth, and began sucking, licking, and slurping it like the girls on the porn movies she'd been watching. As he climaxed, she didn't bother stopping. She sucked him dry. He then fell asleep. She felt good about being able to give her husband pleasure and see a look of satisfaction on his face. Tomorrow, she'd have another surprise for him. She could barely wait.

CHAPTER 17

Big Steve became a member of a church called Holy Assembly located in Moreno Valley. He began studying the Bible faithfully. He was striving for wisdom, understanding, and righteousness. He even began associating with ministers hoping to inherit their biblical knowledge, and a touch of their brotherly kindness.

He had met and studied with the Reverend Joe Black, and openly shared his past drug and street related experiences with him. The Reverend suggested that he give a testimony the following Sunday. Big Steve was grateful to do so.

His parents sat proudly on the third row of the four hundred plus congregation, and sitting next to them was Byron. Byron, for the first time, had the opportunity to go to church with his Pops.

After being introduced by the preacher, Big Steve grabbed the microphone and began talking.

"My name is Steve Pullman. I've never been too much of a strong-minded man, and there was a time in my life when I would fall for just about anything. They say that if you don't stand for something, you'll fall for anything," The congregation voiced their "Amens." He then continued, but this time with more emotion. "Satan had me smoking a crack pipe! He had me drinking alcohol 24/7! He introduced me to gang bangers, prostitutes, street people of all types, and lowlifes from all over the U.S.! He had me lying to my parents and deceiving my wife and son! And because of Satan, I no longer have a wife! You're a liar, Satan, and the truth isn't in you! You're a no good, dirty, low-down liar, and I rebuke you in the name of Jesus! You had my mind and my soul, Satan! But now I belong to Jesus!"

"Amen!" the congregation shouted.

His parents sat calmly, listening to the child whom they raised. His mother couldn't hold back her tears of joy and contentment. His father sat proudly, remaining dignified, but still delighted at his son's accomplishments.

As Steve's speech came to an end, Byron was the first to begin clapping, then the whole congregation joined in. After church services were over, about a hundred members of the congregation caravanned to Hometown Buffet for dinner.

Already there were several single women in the congregation who had their eyes on Big Steve. Each of them waited impatiently for the right time to make their move, and each of them were seeking husbands—godly husbands.

During the ride to the restaurant Byron began asking questions.

"Where'd you learn how to talk like that, Pops?"

"The spirit of God is in me, son," Big Steve explained. "When a person is filled with the Holy Spirit, words and emotions automatically flow from your heart and mind."

"Oh. Me and Mom been to Reverend Joe Black's church before, but Mom always wanted to leave early. That prevented me from getting a clear understanding, you know. Every time the Good Reverend Joe Black started preaching, Mom would always say, 'Let's go.' She said some funny stuff was going on in that church, and until she found out what it was, we weren't going there anymore."

"Is that right?" Big Steve asked thoughtfully, turning into the parking lot of Hometown Buffet.

Inside the restaurant, and already seated were the three fat, undersexed women who'd been eyeballing Big Steve during his speech. They were seated not too far from him, watching him, smiling at him, and discussing him.

"I love a man with a big appetite," Roxanne said while chewing on some pork ribs. She was short, fat, and light-complexioned. "I need a man like him—big and strong, knows how to talk good, and is knowledgeable about the word of God. As long as he knows how to use his joystick, it's all good, you know what I'm saying, girl?"

"Humph," Lisa said, winking at Big Steve. "I think he's giving me some action, girl." She was also short and fat, but was dark-complexioned and unattractive. She'd hit on several men in the church, but was always ignored. She then lied and said, "He blew me a kiss, girl. If I ever get a hold of him, he won't have to come to Hometown to eat, 'cause I've got what he needs to eat right here. Right here." She was pointing between her legs while munching on liver, green beans, cake, and roast beef.

"Big girls have more fun," Lynn, who was the fattest of them all, added. She was talking with a mouth full of food. "Girl, he's about my size and I could give him what he needs, and can damn sure give him what he wants. I could just imagine me and him tumbling around naked in bed, having things our way."

Big Steve smiled at the idea of the women at the next table showing interest in him, and he was actually flattered. But he loved Melody and was not contemplating another relationship.

"Hey, Pops, are we going to church next Sunday?" Byron asked as he ate the remainder of his ice cream mixed with cake.

"Yep. But why do you wanna know? Oh, I know why. I saw you and that girl looking at each other. Do you like her? Is she the reason you want to go back to church next Sunday?"

"Come on, Pops, be serious. She's my friend. Her name is

Christina." Byron then washed down his German chocolate cake and ice cream with some Dr Pepper.

"I thought you were supposed to be studying scripture instead of getting names and ages? Did you get her phone number, too?"

"Next week, Pops. It's all set for next week. We've already talked about it," Byron replied, giggling.

As Big Steve was about to exit the restaurant, the three horny, fat girls smiled and waved goodbye to him. Being a nice guy, he returned their smiles and waves. He then paid the cashier and left.

After dropping Byron back home, Steve returned to his parents' house. He studied his Bible for an hour or so, then fell asleep watching *SportsCenter.*

After several months of regularly attending church, the Reverend Joe Black took money from the church's earnings to pay for Big Steve's tuition to attend a seminary part-time. Once he graduated a year later, he began ministering to churches throughout Riverside, San Bernadino, and Los Angeles counties. He had become extremely knowledgeable about God's words, and spoke clearly and with great confidence. During that time of his life he felt motivated, enthusiastic, and eager to preach the word of God. He thanked the Lord each day for turning around his life and for transforming him into a godly, dignified man of constantly increasing integrity.

On a warm Sunday afternoon, two members of the church, Lynn and Lisa, the fat women who had their eye on Steve, had a brief conversation with Big Steve after services were over.

"I enjoyed your sermon, Minister Steve, and ah, me and my cousin, Lisa, were wondering if you'd like to join us for barbecue later this evening?" She was smiling, desperately wanting Steve to say yes.

"I'm glad you enjoyed the sermon, Lynn. Hopefully you've

digested God's words and will apply them to your everyday life." Steve then smiled. "And barbecue sounds right up my alley. I don't see any reason why I can't accept your invitation. As you ladies can see, I love to eat."

"Good," Lynn replied. Lisa stood next to her cousin grinning. "Here's my address. I've written down my telephone number too in case you get lost. And if you'd like, you can call me sometime and share some of your enlightening words with me."

"Sure, why not," he replied. "We're still babies in Christ, and there's always understanding and wisdom we can gather by studying the word."

"Most definitely," Lynn replied flirtatiously. "So, see you around four. Is that OK for you?"

"Perfect." He then shook the women's hands and walked away.

"We'll be waiting," Lisa and Lynn said in unison, watching his butt as he walked off.

At five minutes to four, Steve was ringing their doorbell. Their apartment complex was located on the corner of Heacock and Dreacea, in the city of Moreno Valley, not too far from his parents' place. It was clean, quiet, and well-secured. The building resembled a small, gated community for senior citizens, but actually it was for people on low income. There was a beautiful swimming pool, a playground, and an open patio area, which contained several barbecue pits. As Big Steve observed his surroundings, he noticed there were no signs of a barbecue.

Maybe they've already cooked it, he thought, and continued ringing the doorbell.

Seconds later, Lisa appeared with a welcoming smile and invited him in. Once inside, she gave him a long, wet kiss. It was far from a holy kiss.

Steve shrugged it off and glanced around the apartment, looking for signs of a barbecue, but there was none.

Lisa was dressed in a pair of shorts, which appeared two sizes too small. She also had on a see-through blouse, which revealed her huge, black breasts.

"Sorry, Steve," Lisa said, "but we didn't have enough money to buy any meat, so all we bought were potatoes to make a potato salad, a couple cans of baked beans, and some instant macaroni and cheese. We hope you're not disappointed."

"That's fine, Lisa. Actually, I love baked beans, potato salad, and macaroni and cheese, too."

Seconds later, Lynn appeared wearing a size 4X see-through sundress. Observing her, Steve noticed she had on no panties or bra.

These fat girls are hot, he thought. *But all I wanted was some barbecue.*

"Just because we can't eat barbecue, doesn't mean we can't have some fun," Lynn suggested. She then walked over, seated herself next to him, and kissed him on the lips. The kissing caused her to get hot and wet between her legs. It had been a long time since she had that feeling. It felt good to her, so she kissed him again, hoping he would respond.

"Easy, baby," he said. But it was no use. The fat girl was hot, primed, and ready.

He had food on his mind, but the fat girls had something else altogether different on their minds—sex. They were as hot as fish grease, and the only thing that could cool them down was some hot sex.

Lisa put on a Snoop Doggy Dog CD and began doing some type of freaky dance. She bent over, put her butt in the air, and shook it from left to right. Lynn paused from kissing Steve and joined Lisa in dancing. Steve was amazed.

Is this what church girls do after service? he wondered. Then the doorbell rang. The fat girls were so into their dancing that they didn't hear it. Big Steve spoke up.

"Lisa! Lynn! Someone's at the door!" he shouted.

Lisa danced over to the door and opened it. Standing there

was Thelma Black, the Reverend Joe Black's daughter. She was carrying two large bags of liquor. Hurriedly, she sat down her bags and joined in with Lisa and Lynn, doing the freaky dance.

Thelma was larger than Lisa and Lynn combined, but she seemed to move a lot swifter than the both of them. Her huge breasts swung back and forth and up and down. Her big, black butt jumped around like popcorn being popped. She was huge, dark, black-complexioned, and had short hair and a pair of tight eyes.

While dancing Thelma suddenly began stripping out her clothes. Once completely naked, she danced her way over to Big Steve and held out her hand.

"Let's boogie, Big Daddy. Show me what you're working with," Thelma said. She then led him to the center of the floor.

He loosened up a little, but hoped and prayed that word of this episode did not get back to the church. Once the song finished, Thelma hurried over to the CD player and put on a song by Naughty By Nature entitled "O.P.P." After turning up the volume full blast, she opened a bottle of peach Cisco, took a long swallow, and continued her freak dancing. Lisa and Lynn followed suit. Big Steve got in the groove of things and began moving to the rhythm of the song. He had totally forgotten about the food. He had also forgotten he was a minister of God. To his surprise, he'd even forgotten about Melody.

He was surrounded by three fat, horny, naked Christians, and somehow, even though he wasn't fond of fat girls, he developed a small erection. Lisa eased up to him and shamelessly began rubbing his penis. Lynn approached him from the side and began licking his neck and ears as Thelma began undressing him. Thelma was highly disappointed upon seeing his small penis.

"Is that all you're working with, Steve?" she asked. Dissatisfied, she hurriedly put her clothes back. "My ten-year-old brother's dick is bigger than that. I'm outta here. Hell, I can get more pleasure using my dildo and watching X-rated movies." She then grabbed the bag of liquor and left.

"Damn!" Lynn shouted, also displeased by the small size of his penis. "Man, your dick looks like it belongs on a baby." She then stormed out the door.

It had been a long time since Lisa had opportunity to be with a man, and there was no way in hell she was about to let him leave without getting her a piece, regardless of the size. She was sick and tired of dildos, porno movies, sex toys, and using her imagination to masturbate. Steve stood there, not knowing whether to put away his penis and leave, or to accept a blowjob from the horny, fat girl. Right away, she helped him make up his mind. She fell to her knees and began sucking his dick the way she'd seen the girls do it on porn movies.

It had been a long time since Big Steve had received a blowjob, and as the fat girl sucked, licked, and slurped, memories of Tastee began flooding his mind.

"I wanna ride it, Steve. Let me ride it," she begged. She took it upon herself to ease him on the floor and then position and mount herself on his penis. She then began riding him like it was the last ride of her life. She had a happy look on her face— a look she had not had in years. The last man she had sex with was also a member of the church. She'd invited him over for barbecue, just like she did Big Steve, but instead of barbecue, they drank Long Island Iced Teas, Old English 800, and smoked a couple of joints. Afterward, the man passed out, which gave her the opportunity to have it her way. Once the man awakened, he was so embarrassed that without saying anything, he grabbed his clothes and left. He never showed his face in church again.

"Let's do it doggy-style, Steve. I want all of it," she said. Looking at her big, black butt he wanted to vomit. He pumped and pumped and pumped, almost reaching the finish line, then suddenly, she pulled away, causing his penis to slip out. She wasn't ready for it to be over. She wanted to make it last—forever, if possible. "No, I don't want you to cum yet," she said seriously. Then she gave him further instructions. "Lie down and let me suck it."

He was angry about her pulling away, and now, since he was limp, he was ready to leave.

"Sorry, Lisa, but I've got to go now." He walked toward his clothes.

"But I'm not finished."

"We've been doing it for over forty-five minutes, and you haven't cum yet?" he asked.

"I've cum lots of times, Steve, but I want to cum once more. Please?" she begged.

"Enough is enough, Lisa. Besides, we've already broken several commandments in the Bible. What we need to do is pray and ask for forgiveness."

"I'm not thinking about forgiveness, goddammit. I want some more dick! OK, I'll tell you what, if you fuck me real good, for one more hour, I'll give you fifty dollars." She was standing with her hands on her hips. Big Steve thought about the offer for a few seconds.

"OK, you've got a deal. But first give me the fifty dollars."

"It's in the bank. When we're finished, we'll go to the ATM and I'll get it. I swear to God."

"OK. I'm going to take your word for it because you're a Christian. But don't be lying to me, Lisa."

"I'm not lying. I swear I'm not. Now come on and let's handle our business," she suggested. Smiling, she then lay on her back and spread her legs as wide as she could.

To Steve, it seemed like the longest hour of his life. During the entire sexual encounter, he showed no interest whatsoever, but she seemed as if she were having the time of her life. She was having things her way, making sure she got her fifty dollars worth and then some.

"Come on, Lisa. Hurry up. Hell, I'm tired."

"Ten more minutes. Just ten more minutes and I'll be finished," she said, continuing to ride him.

After several more orgasms Lisa rolled over, totally exhausted, and fell asleep. Big Steve hurriedly got dressed and tried to wake her with no luck. As he watched her snore and foam at the mouth, he told himself, *Fuck it! It's not worth it.*

He then left. The second he walked out the house, Lisa opened her eyes and began grinning.

Sucka! she thought.

After making it back home, Big Steve threw some leftovers in the microwave, ate, and then fell asleep.

The following day, while at work, he thought about what had happened the day before.

Why? Why did I involve myself in that episode? God was watching me, and I know he's disappointed in me. I was doing well until yesterday. I wonder if Reverend Black knows that his daughter is a drunk and a slut? But actually, this could be the start of something beneficial for me. Since that's how churchwomen want to act, I'm about to put a little twist in the game.

After work, he went to Bible study, met two single, Christian women, and persuaded them that they needed more study in order to increase their spiritual knowledge and understanding. He drove home a woman in the congregation named Laura. Naively, she fell for his bait. He started off by quoting and reading scripture to her, but minutes later, he began kissing and rubbing all over her. Soon she was under his spell, carrying out his sexual demands.

The next day after work, Steve followed the same pattern, and with ease he conquered his second victim. It became a daily ritual for him. As days went by, his devious tactics became easier. Within a month, he had perfected his game.

Each day, the church held some type of service, whether it was Bible study, choir rehearsal, prayer meeting, or services for the youth. Big Steve would always be there offering to give rides home to the single women, and making himself available for one-on-one Bible study with them. Within a three-month period, he had sex with twenty-seven church members. Some were even married. He also had sex with women who belonged to other churches. He promised several of them that he would marry them, but he only deceived them to get what he wanted.

In the eyes of his fellow pastors, reverends, ministers, and other godly men he associated with, his reputation and ability to preach the word of God, and his brotherly kindness still stood strong. Little did they know that he was a fox in the hen house—sly, slick, and wicked.

One day, after having sex with the choir director, Big Steve decided to reward himself by having a drink of Old English 800.

Damn. It's been a long time, he thought. *Let me grab myself a forty-ounce, and sit back and chill.*

One thing led to another and thoughts began stirring in his mind, both evil thoughts and good thoughts. His good thoughts were from God, and his evil thoughts came from Satan. Satan was telling him to go get a hit of crack, another beer, and treat himself to a University whore. God instructed him to pull over, pray, and go home. As the beer kicked in and took control of his mind, it naturally caused him to carry out Satan's suggestions.

Big Steve went by the U, picked up Tastee, bought a fifty-dollar piece of crack, and parked in a secluded area. As soon as he was about to take a hit of crack, loud voices came yelled out.

"Freeze, asshole! Riverside sheriffs!"

Big Steve was arrested, fingerprinted, and charged with possession of a controlled substance and possession of drug paraphernalia. Due to his prior drug offense and a probation violation, the court showed no mercy or leniency, and Steve was sentenced to six years in state prison.

During the first four months of his incarceration, Big Steve wrote Melody several letters, but she didn't respond to any of them. She'd thrown away his last twelve letters without even reading them.

One night, while sipping vodka at her dining room table, Melody finally decided to read Steve's most recent letter. It read:

From your husband.

I don't want to take up too much of your time, Melody, but I hope this letter finds you and Byron in good health and spirits. I'm sorry and regret that my drug problem came between our marriage, but I've overcome it and now I feel I'm a changed man. I realize my mistakes, and I've confessed them to God. He's forgiven me. Can you? I'm still in love with you, Melody, and there's no way possible I can get you off my mind. We can't just forget about our vows. That wouldn't please God. We both need to set our minds on things which please God, in order for us to have a prosperous life together. I'm begging you, sweetheart, for a second chance. That way I can prove my love to you and show you how capable I am of being a father and an outstanding husband. I've forgiven you for all the foul, ungodly things you've done. Please forgive me? Then, we can put all this behind us and move forward as a family. In the beginning we made plans to love each other, honor our wedding vows, and grow old together. I hope we can mend our relationship, Melody. I could never love another the way I love you.

Your husband, the man who really loves you.

Steve

Melody reminisced about Big Steve for a few moments before chastising herself and getting up to refill her drink.

Melody's trifling behavior and Big Steve's departure began taking its toll on Byron. In an effort to bring the spotlight back onto himself and off of her boyfriends, Byron started hanging with the wrong crowd and his grades started to drop. Soon peer pressure and his sense of rebellion got him kicked out of school for fighting. The following day, Melody enrolled him in another school, but his grades still did not improve.

Melody had spoken with Kenneth, his biological father who now lived in Las Vegas. She told Kenneth several times about Byron's attitude, grades, friends, and laziness.

"Send him to me! I'll straighten his little ass out!" Kenneth finally responded.

So, off to Las Vegas Byron went. Kenneth worked as a city official and was an extremely strict man. He was married and raising three teenage boys with his wife, and he wasn't about to take any shit. He felt this was finally a way to do something positive for Byron after years of denying him.

CHAPTER 18

Melody had discussed her financial issues with Michelle, one of her wealthy customers, each time she came in for her beauty needs. Michelle suggested that Melody team up with her, working banks with bad checks and bogus credit cards, in order to make some easy cash.

After involving herself in a few scams with Michelle, Melody realized she could make lots of money, and someday possibly live the rich and flamboyant lifestyle Michelle lived. She had never thought that anyone could make so much money in just one day.

As time passed, through persuasion and persistence, Michelle gradually lured Melody into both her public and private world. Even though an experience with a lesbian was new to Melody, she picked up on it quickly and even began to take pleasure in it.

Michelle's beauty was one of a kind. She was five foot seven and had long, black hair that hung down her back. She appeared to be a mixture of Creole and Brazilian. Her 36DDs matched perfectly with her firm, rounded butt. She was a stunning woman who could easily win first prize in any beauty pageant.

But Michelle was actually a wolf in sheep's clothing. She had obtained a master's degree years earlier, but had never applied her schooling, intelligence, skills, or professionalism to anything positive. Illegal scams had allowed her to live the lifestyle of the rich and famous. She owned a beach home in Newport Beach, a fifty-six-unit apartment complex in Santa Monica, an office complex in Glendale, and had money invested in lucrative stocks and bonds. She also owned a new Mercedes, a Porsche, a convertible BMW, and had enough money in her bank account to live large for the rest of her life.

Michelle made her first sexual advance at Melody one day after they finished one of their scams. While they were stopped at a traffic light, Michelle rested her hand on Melody's leg, looked her in the eyes, then boldly leaned over and kissed her on the lips.

"Would you like to see my beach house?" Michelle propositioned when she saw that Melody didn't resist her touch. "I've told you so much about it, and . . ."

"Why not? Now is as good a time as any."

Michelle's beach home sat in the midst of several half-million to million-dollar homes. It was two-stories and had a white picket fence and well-manicured lawn. Roses, daisies, marigolds, and tulips added to the beauty of it.

Using a remote, Michelle opened her three-car garage and parked the Benz between her BMW and her Porsche. So far, Melody was very impressed.

Damn, she must be rich, Melody thought. *A Mercedes, a Beemer, a Porsche, and a million-dollar home on the ocean—this woman represents money. And she has class too. And to my advantage, she likes me. This could be the start of something big.*

Once they entered the house, two poodles—one black, the other white—stood wagging their tails, delighted to see their mistress. They sniffed Melody and then began barking.

"They like you, babe," Michelle said. "This one is Whitey, and that's Blackie."

Melody smiled and knelt to pet them. "They're so cute."

Michelle then took Melody's hand and led her upstairs to a room she had converted into an office. Out of the blue, Michelle kissed Melody, and then began hugging and caressing her. When Melody showed no signs of resistance, Michelle moved in for the kill. Melody fell into the rhythm, responding with meaningful, wet tongue kisses, while rubbing Michelle all over. They hurriedly undressed each other. While kissing and caressing each other, they tumbled around the room, knocking over the computer monitor, a huge vase, the fax machine, and then the lamp.

Michelle, realizing she had a willing participant, took full advantage of the opportunity. She positioned Melody on the carpeted floor, and aided by sex toys, she licked her all over, caressed her, and made sweet passionate love to her like no one had ever made love to Melody before. Later Michelle handed Melody twenty-five hundred dollars.

"Here, baby, and there's plenty more where this came from. Catch up on your bills, and then treat yourself to something you've been wanting for a long time. If you happen to need more, don't be ashamed to ask. This could be the beginning of something worthwhile."

Since then, Michelle and Melody's scams were going strong, and proving to be tremendously profitable. The procedure was that on Thursdays, Melody and Michelle would go on check-writing sprees, writing checks for much more than the three thousand dollars they'd deposited into the account. When the bank opened on Monday morning, they would then withdraw the three thousand dollars from the account, and still have the merchandise they had purchased. They would then return the majority of the merchandise, all but what they wanted to keep, with a valid purchase receipt, and get back their money. The scam was very lucrative and beneficial for the both of them. Not too many people, especially store managers and cashiers, could catch on to what they were doing.

Melody began making so much money that she had given

away her customers to a couple of her favorite beautician friends, who either worked with her or at other salons. It had been a little over a month since she had been to Creativity. Only three of her long-term clients were allowed to come to her house for their beauty needs. Pat was one of the chosen few. Melody made it a point to continue doing Pat's hair every two weeks, even though she was still sleeping with her husband.

Her relationship with Michelle was improving faster than anticipated. With Byron living with his father in Las Vegas, the green light was on for Michelle and Melody 24/7. Some nights they slept at Melody's place, while other nights they stayed at Michelle's. Their relationship was so deep that Melody had no other choice but to tell Larry about it. She could no longer easily conceal it. She broke the news to Larry one day after they had sex at her home. They were sipping vodka and smoking a joint.

"Baby, we need to talk." Melody said while sitting at the edge of the bed and stirring the ice in her glass.

"What is it, sweetheart?" Larry asked, assuming she was about to ask him for money. Melody took a swallow of vodka to build up her confidence.

"I really don't know how to break this to you. Believe me, this is hard, and—"

Larry sat comfortably next to her, grabbed her by the hand, and looked her in the eyes.

"What is it, sweetheart? Tell me. Do you need more money, or is your husband about to get out again?"

"This, this is hard, baby, and I just don't know how to break the news to you."

"Well, the best way to do it, is first exhale, and then just say it," Larry explained, wondering what she had to tell him.

"OK, I'll try," Melody said. She then took another swallow of vodka, exhaled, and held down her head. "I have another lover," she blurted out.

"Is that all?" Larry then took a swallow of vodka, inhaled the chronic smoke, held it in for a few seconds, and exhaled. "You had me thinking you were pregnant or something, baby." He then showered her with wet kisses. "Sweetheart, I'm in no position to say anything about you having an affair with another man, because after all, I have a wife I sleep with every night, so I can't be mad at you. As long as he doesn't ruin your pussy, I'm cool with it," Larry said with a smile on his face.

She then poured herself another drink, took a swallow, then took a hit of chronic for added courage. "I'm involved with a woman, baby, not a man."

Larry froze. A weird, puzzled look developed on his face. He sat in silence for a minute, thinking about what she had just told him.

"It's cool, sweetheart. What can I say? I don't have the right to call shots on your body, you know." He then smiled, and added, "Besides, I'd rather a woman lick on you, than a man knocking the lining out of your pussy. But what I want to know is, who is she, and why the sudden change of menu?" He refilled his glass, took a long gulp, relaxed, and waited for her to answer. Melody poised herself and replied.

"Her name is Michelle. And to tell you the truth, Larry, I didn't know I was attracted to women until I met her. But she's a good person, and like you, she cares about my well-being and about my financial situation." Melody couldn't believe that she was actually telling Larry all this information.

"Oh, I see," Larry replied. "Is that the reason you haven't been to the salon in over two months, and haven't been answering your phone during late night hours?"

"Yeah, I guess so."

"I figured something was wrong, because lately you haven't been asking me for money. Well, whatever you do, sweetheart, please be careful, OK?" He leaned over and kissed her.

"I'm glad you understand, baby," Melody replied, smiling. "And don't worry, I'll be careful. I promise."

The phone was ringing. It was Michelle calling to let Melody know that she was parked in the driveway.

"Come in, Chelle. Larry's here, honey, and I'd like for you to meet him," Melody said in good spirits.

Michelle was dressed in business attire as usual. She was wearing a beige two-piece pantsuit with a pair of matching pumps. Her hair was absolutely flawless, hanging past her shoulders, with huge curls at the ends. She wore no makeup. She was naturally beautiful.

"Michelle, this is Larry, and Larry this is Michelle," Melody said, glad to introduce her lovers to one another.

Larry was utterly stunned by Michelle's beauty and elegance. *How in the hell can a woman this damn fine not like to be fucked by a man?* he wondered. *Damn, she's one fine bitch.*

Keeping a straight face and not showing any signs of excitement or enthusiasm, Michelle offered a handshake.

"It's a pleasure meeting you, Larry. Melody has told me an awful lot about you."

"Did she tell you the good, the bad, or the ugly?" Larry asked with a laugh.

"Actually, she spoke very highly of you, Larry," Michelle said as she seated herself. "She mainly spoke about how helpful you've been to her and Byron, and I appreciate that." She then held Melody's hand, and added, "And she really appreciates you, but by the same token, there has been a change that I'm sure you're already aware of." She spoke with a stern look, pronouncing each word meticulously and matter-of-factly.

I wonder if Byron knows about her, Larry thought. *Nah, no way. How could Melody tell her son she's fucking another woman? Umph, that's probably why she sent him to Vegas.*

"Nice meeting you, Michelle," Larry said, ignoring Michelle's last comment. "Excuse me, ladies, but I have some business to take care of so I've got to go. And Melody, I'll check with you tomorrow."

Larry did not know whether it would be appropriate for him

to kiss Melody, so he quickly dismissed the thought of kissing her and left. Melody was actually accustomed to being showered with kisses from Larry when he was departing, but because of Michelle's presence, she decided to shrug it off. She walked him to the door and said goodbye. She was still new to the ways of lesbians and did not know how Michelle would respond. She didn't want to do anything to make her angry. She had to be wary of what she did, what she said, and how she carried herself in front of Michelle.

After having sex with Michelle, Melody then followed her home. As they neared Michelle's driveway, Michelle opened her garage door with the remote. Melody parked in the driveway and used her key to let herself in the house.

Unbeknownst to the lovers, parked a few houses down the street, observing her wife accompanied by an unfamiliar face, sat Rosie Martinez. Rosie and Michelle had been married for a little over three years, but they had been lovers for almost twelve years. Rosie was a beautiful Puerto Rican woman who had been employed by the State of California as a supervisor for the Department of Motor Vehicles for the past sixteen years.

Like Michelle, Rosie appeared to be a mixture of black and Mexican. She had an attractive, shapely butt like a black woman, which matched exceptionally well with her firm 36Ds. Her complexion and long, beautiful, straight, black hair made her appear to be a stunning South American woman. Regardless of her beauty, Rosie could be very deceitful, devious, and downright evil if she chose to be. She had proven it before, and wouldn't hesitate to prove it again. She was the type of woman who could not accept rejection. As far as she was concerned, Michelle still belonged to her.

Rosie's jealousy was the reason Michelle had gradually eased away from her. She tried begging and pleading, and even tried to reason with Michelle, promising to change her ways, but

Michelle had heard that same old song too many times before. During a recent phone conversation between Michelle and Rosie, Michelle had clarified the situation.

"The only dealings we have, Rosie, where it would cause us to communicate and to be physically in the same room is our DMV business. I'm paying you generously for what you do for me, so it's not like you're doing me any favors."

Heartbroken, Rosie begged for another chance. "Please, Michelle, please don't leave me. I love you more than you could imagine, and I can't live without you. I'm begging you for another chance. Please, baby."

"For now, Rosie, I need some time alone to clear my head and sort some things out. We'll separate for a few months to see whether your jealousy vanishes or not. If I detect a change of attitude and all goes well, we'll see about mending our marriage. But until then, don't keep hounding me, and don't come over unless I ask you to, and don't do anything stupid."

"Thank you, baby," Rosie replied, grateful that she still had a wife and possibly another chance. "Thank you so much. I'm looking forward to us reuniting soon. And believe me, I wouldn't do anything in the world to screw up my opportunity for another chance."

Michelle had dumped Rosie six months before meeting Melody, and told her that their relationship was over without the possibility of ever being repaired. But Rosie, being love struck, was not ready for things with Michelle to end. If she could help it, no one was going to begin a relationship with Michelle. No one.

Rosie was an extremely jealous woman, and had proven to be loyal, faithful, and totally devoted to Michelle. But one thing Rosie did not approve of was someone messing around with her woman. Rosie sat in her car furiously observing Melody let herself into the beach home she once shared with Michelle. She then fired up her convertible, eased up to Melody's vehicle, quickly jotted down the license plate number, and burned rubber down the narrow street.

While driving northbound on the 405 freeway, Rosie began talking out loud.

"I wonder who that bitch is? I'll find out tomorrow. And when I do, it won't be fucking nice. No one comes between Michelle and me. Nobody! No fucking body!"

Rosie accelerated, reaching 120 miles per hour. She was out of control, driving like she was involved in some kind of high-speed chase. The only thing that slowed her down was a gasoline truck making a slow left turn. After coming to a halt, she collected herself.

"Tomorrow, bitch! I'll deal with you tomorrow! Michelle belongs to me and nobody else!" Rosie yelled.

After taking a long shower together and making love while doing so, Michelle and Melody paraded through the house naked with Blackie and Whitey following behind them. They fixed themselves a drink at the built-in bar, and then went upstairs to the bedroom. It was Michelle's birthday, and Melody was going to see to it that she received a special birthday present and some very special attention. Tonight Melody would be the aggressor. Michelle deserved it.

Sitting at the edge of the bed, relaxing and sipping Dom Perignon, Melody began rubbing on Michelle's back and kissing her gently, while licking and caressing her large, hard nipples. She then positioned herself on her knees and began skillfully licking, tickling, and kissing Michelle's clitoris the way Michelle had taught her.

They made love for close to two hours, and then afterward they fell asleep naked, cuddled up like newlyweds.

The following morning they had breakfast at IHOP, made plans for the evening, and then went their separate ways. Melody's first stop was Target. It was Thursday, the first day of their weekly check-writing spree. She hoped and prayed all went well.

She purchased an expensive fax machine, a thirty-two-inch television, a Hoover vacuum cleaner, and a computer system. The total cost of her purchase $1,443. She wrote the cashier a check, and then made her way to her next stop.

One down and five to go. Her next stop was Home Depot. There she purchased an airless spray painter, an expensive chandelier, twenty cases of high-priced marble tile, a tile cutter, and a costly lawn mower and edger. Her total was $2205. Two down and four to go.

Her next stop was Best Buy, where she purchased a stereo system, which included a twelve-disc CD changer, a boom box, two large high-priced home speakers, a state-of-the-art amplifier, and an equalizer. Her total was a little under $1500.

Afterward, she went to Sam's Club and purchased a Hewlett Packard computer system, another fax machine, and three hundred dollars worth of groceries. Her total was a little over $1500.

Four down and two to go. Her next stop was Circuit City. There she purchased another computer system, this time a luxurious Sony, two HP scanners, a color printer, a camcorder, and a Gateway laptop. Her total was $3,275.

From there, she went to Cerritos Mall, where she purchased $900 worth of women's clothing, then spent an additional $300 on Byron, and another $400 purchasing clothing for her mother.

Next she made a stop at the post office to send off her mother's gifts, and then made her way to Anna's Linen. Even though her mother would be grateful for the presents, deep down inside, she would know that Melody was doing something illegal. A mother always knew her children.

At Anna's Linen, Melody purchased blinds for her entire house, nice towels and rugs, and also comforters for herself, Byron, and for Michelle. The total of her purchase was $624.

During her ride home Melody made plans to spend Saturday

night and Sunday returning the majority of the items she had purchased. Already, she was counting the amount of money she would receive. And then, on Monday morning, when the bank opened, she would close the account and get back the three thousand dollars she had deposited two weeks earlier.

As usual, the DMV was extremely crowded. Since Rosie was a supervisor and had more seniority than the majority of the employees, it was not a problem for her to do what she wanted to do. Nonchalantly, Rosie reached in her purse and pulled out the paper she had scribbled the license plate number on, and then went to her computer. After running the plate number, it came back registered to a Melody Pullman of Moreno Valley. She jotted down Melody's information, signed off the computer, went to her office, and closed the door.

"Bitch! Your ass is mines!" she yelled. "Nobody fucks with my woman! Nobody!"

Rosie took the remainder of the day off. She was annoyed and irritated, and unable to think straight. She needed to come up with a plan, a *quick* plan.

CHAPTER 19

L arry was amazed by the new heights of pleasure Melody had caused him to reach lately. It appeared to him that since Melody became a switch-hitter, her sex had improved from great to magnificent. She had learned new tricks with her lips and tongue, and damn, did it feel good to him.

As he pulled out of Melody's driveway, smiling from the good blowjob he had just received, Michelle pulled into the driveway and parked. Surprisingly, she threw him a friendly wave. As he peeled out, she climbed out of her Mercedes carrying a bag, and then used her key to let herself in the house. Once inside, Melody greeted Michelle with a warm hug and a long kiss. Michelle then reached into the bag and pulled out a small gift-wrapped box with a red ribbon on top, and handed it to Melody.

"Here, baby, this is for you."

Overwhelmed with curiosity and excitement, Melody accepted the box. "What is it, honey?"

Michelle seated herself at the dining room table, remaining calm and giving no hints. "Open it and see, sweetheart."

After opening the box, Melody's eyes grew even larger. A dazed expression appeared on her face. There were four gold bracelets, which had the initials M.M. engraved on each one. Flattered by the bracelets, Melody continued staring at them.

"These are beautiful, honey. I-I-I don't know what to say," She then held the bracelets in her hand, looking them over carefully. "What does M.M. mean?" Melody asked.

"I figured that would be self-explanatory, Mel, but since you had to ask, the first M is my initial, and of course, the second M is yours. They mean that Michelle will always be devoted to, cherish, love, provide for, and care for Melody for as long as we live. These bracelets represent lesbian symbols of love. They are also another way of saying that we belong to each other and no one can come between us," Michelle explained with pride. Melody smiled while slipping on the bracelets.

"Do you give all of your lovers bracelets like this?"

"Nope," Michelle answered. "They never deserved these, sweetheart, but, fortunately, you do."

Melody accepted the compliment, then eased up to her lover and gave her a long, wet kiss.

"Thank you, Michelle. It feels so good to know that someone feels so strongly about me."

"Is that right?" Michelle responded sarcastically. "Well from the look on Larry's face, I'd say that he feels pretty strongly about you too. Don't you think?"

"Actually, sweetheart," Melody said while holding her lover's hand, "since I met you, I could care less about how Larry feels about me. Besides, he could never be mine, because he has a wife."

"But can't you see, Melody," Michelle said, raising her voice a few octaves, "he still has feelings for you and it's interfering with our relationship! And why in the hell does he keep coming over here in the first place? Why Melody? Are you still fucking him?"

Melody had never seen Michelle upset before, and was shocked by her reaction.

"Are you jealous of Larry, Michelle? I've known him for years, and I can't just stop seeing him like that."

Before Michelle could say anything, Melody gave her a kiss while caressing her. "I love you, Michelle, and I'm glad that you are a part of my life. Believe me, baby, I thank God for you every day. My life has changed in so many ways since we've met, and you've given me joy. You've showered me with more pleasure and happiness than Larry could ever give me, and I feel that you're the only person in this world for me. I belong to you, Michelle. That's it, and that's all."

Flattered and pleased by Melody's words, Michelle still felt somewhat betrayed. She pulled away.

"How in the hell can I be the only one in the world for you, and you're still fucking him?" Michelle asked angrily.

The truth of the question exploded in the room like a bomb dropping on Pearl Harbor. Melody sat frozen, thinking of a suitable answer, but didn't speak up quick enough, which caused Michelle to continue her interrogation.

"What are you planning to do with him, Melody? Are you going to continue feeding me this bullshit, or are you going to get rid of him?"

Michelle suddenly seemed like a demon to Melody. It was like her intelligence, kindness, and composed demeanor had been replaced with violence, anger, and rage.

"If it's offending you that much, Chelle, then I'll tell him not to come over anymore. But you knew about him when we first met."

"Annnnd," Michelle replied, holding up her hand. "Is that supposed to mean that I consent to you fucking him?"

"I'm not asking you to—"

"Sorry, Mel," Michelle interrupted," but I have to give you an ultimatum. I refuse to be hurt by anyone, and I most certainly refuse to be second behind a man. I want you to give me his cell number. This matter really needs to be resolved if our relationship is going to continue."

Melody sighed and reluctantly jotted down the number.

"Thanks," Michelle said. "I'll stay at my own home tonight. That should give you time alone to think things out and make your decision. In the meantime, I'll give Larry a call to set things straight with him." Michelle then stormed out of the house. After pulling out of the driveway, Michelle wasted no time dialing Larry's number.

"Hello," Larry answered.

"Larry?"

"Yeah, this is Larry. Who's this?"

"This is Michelle."

"Hey, Michelle, what's on your mind?"

"Are you too busy to meet me at my home? There's something extremely important we need to immediately discuss."

"Uh, well, actually, I was on my way home, but if it's that important, then give me your address and I'll swing by."

Rosie sat a few houses down the street from Melody's home. She had witnessed Michelle leaving Melody's house.

"Bitch, I'm gonna kill you!," she yelled with her nickel-plated .25 caliber automatic in hand. "Michelle's my wife!"

She figured this was not the right time to approach Melody. She wanted them together when she pulled the trigger, so Michelle could see that she loved her enough to kill for her. Michelle had promised that someday soon, they would reunite.

But first, Rosie thought, *I've got to get rid of this Melody bitch!*

Larry made it to Michelle's house an hour later. Taking into consideration the types of vehicles Michelle drove, the stylish clothes she wore, and the image she portrayed, he wasn't at all surprised when he parked in front of her two-story beach house. He approached the front door and rang the doorbell. Moments later Michelle appeared wearing sheer lingerie and a shower cap. Blackie and Whitey were at her feet barking at the stranger. They weren't accustomed to male visitors.

"Sorry, but I didn't think you'd make it here so fast, Larry, but come on in and have a seat in the den. I'll be right with you," Michelle said.

"Thanks," Larry answered, wanting to kick the hell out of the dogs. Fortunately, they followed her.

After making himself comfortable on the leather sofa, he began thinking.

I wonder what she wants with me? I hope she doesn't kill me. I should've told someone where I was going in case I come up missing. But hell, who could I tell?

Michelle reappeared instantly, but this time she was naked. She looked at him with her hands on her hips.

"What is it, Larry?" She then began walking toward him. "What is it you want? Melody, or both of us at the same time?" Larry was in a state of shock. Her wide hips, smooth silky skin, long legs, soft round butt, and shaved pussy aroused him, causing him to have difficulty concentrating on her question. She then repeated the question. "What do you want, Larry? Why can't you leave what belongs to me alone?"

"Are you talking about Melody?" he asked, smirking and still keeping his eyes on her body.

"You know damn well I'm referring to Melody," she replied, annoyed by his ignorance. "Tell me, Larry, why can't you just leave her alone?"

"Well, you know, Michelle, Melody likes to fuck and she enjoys fucking me," he responded, assuming he had the upper hand. "When I found out she was fooling around with another woman, I couldn't believe it, and couldn't see how it was going to work. I mean, I know you've probably got sex toys and stuff like that, but like Marvin Gaye said, 'Ain't nothing like the real thing.'" Larry was still smirking. But Michelle just stood there, completely unashamed of her nudity.

"I'll make a deal with you, Larry. I'll let you fuck me if you promise not to ever again see Melody."

"Is that what this is about? Listen, Michelle, you're fine as hell, and you're damn right I wouldn't mind having a piece of you, but the thing is, I wouldn't want to make you a promise that I more than likely wouldn't keep," he explained honestly. He then massaged his erection, continuing to stare at the luscious looking naked woman standing before him.

"But you're a married man!" Michelle said, offended by his sarcasm. "It's bad enough that you're cheating on your wife, but now you're stepping on my toes and I'm not going to allow it, Larry."

"Annnnd, what's the big deal? Melody's married, too."

"What?" Michelle responded, surprised by what he had said. "What are you talking about?" Michelle was completely dumbfounded.

Instinct told the poodles something was wrong with their master. They sensed her feelings and began barking. Larry spoke up, laughing.

"Oh, she didn't tell you about her institutionalized husband, Big Steve, huh?"

"Wait a minute. I-I-I'll be right back," Michelle said, suddenly feeling embarrassed. She then disappeared and returned minutes later wearing cut-off shorts and a T-shirt.

Larry told her all about Big Steve and his drug addiction, how he and Melody had met, and how he'd been helping her financially from month to month. Afterward, they agreed to let Melody make her own decision as to whom she wanted. Larry clarified that he could care less if Melody chose to keep them both. It was fine with him, but Michelle felt differently.

"Nope, I don't think so," she responded abruptly. "What's mine is mine, Larry. I'm not into sharing precious personal things. Anyway, what makes you think I'll have sex with her after you've shot a load of semen inside her?"

"Well, hell, who's to say you're not doing it now? Let me tell you a little secret, Michelle. I fuck Melody five or six times a week, and we enjoy each other's company and take pleasure in sex. If I haven't let her go by now, even with a paralyzed wife, what makes you think I'll stop fucking her because of you?"

Michelle was offended, but remained calm. "What do you want, Larry? I'll give you anything. Just name it. Is it money? I'll tell you what, Larry, I'll give you ten thousand dollars, cash, right this minute, if you promise to leave her alone from this point on."

"I can't make that promise, Michelle."

"OK," Michelle replied, dissatisfied. "I guess the only way to resolve this matter is to let her make her own decision. We'll do it that way, Larry. Thanks for stopping by. And oh, by the way, she doesn't need to know you were here, nor does she need to know about our conversation."

Around eleven that night Maurice called Melody to advise her he was in town for a few days and was staying at his father's house.

"I feel like reminiscing a little for old times' sake, Melody. Would you mind having some company for an hour or so? Treat's on me," Maurice said, thinking about his past sexual encounter with her.

"Well, actually I've had a pretty awkward day, but since you're treating, what the hell. Maybe you can help iron out a few wrinkles," she said, thinking about his huge penis.

Twenty minutes later, Maurice appeared in uniform at her door, carrying a bag full of liquor. After greeting him with a kiss and a hug, Melody then led him to her bedroom.

"I figured you would be gone a couple of years," Melody said, sitting on her bed. She was wearing a see-through negligee, which revealed her huge breasts and nipples.

"I thought so too, babe, but my father was diagnosed with lung cancer, so I caught the first thing smoking headed back this way," Maurice said while his eyes zeroed in on her breasts.

He then pulled out a fifth of Remy Martin, a large bag of ice, a one-liter Coke, and a large can of whipped cream. Fifteen minutes later, the freak show was on once again.

It was four thirty AM when Maurice left. He had gotten what he'd come for, and had left Melody the remainder of the liquor, along with more sexual memories. Unlike Larry, he wasn't into giving up the money.

Damn, does he know how to fuck! He's got a big, strong dick and more energy than one of those Duracell batteries. Michelle might be my lover, but I still need a dick in my life every now and then.

The following morning at seven thirty-five, Melody's phone began ringing. It rang seven times before Melody checked her caller ID. It was Michelle.

"Good morning, sweetheart. Did you miss me last night?" Michelle asked. Melody thought about her encounter with Maurice and lied.

"Yes, baby, I missed you and everything about you. Good morning to you, and I would like to start by saying I love you." She yawned, then thought about Maurice again.

"I love you more, Melody," Michelle responded. Then she sighed. "While I was asleep, this weird idea popped inside my head. Then as I thought about it, it wasn't so weird after all. I want you to call Larry and see if he wants to fly to Vegas with us tomorrow. Make sure you tell him I'm treating. And just because I'm in a good mood, I'll even supply his gambling money. Give me a call back on my cell after you've spoken with him, OK? I'm on my way to Santa Monica and Glendale to collect rent, but I really need to know your decision ASAP regarding the Larry situation. Get back with me right away."

"OK, sweetheart," Melody replied. "So what is it with this Larry thing, Chelle? Yesterday you wanted his phone number, and today you want him to go to Vegas with us. I know you're up to something."

"Well, sweetheart, I just want the three of us to have some fun together before one of us gets eliminated from our little family, you know. Sort of like a last kiss to say goodbye. That's all," Michelle explained deceitfully.

"I'll take your word for it, Chelle, but it sure seems like you're up to something."

"Nothing to worry about. Call me back as soon as you've talked to him," Michelle instructed, and then she quickly flipped her cell closed.

After Melody spoke with Larry regarding the Las Vegas trip, she wasted no time calling Michelle. Larry lied to Pat, telling her he was going out of town on business, which gave him clearance to go away with Melody and Michelle.

After giving a lot of thought to Michelle's ultimatum, Melody came to a conclusion.

Since I have to choose between both of them, and they'll both be available to me, why not make my decision based on a threesome? That way, my choice will be decided in a pleasurable environment.

As the three of them departed Melody's house, Rosie was again posted a few houses away. She cursed furiously, watching them drive off.

"Where are you assholes taking my wife? She's mine! She belongs to me!" Rosie said out loud. She then peeled off, burning rubber for at least thirty yards, and then quickly turned the corner doing forty miles an hour. She had come prepared, packing her .25 automatic with a full clip. No matter what it took, she wanted Michelle back, by any means necessary. After all, she was her wife, and she had wedding rings and the gold, lesbian symbol of love bracelets to prove it. Rosie was devoted to Michelle, and as far as she was concerned, they were born to be together. She had to do something quickly before Michelle slipped away from her. She was in love, and was not about to let any bitch or man come between her and her beloved wife.

"No! No! No! Hell, no!" she yelled furiously.

* * *

Other than running into a few air pockets, Michelle, Melody, and Larry's flight to Vegas went smoothly and swiftly. Michelle had reserved a suite on the twenty-first floor at Circus-Circus and had arranged for drinks to be delivered to the room at nine.

They had taken a shuttle from the airport to the hotel, which took less than twenty minutes.

"Well, should we try to win some money first, or should we go on to our suite and relax?" Melody asked once they were inside the hotel lobby. She was dressed in a pair of white shorts with a matching white blouse that revealed her cleavage, and a cute pair of white slippers neatly trimmed in gold.

"I'll leave that decision up to you two," Michelle replied, and then pulled a bankroll from her purse, peeled off five hundred dollars, and handed the money to Larry.

"Thanks Michelle," Larry said. "I don't know about y'all, but I'm about to turn this five hundred into five thousand, young ladies. I'll be on the blackjack table or playing roulette."

"Come on, honey," Melody said, leading Michelle by the hand through the casino. "Let's go play Wheel of Fortune. The last time I was here my luck was pretty good."

Four hours later, Melody began getting restless. So far she had won $650 playing Wheel of Fortune and video poker. Michelle won $195 playing the slots, and Larry had come up big in blackjack, winning close to three thousand dollars. He gave back the five hundred dollars to Michelle.

"Here's an extra four hundred, Michelle, since it was your money that allowed me to win," Larry said graciously.

"Actually, Larry, it was your skills and luck that caused you to win, but since you insist, I'll be more than happy to accept," Michelle said as she smiled and took the money. "What's mine is Melody's, you know." She then kissed Melody.

Freaky, sexual thoughts of having two lovers simultaneously aroused Melody, and caused her to tingle between her legs. She then grabbed Michelle by the left hand, and Larry with her right.

"Come on. I have an ultimatum decision to make, remember?" Then she happily led her lovers back to the suite.

The suite was huge, luxurious, and beautiful. It was fit for a king or a queen. It was nine forty-five PM, so the Dom Perignon had been on ice for close to forty-five minutes and was ready to be consumed. Melody played like she was a waiter and wasted no time fixing her lovers' drinks. Larry kicked back on the sofa and relaxed, contemplating what was next.

"Well," Melody said, smiling, "let's toast to a memorable, and hopefully pleasurable night. I hope this will be a night we'll all remember for the rest of our lives."

She was hot and ready to get the party started. Tonight was her night, and she planned to take full advantage of it.

"Tonight's the night my decision has to be made," Melody stated. "This pronouncement will probably affect me for the rest of my life, but I'm sure it'll be best for all of us." She then took a long swallow of Dom Perignon.

"Definitely," Michelle responded agreeably. "But at the same time, sweetheart, your decision will allow your mate to be comfortable and not feel uneasy."

"Yeah, I have to agree with both of you," Larry interjected after taking a sip of the champagne. "Whatever decision you make, I'll have to respect it, whether I like it or not."

As if it were a part of the plan, each of them began taking off their clothes. Melody was excited by the thought of having a threesome, and Larry was energized by the idea of possibly having Melody give him a blowjob while Michelle licked his balls and fingered his butt. The thought alone of fucking Michelle had him erect and ready. This was the chance of a lifetime to Larry.

Larry stood up, approached Melody, and began kissing her. He attempted to climb on top of her, but right away, Michelle objected.

"No, Larry. Sorry, but that's not the way it's going to be done. I refuse to go behind you after you've been inside her. It's against lesbian tradition."

Melody was hot, wet, ready, and desperately wanted them both. She began stroking Larry's erection.

"Come on, Chelle, I want both of you right now," Melody said. She then began rubbing her own clitoris.

"No," Michelle said. "If we perform sex as a threesome, that will mean Larry will be receiving pleasure too, and that's not what this is about. The only way you can determine which one of us gives you the most pleasure is by having one on one sex with us—not a threesome. There's no way in the world you can make a decision by Larry fucking me. Impossible. And I won't allow it." Michelle was standing naked with her hands on her hips.

Sultrily, Michelle eased up to Melody while Larry watched her skillfully go to work on Melody's body. Larry wanted to be a part of this, but Michelle was calling the shots. While watching them lick and suck each other, he stroked his erection.

Damn! I should've fucked this bitch when I had the chance! Just look at her sweet, sexy pussy. Damn! Larry thought.

Michelle moved to the floor on her knees, then eased Melody's legs over her shoulders and began licking her way to stardom. She paused momentarily, grabbed a few sex toys from her purse, and used them on Melody. To Melody it felt like heaven.

Larry was getting annoyed and impatient from not getting a piece of the action. Melody had already had five orgasms and wanted to have five more if possible. Michelle then began licking Melody's nipples, slowly, and then she licked up and down Melody's stomach, following that by slowly and competently licking and sucking her clitoris. Finally, as if she were using her tongue as a paintbrush, she licked slowly down Melody's legs and onto her toes, which caused Melody to go wild. Michelle then topped it off with soft warm kisses. Afterward, she slowly stood up and got dressed as if she were confident she had won first prize in a pussy eating contest. She then had a seat on the sofa, relaxed, and sipped her Dom Perignon. She was confident that Larry didn't stand a chance competing against her.

Impatiently, Larry inserted himself into Melody's hot, awaiting tunnel, but unfortunately, he exploded in ten seconds. All the champagne and waiting for so long to get some action had caused him to lose control.

"No, no! Please don't do this to me, Larry. I need it!" Melody cried. "Come on, daddy. Let me suck it to get it hard again! I need it. Come on, Larry."

"Nope. Sorry, sweetheart," Michelle interrupted, covering Melody's pussy with her hand. "He can't do that. We've already stipulated no pleasure for him. The pleasure is supposed to be all yours, remember, not his." Michelle sensed a victory.

"What kind of bullshit is this!" Larry yelled angrily. He then attempted to eat Melody, and stroked himself while doing so, but it was useless. He couldn't get it up. He then tried jacking himself off, but that didn't work either. Observing his tactics, Michelle smiled while sipping her champagne. Larry's huge penis was a dead soldier, good for nothing but urinating. Usually when this happened Melody knew exactly what to do. However, there were now stipulations and borders that could not be crossed.

"Fuck it! This is bullshit!" he shouted. He then quickly threw on his clothes, grabbed the bottle of Dom Perignon, and turned it up, consuming the rest of its contents. "Fuck both of y'all bitches!" He then stormed out of the suite, leaving the door open.

"Does he always act like that when he can't get it up?" Michelle asked with a smile of victory plastered on her face.

"Nope. Normally he doesn't have that problem." Melody then grabbed one of the sex toys and began rubbing it on her clitoris.

"Forget about him, sweetheart. Come closer," Michelle insisted. And once again it was on.

CHAPTER 20

Pat

Missing pieces of the puzzle had come in flashes of horror to Pat's mind. On one occasion, she dreamed of speaking with a homosexual, but could not remember what the conversation was about. On another occasion she dreamed Larry was having an orgy with two black women and a white girl. She had recently awakened from a nightmare where Larry was having an affair with her beautician. She was sweating, cursing, and yelling.

"How could you? I'll kill you! You phony, slick, deceitful bitch! You fucking husband thief!"

Larry had comforted her. "Calm down sweetheart, it's OK. You're just having a bad dream. Calm down and let me get you a cold towel."

He glanced at his watch while heading to the restroom. It was two thirty AM *Fuck!* he thought. *I think she's remembering.*

That fuckin' Tosha! Larry thought as he ran cold water over the towel. *Damn! That big mouth faggot has fucked me up! I hope Pat doesn't start remembering and begin asking me questions! I can't let that happen! Hell, no. I gotta do what I gotta do. Instead of giving her one pain pill every day, I'll give her two, or maybe three or four. Then hopefully she'll forget about the whole damn thing. Fuck it. I gotta do what I gotta do.*

He made his way back into the bedroom and began wiping her face and neck with the cold towel.

"I'm going to give you some of your medication, sweetheart. Hopefully, you can then relax and sleep more comfortably."

Five minutes after giving his wife three pills, she was out like a light. Lately, Pat had stayed so full of pills she couldn't read anymore, couldn't perform any of her newly acquired sexual fantasies on her husband, nor could she concentrate on watching television. One thing he made sure of was keeping her bi-weekly appointments with Melody. Each time Flora, who was the nurse, maid, and cook, wheeled her into the salon, she dropped her head, ashamed of her looks and condition.

He also made sure that Flora wheeled Pat to the park on Wednesdays and Saturdays, took her to a walk-in theatre on Thursdays, and wheeled her through the neighborhood every day of the week. Pat was completely drained of all self-esteem. She felt worthless, sorry for herself, and ready to give up on life. On one occasion she had even put a gun to her head, but fortunately, Flora stopped her before she pulled the trigger.

"You might as well just let me die," Pat would tell Larry. "I don't want to live like this."

"You'll be out of this in no time, baby," he would say to calm her. "I'm here for you, always. Even in your condition, you'll probably still outlive lots of people, so quit talking like that."

Because Larry kept her full of medication, she sometimes did not recognize him or Flora. With Flora being an experienced nurse, common sense told her the pills weren't necessary, and on a few occasions she brought it to Larry's attention.

"This is what the doctor ordered, Flora," Larry would say. Even though she knew better, from her years of being a nurse, she was paid to follow her employer's instructions, so she did, without questions, comments, or any more suggestions.

The bottom line was, Larry did not want Pat remembering anything, and he did everything in his power to prevent her from doing so. He did not need her telling his daughters bits and pieces, because soon, due to their cleverness, they would figure things out and demand answers from him. They would be angry at finding out he had not only been sleeping with Melody, but had also furnished her home, paid for new carpet and tile, and bought Byron expensive clothes and shoes. No way could he afford to let his daughters find out anything.

Since the encounter in Las Vegas, Larry had been servicing his accounts more diligently, and keeping his mind focused on present and future obligations. He had not bothered calling Melody, nor had she called him. After all, they made Michelle a promise.

He told himself, *If Melody wants to bump pussies with other women, then fuck it!* Actually, it was to his advantage, financially, not to be involved with Melody. It allowed him the opportunity to save more money.

But deep down inside he missed her and craved her company and the sex. He missed her touch, laughing and joking with her, drinking and smoking chronic with her, making long, sweet love to her, hearing her sex cries, and listening to her beg for more. In fact, he missed everything about her.

Lots of days he wanted to call her, but because of the way he acted in Vegas, he dismissed the thought. Even though he was angry about her decision, he would always have an open heart and open arms for her if she ever decided to come back to him. It had been two and a half months since he had seen her, but it seemed like an eternity to him. Whenever he drank, thoughts and visions of her would flood his mind and cause him to be sad. He went from drinking a pint of vodka a day, to drinking a fifth a day. Somehow, he managed to efficiently maintain his accounts.

One night he received a call from Angela.

"Hey, Dad, what's up?" Angela asked in good spirits.

"Hey, sweetie, how you doing?" Larry responded dryly.

"What's wrong with you, Dad? Aren't you glad to hear from your daughter who's about to become a lawyer?"

"Yeah, I guess."

"Are you all right, Dad?" she asked out of concern. She had always known her father to be full of life, excitement, encouragement, and always saying the right words to make people feel good. Instinct told her something was wrong.

"Is it Mom? Is Mom OK?"

"Yeah, she's OK. Everything's fine. You just stay in those books and don't worry about us." His words were slurred.

"You're hiding something from me, Dad. I know you are. Now tell me what's the matter," she insisted.

"Hiding what? You better go and read some of those lawyer books, girl, 'cause you damn sure don't know what the hell you're talking about."

"Quit playin' games, Dad, and tell me what's going on."

"Same old shit, just a different day," he answered. He then took a swallow of vodka.

"You're lying to me, Dad. Let me speak to Mom," she demanded.

Larry took the receiver, laid it on the couch, took another long gulp of vodka, and eventually forgot that Angela was on the phone.

"Dad! Mom! Mom! Dad, pick up the phone! Dad!" Angela yelled. But Larry ignored her and continued drinking straight from the bottle.

Frantically, Angela slammed down the phone. She then made arrangements to catch the next available flight to Ontario airport, which was located an hour away from her parents' home.

CHAPTER 21

Big Steve

Riverside County Jail

Big Steve spent a couple of months in Riverside County Jail before being transferred to the prison. Since it was his first time going to state penitentiary, a few inmates who'd been there several times had given him some advice.

"If your soap falls when you're taking a shower, don't bend over to pick it up. Your asshole will look like a pussy, and inmates won't hesitate to fuck you," one of the men advised.

"Don't hang with crowds. You never know what kind of shit the next man might be involved in," another inmate warned.

"Keep your head up and stay sucka free," another man counseled.

"Always look mean, and walk tough, and nobody will fuck with you," yet another told him.

All that advice caused Steve to be nervous as hell, but he tried hard to conceal his feelings. He didn't want to appear to be a punk.

A few weeks after his arrival, Big Steve witnessed a disturbing incident. While over two hundred inmates were eating lunch, a Mexican inmate passed one of his homeboys a banana, but had reached over a black inmate's plate without saying 'excuse me'.

In jail, that was considered disrespectful and would definitely be dealt with if the person at fault did not make an apology. The black inmate waited a few moments, hoping the Mexican would apologize, but the Mexican continued eating like he'd done nothing wrong. Without warning, the black inmate picked up his tray and clobbered the Mexican over the head.

"I'll kill you! You stupid fuckin' Mexican! No one reaches over my fuckin' plate without saying excuse me! I'll kill you!" the black inmate yelled.

He was kicking and stomping the Mexican. Then suddenly, over one hundred Mexicans sprang from their seats, and like an army, they attacked the black inmate, which caused all the other black inmates to react violently. The riot was on. Deputies stormed in, throwing tear gas and beating the inmates with batons until they had control of the situation.

The riot resulted in twenty-two black inmates and thirty-six Mexicans being taken to the infirmary. After being treated, they were then escorted to solitary confinement. During the episode, Big Steve cringed in a corner, shaking nervously and hoping no one came near him. Due to his proximity to the offenders during the riot, he and the others was sent to solitary.

Solitary confinement consisted of a row of fifty cells, twenty-five on each side, with one inmate housed in each cell. The majority of the inmates were loud, wild, and ignorant. They would yell threats to each other, and would say derogatory things about each other's mothers or family members.

Steve heard one inmate yell to another, "It's only two ugly people in the world, and your mama is both of them!" Big Steve, along with the inmates who'd heard the comment, burst into laughter.

When Big Steve was released from the solitary, he began diligently studying the Bible. The Lord had spoken to him several times in the past and while he was in the hole, but each time Big Steve had ignored his calling. But now he figured if he carried a Bible at all times, inmates wouldn't approach him and ask him all sorts of questions.

But the Bible toting didn't quite do its job. After Steve was transferred to a dorm, while strolling toward his bunk, six black inmates approached him, surrounded him, and asked him where he was from.

"I don't gang bang, man," Big Steve answered. Apparently that wasn't the answer they were looking for. The shortest thug in the group gave Big Steve an evil look.

"Where you live, fool?"

"I-I-I live in Moreno Valley, b-b-but I-I-I grew up in C-C-Compton," Big Steve stuttered nervously, holding his belongings.

"What part of Compton?" another thug asked.

"Actually, fellas, I resided off Long Beach Boulevard and Alondra. However, my residence during the time I lived in Compton was on Poinsetta Avenue."

Upon hearing Big Steve's reply, a big, black dude got excited.

"You from Southside, homey?" he asked.

"Do you know Dexter, Scroncho, Killer Wayne, Lamb, or Keefe D?" another thug asked.

"Yeah, man, I know them," Big Steve replied, hoping his knowledge of the names would earn him a pass. "I went to school with those dudes, but most of 'em are either dead or doin' life in prison."

After a few minutes of conversing about people in the hood, and now accepted by the dorm thugs, Big Steve went back to his bunk to write his daily letters.

He'd written Melody several letters, but unfortunately, the only letters he received were from his parents. They had provided him with a substantial amount of money on his books— actually, more than he needed throughout his term. They refused to turn their back on him due to his drug problem, but they hoped and prayed that he would be OK once he was released. His mother recommended that he enroll in a live-in drug program after his release, in hopes of him staying focused and on the right track. He agreed.

After a week of being in his new dorm the gang-bangers noticed that Steve didn't mingle too much with them, but instead he studied his Bible. Steve began attending daily Bible studies and religiously went to church each Sunday. Because of his enthusiasm to follow the Lord, he became closely acquainted with the chaplain. Even though his mind was focused on good things and a new life when he was released, he could not seem to get Melody off his mind.

The following Sunday, Big Steve testified in church about how he had veered off the path of righteousness

"There was a time in my life when I thought I had it all," Big Steve testified. "I had money, nice vehicles, and a pretty wife. I dressed in designer clothes and could get my hands on as much dope as I wanted. I hung out in ghettos and downtown areas where drug users and sellers congregate. Later on, I began transporting gang-bangers, whores, and basically anyone who wanted to cop drugs, wherever they wanted to go in exchange for a hit of crack, a forty-ounce of beer, or a few dollars.

"I've disappointed my parents time after time, and I also lost my wife and my son, and my home. All of those things happened to me simply because I chose to smoke crack and not follow God. There was a time in my life when I thought I was the man with the plan.

"I thought I had all the right answers, and I thought I had life all figured out. The devil made me think that way, but Satan, I'm here to tell you, you're a liar! You're the master of deceit and you're good for nothing! The devil had me blinded, making me think his blessings were all good, but actually, those were only materialistic things that were here today and could be gone tomorrow.

"Oh yes, Satan will definitely bless you with illegal things that will make you stand out, attract attention, and cause you to feel like you're sitting on top of the world, but actually, you're digging your own grave. He makes you lose your morality, your integrity, and your common sense. You see, you can't buy a family, you can't purchase dignity from your neighborhood store, nor can you order self-esteem or nobility by dialing a 1-800 number. The devil will make sure you're stripped of those qualities. He'll build you up, and then he'll tear you down.

"Even though I'm incarcerated, I'm at peace with myself, as well as with Jesus. Sometimes the Lord will pull us away from what we consider good, and put us in a lowly place, like jail or prison, in hopes of getting our attention. In some cases it works for those who're fed up with living a life of sin, but for those who refuse to take heed to his calling, they'll keep coming back to places like this, and will sooner or later end up dead.

"You see, the Lord has my undivided attention once again, but it took me being locked up again. Believe it or not, people, I'm in love with the Lord, and I take pleasure each day thanking him for saving my life. Thank you, Heavenly Father, and I want to thank all of you for coming and listening to my testimony," Big Steve said sincerely.

After his testimony Big Steve's confidence level skyrocketed. From that day on, Steve held Bible study in the dorm and in the chapel, and held prayer call three times a day. He began ministering to gang-bangers, drug addicts, and anyone who wanted to listen. The spirit of God was in him, and he believed that under no circumstances could Satan's tactics break him down. But the devil was always busy making plans.

CHAPTER 22

Angela

After reaching Ontario Airport, Angela rented a car, and in no time she was pulling in to her parents' driveway. She used her key to quickly let herself in. It was two thirty AM. She turned on a couple of lights, then went to her parents' bedroom. She found her mother sound asleep.

Where's Dad? she wondered.

During the years of her upbringing her parents had always slept together; even after they had an ugly fight. She then quickly checked the other two bedrooms, but still had no luck finding her father.

The den. Maybe he's in the den, she thought. She then made her way to the den, where she found her father laid out like a drunken bum in the street. His mouth was wide open and his tongue hung out like a thirsty dog. He was fully dressed, and his hand was still gripping the empty vodka bottle.

What's come over Dad? I wonder if he blames himself for Mom's accident? I wonder how long he's been drinking like this? Dad has always been a neat and well-organized man. He would never allow the den to be this filthy. I wonder why Flora hasn't cleaned up? I'll definitely have to have a talk with her and Dad tomorrow, Angela thought.

She then went to her bedroom, got undressed, and fell asleep.

The following morning, Angela awakened and began preparing breakfast; it was something she enjoyed doing whenever she came home. She fixed scrambled eggs and mixed in shredded cheese, chopped green onions, and bell peppers combined with a dash of salt and black pepper. Also she made a pot of grits, fried a few spicy hot links, and put six slices of bread into the toaster.

Milk for Mom and orange juice for Dad, she thought.

Larry was still in a vodka coma when she approached him. He immediately awakened at her kiss, exhaling alcohol fumes from his mouth.

"Hey baby, when did you get here?" he asked, excited to see his ambitious daughter.

She frowned at his bad breath. "Ooh, Dad, I can see why you left me hanging on the phone last night. You smell like an alcohol factory."

"Ah, baby, it isn't that bad, is it?" He smiled with reddened eyes.

"Definitely it is, Dad. I think you need A.A. There's no way you're capable of taking care of Mom and this house while you're under the influence. Anyway, I made breakfast for you and Mom, so go wash yourself up. Breakfast is on the table."

"OK, Miss Lawyer. I'll do as I'm instructed," he answered sarcastically.

"You can address me as either counsel or Attorney Myers, but the term Miss Lawyer sounds too chauvinistic," Angela shot back.

While Larry went to the restroom, Angela went to her mother's room.

"Hey, Mom, wake up, it's me." She greeted her mother with a kiss and a warm hug.

Pat opened her eyes slowly and forced a smile to her face. "Hey, baby. Mama's OK. Mama's gonna be all right, girl. Mama's just tired, that's all," She sounded like she was about to die. Angela wanted to cry, but her pride wouldn't allow her to. She reached over and held her mother firmly.

"I'm here, Mom, and everything's going to be just fine. I love you, Mom."

"Mama all right too, girl," Pat replied, shedding tears while speaking weakly. "Mama's all right, girl. Remember when we went to the park yesterday? I had so much fun. You and me had on matching clothes, and we had on the same shoes, and we rode horses too. And we went to New York City, and to Texas. I wish every day could be like yesterday, don't you?"

Angela burst into tears realizing that her mother was delusional.

Why hadn't anyone told me? Why didn't Randy, Dad, or Flora take Mom to the hospital? This was too obvious for them not to recognize, Angela thought.

Wiping away her tears, Angela eased her mother into her wheelchair, and pushed her into the restroom to clean her up. After cleaning her mother and dressing her, Angela then wheeled her to the table, positioned her directly across from Larry, and placed her food in front of her. Pat ignored the food. She also ignored Larry and Angela. She just sat staring at the walls and at the ceiling trying to make sense of what was going on. Angela could no longer hold back her anger and concern.

"Dad, what's wrong with this picture? I thought the doctors said that Mom's brain was all right! The only disorder she is supposed to have is being paralyzed from her waist down, not losing her mind!"

"Well, a few weeks ago," Larry said with a mouth full of food, "I, ah, I—"

"Why didn't you inform me about this? Why didn't you take her back to the hospital?"

"I haven't had time—"

"Are you planning on just letting her rot? Look at her, Dad! Does she seem normal to you? Or is it that you're blinded by the liquor! She needs help, Dad, and for God's sake, you're her husband! You really need to put down the bottle and take responsibility for your wife. Look at her! Is this still the woman you love?" Angela shouted angrily. She then began feeding her mother.

Larry felt so embarrassed all he could do was sit there and look stupid.

"Get dressed, Dad. We're taking Mom to the hospital," Angela demanded.

"Girl, hell, I-I-I've got four pick-ups today. I don't have time to go to no goddamn hos—"

"You're going, Dad, and that's final!" She gave her father a look of dissatisfaction.

Angela was a firm believer in being persistent, and knew how to make things happen. She didn't accept no for an answer, and she didn't believe in the phrase, 'I can't.' She was driven by determination and self-assurance, but her greatest quality was her vocabulary, and her ability to use words effectively.

Forty-five minutes later they were at the hospital. After the necessary paperwork had been filled out, the Myerses were told to wait in the waiting room until Pat's name was called. While waiting, Larry kept glancing at his watch.

"Damn! I'm gonna miss my goddamn money. Hell, I'm the one who pays the damn bills in the house, and here I am sitting at a damn hospital. Un-fucking-believable," Larry complained.

"Is making money more important to you than Mom's health and well-being?" Angela asked, being firm and direct.

"Now you listen to me, Angela, I don't need you—"

"Chill out, Dad, because what you're about to say won't make sense anyway."

Every fifteen minutes Angela stormed up to the desk, annoyed by her mother being neglected.

"Look, I don't know what kind of hospital you people are running, but this is ridiculous! We have insurance and my mother's extremely ill, so what's the damn problem? You people are just sitting on your overpaid asses gossiping on the telephone! I demand to speak with your superior, now, or I'll have charges brought against this hospital quicker than you can wink your eye," she stated to the administrative people. A couple minutes later, two nurses appeared in the waiting room with a chart. One of them called Pat's name. Wheeling her mother through the double-doors, Angela said, "Sometimes you have to act ignorant to get people to listen to you."

"What's your name?" Angela asked the short, fat nurse.

"I'm Nurse Simmons."

"Listen, Nurse Simmons, my mother doesn't need her temperature, blood pressure, weight or height taken. What I'd like for you to arrange, if you have the authority to do so, is a CAT scan. That way, it can be determined whether she has any brain damage. Basically, Nurse Simmons, we can skip the basics and move on to the source," Angela clarified. Angela's words caught Nurse Simmons off guard.

"There are certain guidelines we..." the nurse began.

"I'd like to speak with your superiors or to the doctor in charge at once."

Nurse Simmons desperately wanted to say something unprofessional, but instead she turned her nose up, rolled her eyes, and left the room. She returned a few minutes later with a doctor, but left immediately after introducing the doctor to Angela and Pat.

Doctor Lee sent for Pat's medical records and then escorted them to a room located on the other side of the hospital. Once inside, Larry assisted the doctor in lifting Pat from her wheelchair, and then placing her on a machine that was similar in looks to a rocket ship. The doctor then secured Pat's arms, legs, and torso. He went into another room, pressed a button, and the machine began turning slowly, but fast enough for a person to get dizzy if they were looking at it. The machine twirled for a while, then stopped. Afterward, Dr. Lee and Larry un-strapped Pat and placed her back in her wheelchair. The doctor then gave the Myerses instructions.

"You can either wait in my office, have a seat in the lobby, or you can grab a bite to eat in the cafeteria until I analyze and evaluate her test."

"We'll wait in your office, Dr. Lee, thanks," Angela said. Once inside the doctor's office, unfortunately for Larry, Angela began grilling him again.

"Dad, why does the den look like it hasn't been cleaned in months? That house is disgusting! You know Mom wouldn't have it that way if she were well. It just doesn't make any sense, Dad. It almost seems like you want Mom to die or something. Have you fired Flora, or has she gotten lazy?"

"Listen, Angie, first of all, I'm in no mood to hear your bullshit, OK? And to answer your question, no, Flora isn't fired. And as far as the den is concerned, you know damn well I don't like anyone messing around with my papers and stuff. Hell, lately I've been so damn busy I haven't even had time to tie my own goddamn shoes. Is that all right with you, Miss Thing?" He rested his head in the palm of his hand, irritated by the way she was hounding him.

"Mom kept that house spotless, Dad, and you know it! I don't see why the cleanliness of the house should change because of her illness. There are two adults living in the house who aren't handicapped, and it's just totally uncalled for, Dad. That's not the way Mom would want it. It appears that you have a problem stepping up for her and keeping things in order. It's not complicated to make sure Mom keeps her necessary doctor appointments, and taking care of the basics of maintaining a household. Seeing that you're not handling things in a decent and orderly fashion, what I'm going to do is transfer from Harvard and complete my last year of schooling at Laverne School of Law in San Bernadino. That way I'll be at home every day to make sure that Mom, as well as the house, are taken care of," Angela stated with a stern look.

"Hey, easy now, I am still your father, and I've just about had enough of your miss-arrogant, egotistical, takeover-the-town attitude. You're not gonna just talk to me like I'm a piece of shit.

Goddammit, I'm the one who—" Just then, Dr. Lee entered the office carrying several papers. He had a seat at his desk and began talking.

"I have the results of Mrs. Myers's test," Dr. Lee said as he began shuffling through papers. He remained calm while studying the results, but Angela, feeling both worried and frustrated broke the silence.

"Well?" she asked, walking toward Dr. Lee.

"One moment please," the doctor answered coolly, which only made Angela even angrier. She felt like giving him a piece of her mind, but dismissed the thought after seeing his mouth about to open. He spoke using medical terminology that neither Angela nor Larry understood.

"Dr. Lee," Angela said, standing over him with her hands on her hips, "will you please put this in laymen's terms for us? Your accent, combined with the medical terminology is making it quite difficult for us to comprehend what you're saying. Please simplify it, if you don't mind."

"The test results reflect that Mrs. Myers has suffered some brain damage from her accident. Unfortunately, Mr. and Miss Myers, it will gradually become worse. However, the medication I'm going to prescribe for her keep her mind completely relaxed at all times."

"Just say it, Doc, my mom's gonna be a vegetable, right? Say it!" Angela yelled while bursting into tears and loud cries.

Larry stood and hugged her securely. "It's gonna be all right, baby. Everything's gonna be all right."

Larry was sort of afraid to speak, assuming he might say the wrong thing and Angela would begin blaming him for her mother's condition. Pat sat there expressionless, staring at the walls and ceiling.

After picking up Pat's prescription, Larry, Angela, and Pat made their way home.

The following day Angela flew back to Harvard to take care of all her necessary transfer paperwork. She then arranged to ship her belongings to her parents' house, and caught the next flight back to Ontario Airport, rented a car, and went to enroll at Laverne University of Law.

After taking care of all her business, Angela then went home and met with Flora. Fifteen minutes later Flora was leaving the residence with her belongings, holding her head down and about to cry. Angela had terminated her. After searching the yellow pages, Angela found an agency located in Riverside, which agreed to send her five CNAs for her to interview. Of the five nurses she interviewed, she chose a Vietnamese woman named Selma.

Selma was in her late forties but moved as swiftly as a teenager. She stood four foot four and possessed a pair of eyes that were so tight, they looked like they were closed. She'd been a nurse for thirteen years, and had been happily married for twenty-seven years to a security guard. She had a son and a daughter, both of whom were attending college. Selma and her husband didn't earn much money, but they made sure their children received a college education, even though it caused them to barely make ends meet.

Perfect, Angela thought after interviewing Selma. After discussing her job duties, responsibilities, and expectations, Angela then instructed Selma to report to work the following morning at six.

"No problem, Angela. Consider it done," Selma responded.

Angela then called Melody to inform her that she'd moved back to her parents' house, and she desired to pay in advance for the next six months for both her and her mother's hairstyling.

"That's fine," Melody replied. "As a matter of fact, what I'll do from this point on is make both of your appointments on the same day. Oh, and I'm no longer at the salon where I previously worked. I figured I could cut down on expenses by simply having a few of my choice customers come to my home, and I do consider you and your mother the chosen few."

"You make me feel so special, Melody. I'm totally flattered."

"I'm sorry to hear the bad news about your mother, Angela. If there's anything I can do to be of assistance, please don't hesitate to ask."

"Thanks, Melody. You're a sweetheart and a doll."

"You're more than welcome, Angela. The pleasure is all mine. Give my love to your mom and dad." Melody said. She then quickly hung up.

Melody took a swallow of vodka and began talking out loud. "I can't stand that bitch! I've got to watch what I say around her. Hell, she might have me investigated by the CIA, the FBI, or maybe even the DEA. I know she mingles with the DA and the police, and the bitch probably even talks to judges. Yep, I'd better watch what I say around her. The bitch already thinks she's a lawyer, asking me all those goddamn questions."

CHAPTER 23

Melody

A few months later, Melody became sick. She vomited constantly and began having unbearable stomach pains. Michelle pampered her day and night like she was a newborn baby. Melody had been so busy building up her bank account, she'd overlooked missing four menstrual periods.

Damn! she thought. *I must be pregnant.* She didn't want to bring it to Michelle's attention. She thought it best for her not to know. During the past four months their relationship and love for one another had increased tremendously. Melody had purchased four symbols of love bracelets for Michelle.

"I love you, Michelle. I want you to be a part of my life forever. I want to grow old with you," Melody told Michelle when she presented her with the bracelets.

One day, Michelle had gone to Oxnard, California on business, and had left Melody at her beach house. Melody took advantage of the opportunity and drove to a clinic in Los Angeles. She discovered she was actually pregnant.

Damn! she thought after leaving the clinic. *Who did I last fuck? Was it Larry or Maurice? I think it was Maurice, but he's got his ass in Japan, China, or Korea. How am I going to explain this to Michelle? Fuck it! Let me give Larry a quick call. I'll tell him I'm preg-*

nant by him and see how he reacts. She grabbed her cell and dialed his number.

"Hello," Larry answered calmly.

"Hi, baby. Long time, no hear. How you doing?" Melody asked.

"I'm OK, I guess. Pressure will bust a pipe, you know, but I'll survive."

"Are you still mad at me?"

"Why should I be? I had to respect the decision you made. I've managed to get over it and put it behind me. What does irk me, Melody, is being burned by a woman. But like I said, that was your decision, and I have to respect it."

"Well, baby, I apologize for the way things happened, but I'm glad that we've both gotten over it. Anyway, I called to let you know I'm pregnant by you." She was stuck in a traffic jam on the 91 freeway.

"That's impossible," Larry replied heatedly.

"Why is it so impossible when you've fucked me practically every day for years without using any protection? So why is it so damn impossible, huh?"

"It's impossible, Melody, because I had a vasectomy two weeks after Monique was born, that's why," Larry said harshly. "Maybe your woman got you pregnant? She did have a sex change, didn't she?"

"Fuck you!" Melody replied, and then closed her cell phone.

Well, I guess that's strike one. Damn! What am I going to do? Melody wondered.

When Michelle made it home that evening, she was in the mood for making sweet, passionate love. Melody pretended to be tired and not in the mood.

"I'd better take you to see a doctor tomorrow, baby. Something could be seriously wrong with you, and whatever it is, we need to get it taken care of right away," Michelle said, caressing Melody's breasts while masturbating. "I need you, Melody. I need your touch, your taste. I need to feel your body on top of mine. I need you desperately, honey." She was hot and ready, but tonight, for Melody, just wasn't the night. She caressed Melody's body until they both fell asleep.

When Melody awakened the following morning and realized Michelle was gone, she read the note Michelle had left: *Sorry, babe. Had important business to take care of in Woodland Hills. See you around three. Be ready to go to Kaiser. Call me if you need me. Your wife, lover, and best friend, Michelle.*

Good, Melody thought. She then took a quick shower, got dressed, jotted down a brief note for Michelle, and left.

Damn, L.A. never changes, Melody thought as she entered Los Angeles, heading to an abortion clinic.

While passing Athens Park, memories of an unforgettable high school moment, when her and Maurice would have sex under the trees, flooded her mind. She thought about times she ditched school to go to Athens Park, accompanied by a flock of her hot friends—drinking beer, smoking marijuana and cigarettes, and flirting with young men who were seeking action.

Those were the good old days, she thought.

As she hung a left onto Avalon Boulevard, to her right was Magic Johnson's Recreation Park. It stretched out for fifteen beautiful, well-kept acres, containing an enormous catfish pond, a huge playground, numerous barbecue pits, three separate patio areas, a vast parking lot, and enough room to play any sport. Once she passed 120th Street, she hung a quick right into the parking lot of a clinic, and then parked and went inside.

There was a huge decrepit sign hanging on top of the shabby building that read Kono Medical Group. The building was old and needed immediate attention, but the parking lot was filled with vehicles, which meant business must be good. It appeared that Dr. Kono wasn't putting his profits back into his business.

The building was three faded colors combined with chipped paint and termite infestations, but due to its location, people who required cheap medical services patronized it.

Inside the dilapidated clinic there were twelve women occupying seats. After signing in and filling out the necessary paperwork, she then took a seat and began what looked like was going to be a long wait.

At two forty-two PM, after wasting away her whole day talking to some ghetto women with too many kids and not enough of anything, Melody's abortion procedure was complete. She felt lifeless and had no energy at all. She needed rest desperately before fighting the rush hour traffic back to Newport Beach. She made a sudden decision to go to her aunt's house until traffic died down.

She drove northbound on Avalon and made a left onto Imperial Highway, observing the teenagers who attended Gompers Junior High and Locke High School, and then made a quick right onto Main Street. It had been ten years since she'd seen her cousins—Sherwood, Andre, Evelyn, Pauline—and her Aunt Edna. Her aunt had raised her children without a man, and unfortunately, each child had a different father. There was always some type of drama going on with family members.

Sherwood, who was thirty-eight-years-old, was addicted to PCP, crack, and liquor. He stole cars, shoplifted from stores, and robbed people to support his habits. The week before he had robbed a woman at two thirty in the morning as she attempted to make a withdrawal from a Bank of America ready teller. He passed by her nonchalantly, took a quick scan of the area, and after seeing the coast was clear, he grabbed her and put her in a chokehold.

"Gimme the money, bitch!"

"OK, OK, just please don't kill me! Here, take it, just don't kill me," the woman begged. Sherwood quickly snatched the money out of her hand, and then took off sprinting down Broadway Street. It didn't matter to him that the Seventy-seventh Street

Police Station was two blocks away from where he committed the crime.

Andre, who was Sherwood's younger brother, was a gangster, a car-jacker, had committed a few home invasions, had robbed liquor stores and drug dealers, and had killed numerous rival gang members. A few weeks prior, a rival member, while doing a drive-by shooting, attempted to kill Andre, but he had missed, and instead had riddled Edna's house with AK-47 and Uzi bullets.

Each time Andre left home, whether he was going to the liquor store, hanging out with his homeboys, or just standing in his mother's front yard, he would have his nine-millimeter or his .44 Magnum loaded and ready to be used. Lately his rivals had killed six members from his gang, and were now trying to kill him. He was not only known for doing drive-by shootings, but he was also reputed to walk up to people casually and kill.

Evelyn, one of Edna's daughter's, was a Main Street whore, and had been one since after high school. During her senior year she was homecoming queen. Since then, after getting involved with drugs, her teeth had rotted, her looks had vanished, and she appeared to be a walking zombie. She was medium brown-complexioned, short, had huge bug-like eyes, nappy, unkempt hair, and weighed less than ninety pounds. She solicited sex shamelessly, one block from her mother's house. She was a disappointment to her mother, and had never seen her father.

Pauline, who was Edna's youngest daughter, was twenty-four-years-old. She had five kids, and each of them had different daddies, who were all gang-bangers. Pauline was a fine looking, light-brown complexioned, young lady, but she was naïve and unintelligent. Pretty, but dumb as hell.

Each of Edna's kids lived with her, sleeping in the same room they were raised in.

Edna was a huge, big boned, dark-complexioned southern woman, who had trouble with her kids since they were old enough to walk. They all lacked high school diplomas and plans for the future. Edna made sure she'd taken out insurance policies on each of them, due to the way they were living. She figured their life spans were limited.

Melody made a right on Ninety-ninth, drove down a couple houses, and then turned into the driveway of a green and white duplex. Hearing the sound of the car, Andre peeked out the window, assuming the unknown vehicle was one of his enemies. He had his .44 Magnum in one hand, and his 9mm in the other. Warily, he went out the back door and eased around the side of the house until he had a perfect aim at the stranger.

"What's up, fool! Surprise, muthafucka!" Andre yelled, aiming with precision.

"Don't shoot me!" Melody's screamed as her eyes bugged out. "Please don't shoot me! Please!"

"Andre! Put that goddamn gun away!" Edna shouted as she stormed outside. "Boy, you're gonna give someone a heart attack! Can't you see that's your cousin, Melody, boy?" Edna trotted over and came to Melody's assistance.

"Ah, damn. Hey, Cousin Melody. I'm sorry, cousin, I thought you was those fools who shot up my Momma's house the other day," Andre explained apologetically. He then approached Melody and gave her a hug. He never took his eyes or mind out of observation mode, and he never put away his guns.

"Dre, you scared the hell out of me, boy," Melody managed to say, though she was still somewhat shook up. "Did I come at the wrong time or what?"

"I gotta watch my back, Cousin Melody," Andre replied as he darted his eyes down the street. "It's been a lotta' killin' goin' on around here lately, and it's better them bein' dead, than me."

"Girl, come on in and talk to your auntie," Aunt Edna said as she led Melody inside. "How's your mama doing, chile?" Andre peeked out the window the entire time Melody was there. He slid the window open just enough to stick the barrel of the gun outside. Edna didn't object.

Thirty minutes into Melody's visit, Evelyn walked inside. She was dressed in a short, blue mini-skirt with no panties on, and had on a pair of blue high-heels and a white halter-top. She appeared to be exactly what she was—a Main Street whore.

Without acknowledging Melody's presence, Evelyn headed straight to the rest room and closed and locked the door behind her. She then took a quick hit of crack. Seconds later, she exited the restroom quicker than she went in. She was paranoid as hell and began hallucinating.

"Who's that?" Evelyn asked after walking into the living room. She then scanned the room. "I heard somebody. Is the police out there?"

"Girl, quit looking out the fuckin' window!" Andre shouted.

"Evelyn, don't you see your cousin Melody sitting here? Show some respect and act like you've got some damn sense, girl," Edna said. "Don't pay her any attention, Melody. She's been smoking that shit again. If she only knew how she looks, she'd leave that shit alone. She knows damn well she has to test for that probation officer on Friday."

Two suspicious looking vehicles, an Astro van and a Cutlass filled with gangsters, crept slowly down the street and halted in front of Edna's house. Andre was watching them distrustfully. When he noticed one of the faces as one of his enemies, he yelled, "Get down! Get down!" Gunshots came from both vehicles like they were celebrating New Year's Eve. Andre returned fire, but only hit his neighbor's vehicles. The attackers sped off and were quickly out of sight.

"Damn! Those muthafuckas got away!" Andre yelled.

Melody was so frightened that she urinated on herself. She lay on the floor screaming next to Edna and Evelyn, who were covering their heads and afraid to move.

"Cousin Melody, shut the fuck up and stop all that damn screaming! You're making me nervous with that bullshit!" Andre shouted. "I'm gonna step outside for a minute to see if those fools are gone, then I can get you out of here. This is the wild, wild West around here, Cousin Melody, and some serious shit is about to go down."

Andre then moved stealthily outside with guns in both hands scanning the street.

"Come on, Cousin Melody!" Andre yelled when he didn't see any suspicious vehicles. "Come on while the coast is clear! Hurry up!"

Melody sprung from the floor and ran to her Suburban like she was running for her life.

"I've got to go, Auntie. I'll call you later!" Melody managed to say as she was running. Edna stood at her door waving her off.

"I'm sorry this shit happened, girl, but tell your momma that I said hi, and to stop by and see me sometime."

Yeah, right, Melody thought as she headed to her vehicle. She noticed the back and side windows of her Surburban had been shot out, and there were four bullet holes alongside it, but she quickly jumped in, backed up, and then peeled out, ducking as if she were being chased and shot at. The Astro van and the Cutlass filled with gangsters had spotted her leaving, and speedily moved alongside her. They were on each side of her, giving her a long, hard stare, and then suddenly they accelerated and disappeared.

"What the fuck did I get myself into? Every goddamn time I come to L.A., something happens. It never fails," Melody yelled out loud, still somewhat terrified. Once she entered the 110 freeway, she felt relieved.

I'm not ever bringing my ass back to L.A. as long as I live! I mean that. I give Andre another week or so and he'll be dead! That's giving him the benefit of the doubt. And that crackhead Evelyn, with her nasty, stinkin' self, probably has AIDS, herpes, crabs, syphilis, and some shit they ain't even came out with yet! What the hell am I going to tell Michelle? she wondered as she was now stuck in rush hour traffic.

Two and a half hours later, Melody was pulling into Michelle's driveway. Michelle rushed outside with Blackie and Whitey at her feet. After observing the shot-up Suburban and noticing the worried look on her lover's face, Michelle approached apprehensively.

"What happened, baby? Are you all right? Were you involved in a shootout or something? I thought you were sick. What happened?"

"Am I glad to see you, Michelle. You wouldn't believe what happened," Melody replied, still not believing what she'd been through.

As they entered the house, embracing like husband and wife, Rosie Martinez sat a few houses down observing them. She was highly pissed off at seeing her wife hugged up with Melody.

"Bitch, that's my wife!" she yelled. "Your black ass is mine, bitch! Yeah, you're mine!" she shouted while easing up to the Suburban. She then stopped.

"I see that someone else is trying to kill the bitch, too!" Rosie said. "But she's mine to kill! She's fucking my wife! I'll kill you, bitch!" At the sight of a police cruiser patrolling the high-class neighborhood, Rosie then peeled away, frustrated and wondering who else was trying to kill Melody. It was her job to kill her, and no one was going to get in her way.

Melody ran the scenario down to Michelle, telling her everything except the part about her abortion. That was a secret between her and the doctor.

After a nice, hot shower together, they lay naked across the bed kissing and caressing each other, then conversed for a little while longer and fell asleep.

The following morning, Michelle left early to take care of some unfinished business with a couple of her underlings. She had eight underlings, who went as far as the Bay Area to take care of business for her. She paid them well for their services, but a couple of them weren't bringing in the profits like they should have been. They were simply holding out. One thing Michelle was very capable of doing was operating and main-

taining her business, and figuring out her profits. From her cal-
culations, the money had been coming in much shorter than
normal. She was going to handle this matter her way.

Melody's first stop was the auto glass shop, where she had
her windows replaced. Then afterward, she made her way to
her home. She needed to check her messages and mail. She
put off having the bodywork done on the vehicle until the following day.

After fixing herself a drink and relaxing at her dining room
table, she checked her answering machine and then called
Michelle to tell her that she was going to stay home for the
night to sort things out in her mind.

Melody called Pizza Hut and ordered a pizza to be delivered.
After eating, she took a nice, long shower, lay down, and
grabbed her remote. She scanned through the channels and
stopped at the *Jerry Springer Show.* Ten minutes later, she was
sound asleep.

Rosie was parked a few houses from Melody's, checking her
clip to make sure it was full. Satisfied, she stuffed it in her coat
pocket, put her mask in the other pocket, and then whispered,
"It's show time, goddammit!" As she opened her car door, a
white Taurus pulled up in front of Melody's house and
stopped. The magnetic sign on top of the car read Pizza Hut.
Rosie eased her car door closed and began cursing.

"Fuck! Just when I'm ready to handle my business, some asshole gets in my way!"

It was almost 10:30 PM when Rosie decided to make her
move. She eased out of the car, slipped on her gloves and monster mask, and cautiously approached Melody's house. Sounds
from barking dogs came from nearby as Rosie approached the
side gate leading to Melody's backyard. She crept alongside the
house like a professional cat burglar, ignoring the barks and
the sounds of crickets. She shined her flashlight through the
den window and spotted a computer system, a stereo, a televi-

sion, and a birdcage containing a parrot. She prayed the parrot didn't talk or make loud noises to alarm her victim.

Slowly, she slid open the window wide enough for her to climb through, then eased inside. So far, so good. She then tip-toed to the front door, unlocked the it for her escape route, and then crept to Melody's bedroom, keeping her finger on the trigger. Melody's loud snores were audible throughout the house, which assured Rosie her victim was sound asleep. Rosie stood at the bedroom door, aimed, and fired six times at Melody's naked body. Speedily she fled the scene, leaving the front door wide open. After jumping into her vehicle, she peeled away with her headlights off.

Hearing the gunshots, several of Melody's neighbors ran out-side and scanned the street. Suddenly Patty, a white lady from across the street, spotted Melody's front door open.

"Hey, look!" Patty yelled while pointing at Melody's house. "Melody's front door is wide open! Let's make sure everything is OK!"

She and her husband, along with several other neighbors, moved cautiously inside Melody's house. Melinda, another neighbor, entered the bedroom and saw Melody lying naked in a pool of blood. She screamed as loudly as she could. Her hus-band immediately grabbed the phone and dialed 911.

Minutes later, police cars, ambulances, and fire trucks sur-rounded Melody's home. Melody had been shot once in the head, and once in the buttocks. Fortunately, Rosie had been so nervous that the other four bullets had missed their mark.

Yellow tape was used to block off the crime scene. Two po-licemen, Officer Smith and Officer Boyd, took statements from the each of the neighbors. The information was then passed on to Sergeant Wright, who passed the case to Detective Bell of homicide.

CHAPTER 24

Big Steve

"Excuse me, sir, but you put the ankle and handcuffs on too tight. Will you please loosen them a little for me?"

"You want me to loosen 'em up a little, huh? OK," the deputy replied. He then snatched Big Steve toward him, looked him in the eyes, and said, "Do you wanna fuck with me, asshole? I'll show you who to fuck with!" Then he tightened both pair of cuffs. "Now how's that, porky? They feel better now, don't they?"

The other deputies on the prison transport bus stood back and observed their coworker. They always gave each other that respect. Perhaps the following day, one of them might want to do his thing. One hand washed the other.

Once Big Steve stepped off the bus, the pain in his feet caused him to say, "Shit!" There were two Correctional Officers (C.O.s) at the door of the bus. One was reading off names from an inmate roster, and the other was removing the hand and ankle cuffs.

"Keep moving, convict, keep moving!" one of the C.O.s said to Steve.

After Big Steve was uncuffed, his arms were still positioned like they were cuffed. His ankles were sore, and it hurt each time he took a step. After each prisoner was finally uncuffed, they were then ordered to line up in twos alongside the bus, then they were counted, checked off a list, and were instructed to walk into a building and strip naked. Inside, a different officer was waiting to give them a series of instructions.

"Turn around, bend over, and show me the redness in your assholes! Grab your nuts with one hand, and rake from your asshole to your nuts with the other! Stick out your tongue and wiggle it like you're eating your favorite girlfriend. Bend over and rake your hair from back to front!"

"OK, ten men to a cell!" the officer yelled once they were done. "Don't ask us any fucking questions! We're much too busy to answer questions!"

Naked, Big Steve and nine other inmates entered a holding cell. Steve noticed the other inmates were all focused on one particular inmate—a six-foot-two homosexual with pecs that looked like breasts and a huge penis that hung to his knees. Big Steve did a double take and couldn't hold in his laughter.

"You got a fucking problem, fat boy?" the homosexual asked with an attitude. Big Steve snickered again.

"Who me? Nah, I'm cool," Big Steve replied.

The man then moved to the back of the cell, trying to ignore the gay jokes, the laughter, and the whispering and pointing, but it didn't work.

"Fuck that! I'm gonna kick somebody's ass up in here! The next muthafucka who looks at me, or laughs at me will be sorry, 'cause I might just ram my dick inside him!"

Silence filled the cell from that point on.

A few minutes later, the inmates were given orange jumpsuits, and afterward they were then called out one at a time to have blood drawn and to check for any diseases. Next they were fingerprinted and had their pictures taken. Once they were done, they were then transferred to a larger cell and given a sack lunch.

Five miserable hours later they were still inside the cell. Some of them were asleep on the floor, some were talking about the good old days, and others sat thinking about the years they had to spend in prison.

"Hey! C.O.!" a black inmate yelled. How much longer are we gonna be in here, man? I thought you said we'd be outta here in two hours or less? What's up with that, man?"

"Didn't I say no fucking questions?" the officer responded. "Are you fucking deaf or just stupid? No fucking questions! Understand?"

"Well fuck you, then!" a white inmate shouted.

Hearing the outburst, the officer signaled for three of his coworkers. They then approached the cell.

"Come here, asshole! Yeah, you!" the officer instructed, assuming it was the black inmate. Another C.O. opened the cell door.

"It wasn't me, man," the black inmate explained. "I didn't say anything, man." He then stepped out of the cell. The black officer, who was extremely muscular, grabbed the inmate, tackled him to the concrete floor, and rested his boot on the man's back, while another officer pulled out cuffs and chains and hogtied him. Afterward they carried him to another cell. Another black inmate yelled to the inmate who made the outburst.

"Hey, man, you better tell that fuckin' C.O. that was you, and wasn't my homeboy who said that shit!"

"Hey dude, fuck it, man," the white inmate, who was tall and skinny and had long side burns, replied. "Better him than me. Fuck him."

The black inmate then stormed over to the white boy.

"Muthafucka! I'm gonna fuck you up if you don't tell those officers my homeboy didn't say that shit!"

Big Steve and the other inmates cleared the way.

"Hey, man, I'm not scared of you, dude. You're just another one of those ignorant gang-bangers, dude. No fear, dude. No fuckin' fear," the white boy said boldly. He then squared up with Baby Boy, the black inmate. "Whacha gonna do, you fucking nigger! If you feel froggish, then leap, asshole."

Baby Boy made sure the C.O.s weren't looking. He then cocked his fist back and socked the white boy as hard as he could in the ear, then followed up with a series of punches that sent the man to the floor. Blood poured from the man's face like a gushing water faucet. Observing the fight, one of the officers pressed his panic button. Officers ran from different locations to resolve the matter.

"Over there! Get the black guy wearing the braids!" the Mexican officer shouted. They rushed inside the cell holding pepper spray and shouting.

"Step to the front with your hands behind your back, asshole!"

"Fuck you, cuzz! I'm Baby Boy, fool! Straight outta Watts, cuzz! Fuck you!"

Annoyed, Officer Hernandez sprayed the inmate with pepper spray, then grabbed him and slung him to the floor, and began kicking him. After finally cuffing the inmate, they threw him on a stretcher and took him to the infirmary.

Forty-five minutes later, a C.O. with a thick, blond mustache appeared at the cell and began calling names off the roster.

Big Steve was assigned to cell 201, which was located on the upper tier. After being escorted to his building, Big Steve stood by his cell door holding his property. Inmates in other cells immediately began directing yells toward him.

"Where you from, cuzz?" one voice shouted.

"Hey, Blood, what set you from?" another voice yelled.

"Where you from, fool?" another voice sounded, then his cell door suddenly opened. Cautiously, he stepped inside and closed the door behind him.

The cell was twelve by seven, and there was very little room to move around. The cell was unoccupied at the time, but there were pictures on the wall of women lying on their backs holding their legs open, pictures of naked women positioned like they were about to hike a football, but instead they showed their rectums and vaginas, pictures of gang-bangers kneeling or standing next to a low rider with gold Dayton rims, and a picture of a Ford Explorer with gold spoke rims. There was also writing materials and food on the steel table. After making his bed and putting away his belongings, Steve stood at his cell door listening to the inmates yell from cell to cell, then suddenly one of the yells was directed at him.

"Hey, 201! Where you from, cuzz?" a gang-banger shouted from a cell thirty yards away.

"201! 201! Where you from, fool?" another gang-banger yelled.

Steve ignored the voices. He then sat down and began reading his Bible until the cell door popped open. A black youngster appearing to be in his mid-twenties walked inside.

"What's up, O.G.?" Youngsters referred to anyone over thirty as O.G., which means Original Gangster. A person did not have to be a retired gang member to be considered an O.G.—just over thirty-years-old.

Steve put down his Bible, stood up, and shook the youngster's hand.

"How you doing, man? I'm Steve."

"I'm Killer Karl, cuzz. Eight Tray Gangsta," the youngster replied. He then meticulously scanned his picture wall, making sure there were none missing.

Killer Karl was short, medium-brown complexioned, wore his hair in a short natural, and weighed about 130 pounds. Once he'd finished taking a quick inventory, he sat at the edge of his bunk and began talking.

"Where you from, cuzz?" Killer Karl asked.

"I'm from Compton, but I've turned my life over to the Lord, man, and now I claim Jesus," Big Steve replied sincerely. Killer Karl snickered.

"Ah, nigga, you wasn't claimin' Jesus on the streets, but now that you got busted, you wanna start claimin' Jesus. Y'all niggas tickle me with that shit, homey." Killer Karl laughed. "How much time you got, man?"

"They gave me five years."

"What you busted for?"

"Possession and possession for sales."

"Ah, nigga, you was a crackhead on the streets." Killer Karl laughed even louder.

"If that's what you want to call it."

"Ah, cuzz, you ain't gonna do nothin' but thirty-one, thirty-two months on five years, so quit stressing, man. But I bet that when you get out, you start smokin' that shit again, homey. Once a crackhead, always a crackhead. The only reason you ain't smokin' crack this minute is because you're locked up. And that's the only reason you're claimin' Jesus."

"Whatever, man. I told you my life belongs to the L—"

"Bullshit, cuzz! You know damn well you wish you had a hit right now!"

"Those days are over, Karl, and that life is behind me," Big Steve said earnestly.

"Killer Karl, homey! Don't just call me Karl. The name is Killer Karl!"

"Anyway, man, how much time do you have?"

"They gave me life, man, and I ain't never going home, cuzz. Never!" Killer Karl emphasized.

"Never say never, Karl!" Big Steve replied sympathetically.

"Killer Karl, nigga. My name is Killer Karl. Don't get that fucked up, homey!"

"Would you like me to pray for you?"

"I don't want you to do a muthafuckin' thing for me! Just do your program and stay the hell outta my way!" Killer Karl said. He then stood up, reached underneath Steve's bunk, and pulled out a T-shirt containing a large trash bag full of a liquid substance. He quickly opened the bag and dipped a coffee jar inside, filling the jar with the substance. He then took a swallow.

"Here, man, you want some?"

"What is it?" Big Steve asked curiously.

"Pruno, nigga. Haven't you ever drank pruno before?"

"Unh unh. What is it?"

"Liquor, cuzz. This shit will get you f-u-u-cked up," Killer Karl emphasized. He then took another swallow. "This is the next best thing to Old English, homey. I was a rider when I was on the streets, homey, and I killed a lot of people in my days. I'd do it again if I had to, homey. Everybody in the hood knew me, and I mean everybody. The worst thing about it, cuzz, was that my enemies lived a few blocks from my hood. Man, I used to cruise by the liquor store in the hood to see if any of my enemies were hangin' out, and if they were, I'd let them have it, homey. Tac-tac-tac-tac-tac-tac-tac!" Killer Karl shouted, excitedly aiming his index finger at the cell door.

So far, he had drank three coffee jars full of pruno and was feeling good and talkative. He looked around the cell, admiring its cleanliness, then frowned.

"Check it out, homey. Every time you use the sink, you gotta use that towel to wipe it dry. Use the other towel to clean the floor and wipe the walls, and that way, the crib can stay intact, you know what I'm sayin'? You got to understand, homey, that you're just passin' through like the rest of those short time fools, and no tellin' how long I'll be here. Everybody who comes through here has to comply with my rules, you know what I'm sayin'." He paused to take another long swallow, then continued. "And another thing, homey, don't be farting, 'cause I don't wanna smell your shit! If you've got to fart, sit on the toilet and flush when you're done. And each time you drop a turd, flush it. Simple as that, homey."

Big Steve felt kind of stupid taking instructions from a

youngster. He was actually supposed to be housed in a dorm with low security inmates whose sentences ranged from sixteen months to five years, but presently those dorms were filled, which caused him and several other inmates to be housed with lifers like Killer Karl until bed space became available in the low custody dorms.

Big Steve was curious about a few things, and began asking questions.

"Man, how do you make that nasty smelling stuff you're drinking?"

"Easy," Killer Karl said. "First, homey, you get a trash bag from one of the porters, then take about thirty or forty apples or oranges and put them in a sock and crush them with your fist or beat them against the wall. Then, you dump them in the trash bag. Then add bread, sugar, fruit juices, or the fruit cups we get at dinnertime. Make sure you save 'em and bring them back with you. Then, homey, all you have to do is tie up the bag, wrap it good and tight so it'll cook. Keep it warm and let it sit for about a week or so, then take it to the throat," Killer Karl explained confidently. He then finished the remainder of the pruno.

"What if the C.O.s find it?" Big Steve asked, concerned about being blamed and going to the hole.

"They ain't gonna do nuttin' but take it from you. Hell, you're already in prison, so what more can they do to you?"

"They probably can't do anything to you because you got life, but they might take some time away from me and throw me in the hole."

"So what you sayin', homey? If you scared, go to church, nigga! I ain't gonna stop drinkin' or makin' my pruno for you or nobody else! If the C.O.s find it, then I'll cop to it, so quit trippin'!" Killer Karl replied animatedly.

Killer Karl's stories and conversations were neverending. He boasted about how many rival gang members he had killed, how many women he had sex with, bragged about his low rider and his Explorer, how much money he spent on attorneys, and how he got busted.

Big Steve fell asleep listening to Killer Karl's war stories, but awakened a few hours later and started praying that Melody would write him. He then fell back asleep. So far, he'd written her thirty-eight letters, and had not received any in return.

The following morning at six thirty a loud voice yelled through the PA system.

"Chow time! Chow time! Get up, get dressed, and get ready for chow! Chow time!"

Big Steve immediately jumped up and began getting ready. Killer Karl had already left for work. While waiting for his cell door to open, Steve prayed, then the voice yelled once again.

"201. Step out and close your door behind you!"

Steve grabbed his chair and seated himself once he reached the cafeteria. There was an officer in a gun tower, and another C.O. overseeing the inmates eating.

Scanning the building, Big Steve spotted Killer Karl mopping the floor, but his attention was then distracted by someone directing a yell at him.

"Where you from, homey?"

"Hey, homey! Where you from?" another voice shouted,

Steve ignored them and continued eating. Annoyed by being ignored, the inmates shouted again, but louder this time.

"Hey, man! I know goddamn well you hear me!"

Killer Karl overheard the comments and mopped his way over to the inmates who were making the comments.

"Quit trippin' on my cellie, y'all," Killer Karl said. "I've already checked him out, and he's cool, so leave him alone." Killer Karl then walked over to Big Steve. "Fuck those niggas, homey. They ain't kickin' up no dust, you know what I'm sayin'. If they give you any problems, jus' hollar at me, cuzz." He then continued mopping.

A thug sitting at another table looked at Steve.

"I'm Ken Dog, homey. Eastside Main Street Mafia Crip." That was a gang-banger's way of introducing himself. They would first state their gang name, and then state what gang they were from.

"Freak Daddy. Lynwood Pope Street Crip, cuzz." Yet another thug introduced himself.

"Bay Rob, Santana Block Compton Crip," another offered.

After the introductions, the inmates sat waiting for Big Steve to introduce himself, but he was too busy eating french toast.

"So where you from, homey?" Ken-Dog asked after impatiently waiting for Steve to introduce himself.

"Well, actually guys," Big Steve said, "I grew up in Compton, but I don't gang bang. I lived in Southside neighborhood, but—"

"No shit," Bay Rob said excitedly. He then yelled to an inmate at a different table. "Hey, C-Rock! One of your homeboys is here! Do you know Bozo, Big Black, Solo, Scroncho, and Big P?" he asked Steve.

"Nah, man, I don't know any of those dudes. I gave my life to God, you know, so I have to eliminate negative people and harmful things from my life, which is why I moved from Compton," Big Steve replied, still munching on french toast.

"If you from the South, man, then you got to know the homies I just mentioned, 'cause they're runnin' things in the South, homey. You know Kefee-D and Slep-Rock?"

"I went to school with both of them, but like I said, it's been a long time since I've seen any of those dudes."

The voice through the PA system suddenly announced, "First row pick it up!" Chow time was over.

While walking back to their cells, a voice from the lower tier yelled out.

"Hey Ken Dog! Where is that fool from?"

"He don't gang bang, homey, but he's from Compton. He talking 'bout he a preacher and shit," Ken Dog replied, laughing.

246 of Samuel L. Hair

"Seems like niggas want to follow God when they come to jail, but as soon as they get out, they put God on a shelf and go back to doing whatever they were doing that got them here. Those kinda niggas come through here like ants runnin' to a pile of shit, you know what I'm sayin'," the inmate yelled.

Big Steve returned to his cell, prayed, and then fell asleep. Eight days later, he was transferred to another part of the prison and housed with inmates with lower security levels like himself. Again, he was housed on the upper tier and was assigned to an upper bunk.

After making up his bed, he sat and began observing the inmates. He wasn't quite ready to meet them yet and to be asked, "Where you from? Or do you know such-and-such." He just wanted to relax and think about the Lord and Melody.

A short, black man with long braids and a loud mouth passed Steve while singing a rap song.

"Six in the morning police at my door, six in the morning police at my door, six, six, six in the morning police at my door," were the lyrics.

To Big Steve's right, three feet away on the top bunk, was a Cuban reading a book. To his left was a humble looking Mexican studying his Bible.

Good, Big Steve thought. *Someone else believes in God other than me.*

Big Steve then decided to go to the dayroom, which was the area for game playing and television viewing. Black inmates playing dominos occupied one of the tables, while Latinos playing spades occupied another, and on another table were white inmates playing pinochle. There were chess games going on at a couple other tables, and inmates talking and telling each other lies occupied another table.

Big Steve had a seat and checked out each black inmate. He figured he could learn a little about their character by observing them. His focus was suddenly on a bald, peanut butter-complexioned brother, who had a professional demeanor.

He's not like the others. He's cool, calm, and controlled. Maybe I'll have an opportunity to speak with him one day, Big Steve thought while still studying the man.

Twenty minutes later, he went back to his bunk and began reading his Bible, but was soon interrupted.

"I'm Cuban P. What's happening, man?" the Cuban occupying the bunk next to him asked. The inmate spoke with a New York accent. Big Steve offered a handshake.

"I'm Steve. Nice to meet you, Cuban P."

"Likewise," Cuban P. replied with a toothless smile.

Big Steve was glad to be greeted by someone without being asked, "Where you from?"

"Hey man," Cuban P said, "this place is kinda crazy, you know. Just roll with the punches and you'll be all right, you know what I mean?" Cuban P then jumped off his bunk, lifted his own mattress, and grabbed a balled-up piece of paper. "Watch out for me, Steve. Tell me if a C.O. comes this way. Hey, you wanna hit this?" he asked while about to smoke dried up banana peels. Inmates swore they were high when they smoked dried spinach, apple seeds or dried banana peels.

"Nah, man, you go right ahead," Big Steve replied, shaking his head in disgust.

"This is some good shit, man. Straight nature, you know what I mean? Grown in the fucking ground, man." Cuban P emphasized.

On the other side of Big Steve was a Mexican reading his Bible, and another Mexican drinking a nasty smelling substance. It had the same odor as the pruno Killer Karl had been drinking.

Ah, man, Big Steve thought. *I'm surrounded by evil.*

Suddenly, Steve's bunkie began singing rap songs.

"In my younger days, I used to sport a rag, back pack full of cans, and foe-foe mag, flamed up from the feet up, blued up from the suit up, is how I grew up..."

A Mexican covered with tattoos, approached the bunk next to Steve and spoke to another Mexican.

"Fill it up, homes." He handed his cup to the inmate drinking the pruno.

Irritated, Big Steve climbed out of his bed and went back to the dayroom. He could no longer tolerate the smell of banana peels, apple seeds, spinach, and pruno. He approached the bald, intelligent-looking man, and started to introduce himself, but decided against it, not wanting to distract him while he was playing chess. Acknowledging Steve's presence, the man introduced himself.

"Hi, I'm Maxwell," the man said in a soft-spoken, intelligent voice. Steve accepted the handshake.

"Nice to meet you, Maxwell. I'm Steve."

"How much time do you have?" Maxwell asked, never taking his focus off the chessboard.

"Five years," Big Steve replied.

"What sort of case did you have?"

"Possession for sales, and possession of paraphernalia.

"They gave you a break, man," Maxwell replied. He made a move, looked at his opponent, and said, "Checkmate."

Within forty-five minutes Maxwell had defeated six challengers. There were several other inmates waiting to play him, but they were the same inmates who tried to beat him each day.

Maxwell stood five-ten and weighed two hundred pounds. He had a peaceful expression. He convinced Steve that he had three wives and twelve girlfriends, a home in Mexico worth eight hundred thousand American dollars, a million dollar home on the beach in Santa Monica, a twenty-two unit apartment complex in North Hollywood, and eighteen nightclubs scattered throughout the U.S. In addition to that, Maxwell told Steve he owned a Rolls Royce, a Roadster, and a Lamborghini. He also said that he wore six hundred dollar anteater, shark, and ostrich shoes. Each of his supposed nightclubs were named Maxville. He said 90 percent of his employees were dope fiends and were paid in drugs instead of cash, and that they were also ex-felons who had all been to prison for various reasons.

In the beginning, Maxwell only dealt with small amounts of drugs, just enough to pay the workers at each location, but as time passed, Maxville became a whorehouse, and a spot to purchase ounces and kilos of cocaine and heroin. His weekly gross had increased from fifty thousand legal dollars, to two hundred thousand illegal dollars, and that was only at one location. His days were spent flying from location to location throughout the U.S. He had hired a right hand man, but felt the guy was not 100 percent loyal, and was holding out on large amounts of cash. A jealous girlfriend, who knew about Maxwell's operations, snitched on him and turned state's evidence against him. That was the actual reason for his incarceration. She had warned him many times that she was sick and tired of being the other woman. His response was always, "I love you more than any of my wives, Lydia. We have something solid and unbreakable. Soon I'll be divorced from the others, and I promise you that you'll be my one and only wife," he lied. Lydia had heard the same lie for eight years.

After a two-year investigation, enough evidence was gathered on Maxwell, and with the testimony from Lydia, he was put him away for fifteen years. This was the beginning of his term.

After hearing the rise and fall of Maxwell, Big Steve shook his hand.

"Be cool, Maxwell. I'll talk with you later, man." He then walked away and sat by himself at one of the tables.

Two brothers then approached Big Steve.

"How you guys doing? I'm Steve."

"I'm D-Mac, homey," the short, light-complexioned inmate said after shaking hands.

"What's up, homey? I'm Smiley from Du-Rock," the taller one said.

D-Mac was eighteen-years-old and had been arrested for robbery and assault. He was sentenced to five years in prison. He stood five-five, and had a pair of hazel eyes and short hair. He did not have the appearance of a gang-banger, but desired to become one. Gang-bangers were his mentors. Everyone wanted to be a tough guy, but most of them couldn't read or write. When they received mail or wanted to write a letter to a friend or a loved one, they would get an educated inmate to do it for them. One would wonder how a man like that was going to help his children with their homework, or get ahead in society using slang as their daily vocabulary. Big Steve sat thinking of all the things his parents had instilled in him at an early age.

Smiley was in prison for robbery. His days were spent in prison drawing pictures of cartoon characters. Using his imagination, he could draw just about anything. If he hadn't chosen to live a life of crime, he could've been an artist. But he'd made the choice earlier in his life to use his fingers to pull a trigger instead of using them to utilize the talent he was blessed with. Hopefully, the ten years he was sentenced to would give him enough time to reconsider his career.

Suddenly, a dark, baldheaded brother with beady eyes approached Big Steve. He extended his hand.

"I'm Alex. How you doing, man?"

Big Steve accepted the handshake.

"Fine, thank you. I'm Steve. Glad to meet you, Alex."

"Likewise," Alex said. "How much time you got?"

"Five years."

"No shit."

"Yep, but I can't complain, you know. I did it to myself. It could've been a lot worse."

Alex then had a seat next to Big Steve and continued talking.

"Yeah, I know what you mean, man. I was smoking crack on the streets, you know, but I'm convinced the Lord sent me here to make me focus more on him, and take my mind off things of the devil," Alex explained sincerely. Big Steve was shocked to hear someone admit to smoking crack and mention the Lord. Normally, inmates would lie and say they were dealers instead of users, but their character reflected what type of person they were on the streets.

Alex was originally from Brooklyn, New York. He was one of those guys who came to Cali for vacation, but ended up on probation. In his case, he ended up in prison. He was forty-four-years-old, stood five-nine, and weighed 175 pounds. He was swift on his feet and had won several boxing titles before beginning a life of crime. He was considered the jailhouse preacher, the black M.A.C. Rep, which meant the representative for the black inmates, and he was a rapper, a speaker for A.A. and N.A., and he was also a compulsive gambler. He made bets on all sports and played cards and dominoes practically all day. His winnings would be paid in soups, coffee, tobacco, stamped envelopes, or whatever an inmate had of value.

Big Steve conversed with Alex for a few minutes until a young thug from afar, shouted, "Hey, O.G.! Come over here and make a beat while I rap." A group of youngsters were waiting on Alex.

"I gotta go, man. I'll talk to you later," Alex said, and then sped over to the crowd of thugs.

D-Mac and Smiley were doing push-ups with a brother from Vallejo named Domino, and weren't paying attention to passing inmate traffic. Two Mexicans attempted to pass them, but one was accidentally struck in the face by D-Mac when he jumped up to do lunges.

"Hey, homes, are you going to apologize or what?" the Mexican said furiously. His nose was bleeding. Smiley stood flexing his muscles, hoping to intimidate the Mexicans. D-Mac spoke up boldly.

"It was your fault for walking down the aisle while we working out! If anything, y'all should've went around or waited till it was cool to walk by, you know what I'm sayin'?"

"Are you going to apologize or what, homes?" the Mexican said as he balled up his fist.

Continuing to flex his muscles, Smiley interjected.

"So how do you want to settle this shit, homey?" He was directing his question to the bleeding Mexican. Law Dog then approached the scene.

"What's really going on, cuzz?" D-Mac stood with balled fists ready to take a swing, as Domino began explaining things.

"This Mexican wants D-Mac to apologize to him for hitting him in the nose by accident." Over fifty Mexicans suddenly appeared. Just about every inmate in the dorm was watching, but the C.O. hadn't noticed yet. He was too busy eating donuts and looking at *Playboy* magazines.

"Wait a minute, cuzz! Fuck that!" Law Dog shouted. "Silent, let me holler at you a minute." Silent was the shot caller for the Mexicans. He and Law-Dog stepped into the restroom, made a quick decision as to how to resolve the situation, and then returned to the crowd.

"Hey, Dreamer," Silent said. "You and homeboy go to the restroom and handle your business, you know what I mean. The best man wins, you know what I mean?" Law Dog interjected.

"Handle your business, D-Mac. Dynamite comes in small packages, my nigga, so show him what you workin' with."

The C.O. still wasn't paying attention to what was happening. D-Mac and Dreamer stepped into the restroom and squared up, then Dreamer swung and quickly connected to D-Mac's eye. He followed up with a hard kick to his balls.

"Ah, ooh, ah!" D-Mac cried out, kneeling.

"Get up and fight, nigga!" Law Dog yelled from a distance, but Dreamer didn't allow him the opportunity. Dreamer then got into a kick-boxer stance and attempted to kick D-Mac in the face, but D-Mac caught his foot, dragged him a few feet, and dove on top of him.

"Get up! Get up Dreamer! Kick his fucking ass!" Silent yelled. Dreamer then eased out of the hold, got to his feet, and rushed D-Mac with a series of punches striking him several times in the head. D-Mac was stunned and could barely see. His left eye had closed.

"Get him, cuzz! If you let him kick your ass, then me and the homies are gonna kick your ass!" Law Dog yelled angrily.

D-Mac quickly regained composure, squared up once again, and rushed Dreamer with his head down, landing a few lucky punches to his opponent's eye, mouth, and nose. Then he grabbed a cup and rushed Dreamer again, but this time he beat him in the head with the cup. He then grabbed Dreamer and put him in a headlock.

"Let him go, homes! Let him go!" Silent yelled. The fight was over.

After observing the scene, Big Steve went back to his bunk. Cuban P was pacing back and forth reciting Al Pacino lines from the movie *Scarface*.

"Take a good look at tha bad guy, 'cause this tha las time you gonna see a bad guy tha loo like me. Manny, I tol' you sanitarium, not sanitation. Why you tahking crasse for? I eat so much octopussy, I got octopussy comin' outta my fuckin' ears!" Cuban P recited. He then approached Big Steve's bunk, looked him in the eye, and recited another line.

"Hey, Steve! Delano is nothin' but a great big pussy jus waitin' to get fucked!"

Afterward Cuban P lifted his mattress and pulled out some spinach he'd been drying out, grabbed a pinch, then rolled it using Bible paper, lit it, and began smoking.

"This some good shit, Steve. It makes you feel like you smoked some crack or PCP," Cuban P said. He then took another long drag, held it for ten seconds, then exhaled. "Damn, this is some good shit. I'm f-u-u-u-cked up." A few minutes later he then climbed on his bunk and fell asleep.

After showering, Steve lay down and called it a night. He began to dream. He dreamed about Melody and his parents. He also dreamed about his adventures on The U. He then dreamed he was preaching to a large congregation. His dreams were suddenly interrupted by the sound of someone beating on a bunk. It was the wannabe rapper.

"Six in the morning police at my door. Six, six, six in the morning police at my door!" the man sang.

Steve turned over and lifted his head.

Don't these people have any respect for someone who's sleeping? His neighbor to the right of him was studying his Bible, but after glancing at Steve, he set down his Bible and began making conversation.

"Sorry for not introducing myself earlier, but I'm Nick," He then offered a handshake.

"I'm Steve. Nice to meet you, Nick."

"Do you believe in God?" Nick asked out of the blue.

"Do I? Yes. Actually, he's responsible for me being here."

"What do you mean by that, Steve?"

"Well, my life was what you call on the wrong track, Nick. God tried to get my attention several times in the past, but I was too blind to see it, and too dumb to realize it, so he let me continue to roam around and serve the devil, doing everything ungodly under the sun—smoking crack, committing adultery, sleeping with whores, hanging with lowlifes, and selling drugs—until eventually I hung myself, and here I am.

"God had already known this was going to happen, you know. But this is his way of getting my attention. He's showed me that there's a better way, a more peaceful way, a way of righteousness, truth, and understanding that will give us wisdom and help us make good decisions. He's taught me that you can't serve two masters. You can only love one and hate the other.

"So far, Nick, I feel good about myself even though I'm incarcerated. Drugs caused me to lose my wife and prevented me from having a good paying job and living a normal life. I might as well say that drugs caused me to die. But thank God, I've been born again, but this time, I have Jesus Christ in my life."

Nick looked at Steve surprisingly.

"Praise God, brother. Praise God," Nick said.

Nick stood five-nine and weighed 190 pounds. He had

brown eyes and was soft-spoken. He also had a warm personality and was very friendly. Since he'd been in prison, his personality had gotten him in trouble a few times with his own race. The Bible taught him to love his neighbor, to always show brotherly kindness, to be honest, and not to hate. But his race felt differently.

One day a couple Mexicans approached Nick.

"Who are you gonna run with? The South-Siders, the Border Brothers, or the blacks? You've got to choose one or the other. You can't be talking to those black guys, and you can't be attending prayer meetings or Bible study with them. You're a South-Sider, man, and we don't do it like that, you know what I mean? What if a riot breaks out right this minute? Who are you gonna go down with?"

"God said not to be prejudiced. He said to love and not to hate." Five Mexicans jumped him, giving Nick two black eyes and a busted nose. Afterward they threatened him.

"You heard what the fuck we said, homes! Don't have us come back and throw you over the fucking tier!"

Later that evening, Nick went to church with four black guys, three whites, and two Mexicans. *I'm a follower of Christ, not of men. I refuse to do what men tell me. I do what Christ tells me to do,* Nick thought.

"Tomorrow after lunch we're having Bible study, and I'm giving a testimony, Steve," Nick said after Steve and Nick conversed for another forty-five minutes. "Would you like to join us?"

"Sure, of course. That's about the best thing I've heard all day," Big Steve replied. He then said good night to Nick and fell asleep.

Two months later, Big Steve was transferred to the California Correctional Institution in Tehachapi.

CHAPTER 25

Detective Bell

Detective Robert Bell was a huge, black man. He stood six-four, weighed 342 pounds, and had a potbelly. Regardless of his weight, the detective was extremely quick on his feet. He was dark-skinned, had a pair of huge, serious eyes, and a cold, hard stare that was known to make the guilty confess. Bell had been working homicide for a little over ten years. Prior to that, the detective worked as an undercover narcotics agent, and before that he was a street cop. He had a reputation in the department for getting the job done. He was also known for his diligent detective strategies and tactics.

In addition to his years of police and detective experience, Detective Bell had a serious drinking problem. Each day before going home he would stop and buy himself a fifth of Wild Turkey. Then he'd go home and begin talking out loud after taking a few swallows, forming opinions about suspects, cases, judges, and lawyers. He would pace his den floor talking to himself and occasionally even answering. In spite of his drinking problem, Detective Bell took each case personally, and he was extremely careful about everything he did. He was a man of instinct, theory, and philosophy, and most times he was absolutely right when forming opinions about suspects. Due to his years of experience, Detective Bell had seen and heard it all. At least that's what he thought up until his current case.

There were lots of questions that needed answers regarding the Pullman case. The fresh bullet holes in the Suburban, the fake ID cards he'd found inside Melody's purse, and the whereabouts of her son. After going through Melody's house with a fine-toothed comb, instinct and experience told the detective there was more to this case than met the eye.

He began his investigation by writing down phone numbers from Melody's caller ID that had been made to the residence within the last week. So far, there had been no fingerprints found, nor were there any clues from the skid marks, which made things pretty difficult for the detective. He then phoned the telephone company to have Melody's phone records faxed to his office.

As the detective sat behind his desk, something troubled him about this case. While going over Melody's phone records, he thought, *This wasn't a robbery because nothing was taken and there aren't any signs of forced entry. Someone wanted her dead, but who and why is the question. From the looks of the bullet holes in the Suburban, someone tried to kill her before she made it inside her house. If Mrs. Pullman makes it, me and her have a lot to talk about. Hopefully she'll be out of the coma soon.*

He was on his way to Special Touch to question Tosha and the owners of the salon. After pulling Melody's records, he learned of her fight with Tosha. He hoped either Tosha, or the owners could give him more information.

After entering the salon, the detective stood eyeing each worker meticulously. The owners observed him, and instinct told them he wasn't there for a manicure, a pedicure, or a new hairstyle.

As usual, all sections of the salon were filled with customers, including the waiting area. The pedicurist, who was closest to the entry, was doing a pedicure on a fat lady, but she paused to greet the detective. Ignoring her, Detective Bell continued scanning each beautician, and had no problem spotting Tosha. He took deliberate steps toward Tosha, never taking his eyes off him. Nearing him, the detective wondered if a homosexual was capable of committing murder. He flashed his badge.

"Detective Bell. Riverside Homicide." Tosha smiled, continuing doing his customer's hair.

"Ump, where's your uniform, officer? I just love a man in uniform. They just look so, so manly, and so macho, and so—"

"Perhaps you'd like to come down to headquarters to answer my questions, sir?"

"You promise to handcuff me?"

"Enough of the bullshit," the detective announced angrily. All eyes in the salon, especially the owners, were on him.

"Damn, Tuffy, you don't play around, do you? I'll bet you're a real tiger in—"

The Detective's stare warned Tosha not to finish the comment. Smirking and setting down his styling tools, Tosha acquiesced.

"I'll be right back, Lisa. Hang tight for a minute while I see what Big Daddy wants. If I'm lucky, maybe he'll take me for a ride around the world, if you know what I mean," Tosha said sarcastically.

The detective then led Tosha out of the salon. Tosha had actually been enjoying the attention, but Detective Bell had no time for bullshit. He needed answers. Quick answers. Tosha was dressed in a pair of skin tight jeans, pink and white tennis shoes, and a white shirt, which was opened wide to reveal a tattoo on his chest.

"Am I under arrest?" Tosha asked smiling.

"Should you be?"

"That depends."

"Depends on what?" Detective Bell asked, glaring at Tosha.

"Well, I might have a couple of unpaid traffic tickets, but

that's about it. Anyway, Detective, ah, er, sorry, but I forgot your name. What's this all about?"

"Bell. Detective Bell is the name. Where were you last night between10:30 PM and 1:00 AM?"

Tosha smiled. "Humph, probably making love with my man, or just finishing. Me and my man can go on and on and on and—"

"Yeah, yeah, yeah, that's not sweet music to my ears, you know. Actually, I think it's rather disgusting. I know Tosha isn't your birth name, so for the record, let's have it," the detective demanded.

"Timothy Carter. But, please, Detective, don't tell anyone inside the salon."

"That depends on you. Now, back to the question. I take it you have an alibi for between ten thirty and one in the morning, correct?"

"Definitely. My man can—"

"What do you know about Melody Pullman? And be specific, Mr. Carter."

"Don't call me that, please," he requested. "Call me Tosha."

"Yeah, whatever."

"Humph, I'm trying to think of where to start. Well, let me start by saying that I can't stand that two-faced, phony bitch. Did you know she caused a long-term customer of hers to be paralyzed? That bitch isn't going to have nothing but bad luck. Believe me, Detective, someone's going to kill her if she doesn't stop doing what she's doing."

Detective Bell gave him a hard stare. "Sounds like you've got a lot of hatred for Mrs. Pullman, Mr. Carter."

"Don't call me that, Detective. I'm serious."

"I'll try not to forget. Anyway, who are the major players involved in Melody's love life, since you seem to know so much about her affairs?"

"Bottom line, Detective, Melody is a heartless husband thief.

The bitch has fucked many of her customers' husbands, and is still—"

"Have you ever joined her on an, ah, threesome or something? How would you know all of this? Were you there?"

"Nope, I wasn't there, but it's obvious. Anyway, I told her customer, Pat, about what I knew. I offered to take her in my car so they wouldn't spot hers. That way, she could see for herself that her husband was a no-good, low-down dog, and she could also see that her beautician was fucking her husband." Tosha paused. "What has the bitch done? Knowing her, like I said, the bitch might be—"

"She's in a coma. Last night someone tried to kill her in her sleep."

"No shit! Damn! I knew it, I knew it, I knew it. So that means that, hey, wait a minute," Tosha said. "It couldn't have been Pat, because she's paralyzed."

"Was it you?" the detective asked. "Sounds to me like you hated her." He studied Tosha's body language, waiting for a response.

"You're right, I did hate the bitch, and I hated her enough to kill her, but I didn't get the pleasure of doing so. I kicked her ass right here in the shop, but I didn't kill her. You see, I knew that sooner or later someone else would. It was just a matter of time. Humph, Pat's daughters may have tried to kill the bitch. I don't think they would've appreciated their beautician fucking their father, you know. Both of his daughters are attending college, and her son lives in Long Beach. Actually, I think they'd have a damn good, ah, what's the word I'm looking for?"

"Motive."

"Yeah, motive for killing her. Don't you?" Tosha asked, smiling and staring at the detective's crotch.

"It's not my question to answer, Mr. Carter."

"Quit calling me Mr. Carter, Detective. Show me some respect for what I am," Tosha snarled, holding his hands on his hips.

"Yeah, whatever. Anyway, do you by chance know the names of her daughters?" Tosha smiled.

"I take pride in memorizing names. Angela and Monique are the daughters' names, and the son's name is Randy. Angela's the oldest, and from what I hear, she's the smartest. Melody has a lot of damn nerve, because I heard through the stylist grapevine that she's been doing Angela's and Pat's hair every two weeks.

"I'd be willing to testify in court against Melody, Detective, because what she's been doing just doesn't make any damn sense. That is, of course, if she lives. I'd like the attention, you know, being the star witness in an attempted murder trial. Humph, do you think I can be on TV all over the world, like O.J.?"

Detective Bell spent another hour or so talking with Tosha, getting all the information he could possibly get.

"Give me an address and phone number where I can reach you," Bell said when he was finished. "I'll talk to a friend of mine to see about getting your picture on the front page of the local newspaper. I'll be in touch, Mr. Carter." He then handed Tosha a business card and walked away, heading back to the station.

It was 2:30 when the detective sat down behind his desk. His boss, Lieutenant Sparrow, spotted him and immediately buzzed him into his office for a conference. Detective Bell was his most reliable homicide detective.

"What's up LT?" Detective Bell asked, shuffling through papers.

"That's what I'm trying to find out, Bell."

"I rounded up a few bits and pieces, but still nothing solid yet." Detective Bell approached the LT's desk. "Got some interesting info from a fag she used to work with, but I have to do some follow-up to make sure things check out. He says that, ah, our victim was screwing her long-term customer's husband. That opens a door for motive. Also, I spoke to an old customer of hers who claimed our vic was bumping pussies with another woman. There's still a few bases I need to cover before I start bringing in suspects."

"I see. Well, I need you to stay on top of it, Bell. The Captain's in my ass about this case, and he wants someone to answer for it. Keep me informed, will you?"

"You bet," Detective Bell replied. He then turned and walked out of the LT's office.

After retrieving his faxes, Detective Bell went back to his desk. The phone records revealed all calls that had been made from and received at Melody's address for the past month. As the detective examined his list he put a check mark by Tosha's name, reminding himself that he'd already spoken with him. Relaxing in his high-back leather chair, he began thinking.

One down, six to go. Next I'll see what Larry and his daughters have to say. Then I'll speak with Pat. I'll save the mystery lesbian woman for last. There's still lots of pieces missing to this puzzle. The bullet holes in the Suburban, for starters. I really need to talk to Melody, but that's impossible at the moment. I'd better phone the hospital, talk with her doctor, and instruct him to give me a call when she's conscious.

After speaking with Melody's doctor, Detective Bell then dialed Larry's cell number.

"Hello," Larry answered.

"Larry Myers?" Detective Bell asked and then identified himself. "Detective Bell, Riverside Homicide. We need to talk. Immediately."

"About what?"

"Melody Pullman, sir. We can do this the hard way, by having you picked up, or we can do it the easy way by arranging an immediate meeting." The detective was very firm.

"Sorry, detective, but I—"

"No problem, Mr. Myers. I'll have a squad car pick you up and bring you to me, since you don't want to cooperate."

"All right, all right, you win. Where and when do you want to meet, detective?"

"You name the place."

"OK, but I don't have all day. There's a dollar store on the corner of Alessandro and Perris Boulevard. I'll be sitting in front of it in a white Ford pickup."

"Stay there," the detective ordered. "I'm driving a white Plymouth."

"Yeah, OK. But what is this—" The line went dead.

Twenty minutes later, Detective Bell was parking in front of the dollar store. Instinct told him that the high-yellow complexioned man leaning against the white truck was Larry.

"Larry Myers? Detective Bell, Riverside Homicide." He offered a handshake. "Do you like Chinese?" Bell asked out of the blue.

"Nope. I'm a fish and chicken man," Larry replied with folded arms.

"It's my treat," the detective offered without any expression.

"Hey, man, listen. I've got hundreds of things to do much more important than having a worthless conversation with you. I've never been in trouble with the law in my life, and—"

"Easy, Larry, easy," the detective said. He was aggravated by Larry's tone and choice of words. "Maybe you'll be more comfortable at my house, Larry, if you know what I mean. Now let's cut the shit and this won't take long. It wouldn't be too nice, Larry, if your wife finds out you've been fucking her hairdresser for the past four or five years, would it? Believe me, I have witnesses who'll be more than happy to testify to your affair. Can we sit and talk, or do we take a ride to the station and call the wife to join us?" the detective threatened.

"Come on, man, let's get this over with," Larry replied. He then followed the detective through the parking lot.

"You've been having things your way, huh, Larry? I mean, a wife and a mistress. Some guys have all the luck, huh?"

"What's this all about, man? I've got a business to run." They were entering the restaurant.

"Where were you last night between 10:30 PM and 1:00 AM?" the detective asked firmly.

"At home, in bed, sleeping," Larry replied.

"Home alone? Oh, I'm sorry, Larry, I forgot you're a married man," Detective Bell said sarcastically. "By the way, someone tried to kill your mistress last night. You wouldn't happen to know anything about that, would you?"

"Melody?" Larry responded, shocked. "Someone tried to kill Melody? Where is she? Is she all right? Who would want to kill Melody?"

"For starters, Larry, try your wife. Secondly, try your daughters or your son."

"My wife? My daughters? My son? Are you crazy?"

After being seated and going over the menu, Detective Bell continued his interrogation.

"Was your wife in bed with you?"

"Of course she was. She's paralyzed. She couldn't leave if she wanted to."

"Where were your daughters and son?" Detective Bell was studying Larry with an experienced eye.

"Angela was home sleeping, Monique's in Florida attending college, and Randy was more than likely at home with his family in Long Beach. You couldn't possibly think my son or daughters tried to kill Melody."

"At this point, everyone's a suspect," the detective replied.

The Chinese waiter appeared, took their orders, then disappeared.

"Tell me more about Melody. Is she OK or what?" Larry asked, concerned.

"She's in a coma," Detective Bell answered, still studying Larry. "Yep, like I said, everyone's a suspect."

"Now seriously, detective," Larry said, "you've got to be kidding if you think anyone in my family tried to kill Melody. We're all law abiding citizens, not killers."

"I'll need your son's phone number and address. Also, I need to speak with your daughters, and I absolutely need to speak with your wife to verify your alibi, and to answer a few questions as well. You wouldn't have a problem with that, would you, Larry?"

"Not at all, but I hope you're not planning on bringing up my affair with Melody to my wife or kids. Besides, it ended over five or six months ago."

After their food was delivered, Detective Bell continued.

"So, you haven't tapped that ass in five or six months, huh? Did she find someone new, or did she find someone with a larger pipe?"

"Man, to tell you the truth, Melody somehow got hooked on pussy," Larry replied, shaking his head in disgust. "She met some rich bitch named Michelle, who has a house on the beach and drives a convertible Mercedes."

"Is that right? So, if you were banging Melody, then how would you know where this rich lesbian chick lives?" the detective asked while chewing a piece of orange chicken. "Oh, don't tell me, Melody told you where she lives, right?"

"Hell no, man," Larry replied while munching chicken chow mein. "You're not gonna believe this, but—"

"I probably won't," the detective interrupted.

"I received a call one day on my way home from Melody's. It was Michelle telling me we needed to talk urgently. She gave me her address and told me to meet her ASAP at her beach home."

"Don't tell me," Detective Bell interrupted. "She wanted to test you in bed, right?"

"Damn right she did, but like a damn fool, I didn't fuck her," Larry said, shaking his head.

"You mean to tell me you turned her down?"

"Yep."

"Why?"

"Because the bitch wanted to play 'Let's Make a Deal,' and I wasn't down for it," Larry replied. He washed down his food with a glass of water, then continued. "She offered me her pussy if I promised to stop fucking Melody, but I didn't want to make a promise I probably wouldn't keep. I mean, man, she got naked and threw the pussy all in my face. But once she saw I was turning down her pussy, she offered me ten grand, man. Ten fucking thousand dollars to stop fucking Melody. Can you believe that shit?"

"Not really. Sounds like a bunch of bullshit to me, but keep talking."

"Think what you wanna think, man, but I'm telling you the honest to God truth," Larry said, eating his last piece of sweet and sour chicken.

"I'll let you know when to come down to the station, but for right now, I'm about to see if your alibi checks out by asking your wife and daughters a few questions. I'll get to your son later."

After bringing their lunch and discussion to an end, Detective Bell looked at the bill and smiled. *Not bad considering the info I got,* he thought.

After paying the tab and leaving a non-generous tip, Detective Bell and Larry left. While walking to their vehicles, the detective thought of a last minute question.

"By the way, Larry, do you still love her?"

"Who?" Larry asked, not knowing whether the detective was referring to his wife or Melody.

"Your mistress, Melody."

"I told you, Detective, I haven't been with Melody in five or six months. As a matter of fact, she called me with some shit about being pregnant by me, but when I told her I'd had a vasectomy after my last child, she cursed me out and hung up."

"Seems to me like the ball bounces in your favor pretty often, Larry. Some guys have all the luck. Some guys get all the breaks, huh?"

"What can I say?" Larry answered.

"Yeah, whatever. Anyway, I need a contact number for your daughter in Florida. Oh, and something else, do you plan on going to the hospital to see Melody?"

"If she's in a coma, she wouldn't know me from the man on the moon, right? I don't know. Maybe, maybe not."

Asshole, the detective thought. *I don't like assholes like him.*

Driving down Perris Boulevard, going to question Pat, Detective Bell thought about Melody.

The bullet holes in her vehicle, the fake IDs, Larry, her lesbian lover—something just doesn't add up. None of this actually motivates someone to murder. The only person who has a good motive is Larry's wife, and she's not capable of pulling it off alone. Something's missing. Hopefully I'll find out after talking to his wife and daughters. Once I've questioned everyone on my list, I'll do a background check on them. Sooner or later something has to break.

He parked in front of the Myers' residence. The house was light green, trimmed with dark green oil-based paint that shined like it had recently been buffed. It sat on five acres of well-kept grass, and had a circular driveway which held a Lexus, an Astro van, a 1964 convertible Corvette, and a new Honda Accord.

Approaching the front door, the detective noticed two red Doberman Pinschers, one at each end of the house, about to charge him, but they were stopped by a chain that only allowed them to go a certain distance. Quickly, he pulled out his pistol. The dogs were barking and growling viciously at him when Angela appeared on the steps.

"Boy! Girl! Get out of here! Get out of here!" she yelled to the dogs.

"Apparently they knew I was coming, huh?" the detective

said after putting his gun away. "He then introduced himself. "Detective Bell, Riverside Homicide," he said as he extended his hand.

She stared at him curiously and accepted his handshake.

"I'm Angela Myers. How can I help you, Detective?"

"I'm investigating an attempted murder on Mrs. Melody Pullman. I need to ask you and your mother a few questions. Your names and phone numbers were in her phone records, Miss Myers. That's how I found your address."

"Someone tried to kill Melody?" Angela responded hysterically. "Who? Why? When? She's me and my mom's beautician." After a moment Angela quickly regained her composure. "Come in and have a seat, Detective," she said politely.

"Thank you, Angela." He followed her inside.

"Have a seat, Detective Bell, and I'll go get my mother."

"Fine."

As Detective Bell sat on the white, antique furniture, he couldn't help but notice how uniquely the living room was furnished. On the wall facing him there was a huge glass mirror trimmed in a shiny gold that matched perfectly with the furniture. An expensive chandelier made of glittering crystal hung attractively from the ceiling, and a china cabinet made of redwood sat prominently in the corner. A picture of Martin Luther King, Jr. was on the wall to his right, while a huge, colorful picture of Nelson Mandela hung on the wall to his left.

Seconds later Angela reappeared, wheeling Pat into the living room.

"Mom, this is Detective Bell. Detective Bell, this is my mother," Angela introduced.

The detective stood up, approached Pat, and graciously extended his hand. "Nice to meet you, Mrs. Myers."

She accepted the handshake. "Likewise, Detective. How may I help you?"

The medication Pat had been taking was doing its job well. Gradually, thanks to Angela, Pat's mind was getting back to normal. Her medication was now given to her properly, and Selma had been doing an outstanding job of taking care of her needs, as well as the needs of the house.

Pat's hair was looking marvelous and her self-esteem and motivation were being restored daily. Bits and pieces of her memory were coming back to her, but unfortunately, the nightmares of conversing with a homosexual continually flashed through her mind. She had discussed the nightmares with Angela, but could only guess at what was causing them.

Pat was positioned directly in front of Detective Bell. Angela seated herself in the high back antique chair. The detective studied both women for a few moments.

"I'm here, Mrs. Myers, regarding an attempted murder on Mrs. Melody Pullman," he began. "I'm going to try to make this as brief as possible. Ladies, I need to know your whereabouts between 10:30 PM and 1:00 AM last night."

"What!" Pat responded frantically. "You mean someone tried to kill Melody? My beautician, Melody?"

"I'm afraid so, ma'am."

"Why? She's been, oh my God. I-I-I was here in bed with my husband, Detective, and my daughter was in her room asleep. I don't understand what our whereabouts have to do with an attempted murder on Melody."

"I'm questioning everyone who's had contact with Mrs. Pullman in the past month, Mrs. Myers."

"Is she all right? I mean, you're from homicide, and—"

"She's in a coma at the moment on the fifth floor of Riverside General Hospital. Homicide Division, Mrs. Myers, handles murder cases as well as attempted murder cases."

"I hope she'll be all right. Oh my God. Well, to satisfy you curiosity, Detective, I called Melody to set up an appointment. That would explain why my number is on her phone records." Pat stuttered slightly, still not believing that Melody was almost killed.

"Do you normally stutter, Mrs. Myers?" He studied her carefully.

"What are you insinuating, Detective?" Angela interrupted. "My mother is not capable of committing murder, if that's what you're getting at! You're climbing the wrong tree, Detective, and I would appreciate it if you—"

"Calm down, Angela, calm down. I never said your mother was capable of committing murder. Please keep in mind that I'm investigating an attempted homicide, and there are certain questions I have to ask," the detective explained evenly.

"But you're questioning the wrong people, and I won't allow—"

"How can I tell?"

"Because, Detective, we're law abiding citizens. As we speak, I'm in my third year of law school and studying for the state bar exam. Soon I'll be a district attorney. And I hope like hell I don't get cops like you bringing me suspects you assume committed a crime. Both my mother and myself are people of integrity and dignity, and it would very well please both me and my mother if you would leave. Now!" She stood with her hands on her hips, giving him an I-wish-you'd-hurry-up-and-get-the-fuck-out-of-this-house look.

"You'll both be notified if we need to ask you some more questions. Don't leave on any unplanned vacations." Detective Bell said before Angela could slam the door behind him. The Dobermans charged at him once again, but the chain prevented them from getting to him. But just in case, he drew his weapon.

After the detective left, Larry came out of the garage, pretending he hadn't known the detective had been there. He had been listening for Bell's vehicle to leave.

"What's the matter, Angela? Did I hear you arguing with someone?"

"Yes, you did, Dad. Get Mom ready, quick. I'll tell you about it on the way to the hospital. Someone tried to kill Melody last night and we're going to visit her."

Larry did an excellent job of playing dumb.

* * *

Once the detective made it home, he poured himself a glass of Wild Turkey and sat behind his desk. There were still lots of unanswered questions and missing pieces to the puzzle. After a few sips he began thinking.

I guess I'll eliminate the future D.A. and her mother, but for the record I'll still keep them in the back of my mind. Larry is just an unfaithful asshole and that fucking faggot is a freak by nature. Now, I ask myself whether I think any of these suspects attempted to kill Mrs. Pullman. The answer is no. Now, let me ask myself whether I think any of the suspects conspired to kill Mrs. Pullman. Nope, none of them. That means that my job isn't anywhere near complete. Like Angela said, I'm climbing up the wrong tree. Maybe the answer lies with Michelle or her son's father. Hopefully it does.

Two glasses later the detective was out like a light.

The following morning, after coffee and a heavy breakfast, Detective Bell went to his office and dialed Kenneth's phone number.

"Hello."

"Is this the Coleman residence?"

"Who's calling?" Michael, Kenneth's son, answered.

"Detective Bell, Riverside Homicide."

"Detective who? River who, homo who?"

"Is your father home?"

"Who's calling?"

"Are you his secretary or his answering machine?"

"Who is this?" Kenneth asked as he snatched the phone from Michael.

"Detective Bell, Riverside Homicide."

"This is Mr. Coleman. How can I help you, detective?"

"I'm calling from Riverside, California, Mr. Coleman, and I'm afraid I have some bad news for you, but for now I need to ask you a few questions."

"What kind of bad news, Detective? I have no business in Riverside."

"Isn't Melody Pullman the mother of your son?"

"Yes she is, but what—"

"Someone broke into her house and attempted to kill her while she was asleep."

"What? You've got to be kidding."

"She's in a coma at Riverside General Hospital, Mr. Coleman. I already know the situation with your son. How soon can you make it to Riverside?"

"Well, I'm five hours away, and it's 10:15 now. With traffic and all I should be able to make it there by six."

"Excellent. My number is 555-0099, and the station address is 122 Police Plaza. If you will, Mr. Coleman, stop by and talk to me before going to the hospital."

"Will do," Kenneth replied.

Five minutes later, Detective Bell was dialing Michelle's number.

"Hello," Michelle answered.

"Michelle, please?"

"Yes, this is Michelle. Who's this?"

"Detective Bell, Riverside Homicide."

"Is this regarding Melody?"

"Yes, how did you know?"

"I arrived at her home a few minutes ago, and I'm presently talking to three of her neighbors. Sorry, Detective, but I've got to go to the hospital," Michelle replied and then flipped her cell phone closed.

"Damn!" the Detective shouted. "I guess I'm on my way to Riverside General, but first I'll run a CBC (Criminal Background Check) on the suspects I've already questioned."

After searching for over an hour, Detective Bell discovered that neither Larry, Angela, Pat, nor Kenneth had a criminal background.

What the hell's going on? Everyone's clean. Shit. Something has got to give, he thought. He then redialed Michelle's number.

"Michelle, this is Detective Bell."

"Yes?"

"How's she doing?"

"She's still in a coma, but I've spoken to Dr. Maxwell, and he told me that if she does happen to live, the bullet would have to remain inside her head. He said it couldn't be removed without causing severe brain damage. But the good news is that she could possibly still live a normal life even with the bullet inside her head," Michelle explained.

"How long are you planning on being there, Miss, er, ah—"

"Green. Michelle Green. I assume you have some questions for me, right, Detective?"

"Yes, I do have questions for you, Miss Green."

"In that case, what time will you be here, Detective?"

"Is one thirty OK?"

"Perfect."

After hanging up, Detective Bell smiled at his cleverness in getting Michelle's name. He then ran her name through the CBC process. As he stared into his computer monitor he couldn't believe his eyes. Michelle Green was not only married to a Rosie Martinez Green, but she also had an arrest record as long as Interstate 10.

"I'll be goddamn!" the detective said out loud. "Michelle Green had been arrested for fraud, grand larceny, grand theft personal property, and commercial burglary. She's spent four and a half years in prison, and two and a half years in L.A., Orange, and Riverside County Jails each. "She's a fucking career criminal."

CHAPTER 26

Big Steve

The bus had finally arrived at California Correctional Institution in Tehachapi. During the entire bus ride all Big Steve thought about was Melody. She was actually all he wanted to think about.

My Melody, he thought. *I wish she would write me. I wish she would treat me right and love me like she promised to. I don't care if she had an affair with someone else, I'm still in love with her and I can't deny it. She was my first and hopefully she'll be my last.* He'd fallen asleep and dreamed about her.

Due to overcrowding, Steve, along with eight other inmates, were sent to a level four yard, which is the highest security level in the prison system. Walking down the tier to his cell, Big Steve felt tense.

Why did they send me around prisoners with life sentences? I've got to talk with the warden about this. Maybe he'll let me sleep in the church. I'm scared. He felt like he was entering the point of no return. Lifers appeared at their cell doors as Steve walked toward his cell. The warden had asked each lifer if they wanted a cellmate, but all of them had responded, "Hell no!" All but one inmate. His name was Tiny.

Even though Big Steve was nervous, he built up his confidence and began walking coolly and with toughness. He told himself that if someone asked him when his release date was, he would lie and tell them he had thirty-five years left. He knew he couldn't let these lifers know his date was in a couple years. A lifer didn't want to hear any shit like that.

A lifer named Black suddenly yelled out.

"If they open this fuckin' cell, I'm gonna snatch you in here and beat the hell outta you!" Black had killed four police officers in the early sixties, and was serving a life sentence.

Steve continued his cool, tough stroll, then developed a mean look. He began mumbling things like, "What's up, fool? Yeah, that's right. Yeah, we gonna do the damn thing, you know what I'm sayin'," but another lifer still tested him.

"Man, you ain't shit!" a lifer named Tuffy yelled. "I think you're as soft as cotton, punk! You're lucky you ain't comin' in here, 'cause I'll ride you like Lone Ranger rode Silver!" Tuffy had been locked up for twenty-five years, and he still had another twenty-five to go.

Big Steve ignored his threats and kept strolling.

Then another lifer named Meat Loaf yelled out. "I smell bloody pussy! I think you're on your period, nigga. You better change your Kotex! Whatcha gonna do, huh? Whatcha gonna do, fool?"

The other lifers waited for Steve's reaction. Realizing he was on the spot Steve dropped his blanket, sheets, and personal property, and began parading swiftly back and forth.

"Who said that?" Steve yelled. "Who's the bad muthafucka on this row that said that? Speak up, coward! Is your tongue stuck in your mama's pussy or sump'n?" He stormed up to each cell, looking each lifer in the eye. "Speak up, bitch! You were talking all that shit a minute ago. What's up, fool? Talk, muthafucka, talk!" No one said a word. Big Steve then picked up his belongings and walked back toward his cell.

"I got thirty-five years to do in this muthafucka," Steve boldly yelled. "And I can see I'm gonna have to kill a whole bunch of fools while I'm here! I guess y'all ain't read the front page lately, though, 'cause I'm that nigga! Read the front page, muthafuckas, then come talk to me!" Deep inside he was nervous as a puppy in the ring with four killer bulls.

Cell number 289 finally opened for him. Blocking the entry was a 380-pound, seven foot, jet black man, who looked like he belonged in a jungle with a gorilla family. Big Steve glanced at his bare feet and guessed they had to be anywhere from a size eighteen to a twenty-four. Steve wanted to drop his belongings, turn around, and run, but the huge man stepped aside.

"Hi, my name is Tiny," the giant said in a soft voice. "What's yours?" Steve was shocked by the soft, squeaky voice that came from this behemoth man.

"I'm Steve. How you doin', Tiny?" They shook hands. For a few moments, silence filled the room. As Steve began situating his belongings, Tiny stared at him and then began asking questions.

"Hey, Steve, tell me how the streets is, man. I been locked up for years, and you're about the closest thing I'm gonna get to the streets." Tiny was now sitting on the edge of the toilet. "I'm just a big ole country boy from Crockett's Bluff, Tennessee. Those white folks said I did, though, but man, I'm tellin' you, Steve, I didn't do it. But I'll tell you what I did do, though. I killed me two white policemen back in 1959 on the outskirts of Greenwood, Mississippi. Yep. I sho' did. I was walkin' down the road comin' from my Auntie Georgia Mae's house, you know. I had just picked me some lemons so's I could make me some homemade lemonade. Anyway, those sons of bitches stopped me, talking 'bout I slapped a white woman. I told 'em I ain't slapped no white woman, and I told 'em I ain't even seen no white woman in three, four years, but they didn't believe me, Steve. They said I fit the description, so they tried to handcuff me, talkin' 'bout I'm fixin' to go to prison for the rest of my life, but I couldn't let 'em do it, Steve, so's I grabbed both of 'em by the neck and squeezed them till they didn't breathe no mo'. Then I threw 'em down a cliff, then pushed they car down there too, and then I went on 'bout my way to make me some lemonade."

Big Steve did not doubt what Tiny had said. Instead of dwelling on that, he asked what Tiny wanted to know about the streets.

"Man, jus' tell me 'bout the streets, man," Tiny smiled, revealing a row of small teeth, which appeared to be too small for his huge head.

Each lifer on the tier waited impatiently to hear Steve talk about the streets. It had been over twenty years since many of them had talked with anyone who had recently left the streets.

Glad to be accepted, Big Steve stood in front of the cell door and began telling street tales.

"OK, Tiny, check it out. A while back, I had three bitches suckin' my dick at the same time. A bitch named Tastee pulled out her false teeth, and man, she gummed the hell out of my dick, man. At the same time another bitch was licking my balls and twirling her finger inside my ass, and another bitch was sitting on my face. Man, those bitches showed me the time of my life." Tiny busted out in laughter, and so did the tier of lifers.

"Tell me anotha' story, man. Tell anotha' one," Tiny begged, smiling. All the lifers yelled, "Yeah, tell anotha' one!" Getting all this attention made Big Steve not only feel accepted, but also more at ease. He hoped and prayed his stay on the level four yard would go quickly and smoothly.

"OK, Tiny, check this out," Steve said. "Man, people are doing just about anything for crack nowadays. I mean anything, man. People are stealing from their mamas, grandmothers, and kids, and even setting up family members, man. Women is out there sucking dick for two dollars, lawyers and doctors are on the shit, people are even dropping out of college, man. I've got an uncle named Kirk who's confined to a wheelchair. He had a five bedroom house that was paid for, right? His wife died ten years ago, but somehow he hooked up with a bitch on crack, and a week later, he started smoking it. It took him fifty years to start using drugs. He lost his house and his car behind that shit, and on top of that, the crackhead bitch left him too."

"No shit, man?" Tiny asked.

"I'm telling you some real shit, man," Big Steve said.

"Tell me anotha' one, man, tell anotha' one," Tiny begged again.

The lifers on the tier enjoyed Big Steve's stories so much they began passing him soups, stamped envelopes, cans of tuna, and pouches of tobacco and coffee to show their appreciation for being entertained. Steve told them street stories until four in the morning.

The following morning after breakfast, a C.O. came to escort the tier to the yard. The prisoners discovered that the weights had been taken off the yard for security reasons, and they went ballistic.

"Ah, hell no!" Black shouted angrily.

"What the fuck!" Tuffy yelled furiously.

"Somebody fixin' to die around here! Ain't nobody but those fuckin' white folks!" Meat Loaf shouted.

Tiny didn't care too much about weights because he was already big and strong. As long as they didn't take his punching bag, he was fine.

Big Steve walked side by side with Tiny toward the punching bag, but suddenly came to a halt when he witnessed a group of prisoners charging a C.O.

"Lie down, Steve!" Tiny instructed. The riot was on. A group of prisoners grabbed the C.O., stuck him several times with prison-made weapons, then stomped him, but shots from a mini-14 quickly quelled the riot, killing several of the prisoners.

Counting the C.O., twelve lifeless bodies were lying on the ball field. The yard went on lockdown pending an investigation.

A lifer named James Johnson, who went by the name of J.J., worked as a clerk in the operations office. For some reason, J.J.

envied Big Steve. He didn't believe he was a killer, nor did he believe he had thirty-five years. To J.J., Steve just didn't seem capable of being a killer, so he took it upon himself to do a little investigating.

"I'm tellin' you, Red," J.J. had said to a prisoner in the next cell, "he ain't no killer! He's a goddamn clown, if anything! He laughs too much and tells too many jokes to be a killer! Ain't no muthafucka in the world who got thirty-five years to do, gonna laugh 24/7! I'm tellin' you, Red, it's sump'n fishy 'bout that nigga, man! When I get the chance, I'm gonna check out that fool's file."

The following day while working, J.J. obtained Big Steve's file.

I knew it! J.J. thought. *I knew he wasn't no killer!* He then made up an excuse to get off work early, telling his boss, the lieutenant, that he had a headache and wasn't feeling good. The lieutenant, because of J.J.'s loyalty to him, granted his request. J.J. had been the lieutenant's clerk for the past eleven years. There was nothing that went down on the yard that J.J. didn't know about, which meant that there was nothing the lieutenant, captain, and warden weren't aware of. J.J. was somewhat indispensable to his superiors. He had earned plenty of clout during his reign as a lieutenant's clerk, and he had always taken advantage of opportunities to find out what each prisoner was convicted of, how many times they'd been to prison, and the length of their sentences. Even though he played the tough guy role he was nothing more than a snitch.

J.J. reported all illegal activities to the warden, which was another reason he made $250 a month, when the average inmate only received fifty dollars a month for his job. If he knew where any shanks were hidden, whether they were hidden in an inmate's cell, or on the yard, J.J. would report it to the warden. If he heard news about a fight, or a riot about to take place, the warden would always be informed. J.J. considered himself an asset to the prison. His rewards were small favors—being able

to occasionally use the office phone, being able to be transferred to any cell he requested, having frequent snacks, such as
cookies, potato chips, peanut butter and jelly, and jars of coffee, and he was even given a pack of Kools from time to time.

J.J. strolled down the tier like he was late for dinner, and before he got to Steve's cell, he began talking loudly, sharing with
the other lifers what he had discovered.

"I knew it! I knew it! I fuckin' knew it!" J.J. yelled. He was
now standing at Tiny and Steve's cell. "You artificial muthafucka! You're phony, a liar, and a bitch on top of that! I pulled
your card, nigga! You ain't got no fuckin' thirty-five years! Your
record wasn't hard to read because it's only one sheet of
paper!"

Tiny looked bewildered, and Big Steve was embarrassed. He
was put on the spot in front of an audience who enjoyed his en-
tertaining skills, and now he was at a loss for words. He thought
about telling more street stories to divert the listeners' attention, but the bomb had already been dropped, and it was too
late. J.J. continued revealing everything about Big Steve.

"He only got five years, y'all! Five little punk years! I'm gonna
beat your ass, man. As soon as you step out of that cell, I'm
fuckin' you up, man, you can believe that!" J.J. threatened.

Tiny glanced at Steve, then at J.J., and then back to Big Steve.

CHAPTER 27

Melody

Four-and-a-half months after he shooting, Melody came out of the coma. When she first opened her eyes, the faces surrounding her were blurry. Stella, her mother, had been rubbing her forehead for the past half hour, and she was actually the first person Melody had a clear vision of. Then Michelle and Pat's faces came into view, then Antoinette and Tony, and then Kenneth, Byron, and Angela. The last person she noticed was Larry.

A few minutes prior to her awakening, Angela had been reviewing paperwork for a case she was about to try. She had passed the state bar exam a couple of months earlier, and had been hired as an assistant D.A. for Riverside County.

Angela moved closer to Melody and looked into her eyes.

"Girl, you'd better get out of this bed so you can do me and Mom's hair. As a matter of fact" she said, looking at the other women, "it looks like all of us need immediate hair attention, and I don't think any of us are about to let anyone else touch our hair, so hurry and get well soon, Mel. There's lots of green to be made."

Michelle moved closer and began stroking Melody's arm. "You're going to be all right, Mel. Hang in there, OK?" She then began rubbing her forehead and smiling. "And have I got a surprise for you when you come home."

Melody's eyes slowly shifted from Michelle to Byron. She wanted to squeeze his hand and tell him she loved him. He approached her bed and kissed her. She then looked to her left and saw Kenneth. Her migraines wouldn't allow her to think. First of all, she couldn't figure out why she was in a hospital bed. Why were these people who were a part of her life surrounding her like she was about to die? Her head was hurting much too badly for her to figure it out. Then Antoinette approached her.

"Hey, sis, what's up? Your nieces and nephew ask about you every day. They be saying, 'I wanna go to Auntie's house, Mommy, so she can take me to the movies and buy me some candy and some McDonald's and a bubblegum machine.' I sure wish you would hurry and come home so they'll quit bugging me every day. Besides, I'm due for a perm, sis, and you know I'm not about to let anyone else touch my hair."

Tears ran from Stella's eyes as she looked at her daughter lying there in misery.

"Chile," Stella said, "I sure wish you would come on home so I can fix you some collard greens, some black eyed peas, banana puddin', and some dressing and macaroni and cheese and . . ." Stella then burst into tears. "Why? Why, baby? Why would somebody wanna try to kill you?"

Both Antoinette and Byron embraced her. Melody's mind wasn't stable enough for her to understand what was going on. She just lay there trying to make sense out of the wires that were connected to her. She wanted to ask questions, but she didn't have the strength. She lay there, puzzled, staring at the ceiling like the answers to her questions were about to drop down on her.

Michelle had been paying Melody's bills, including her mortgage payment, since she had been in the hospital. She felt that that was the least she could do for her. She had also bought a fixer-upper commercial building and had it completely re-modeled and converted into a salon. That was the surprise she had for Melody. The huge sign on top of the building read: Melody's Extraordinary Hair, Nails, and Feet. The building was a bank repo, so Michelle had gotten a pretty good deal on it. The equipment and furnishings had run her a little over ten thousand dollars, and the remodeling and custom work ran another twenty thousand. She had purchased the building for less than seventy-five thousand dollars, which was the deal of a lifetime.

One day, before Melody came out of the coma, Michelle went to Melody's home to pick up her bills so she could pay them. While she was there, she had a brief conversation with Stella and Antoinette, who were staying at Melody's place while she was in the hospital.

Stella was a sweet old lady who was born in the south and looked ten years younger than Melody. She was smartly dressed, wearing a two-piece short pantsuit, sandals, and a pair of prescription glasses that accented her appearance. She was a short, swift woman, who talked fast and moved even faster.

Stella had heard through the grapevine that her daughter was messing around with a wealthy lesbian woman. She was already aware of Melody sleeping with her customer's husband, and she didn't approve of it, but she still loved her daughter.

"It's her life, and if that's the way she wants to live it, then that's on her. As long as she doesn't bring that bullshit around me, I could care less what she does. But she needs to take her ass to church and find herself a real husband. That's what she needs to do," Stella would say.

Stella wasn't into the lesbian/gay thing, and she damn sure didn't believe in 'don't knock it until you try it,' especially not any uncivilized shit like that. When Melody's older brother, Tony, had first told Stella about his sister's affairs, Stella had shouted, "Don't come tellin' me no shit like that, boy! I don't wanna hear it!" Tony had lied to her so many times in his forty-one years that Stella hardly believed anything he said. Actually, in this case, she didn't want to believe him. Even though he was the oldest, he was considered the snitch of the family. He couldn't keep a secret, and he couldn't wait to tell a family member what another family had done, or was doing.

Melody's sister, Antoinette, who was a police officer, had been sitting at the dining room table when Michelle entered. Antoinette was also aware of, and disapproved of, her sister's relationship with a married man. Unlike her mother, Antoinette was a snotty bitch with an attitude. She was happily married with three beautiful children—two girls and a boy—but she paraded around on earth like her shit didn't stink. She was light-brown complexioned, had long, pretty hair, stood five-seven, and was blessed with a bountiful chest. To add to that, she had a trim waistline, a nice butt, and a pair of big, brown, intelligent eyes. Her look was always serious, and she hardly ever smiled.

"Hi," Michelle said cheerfully.

"Hi, how you doing?" Stella replied with a warm southern smile.

Antoinette turned up her nose and walked away.

"I didn't mean to intrude on you and your daughter's privacy, but I just came over to pick up the bills so I could pay them. Melody's credit was pretty bad when I first met her, but together we straightened it out. Now it's A-1," Michelle proudly said.

"Yeah, I know what you mean, girl. The way that girl's credit was, she probably couldn't buy a damn skateboard on credit, chile," Stella replied.

"Oh, and by the way," Michelle said while scooping up eleven letters with *California State Prison* stamped in huge print on the front of the envelope, "I ran across a good deal on an old building and had it converted into a hair and nail salon for her. Here, I even had her business cards printed. Why don't you and Antoinette stop by and take a look at it? Here are the keys. It's less than five minutes away," Michelle said, smiling.

"Girl, you gotta be kiddin' me. You know that girl been doin' hair ever since she was nine, and she always talked about having her own shop one day. Hell, but with her always bein' up to her neck in bills, and bein' a single parent, she just couldn't afford it. I know she's gonna be grateful for it, Michelle. Praise the Lord, chile," Stella said happily.

"I'm sure she will. I figure she should be healthy and ready to return to work in less than a month or so if she's lucky."

"I hope so, chile, 'cause she's sure been through a lot, you know. I sure hope everything turns out all right."

"Well, Mrs., ah?"

"Swift. Stella Swift, chile, but everybody calls me Stella."

"Stella, we're going to do everything in our power to make sure Melody comes out on top of things, but for now, I have to go take care of these bills, then I have to resolve a problem at one of my businesses. You take care, Stella, and I'll most definitely be in touch. Here's my card. If you ever need anything, and I mean anything, don't hesitate to call. See you around," Michelle said, and then shook Stella's hand and left.

Antoinette reappeared and began mocking Michelle.

"'If there's anything I can ever do for you, I mean anything, don't hesitate calling. I'm going to do everything in my power to see that Melody comes out on top of things. I have to go resolve a problem at one of my businesses.' Mama, you better watch out for that gay bitch, because before you know it she'll be trying to bump pussies and grind on you."

"Quit talking crazy, chile."

"Just watch out for her, Mama. I don't want to have to kill that bitch!"

"Cut it out now, Antoinette. All she's tryin' to do is help your sister. Now come on, take me down here to see this girl's new salon, chile."

Michelle read the letters Steve had written to Melody one by one.

I need to take care of this before it escalates into something more, or before he gets misled or builds up false hopes. Melody belongs to me and only me. I'll make damn sure this Big Steve character knows it!

She pulled into an Office Depot parking lot, and using her laptop, composed a letter to Big Steve. It read:

To: Big Steve
From: Michelle / Melody's Lover
This is not a letter that requires pleasantries. You've blown your chance with Melody. You chose drugs over her simply because you loved smoking crack more than you loved her and Byron, so buzz off. She's given you several opportunities to prove yourself, but you've failed each time. Buzz off, crackhead. She belongs to me. And yes, I am a woman. I'll have my attorney send you the divorce papers ASAP. Also, I'll send you a couple hundred dollars in good faith. No more letters from you. She officially belongs to me. Ask her mother. It's over. Get a life.

She then stamped and addressed the envelope and dropped it in the mailbox.

When Stella and Antoinette arrived at the new salon they couldn't believe their eyes. The first thing that attracted their attention was the huge sign out front. They parked and went inside.

"Unbelievable," Antoinette said. "Totally unbelievable."

"Lord have mercy. This place look like it belong somewhere in Beverly Hills," Stella commented.

The floor was completely tiled in black and gold, Melody's favorite colors. Each wall was fully mirrored. On the left were five hair dryers, and on the right was a display counter holding beauty supplies and the cash register. Farther back on the right was the manicure area, and on the left was the pedicure area. At the rear of the salon there were four chairs, which were set up for hair styling, and also two barber chairs. There were six ceiling fans neatly hanging from the ceiling, and a thirty-two-inch television was professionally built into the wall. There was also a huge stereo speaker sitting in the front area of the salon, and its mate sat in the rear. They were connected to a ten-disc CD changer.

Walking toward the rear, Stella stared at the huge print reading *Mama's Chair* that was neatly engraved into the leather of a unique styling chair.

"Look at this, Antoinette," Stella excitedly said. "Isn't this sump'n? That Michelle sure has taste, doesn't she?"

"Mama, can't you see that this isn't anything but bait! If Melody accepts this salon from her, she'll owe that bitch for the rest of her life. I'm sorry, Mama, but I wouldn't accept it if I were her. I don't want anybody holding anything over my head."

"I'm sure, chile, that Melody can make enough money to pay her back, so quit bein' so damn negative. You sound like your Uncle Fitzgerald. Always complainin' 'bout sump'n, and always talking negative 'bout people," Stella said, defending Melody.

"Just think about it, Mama. This place is going to keep her connected to Melody until God knows when."

"Well, chile, if that's how she chooses to live her life, then so be it. What if you decide to drop your husband for a rich, attractive woman? What am I s'pose to do then, hate you? Nah, chile, I don't think so. I'd jus' have to accept and live with whatever choices y'all make."

"Mama, she's tripping."

"You the one trippin', chile, and to tell you the truth, I think you're a bit jealous."

"Jealous of what? Let's go, Mama. I've seen and heard enough for one day." Antoinette now had an attitude.

It had been several days since Melody came out of her coma. Dr. Maxwell stood over Melody looking over a series of papers.

"Hi, I'm Dr. Maxwell," he greeted. "How do you feel today, Mrs. Pullman?" She managed to nod her head once. "You should be ready to go home any day now. Would you like that?"

Melody lay there confused, still trying to figure things out, but the pain in her head prevented her from doing so. She took her eyes off the surrounding faces and stared at the ceiling, but still she found no answers.

"She's going to be just fine, Mrs. Swift," Dr. Maxwell said, looking at Stella. "Within the next week or so she should be recovered enough to go home. As you all know, the bullet cannot be removed due to the damage it may cause to her brain. She's very lucky, and God spared her life for a reason. The bullet is less than a sixteenth of an inch from her brain. If the gun had been a larger caliber, there's no question that she'd be dead."

As Dr. Maxwell was about to leave the room, Michelle spoke up.

"Dr. Maxwell, may I speak with you a moment in private, please?"

"Sure, follow me to my office," Dr. Maxwell replied, leading the way.

Curious looks were on everyone's faces. They were all thinking the same thing: *What does she need to speak to the doctor about? How is it that Melody's own mother didn't ask for a private conversation with the doctor, but this woman does?*

Michelle reappeared twenty minutes later. Everyone put aside their thoughts.

"Sorry to make it seem like I'm being secretive," Michelle said, "but I'm not. I've been a very close friend of Melody's for quite some time now. I take care of a lot of her business, personally, to make sure it gets done."

Antoinette gave her a snotty look, turned up her nose, and left the room.

Michelle ignored her and continued. "Melody and I are very intimate, and have been for a good while."

Stella dropped her head, and everyone else looked at each

other, bewildered. Now they understood why this woman was deep into Melody's affairs.

Kenneth then spoke up. "Byron, here's ten bucks. Go to the cafeteria and get you something to eat."

"But I'm not hungry, Dad." Kenneth gave Byron a stern look, and Byron hurriedly left the room.

"That's one of the reasons I'm not letting Byron come back to live with you," Kenneth said. "I refuse to let my son be raised in a fruity-tootie household!" He then stormed out of the room.

Larry, hoping Michelle didn't spill the beans on him, stood next to Pat.

"I hope none of you hate me because of what I am," Michelle continued. "After all, I am still human. Oh, and by the way, I asked Dr. Maxwell whether Melody would be on any strong medication that would prevent her from running the business I bought for her. His answer was no. Here are some business cards I had made for her, and I'm hoping all of you will patronize her business." She then left.

The room was in an uproar with everyone expressing opinions until Angela took over.

"Melody's sexual preference is not the issue here, and I think we're wrong for stereotyping her. We've all known her to be sweet, resourceful, sociable, and extremely caring. And on top of all that, she's a top-notch beautician. Let's please remember her like that, OK? I think this issue will then be a lot simpler for all of us to accept and deal with." Everyone shook their heads in agreement.

Larry felt relieved after Michelle had gone. He then disappeared to the restroom to wipe the sweat from his face.

CHAPTER 28

Detective Bell

He now felt that he was on to something. He ran a CBC on Rosie Martinez, but she had no record. But what he did find out was that she was employed by the Department of Motor Vehicles. He hurriedly jumped in his car and headed to the hospital.

Now I'm beginning to see through the cracks. The pieces are forming little by little. Rosie Martinez, the wife, or should I say the jealous wife, of Michelle Green, works for DMV, huh? OK, that explains the fake identifications. Yep. Let's say Michelle gave Rosie the boot, but Rosie didn't accept it. Rosie finds out Melody is bumping pussies with her wife. It wouldn't be hard at all—with Rosie having access to information like addresses, social security numbers, and phone numbers—for her to find out where Melody Pullman lived. I'll put my life on it that Michelle introduced them so that Melody could get fake ID cards, and nine times out of ten Rosie couldn't accept the fact that her wife was bumping pussies with another woman, the detective thought. *I'll put my life on it!*

When Detective Bell stepped into Melody's room, Michelle was standing over a sleeping Melody, shedding tears and sobbing like Melody had died. He was stunned by her beauty. She was dressed in a beige, two-piece pantsuit with a pair of matching pumps. Her shoulder-length hair was flawless. He then zeroed in on the unusual golden bracelets on her arm, and then he glanced at Melody's arm and noticed she had on the same exact bracelets.

Hmm, I've got to check into that. He continued thinking while studying her from a side view. *Larry has to be out of his fucking mind to pass up an opportunity to bang this dime-piece. Just give me one minute with her, and I'll have her hooked on dick for life. Just one fucking minute!*

Once Michelle became aware of the detective's presence, she introduced herself.

"Hello, I'm Michelle Green. And you are the detective, I assume?" She then offered a handshake.

"Detective Bell, Riverside Homicide. It's a pleasure meeting you, Miss Green. I've heard lots about you."

"I'm flattered, Detective. But how, may I ask, have you heard about me?"

He took off his flirtatious mask, remembering he was investigating a homicide and Michelle was a suspect.

"Let's go to the cafeteria for a few minutes, Miss Green. I'll buy you lunch."

"Lead the way, Detective."

After they were seated, Michelle led the conversation.

"So, what do you think, Detective? Do you have any leads or suspects?"

"Yep," he replied, reading the menu.

"Have you arrested anyone?" Michelle asked apprehensively.

"Nope, not yet." He then looked at her sternly. "It's my turn to ask you a few questions now, Miss Green. It's possible that you could shed some light on this case. Before I get into the specifics of the case, I want you to be aware that I've run a background check on you." He gave her time to digest his words, and then continued. "I'm aware of your criminal history, Miss Green." She remained cool, calm, and controlled.

"I'm not at all surprised, Detective. As a matter of fact, I was expecting you to say that. Yes, I've had legal problems in the past, but those days are long gone. It feels good now to be a law-abiding citizen and not to have to look over your shoulder wondering whether the sirens you hear are coming after you. Yes, Detective, my life of crime is far behind me," Michelle lied.

"Where were you Thursday between 10:30 PM and 1:00 AM?" he asked, studying her diligently.

"Home alone, detective. Actually, if you've done your homework by checking Melody's caller ID, and by checking her phone records, you should have noticed my number at least twenty-five times. Melody told me she wanted to be alone on that particular night. She said she needed time to sort things out. When I hadn't heard from her by ten thirty or eleven, I began calling her constantly, but she never answered."

"Interesting," Detective Bell replied. "So do you know how her vehicle got filled with bullet holes, recent bullet holes?"

"That morning Melody went to Los Angeles to visit her aunt and cousins she hadn't seen in years. She told me that one of her cousins was into gang banging, and that while she was there, a rival gang shot up her aunt's house. Unfortunately, her Suburban was caught in the gunfire. I guess she was in the wrong place at the wrong time."

This bitch is cool as ice and smooth as silk, but I know she's a god-damn crook. How else could she afford a fucking two-story house on the beach, a brand new Benz, a fucking BMW, and wear two hundred dollar pantsuits and three-hundred dollar shoes? She's a wicked crook that just hasn't been busted yet. Here I am, a fucking detective, driving a piece of shit car, living in a raggedy ass two bedroom house that needs new carpet, plumbing work, and a fucking garage door, and this smooth bitch cruises in luxury and has a goddamn house on the Pacific. What kind of shit is this? Detective Bell wondered.

"How are you and your wife Rosie Martinez doing?" He studied her intently.

"I guess you have done your homework, huh, Detective?"

"Always, Miss Green. Always."

"To tell you the truth, Detective—"

"Please do, Miss Green, because the truth has a way of coming out, you know."

"As I was saying, I haven't seen or heard from Rosie in over seven months."

"Is that right? Well how do you explain the fake ID in Melody's purse? The way I see it, Miss Green, you couldn't have accomplished your illegal scams without Rosie Martinez. Her employment at the DMV allowed her to make perfectly legal looking, but illegal ID cards in whatever names you chose. It was a brilliant idea, Miss Green, but didn't your parents ever tell you that you can only do wrong for so long before it catches up with you?"

"Are we here to talk about the attempted murder on Melody's life, or are we here to discuss my background, my wife, and my wife's job?" she responded irritably.

"Actually, it's good to discuss them both. Don't you think so, Miss Green?"

"I'll tell you what, Detective, you say that you have the phone records, right? Well then use them. Those records will not only prove my innocence, but will also be my alibi. I phoned her from my Newport Beach home that night, not from my cell. Check it out."

"I'll bet it is, Miss Green. I guess that's all for now, but I'll definitely be in touch. Oh, and by the way, have you ever met Melody's husband? I've heard he's been in and out of prison for the last few years. You might be playing on deadly ground, Miss Green. I mean, you know, messing around with someone else's significant other can be extremely dangerous. Actually, I think this case is proof of that," the detective said, smirking.

"Detective, your insinuations are unnecessary."

"I think they are necessary, Miss Green. Anyway, I'll be in touch in a few days." He then stood up and walked away.

When he arrived back at his office, he turned on his computer and began searching for the location of the DMV that employed Rosie Martinez. Seconds later, he found out that she was employed by the DMV office located in the City of Commerce, and he also discovered that she owned a home in La Puente. Instinct told him he was on the right track. He could smell it.

"I'll bet my life on this being the murder weapon! And I'll bet my pension that the slugs taken from Mrs. Pullman's torso and bedroom walls match this gun!" the detective said, staring at the gun.

Driving to the lab, Detective Bell felt a sense of victory. He wanted to call Michelle and say, "You're next, slick," but dismissed the thought. He wanted to see the expression on her face.

The slug matched the gun perfectly. Rosie Martinez was convicted of attempted murder, assault with a deadly weapon, and assault causing great bodily injury. She paid forty thousand dollars to her lawyer, hoping to avoid going to prison, but the cards did not fall in her favor. After Michelle's convincing testimony and the indisputable forensic evidence, it had only taken the jury twenty minutes to reach a verdict—guilty.

CHAPTER 29

Big Steve

"What's up, Steve? Is it true?" Steve wanted to drop his head, but was afraid Tiny might yank it off.

"What's up, Tiny?" Big Black yelled from another cell. "Your cellie lied to you! You gonna let him get away with it?"

"Beat his ass, Tiny!" Tuffy yelled.

"This man ain't done nothin' to us but made us laugh since he's been here," Tiny said, coming to Big Steve's defense. "He's told us some things I couldn't imagine with my own mind, and he even gave me a couple church girls' addresses, so I can write 'em. This man is aright with me, and J.J., you ain't gonna do a goddamn thing to him, and nobody else is either. This man had all y'all laughin' like he was Richard Pryor. Ain't nobody made us laugh that damn hard in over ten years. Y'all ought to be grateful a man like him came our way. If he lied, maybe he had a good reason to, and I ain't gonna hold it against him."

Disappointed, J.J. made his way to his cell. Big Steve then began explaining to everyone his reason for lying, and fortunately everyone understood and didn't hold it against him. They all said they would have done the same thing.

Later that night after the lights went off, a lifer who went by the name of Dog, shouted from his cell.

"Hey, Steve! Tell us some more about the streets, man!" The

prisoners who were asleep had quickly awakened in hopes to hear more street stories.

"Yeah, I need a laugh, man. Tell us some more stories!" a lifer named Big P, who had murdered and raped seven white girls in the early 1960s, shouted.

"Yeah, Steve," Tiny said, "tell us some more, man. Tell us some more."

"OK, y'all, I'm about tell y'all some shit that's gonna have y'all laughing like hell." The lifers had begun laughing before Steve even got started. "One day I was at church, and these big, fat girls kept checking me out while the preacher was preaching. Anyway, two of the fat bitches approached me after church, handed me their address, and invited me to their house for barbecue, potato salad, hot links, pork and beans, and shit like that, right? Anyway, I gets to their house about five or six o'clock, you know, but I figured sump'n was funny, 'cause I didn't smell any goddamn food. Anyway, I knock on the door, and the fat one who gave me the address came to the door wearing a see-through negligee, showing her big, juicy, watermelon titties and her hippopotamus stomach, right? Anyway, I went in and had a seat, and the next thing I know, the other fat girl appears wearing panties and a bra, and started doing a dance those fat girls be doing called who-chee dancing. Man, they put on some hip-hop music and started dancing wild, man. They were all over me like white on rice. Then the doorbell rang." Steve stood and gestured as if he were on stage in front of millions of people. "And y'all wouldn't believe who it was," he emphasized.

"Who was it, man?" Tiny asked excitedly.

"It was the preacher's daughter, man. The bitch had a grocery bag full of liquor. Anyway, she walked in and started dancing too. Then those bitches started drinking and dancing around, and the next thing I know they started taking off their damn clothes. Then, man, they grabbed my hand and led me to the middle of the floor. Three oversized, naked bitches surrounded me, man—six humongous titties, and three big, lumpy asses. Anyway, the preacher's daughter, out of the blue, unzipped my pants and pulled out my dick, but the bitch musta got nervous when she saw it." Everyone burst into laughter, and then Steve continued. "But I was glad, man, 'cause ain't no way in hell I could've handled those fat, horny bitches anyway. The preacher's daughter and one of the fat girls split, but the short, ugly sister was drunk, and she wanted to fuck. I told her I didn't want to fuck, but she promised me fifty dollars to fuck her for two hours, but I never did get that money. Man, that was the worst ride of my goddamn life!"

The lifers, all except J.J., burst into laughter. J.J. figured it was just another lie. He was still angry because things had not gone his way. He figured Big Steve should be getting his ass kicked, instead of getting laughs from these goddamn idiots.

The following morning after breakfast, Big Steve was transferred to the level one yard. He felt a sense of relief, but his level four audience felt like they were back in prison again. There were no more laughs or entertainment—only mean looks, loneliness, hatred, and everyday, ordinary prison life. They were all thinking the same thing.

Damn, I wish Steve would come back for just one more day, or even one more hour.

Tiny was recognized on the four yard for his ability with the punching bag, but he now received even more recognition since having Steve as his cellmate. When the yard finally re-opened, nine months after the investigation of the murders, prisoners approached Tiny, while he worked out on the punching bag, and asked him things.

"Tell me what else Steve talked about while you guys were in the cell," one of the lifers said.

"Did he ever talk about his wife and kids?" another one asked.

"You said he was church man, huh? What religion was he?" another inmate asked.

"What was he really in jail for, Tiny?" yet another prisoner asked.

Tiny would always smile, and reply, "I can't tell you, man. It's a secret."

Big Steve, along with seven other inmates who came from the four yard with him, were housed in the gym on the one yard until bunks became available in one of the dorms. Once Steve was issued a bunk in the gym, he made it up and put away his personal items.

I need a shower, he thought. *I only showered four times in nine days and I stink.* He grabbed a clean change of underwear and his towel and soap, and made his way to the shower room, but after entering, he could not believe his eyes.

There was a skinny black man bent over giving a Mexican a blowjob, while a white boy was fucking him at the same time. The homosexual was too caught up in what he was doing to acknowledge Big Steve's presence. The white boy observed Steve watching, but only sped up his rhythm.

"Hey guy, you wanna join the party? It's good, man. It's all fuckin' good." Steve stood paralyzed and amazed, still not believing what he was witnessing. He quickly turned around and went back to his bunk.

Damn, he thought. *I thought all the crazy shit went down on the four yard. One thing for sure, I guess there's no prejudice in here. Well, I might as well take a stroll around the yard to check things out. I'll shower later.*

The yard consisted of nine dorms that housed two hundred inmates in each dorm. There were trees scattered throughout the yard, which provided shade. The temperatures were known to reach as high as 130 degrees. There was a baseball field that was used six days a week for dorms to play against each another. They even had playoffs and championship games. There was also a field, which was used to play football until too many serious injuries kept occurring. There were basketball courts, work-out areas, a library, and an area used by the prisoners to throw picnics.

As Big Steve strolled through the yard he observed a few inmates playing dominos on benches and tables, some working out in groups, some walking around the track, some talking, and some just lying on the grass relaxing or reading. Lots of inmates were watching a softball game between dorm nine and dorm seven. There were bleachers filled with spectators set up along both sides of the field. Lots of inmates had to stand to watch. The tycoons of the yard, inmates who were supposedly big drug dealers with lots of money, always had the comfort of their pillows for cushions and their own personal spot on the bleachers. They gambled on every single game, whether the team was good or sorry. The bets were large by prison standards—cartons of cigarettes, three to ten jars of coffee, a hundred stamped envelopes, twenty to fifty cans of tuna, oysters, crabmeat, or cans of tobacco.

Big Steve decided to blend in with the standing observers and began watching the softball game. It was the ninth inning and the score was tied at five. There was a runner at second base and one out. One ball and two strikes was the count. Benzo Al had a bet with a brother named Tailor-Made for two cartons of cigarettes and two jars of coffee. Benzo Al had put his money on dorm seven, and Tailor-Made's money was invested on dorm nine. Another brother named Richie Rich had bet with dorm nine and had put five cartons up against Corvette Keith, who had his money on dorm seven. There were also small-time gamblers occupying the bleachers.

Dorm nine was at bat. The ball was pitched and hit deep to left field, allowing the runner at second base to score. The game was over. Dorm nine had done it again. Tailor-Made and Richie Rich gave each other thumbs up and walked away with another victory under their belts. Big Steve made his way back to the gym, hoping to have clearance to take a shower.

After showering, he gathered his writing materials and wrote Melody a letter.

Dear Melody,

May God bless you and Byron. I pray each day that you and I will soon reunite. I love you very much, Melody, and I'm doing my part to live up to my wedding vows. I forgive you, Mel, for whatever you've done wrong. By the way, I received a letter from Michelle. She informed me of your relationship with her, but deep in my heart I know she's not really what you want. Please write me. Just one letter from you and I'll feel like I own the world. Please, Melody, write me. I will then be content. Remember, sweetheart, I belong to you, and we promised to love one another until death do us part. I'm waiting for some love-by-mail from you. I love you, Melody.

Your husband,

Steve

The gym housed 320 prisoners, and all except three bunks were occupied. It was one thirty in the morning when Big Steve rolled over and opened his eyes. He turned his head, slowly to his right and observed the black homosexual, who he'd witnessed earlier in the shower, lying on his bunk giving an inmate a blowjob. He then saw five thugs waiting in line for the same treatment. He covered his head, but left an opening in the cover so he could watch.

Twenty minutes later, the homosexual had taken care of everyone in line. Big Steve rolled over and fell back asleep.

The following morning after breakfast, Steve was sitting on his bunk reading his Bible when suddenly he observed five homosexuals approaching the gay boy's bed.

They really think they're women, Big Steve thought. *Help them, Lord. Please help them.*

Steve's attention was sidetracked by an argument a few bunks away between two black inmates. They were arguing over religious differences. Listening, Steve learned the Muslim inmate's name was Jabar, and the Christian he was debating with was named Samuel. They were standing face-to-face yelling their opinions and beliefs at one another.

"The Lord Jesus Christ is the son of God! He died on the cross for all of our sins! You should be praying to him and thanking him each day!" Samuel voiced.

"Jesus was a prophet!" Jabar replied angrily. "He was a man, stupid! Nowhere in the Bible does Jesus tell you to worship him! The Ten Commandments state that you should have no other God, but God. Jesus Christ was a man, you goddamn idiot!" Samuel then moved closer to Jabar.

"You ignorant, uneducated Muslims worship Oula, Bula, Cudulla, or whatever his goddamn name is, and—" Jabar's punch was so quick and powerful Samuel didn't see it coming. The blow came like a bullet with deadly force and knocked Samuel out. Jabar noticed Big Steve watching.

"Hey, man! Help me take this fool to his bunk before the C.O.s come!" Steve didn't want to be involved in anything, but on the other hand, he didn't want to receive the same treatment as Samuel.

"All right, but let's hurry," Steve replied nervously.

"Thanks, homey," Jabar said. Afterward Jabar offered a handshake. "I'm Jabar, man."

"I'm Steve. Nice to meet you."

"Right on, Steve. Thanks again, man. I'll check you later."

Other than Steve, the homosexuals were the only other inmates who had observed the incident between Jabar and Samuel, and they were aware of what happened to snitches.

There was an occurrence which had taken place years earlier in Folsom State Prison, involving a homosexual who had snitched. Someone overheard a homosexual snitching, and two days later the homosexual was found dead, lying in the shower with a broomstick rammed up his rectum. Word had spread quickly throughout the homosexual population in the prison system. That put an immediate halt to gay snitching.

As Steve walked the yard he observed a church.

Cool. They got churches in prison, he thought. *Let me go in and check it out.* Inside there was a long hallway with small tables on both sides containing religious literature, calendars, and both Spanish and English Bibles. Posted on the wall there was a schedule for Protestant, Catholic, and Islamic services. At the end of the hallway was the entrance to the church itself. There was no one else there, so Steve felt it would be all right to go to the altar and pray. While praying, he didn't notice the Chaplain observing him.

Once Steve finished, Chaplain Acres approached him and said, "Amen." The Chaplin then reached for Steve's hand and began praying with him, then afterward led him to his office where he jotted down his name, prison number, and housing location. He then handed him some religious literature to read.

"I'll see you at Bible study tonight, Chaplain Acres," Steve said as he was getting ready to leave. The chaplain smiled.

"God would love that, Steve. I'll see you then."

On the way back to the gym, Steve felt good about talking with Chaplain Acres. Already he felt like he'd been born again and had an altogether different purpose in life. He felt transformed and energized with Christ. He walked back to his bunk, picked up his Bible, and began reading the book of Proverbs.

Marva, the homosexual who slept next to Steve, approached him.

"I'm Marva. You're new, huh?" Steve didn't want to be rude and ignore the homosexual, but he didn't want other inmates to see them conversing and get the wrong idea. Keeping it brief and simple, Steve replied, "Yeah, I'm new."

"How much time you got?" Marva asked, smiling.

Steve looked around to see if anyone was looking. "Five years," he replied succinctly.

"Well, anyway, if you need anything, and I mean anything, don't hesitate to ask me, OK?" Marva's smile had gotten even bigger.

"OK, thanks," Steve replied. He went back to reading his Bible.

Marva walked away with a femine twitch in his stride. His gestures were those of a sexy woman. There had not been a day during his imprisonment that someone naïve, new, or curious didn't get drawn into Marva's web of deceit. Several married inmates had received blowjobs from Marva. Some had even had anal sex with him. Marva had a way with words, as well as with his hands and lips. He had broken down many strong men, and had them doing things they could never imagine themselves doing.

After reading his Bible for an hour or so, he wrote his parents. He told them about his encounter with Chaplain Acres, and also informed them of his new feelings of godliness. Chaplain Acres had promised him a job working as his clerk, which made him feel even better. He told them his dream was to someday have his own church and continue to preach the word of God to people.

Once Steve was finished writing his letters, he then went to Bible study. Afterward, he returned to his bunk, studied his Bible for a while, and then fell asleep thinking about Melody.

Two days later, Steve received a slip of paper instructing him to report to work each day at the church from four PM to nine thirty PM. He was assigned as Chaplain Acre's clerk.

Within a month, inmates began referring to Steve as "Preach." He became very strong in the Lord and had gained lots of confidence in preaching. Inmates who were beginners to Christianity sought him out for guidance. He was grateful that Chaplain Acres had taken him under his wing and taught him how to be more concrete in the Lord, but he just could not seem to get Melody off his mind. Of the fifty-nine letters he'd written her, he received only one reply, which was the letter informing him she no longer wanted him. But he still loved her.

No matter where Steve was on the yard he wouldn't hesitate preaching or having Bible study.

A few months later word got to several inmates that a black

inmate named Robert Strong had been writing obscene letters to their wives and girlfriends. Robert was one of Steve's faithful Bible study participants.

Robert Strong worked alone as a janitor in the visiting room. An hour before he got off work each day, the mail was delivered to the visiting room. It was to be picked up by the C.O.s who worked the afternoon shift so they could take it to their assigned dorm and pass it out.

One day, while thinking about the pittance he was paid for working, a plan began forming in Robert's mind.

Shit! There's nine bags of mail altogether, and a lot of the manila envelopes probably have stamps or stamped envelopes inside them. I'll open them all and check. I can pull the stamps off, and either sell or reuse them. And if I get lucky, I might even write a few bitches. I wonder if they'll write me back.

Robert's thoughts became his actions. Checking the clock one day, he realized he had fifteen minutes before anyone arrived. The mail had already been delivered. He trotted to the door and peeped out. The coast was clear. He then rushed over to the mailbags, grabbed the first one, and sprinted to the restroom. Inside the bag there were three large envelopes. In one of the envelopes there was a book of stamps. There were twenty stamped envelopes in the second, and ten pictures of naked women in the third. He hit a jackpot on his first try. He then tore the manila envelopes into small pieces, flushed the pieces down the toilet, then furtively took the mailbag back to where he'd gotten it. He glanced at the clock. There wasn't time to hit another bag. He called it a day. Tomorrow he would do a repeat. He left the room, making sure he had left no evidence of his thievery.

Should I sell 'em or keep 'em? Robert wondered while on his way back to his dorm. *Maybe I should just keep 'em, let 'em pile up every day, and see how many I have by the end of the week. Shit, I can trade 'em for coffee, cigarettes, soups, and tuna, and hell, I can even gamble with 'em. I'm a lucky, lucky man.*

He strolled to his dorm, put away his ill-gotten gains, showered, then sat in the dayroom and watched TV. Robert Strong
felt pretty damn good about his accomplishments, and about
himself.

After dinner, Robert heard an announcement over the inter-
com.

"Protestant Bible service is being held in the chapel! Protestant Bible service is being held in the chapel! All inmates wishing to attend should report to the chapel!" Normally when
Robert heard church announcements, he ignored them. But
for some reason, that particular evening, he desired to go to
church. He felt he needed prayer. He had a couple of scriptures memorized, but didn't live by them.

As he stepped into the chapel that day, Big Steve greeted
him.

"How you doing, my brother?" Big Steve asked, offering a
handshake.

"Fine, thank you. You must be Steve Pullman?" Robert asked,
accepting the handshake.

"I'm not wanted by the FBI or the CIA, am I?" Big Steve
asked, smiling.

"Nah, man, not at all. I heard about you from a few brothers
and Mexicans, and I've been dying to meet you. It's a pleasure
meeting someone like you, Steve. Man, I hear people talking
'bout you in the dorm, in the chow line, in the library, and even
heard a brother speak of you when I was sitting on the toilet
one day."

Big Steve smiled. "Is that right?"

"Yeah, man, I'm not kidding. Anyway, Steve, I'm Robert
Strong. I plan to begin coming to church every Sunday, and attending daily Bible studies as well"

"It's not how many times you come, Robert, it's what you
learn and digest, and whether you apply the good Lord's words
to your life accordingly. If a person goes to church seven days a
week for four hours a day, and they're still not walking or think-

ing according to the scriptures, then their presence in the church, and all that they've heard, is in vain. Let's say a person went to church only once in his entire life. He learned what God expects of him, and he left the church a brand new man. His thoughts were different, he walked with surety, and from that day on his whole outlook on life was different. That's a man who pleases the Lord and whose path will be blessed," Big Steve explained.

"Well, I need God in my life, like yesterday. Because sometimes my mind tells me to do things I know I shouldn't, but I find myself doing them anyway. I know it's the devil."

"I know exactly what you mean, Robert," Big Steve said. He then sighed and added, "Been there, done that."

In the midst of conversing, inmates began coming into the chapel by the dozens. Each of them, no matter their race, greeted Big Steve with a handshake, then made their way into the chapel and took a seat. Big Steve felt where Robert Strong was coming from and realized that this man was seeking the Lord. He showed Robert brotherly kindness by recommending he study the books of Proverbs, James, and a scripture from the book of Romans 7:15. The verse reads, "I do not understand what I do. For what I want to do I do not do, but what I hate I do."

Steve was on stage preaching. He paced the stage, mic in hand, preaching and teaching about how Satan operates. His audience gave him their undivided attention. Chaplain Acres was extremely proud of Steve. He had known from his first meeting with Steve that this was a man who could attract lots of seekers of the Lord, and who was also capable of tending his clerical needs as well.

"Praise the Lord," Chaplain Acres said, proudly watching Steve from the front row.

Robert Strong felt good after he left church. He didn't quite feel like a brand new creature in Christ, but he felt good about confessing his sins and asking forgiveness. He also felt good about meeting Steve. He felt he could talk to Steve about problems at home, problems with inmates, personal problems, or just about anything. He felt that Steve was not just a minister of God and an excellent teacher and counselor, but he also considered him a friend.

The following day, while buffing the floors of the visiting room, a battle took place in Robert's mind. The battle was between Satan and God, right or wrong. One voice said to him, "Do it dummy! Just do it! You've got to get ahead somehow! You don't make enough to buy a goddamn stick of deodorant! There's nothing to think about, so just do it! What is it? You've gotten honest all of a sudden since you came to jail? Bullshit! Any other inmate with this golden opportunity would do the same damn thing! Do it!"

The other voice was softer and said to him, "Satan is a liar and the truth isn't in him, Robert. Rebuke Satan in the name of Jesus. Turn from your old wicked ways. Blessed is the man who endures temptation. A double-minded man is unstable in all his ways. Do not be deceived, Robert. Satan has many tactics and he's trying to use one on you now. Can you imagine what will happen to you if an inmate or a C.O. catches you? Walk with the Lord, Robert. Judgment day is near."

Even though Robert wanted to follow God's words, the temptation of Satan overruled.

At 1:45, Robert made sure the coast was clear. He then grabbed two mailbags and sprinted to the restroom. Quickly and nervously, he rummaged through them. This time he found fourteen huge manila envelopes. Each manila envelope contained twenty stamped envelopes. He felt like he'd hit another jackpot. Hurriedly he shredded the manila envelopes into small pieces and flushed them. He then hurried out of the restroom and placed the mailbags in their designated area. After he made sure things looked normal, he left.

The next day, Robert repeated his criminal act, but this time he did something a little different. He took letters that were addressed from Mexican, black, and white girls, which were sent to their husbands or boyfriends. Robert was a freak and he enjoyed reading sex letters. An inmate once let him read a sex letter that was sent to him from his girlfriend. The letter had been so sexually descriptive that immediately after reading it, Robert masturbated. From that day on, whenever he wanted to masturbate, he'd imagine the words written in the sex letter.

On the way to his dorm, he began thinking.

Good. Out of seventeen letters, maybe I'll get at least five or six sex letters. Yes! He then smirked. *It'll be nice to get one every day. Yes!*

He lay on his bunk, reading each letter as if they were written to him. Eight of them were extremely descriptive sex letters. On a sheet of paper, he wrote down each sender's address, then took the envelopes outside and stuffed them in the bottom of a trashcan. He then took a shower, and afterward he wrote erotic letters to each of the women. He dropped the letters in the mailbox and lay back down. He felt good about his cleverness.

Damn, I'm good. Those bitches write good sex letters, but I can write even better ones. Nine times out of ten, the men they're writing probably can't spell or write. I'm going to have these bitches writing me, instead of whoever they're writing. I should have a response back in a couple weeks. But in case I don't, tomorrow I'll take twenty more letters, and write all twenty women. I'm sure to get responses that way.

Each day for the next two weeks Robert sent out sex letters to various women of all races. He also continued to steal books of stamps and stamped envelopes, but he made it a habit to attend church and daily Bible studies, and to hang with Big Steve, hoping to gain more spiritual knowledge. Big Steve had become somewhat of a mentor to him.

Johnny, who went by the moniker of Pup, was known as the Al Capone of the 2000 Era. His reputation in his hometown, Whittier, California, was of unbridled viciousness. He had a dazzling smile, but beneath that smile was an extremely ruthless man. He was not only a big-baller and a shot caller, he was also a man with no conscience. "I don't give a fuck!" was a phrase he used at least twenty times a day. Pup supplied many of Whittier's drug dealers with heroin, cocaine, and crystal meth, and now he supplied prison addicts with drugs through a scam he was running in the mail room. Whenever Pup spoke, everyone, especially the Southern Mexicans, listened. He was definitely the man.

Monday evening when mail call was announced, Robert listened for his name. Unfortunately, it wasn't called. Johnny, who lived in the dorm next to Robert, received a letter from his wife that had him irate.

The letter informed him that she had received a letter from an inmate named Robert Strong, with the prison number of P-76161, who was housed in dorm five. Johnny wasn't the type of man to fuck with. And to fuck with his family was definitely a no-no.

When his wife received the letter from Robert, she couldn't believe her eyes. The letter was obscene and disrespectful. One thing Pup didn't tolerate was disrespect. Especially disrespect to his family. His wife sent him the letter Robert had mailed to her, and Pup was furious. He tried to control his anger, but couldn't, especially after reading the letter.

Heatedly, Pup balled up the letter, stuffed it in his pocket, then stormed through the dorm in search of his two minions, Bubba and Spanky. Inmates of all races figured something was wrong because they'd never seen Pup in such a rage. He stormed into the dayroom and spotted Bubba and Spanky playing cards. He looked at them and shouted.

"Fuck the card game! Come on, both of you! We've got business to take care of!" After leading them to a secluded area, he showed them the letter.

"Let's kill the muthafucka!" Bubba said, wanting desperately to shove a piece of iron inside the man who had insulted his superior.

"Let's go take care of this fool, Pup," Spanky, a huge Mexican who enjoyed fighting and being involved in riots, suggested.

"No," Pup said, holding up his hand. "I'm going to have the pleasure of taking this asshole out with the help of his own people. I want both of you to spread the word to all the South-Siders, and let 'em know what's going down. In the meantime, I'm going to let the black shot caller know what's up."

Even though Bubba was from Baldwin Park, and Pup was from Whittier, they clicked together like links in a chain. Bubba had a reputation for cutting his enemies' throats, and shooting to kill, which was the reason Pup had chosen him to be his right-hand man. Unlike Pup, Bubba rarely smiled. He had a mean look and a meaner attitude. There was nothing he wouldn't do to win Pup's approval. Bubba was responsible for collecting debts, as well as for disciplining those who were late in paying. He took much pride in his position.

After searching the yard for five minutes, Pup finally located Bricc, who was the shot caller for the blacks, and also the M.A.C. (Men's Advisory Council) representative.

"Let me round up a few of the homies, Pup," Bricc said after reading Robert's letter. Meet me in front of dorm six in fifteen, twenty minutes."

"For sure, homes," Pup responded.

As Bricc rounded up his crew, both black and white inmates began approaching him, showing him letters written by Robert Strong that were addressed to their wives and girlfriends. They wanted to take care of Robert Strong personally, but the proper prison procedure in handling such matters was to notify the shot-caller or M.A.C. rep first. Inmates weren't allowed to take matters into their own hands. That would be a violation that would definitely cause harm to the violator.

Bricc was furious. While standing in front of his dorm, waiting for his crew, he asked himself, *How in the hell did this stupid muthafucka think he could get away with something like this? I wonder if he thought that the girlfriends or wives weren't going to say anything to their men. He's got to be the stupidest son-of-a-bitch in the world to put his prison number, dorm, and bunk number on the letters. Well, Mr. Robert Strong, you're a dead soldier. A dead fuckin' soldier.*

Seconds later, seven evil looking white boys, Pups, Bubba, Spanky, nine other Mexicans, and eleven blacks, both Crips and Bloods, approached Bricc.

"I'm gonna kill that motherfucker!" a muscular, white inmate yelled. "That black piece of shit wrote my wife a fucking letter, talking about how big his dick is, how good he knows how to fuck and eat pussy. The motherfucker even lied and told her I'm writing two black chicks! Here's the fucking letter, Bricc. I'm gonna beat this motherfucker's ass personally!" The white guy's name was Ace. He was a member of the Aryan Brotherhood, which is a white gang that hates black people.

Nonchalantly, they all plotted vengeance against Robert Strong and came up with a perfect plan.

Big Steve had recently spent forty-five minutes in a one-on-one Bible study with Robert Strong. Robert had been building up his spiritual account since he'd met Big Steve and actually felt that he was growing in godliness, even though he still did evil things. He would tell himself, *God will forgive me no matter what I do, because God is a forgiving God. He forgave Paul, who used to kill Christians. What I've done doesn't compare to murder, so I know he'll forgive me.*

One day Bricc got word that Robert was in church and had been there for close to an hour. With that information, he approved a hit man from each race to go into the chapel and wait for the right time to make their move. Ace, Bubba, and Killer Rat were chosen to represent their races. Subtly they made their way to the chapel. They went to different rows and got down on their knees like they were praying. When they saw Robert shake hands with Preach and Chaplain Acres, they knew it was almost time to make their move. Robert was feeling like a brand new man with a brand new plan. As he exited the first set of double doors, Bubba stood and reacted first.

"Hey, Robert. Can I ask you something, man? It'll only take a second."

"Sure. What's up?" Robert asked.

As Bubba approached Robert, Ace and Killer Rat stood and joined their crime partners in the hallway. As Bubba held a brief conversation with Robert, Ace and Killer Rat moved toward Robert from behind, then dug sharp, long pieces of irons into Robert's body several times, making sure he wouldn't live. Killer Rat plunged his weapon deep into Robert's neck, Bubba jabbed him three times in the heart, and Ace stuck him in the kidney. Robert Strong's lifeless body fell to the floor, with blood flowing quickly from his wounds. Quietly, the killers left the chapel.

After finishing a long prayer with Chaplain Acres and catching up on some paperwork, Big Steve walked through the first set of double doors and saw Robert's body lying in a pool of blood. He wanted to scream. Instead, he turned and ran back into the chapel to inform Chaplain Acres.

The prison officials notified Robert Strong's parents about his death. They were instructed on how to go about picking up his body. They wanted explanations, but after a sixty-four day investigation, there were still no answers for them. No witnesses, no murder weapon, no suspects. Case closed.

CHAPTER 30

Melody was released a couple weeks after she came out of the coma. Her brain was functioning well and she no longer had the migraines. Even though she felt she was fully recovered, Stella decided to spend a couple more weeks with her before returning to Mississippi.

Each day, after Michelle had finished taking care of her business, she would call Melody and Stella and ask what they wanted for dinner.

After taking their orders, Michelle would stop by a restaurant, pick up the orders, and deliver them. Whenever she spent the night, which was most of the time, Michelle made it a point not to be open with her sexual approaches toward Melody. Antoinette's suspicions led her to call Melody's home at least three times a night to make sure things were OK.

Michelle went to Staples a week prior to the opening of the salon and had five hundred flyers printed to advertise the grand opening. Melody was back on her feet, feeling like a million bucks and a queen, both mentally and physically, and excited and eager to run her business.

When she had found out what had really happened to her, she and Michelle began arguing on a daily basis. Even though

they both admitted to being wrong for concealing their mar-
riages, it didn't lessen the severity of the arguments.

"You could've told me! Your fucking wife tried to kill me,
Michelle!" Michelle would always try to calm her by caressing
her, but most times, Melody rejected her touch.

"No! Stop, Michelle! I'm serious! You could've gotten me
killed! It would've been all your fault! You expect me to act like
nothing's happened, but I'm sorry, I can't!"

"Stop your bitching, Mel. Hell, you weren't honest with me
either. You could've told me you were married, but you chose
not to. Am I constantly riding you for that? No, I'm not, because it's in the past. If we continue to keep dwelling on this,
it's going to prevent us from moving forward. I want us to grow
old together, OK? I want us to be lovers, not fighters. Keep in
mind that these bracelets are symbols of love, not of hate."
Michelle said.

Things would be all right for a day or so, and then suddenly
the shit would hit the fan again.

Before Stella left to go back to Mississippi, Tony called a family meeting. Once everyone was seated at the dining room
table, Tony took a sip of water and began.

"I think you need to cut the line, sis. This new life you're
leading almost cost you your life, and it's just not worth it. It's
unhealthy, and basically it's a fucked up way to live, especially
while raising a child."

"Who in the fuck—" Melody yelled.

"Y'all cut out all that cussin' and carryin' on!" Stella interrupted. "I raised y'all better than that! Get your point across,
Tony, without talkin' all that filthiness, boy!"

"You may be my big brother," Melody said, "but you damn
sure can't tell me how to live my fucking life!"

"That's the point, sis, that's the goddamn point!" Tony said,
annoyed by his sister not listening.

"Tony! Watch your mouth, boy!" Stella shouted. "I ain't

gonna tell y'all no more about y'all mouths! Y'all sound like one of those kids raised in the projects or sump'n!"

"The point is," Tony continued, "you haven't been running your own life. You may have struggled when you were by yourself, but you showed independence," Tony said, then shook his head in disgust. "That is until you started fucking your customer's husband, and—"

"Tony!" Stella interrupted again.

"OK, Mama, I'm sorry."

"I don't have to sit here and listen to this bullshit!" Melody yelled, then attempted to stand, but was held down by Stella. "Sit down, Melody, 'cause I've got sump'n to say about this matter too."

"Calm down, Melody," Antoinette interjected. "Because actually, I think we've all got something to say." Antoinette composed herself. "We love you, sis. The same blood is running through all our veins, which means we are family. We—"

"You guys can talk all you want, but that doesn't mean I'm going to agree with you," Melody interrupted.

"All I'm trying to say is that we all love you and don't want to see anything happen to you," Tony said. "You were playing it close when you were sleeping with Pat's husband, you know. What do you think would have happened if Pat, Angela, or Monique had found out about your affair with him? But that's history. Michelle's wife tried to kill you, and who's to say she doesn't have another lover somewhere who may be even more jealous than her wife was, and—"

"OK, Tony," Stella interrupted. "You've made your point. Melody, you'd better take heed, chile. If you listen, you might just live a little longer. You're right about it being your life and all, but chile, if I were you, I'd be scared as hell to walk outta my front door, thinkin' somebody might try to kill me. Now, don't get me wrong, chile, cause I do kinda like Michelle, but it seems to me that she thinks she owns you. I've been really

Samuel L. Hair

thinkin' hard 'bout this whole thing lately, but I jus' ain't said nothin' to you yet. Now I don't mean to hurt you, Melody, but I don't think I could stand seeing you get hurt again. Now sump'n gotta be fishy, chile, 'cause why else would a woman go out of her way and spend hundreds and thousands of dollars on another woman? I mean, I know y'all s'posed to be, ah, whatever you wanna call it, but chile, I'd rather be on welfare and have one eye than to live the way you're livin'.'"

Melody listened, but showed no signs of interest. Antoinette spoke up again.

"Personally, sis, I don't care whether you choose to sleep with men or women. My main concern is for Byron. Now we've had our differences in the past, Melody, but we always seem to get back together through love, understanding, and on the strength that we're family. So please, sis, listen to us. We're not trying to steer you wrong. We're simply trying to advise you on what's best for you and Byron."

"I've listened to each of you like you all wanted me to, and believe me, I do understand," Melody replied thoughtfully. "But it's not as easy as you guys think to just walk away, especially from something like this."

"Like I said, chile, I'd rather be broke, on welfare, and have one eye than to have somebody have sump'n hangin' over my head, forcin' me to do sump'n I don't wanna do. That's blackmail," Stella said.

"I'll think about it, but I'm not making any decisions or promises this minute."

"Well think about it, chile. That's all we can ask."

"All right. Now come on, Mama, before you miss your flight."

While Tony and Antoinette were loading Stella's luggage and boxes into Melody's Suburban, Stella led Melody to the den, gave her a hug, and then had a few motherly words with her, crying as she spoke.

"Give it up, baby. It jus' ain't worth it. That woman thinks she bigger than life, and thinks she owns you. Can't you see it? For your own sake, and for the sake of Byron, give it up, baby. I don't care if you have to give back everything to her and be strugglin' again, it jus' ain't worth it." Stella embraced her daughter. "Do that for Mama, OK, baby?"

Melody just hugged her mother tightly, keeping her silence.

During the ride back home from taking her mother to the airport, Melody began thinking.

Maybe they're right. Maybe I need to give up this gay bullshit. God created me to be loved by a man, not to be sleeping and having sex with a woman. Hell, I can't even get me a piece of dick unless it's plastic or rubber, and Lord knows I like the real deal. But dick isn't the issue here. I've hurt my mother and I'm possibly about to lose my only child, all because I chose to be with a dyke and married a crackhead. But how can I be a dyke if I still have desires for dick?

Damn, I miss Larry. I wonder if he'd talk to me if I called him. I wonder if he'd dick me down if I asked him to? Hell, why do I keep thinking about dick so much? Maybe I'm not gay after all. Maybe it's just a fatal attraction. Maybe I'd better take my family's advice. But if I do decide to take their advice, hell, I won't have my own business, and I'd have to live struggling again from day to day, dealing with final notices, groceries, Byron's expensive taste, gasoline, and all kinds of other shit! I can't imagine living like that again. Mama talking about she'd rather be broke, on welfare, with one eye, and all that bullshit, but there's no way in hell she'd want to go from powerful to penniless.

I've always wanted my own shop, and now that I've got it, I'm going to do everything in my power to keep it, even if it means paying back Michelle in monthly payments. But she wouldn't take it. Nope, she wouldn't. If she couldn't have me and have control of my world, she'd want to see me fall flat on my face. She would want to see me struggle so I'd come crawling back to her, begging her, on hands and knees, for the flamboyant lifestyle I once lived. Bitch! But I got a remedy for that. I'm going to make me some quick thousands, bank it, then dismiss her and buy my own salon. Like Mama said, the bitch thinks she owns me. I've got to walk around with a bullet inside my head for the rest of my life be-

cause of her. Yes, it's definitely time to play the player, and it's time to bail out of this lesbian bullshit. But I've got to do it on the down low.

The grand opening of the salon was scheduled for Saturday, two days away. Fortunately, all lights were green and the salon was ready for business. In Melody's personal life she still had lots of unfinished issues to take care of. She thanked God that Michelle had paid her bills while she was hospitalized. But she felt all good things must come to an end, all but her new business.

Angela and Pat had been very supportive in assisting Melody with the grand opening. Angela had walked through a couple malls and shopping centers handing out fliers advertising the opening. Pat helped out by rolling around in her electric wheelchair passing out fliers at banks, churches, and at a couple parks. Melody phoned each of her old clients to inform them of her new location. Seventeen of them made appointments. There was a huge gospel concert at the Riverside Auditorium and Melody was on the scene handing out fliers to everyone who entered. Everything was going well.

One day after Michelle had taken care of her scam business, she stopped by the salon and observed Angela interviewing eight applicants. Deep inside she was furious, but she tried to conceal it. Melody was interviewing applicants as well, but what Michelle had to say could not wait. She marched over to Melody.

"How dare you have that bitch interviewing applicants to run a business that I made possible for you! I won't tolerate it, Melody. Under no circumstances will I allow her to have anything to do with what I'm part of!"

Melody frowned. "Excuse me, Mrs. Fong," Melody said to the woman she was interviewing. "I'll be with you in a few minutes." She then turned her attention to Michelle, who was standing with her hands on her hips. "I think it'll be more appropriate for us to step outside and talk." Melody led the way out the front door.

Angela overheard Michelle's outburst, but continued interviewing the applicant.

Melody pointed her index finger in Michelle's face. "That was very unprofessional and uncalled for, Michelle. What's wrong with you? Are you on drugs or something?" Michelle's pride dropped a few notches.

"I'm sorry, sweetheart. It's just that lately we haven't been spending much time together and-and I-I need you, Melody. I mean, maybe this whole salon thing was a mistake, because it seems to be pulling you away from me." She was sobbing, looking into Melody's eyes.

Observing them through the window, Angela shook her head in disgust.

Michelle reached for Melody's hand. "I see how she looks at you, Mel, and she doesn't fool me one bit. I've watched her look at your butt, and I've caught her undressing you with her eyes a few times too. The bitch wants you, Mel, and I think you know it."

"You're crazy, Michelle. I really think you need help."

"Oh, I need help? Me? No, Melody, I think you're the one who needs help if you can't see that bitch wants you. But you know what, Mel? Actually, I think you're the stupid one. You know why I think you're stupid, because you don't recognize the hand that's been feeding you. Did she pay your fucking house note when you were in a coma?"

Angela came out to let Melody know Stella was on the phone, but Michelle continued speaking her mind.

"Did she have anything to do with financing this place or furnishing it? Hell no, she didn't! She wants you, Mel! She wants you, but you're too damn blind to see it! Wake up and smell the coffee!"

"Excuse me, Michelle," Angela interrupted, "but you've got me mixed up, because I don't operate that way."

"You're a fucking liar, bitch!" Michelle yelled. "You don't have a husband, a boyfriend, or even a dog in life! I know you're after what's mine, but you can't have her. She belongs to me."

"Michelle!" Melody yelled. "Would you please leave! Now! Leave, Michelle!"

"No, Melody, it's OK. I'll leave," Angela offered. "Mom warned me that this might happen, and I should've taken her advice."

"No, Angela, don't leave. Please don't."

"Now you're begging the bitch to stay! Let her go, Mel! We can manage without her."

Angela went back inside, excused herself from the applicant she was interviewing, grabbed her keys and purse, and stormed out of the salon. Michelle was now satisfied, feeling like she had won.

When Melody made it home from the salon, Michelle was lying in the bed naked, impatiently waiting for her.

"Hi, baby," Michelle said with a huge smile like nothing had ever happened. But Melody wasn't in the mood for socializing, and she damn sure was not in the mood for sex, at least not with Michelle.

"My day was going well until your unnecessary disruption," Melody replied dryly. "You've not only made me lose a customer, Michelle, but a friend as well."

"You're still tripping on that Angela bitch, huh? I knew you two were fucking around. I knew it. I'll kill that bitch, Mel! I swear to God, I'll put her out of her fucking misery! She doesn't know who she's fucking with. She has the right idea, but she's got the wrong bitch!"

"So now you're a killer, right? Over jealousy, right? Just like your fucking wife," Melody said.

"Mel, you've got to believe that I hadn't talked to Rosie in over six months. I had no idea what she was thinking, or what she was up to, so don't keep bringing that bullshit up to me!"

"But instead, just drop it, right? It'll be easier for you if I just forgot all about it, won't it?"

"You've really been acting like a bitch lately, Mel. I think that salon and your relationship with Angela is pulling us apart. We've only made love three times since you've been out of the hospital, and we used to make love two to three times a day. I've had it, Mel, and I'm fed up to my fucking neck. I feel you're not happy with me anymore. Is that it? Is that it, Mel? You've chosen that bitch over me, haven't you?"

"You're sick, Michelle. You need help. Good fucking night. I'm sleeping in the other room," Melody said, and then left the room

When Melody made it to the salon there were eleven of her old customers and seven new ones standing in line. She had hired two manicurists, two pedicurists, a barber, and two other hair stylists. She approached each of her long-term customers and greeted them. Pat was first in line, but Angela, who had also had an appointment, didn't show up.

"Hey everybody," Melody greeted in good spirits. "Welcome to Melody's Extraordinary Hair, Nails, and Feet! For those of you who've experienced my tardiness in the past, as you can see, I'm here ahead of schedule and ready to rock and roll. Let's get this party started!"

Larry, who had driven Pat to the salon, climbed out of his truck and went inside. He had heard a lot about it from his wife and daughter, but he wanted to see it for himself. Melody put on a CD by Marvin Gaye, and then walked over to Pat and began making small talk with her while starting to do her hair. The waiting customers were being entertained by the music, while Larry sat there undressing Melody with his eyes.

"Where's Angela?" Melody asked Pat.

"She wasn't feeling well. She said she'd call you and reschedule," Pat lied. The truth was that Angela found another salon.

She'd told her mother that as long as Michelle had anything to do with the salon, she wouldn't come near the premises.

All the chairs in the waiting area were filled, so filled that three waiting customers had to stand.

Tomorrow, Melody thought. *I'll bring a couple more chairs from home.*

Occasionally Larry and Melody shot glances and smiles at each other, but of course, Pat was underneath the dryer and couldn't see them. Business had been constant all day. Closing time was at exactly 6:45 PM. Afterward, Melody locked herself inside and put on another CD by The Isley Brothers. Happily, she began singing along to the lyrics.

She felt fantastic. She danced around the salon until she remembered the bottle of vodka in her Suburban, then she quickly stepped out to get it. When she returned, she took a few sips, threw on a Luther CD, and began singing along to the lyrics.

She felt so good and so at ease, but something was missing. Larry. Smiling, she picked up the phone and dialed his cell number.

"Hello," Larry answered.

"Hi, baby," Melody said excitedly. "Can you talk?"

"Yeah, what's up?" he asked after he made sure Pat wasn't around.

"I just called to tell you I miss you. When I saw you today, I melted, baby. I found myself reminiscing about our past sexual encounters." She giggled.

"Is that right? I miss you too, sweetheart. When I saw you today you were looking absolutely beautiful. And congratulations on your new shop, too. You deserve it."

"Thank you. Well anyway, can we meet? I need you."

"Now?"

"I told you, I miss you and I need you. If you want me to beg for it, then I will, but I need you right this minute."

"Your house. Twenty minutes," he replied.

"Not my house. Michelle might pop up. I want the feeling and memory to last this time. No telling when there will be a next time, you know what I mean?"

"OK, ah, all right. Meet me at the Travelodge in thirty minutes. You'll probably beat me there, so go ahead and pay for the room, and I'll reimburse you when I make it there. And let whoever's working the window know I'm on my way so they can direct me to the room."

"Got it." Now she really felt happy.

The key was waiting for him when he arrived. Like old times, he had a fifth of vodka, a bag of chronic, a bouquet of roses, a box of chocolates, and a huge I-miss-you card. He was dressed in a tight pair of jeans and a T-shirt, with an oily pair of tennis shoes on his feet.

"Hi, baaaby," Melody greeted excitedly as he entered the room.

"Hey, sweetheart, how you doing?"

He handed her the bouquet of roses, the chocolates, and the card. She was already naked, hot, and ready. Pushing the gifts aside, she eased out of bed, gave him a long, slow, wet kiss, and then unzipped his pants, pulled out his penis, and sucked it like there was no tomorrow.

"I miss it," she said, "but I miss you more." Once again it was on.

After sex, they engaged in small talk over vodka and a joint. When they departed it was almost midnight. They both had some explaining to do when they got home.

Michelle had called the salon several times, but no one answered. At first, she was in the mood for making love. Now she was in the mood to kill. She'd been pacing Melody's house, in panties and bra, waiting impatiently for the sound of the Suburban. Seven o'clock passed, then eight o'clock, then nine o'clock, and then finally it was ten o'clock. When the clock struck eleven, she threw on one of Melody's robes, ran outside to her Mercedes, grabbed her pistol, and then went back inside the house.

"This bitch doesn't know who she's fucking with! Bitch, do you know that I'm a fucking convict! If you didn't know, you're damn sure going to find out tonight!" Michelle yelled furiously while continuing to pace, now with her pistol in hand. "I know she's with Angela! She thinks I'm stupid, but I'll show her who's stupid!! You had the right idea, but you're fucking with the wrong bitch!" she yelled again.

At ten minutes after midnight, Melody walked through the front door. Calmly, with both hands behind her back and pistol in hand, Michelle approached her.

"How was she, Mel? Was she better than me? Did she give you a good licking?"

"Chelle, quit being so insecure," Melody replied, ignoring Michelle's assumptions.

"I said, was she better than me?" Michelle stepped in front of her, still concealing the pistol.

Melody shoved her aside and walked toward her bedroom, but that only made Michelle angrier.

"You know what your problem is, Mel? You don't take me seriously. But I'm here to tell you that you really don't know who you're fucking with!" Michelle said. She then aimed her pistol at Melody's face.

Melody screamed and stood in a state of shock, not knowing what to do. She screamed louder, hoping to attract the attention of someone. "Well, Mel, that was your last orgasm, bitch," Michelle said, then pulled the trigger once, then again. It was jammed.

Melody sprinted for the front door, but Michelle threw the pistol at her, hitting her in the back of the head, causing Melody to stagger. Melody managed to grab hold of the door-knob and turn it, but then the security door was double locked, which gave Michelle time to grab her by her hair, pulling large portions of her weave loose. Melody quickly turned, now fighting for her life, and threw a punch, connecting with the side of

Michelle's face and causing her to drop the pistol. Melody punched her again, knocking her to the floor and leaving her there.

"I'll kill you, bitch! I'll kill you!" Michelle yelled. Michelle was stunned long enough for Melody to unlock the security door and dash to her neighbor Patty's house. Michelle hurriedly retrieved the pistol, chased Melody a few yards, then pulled the trigger again, but the pistol was still jammed. Michelle then ran back inside the house and grabbed her clothes and keys. She sprinted to her Benz, climbed in, and peeled off.

"She tried to kill me!" Melody frantically yelled to her neighbors, then collapsed on Patty's living room sofa. Patty dialed 911.

Detective Bell had a hunch that the Melody Pullman case was far from being over. He had left word at the station, and had written in huge print inside the briefing room for anyone to call him immediately if a call was received regarding Melody Pullman. It was 12:49 AM when he received that call.

After questioning Melody, Detective Bell knew it was another case of a jealous lovers' quarrel. He then put out an all points bulletin on Michelle Green. That morning he got search warrants from judges located in the cities Michelle owned property, and in no time, her home in Newport Beach, her twenty-two unit apartment complex in Santa Monica, her twenty-four unit complex in Long Beach, the nineteen units she owned in San Bernardino, and her cabin in Big Bear were all surrounded by police.

Tony and Antoinette had come to aid and comfort their sister, and they had also contacted Stella. Detective Bell, with the aide of Tony and Antoinette, persuaded Melody into turning state's evidence against Michelle. Then she told the detective all she knew about Michelle's fraudulent operations, and the detective immediately confiscated Michelle's personal computer and laptop, her filing cabinets, and ten hard drives containing enough information, combined with her extensive arrest and conviction record, to put her away for the next twenty years.

Because this was another attempted murder on Melody's life, Detective Bell was on the case, working closely with a fraud detective named Ohno. They ordered stakeouts at each of Michelle's properties, and also at other places Melody informed them that her lover might go.

As time went by, Ohno and Bell discovered that Michelle had somehow sold six homes, a restaurant, and twenty acres of commercial land that wasn't hers.

Melody's new business had been running much better than expected. She was raking in thousands of dollars weekly. Her only fear was that the building might get confiscated with the rest of Michelle's illegal assets.

Detective Ohno and Bell had used various tactics to apprehend Michelle, but each attempt had failed. They had ordered taps on Melody's home and business phones, and twenty-four hour surveillance on Michelle's properties, but still they had no success. Detective Bell actually enjoyed the challenge of searching for her, but he could tell by her record and wealth that catching her wasn't going to be easy.

Detective Ohno was a Korean who had been working fraud for a little over eleven years. He was a quick thinker and a man with excellent strategic tactics. Unlike Detective Bell, Ohno was not an alcoholic. He took his work seriously, but this case was much different from all the others. Michelle Green had nineteen aliases and no telling how many identities.

Since Ohno had been assigned to the case, he had stapled pictures of Michelle on every wall of his apartment, even in his restroom. No matter what room he entered, he would see her. He also had copies of documents—check books, credit cards, and other paperwork linking her to over thirty-five fraud operations—lying neatly on his table. Ohno, like Detective Bell, was obsessed with catching her.

"We've got her by the tits, Ohno, that is, of course, if we catch her. We have enough evidence to put her away for life," Detective Bell told his partner.

"No doubt, we've got her. But first, we've got to catch her. We're not dealing with an average criminal, here. We're dealing with a smart criminal with mucho dineros. The bitch has money to burn, Ohno, and those are the hardest kind of criminals to catch."

Michelle had changed her identity as well as her appearance. She had a variety of looks, and thanks to Rosie Martinez, she had even more identities. She cut her hair short, and dyed it red, and rode in an electric wheelchair everywhere she went. She had arranged for her vehicles, before the search warrant, to be picked up and stored at a nearby storage facility. She was so sure of herself, and so full of courage, that she moved into one of her vacant Santa Monica apartments, and had been living there since she had been on the run. It didn't take her long to figure out who the undercover policemen were that were staking out her building. Each day she rolled by them, and had even spoken to them, appearing to be an elderly, red-haired, innocent woman. They made small talk with her occasionally, not realizing they were conversing with the woman they were after. If she had somewhere far to go, she'd call a cab, and for her local runs she caught the bus.

Cops are so damn stupid, it's pathetic! They're so damn macho, but yet so goddamn stupid, Michelle thought.

CHAPTER 31

Things had been going quite well for Melody. Her business was successful and her love life, even though she was still fooling around with someone else's puddin', was fulfilling. As far as she was concerned, it had never been better.

Finally, after all of her years of working for others, she was now a successful entrepreneur. The government had seized the salon building, but her customers agreed to come to her home for their beauty needs. The seizure and auction process had taken two and half months. Melody saved money, preparing herself financially to purchase the building. Her patience finally paid off, and the building was rightfully hers.

Faithfully, Pat and Angela continued to keep their appointments once every two weeks, and like old times, Melody and Larry resumed their relationship. Sex with Larry was so good this time that she had even given him the keys to her salon, as well as the keys to her home.

One Sunday morning, after a long night of drinking vodka and smoking a joint, Melody awakened and decided to go to church. While getting dressed, her telephone rang.

"Hello," Melody answered.

"Hey girl, how you doin'?" Stella asked.

"I'm fine, Mama, just trying to get ready for church."

"Church?" Stella answered, shocked. "What happened to you, chile? You had a vision in the middle of the night or sump'n, or you just been doin' so much wrong, you think it's time to go to the altar and confess?" Stella said, smirking.

"Jesus, Mama, do you give me credit for anything? You criticize my thoughts, my plans, my men, and everything I do."

"I ain't criticizin' you, chile. I jus' call it like I see it."

"How can you see it, Mama, when you're over two thousand miles away, unless you're like Superman and have X-ray vision?"

"There's one thing I don't need X-ray to see. I'll bet you've been drinkin' all night, haven't you?"

Melody didn't want to lie, but she didn't want to confess either. "Aaand? I'ma grown woman. If I choose to—"

"I raised you, chile," Stella interrupted. "You can't fool me."

"Mama, get off my case, OK?"

"I'm jus' sayin', chile, that you can't drink, cuss, and do everything wrong under the sun, then run to the Lord's house on Sunday mornin' all dressed in white, talkin' 'bout you blessed, or expectin' a blessin' from God. It doesn't work like that, chile."

"Anyway," Melody said, "let me finish getting ready. I'll call you when I get back from church."

"You tryin' to rush me off, now, huh? Have you talked to Byron lately?"

"Not for a couple weeks.'

"Why?"

"I've been too busy, Mama."

"Too busy to call your son?"

"Mama."

"Don't Mama me, chile, jus' do what you s'pose to do."

"Mama, you're gonna make me late for church."

"Since when have you cared about bein' on time, chile? You'd be late for your own funeral if you wasn't already dead."

"Yeah, Mama, whatever."

"Say a prayer for me, chile, and I'll talk to you later."

"Humph. You need prayer, huh? What have you been doing wrong, Mama?"

"You better ask yourself that question. I've lived my life, and I'm proud to say that I'm a very fortunate and blessed woman. You can take that to the bank."

"Talk to you later, Mama." She then hung up and continued getting dressed.

The church was packed with people there to hear Reverend Joe Black preach. Melody scanned the faces in the church. Fortunately, there was no one there she knew. She was wearing a red and white dress, a pair of white high heels, and had red and white ribbons neatly tied in her hair. She examined herself before leaving home and was completely satisfied with the way she looked.

Reverend Joe Black began preaching, but it didn't take him long to start hollering.

"I say, some of you partied last night, defiling the body of Christ with alcohol and drugs, and you got the nerve to sit on the front row! You think you're fooling God, don't you? Unh unh. No, no, no. You're not fooling anyone but yourself. Oh yes, God acknowledges your presence in his house, and he also sees what you're doing when you leave here. Clean up your act, people! Clean your hearts and minds with the word of God. Live right! You can't label yourself a Christian if you're using devilish words. Turn from your wicked ways, you hypocrites! Cut out the alcohol, the lying, the drugs, the fornicating, and the adultery! You can't get to heaven if you don't please God while you're on earth! God is watching you! It doesn't matter if you're in a building, a house, a hospital, a jail, an airplane, or a boat. God is watching you!"

The Reverend Joe Black continued preaching for the next forty-five minutes or so. The entire congregation, including the choir, had given him their undivided attention. For the first time in three years, Melody sat through the sermon even though she wanted to leave. After church, members of the congregation gathered in the parking lot and made small talk, but not Melody.

She climbed into her Suburban and went home. When she made it there, Larry's truck was parked in her driveway. She smiled and thought, *Damn! Here I go sinning again.*

She parked, then walked into her house. The smell of spaghetti, garlic bread, and sweet potato pie permeated the air. Larry was standing almost completely naked at the stove, stirring the spaghetti. The only thing he had on was an apron.

"Hey, baby cakes. What's going on?" Larry asked when he observed her staring at him.

"Hey, baaaby. Whatcha cooking, good looking?" She then gave him a long, wet, kiss.

"Just hooking us up some spaghetti, babe. I figured you were at church when I kept calling and you didn't answer, so I thought I'd surprise you by making dinner. You aren't mad at me, are you?"

"Why should I be? You make me feel special." She smiled. "I'm flattered, honey, but you can't start something you don't plan to finish, you know."

"What are you talking about, sweetheart?"

"Well, what about rolling out the red carpet for me, the champagne, bubble bath, and candle lights?"

"Aw, OK, you got me. Next time I'll be more thoughtful."

"You tried, but I'll tell you what, you can make it up to me in bed. Deal?"

"Deal!" he replied.

After dinner and sex, they fell asleep, exhausted. When Larry awakened, it was almost eight.

"Damn!" he cursed. He then quickly dressed, kissed her good-bye, and hurried home to Pat.

Chapter 32

Michelle

When Michelle received notices of forfeiture for all her properties, she wanted to cry, but she knew crying wouldn't do her any good.

I have one week to move, she thought. *Damn! I should've never fucked around with that bitch! Now she's cost me property and my fucking life! Bitch! I can't wait a week, I gotta do something soon!*

Earlier Michelle had purchased a rundown 1985 Buick Century, which was uncharacteristic for her. She figured the police, especially Detective Bell, would be expecting her to drive luxury cars and wear expensive jewelry and clothing, but she had them fooled. The windows on the Buick were tinted so dark that you couldn't see inside the car. She sold all her jewelry, handbags, and clothing to friends. Both her vehicles were in storage, and she had closed her bank accounts, netting a little over six hundred thousand dollars. She had planned everything perfectly.

"They're never going to catch me!" Michelle said out loud while sitting in her apartment. "Cops are fucking brainless. Even that goddamn Detective Bell. They're all stupid! No education higher than a fucking high school diploma! No brains! I've got street sense, book knowledge, and way too much common sense for those brainless cops to ever catch me! Catch me if you can, copper! Catch me if you can!" The undercover officers were posted right in front of her apartment, and they didn't even know that she was right under their noses.

After having a new engine, transmission, and tires put on the Buick, she hopped on to Interstate 10, eastbound, and headed toward downtown Los Angeles. While driving, she thought, *I've lived the lifestyle of the rich, once, and I can do it again, but I have to lay low and portray the image of a derelict for a while. Those slow-thinking cops will never catch me. Brainless motherfuckers!*

She took the Alameda Street exit, made a left, traveled a few blocks, then parked. She was now in the Garment District. The Garment District was an area of downtown Los Angeles where wholesalers sold merchandise on sidewalks and in alleys. People came from far away cities to purchase clothing and merchandise of all kinds. Michelle already knew exactly what she wanted to purchase, so she walked to Maple Street where sporting goods, luggage, and stationary supplies were sold. The sidewalks were crowded with so many people—shoppers, shoplifters, undercover cops, and dope fiends—that Michelle was forced to walk in the street. As she stood looking at the gazebos and tents, she pointed to a beige tent, then signaled for the salesman.

"I want that one," she said. The clerk, a five-foot, Hispanic man, smiled, revealing a mouth full of rotten teeth.

"No Ingles, no Ingles. No comprende, no comprende."

Michelle wondered how a person could run a business in the United States without at least a rudimentary understanding of English. She smiled politely, pointed at the tent, then back at herself, then back at the tent. The salesman then understood.

"Si, si, senorita, si," he answered, smiling. "Cincuenta, senorita, cincuenta." She thought, *I should've taken a Spanish class. This is totally fucked up!*

"How much, amigo?" Michelle asked.

"Cincuenta, senorita, cincuenta."

"How much?" she repeated, getting exasperated.

"Cincuenta, cincuenta, cincuenta, cincuenta," the salesman

said, getting irritated. A pedestrian observing the exchange, approached and quickly settled the confusion.

"Fifty dollars, ma'am. He says the tent is fifty dollars."

"Thanks," Michelle said to the man. "Will you please tell him I would like to buy it, and that I'll pay him to have it carried to my car?" She then peeled a crispy fifty-dollar bill from her bankroll and handed it to the salesman. After collecting the money, he disappeared through a small door and returned seconds later, escorting a huge, barefoot Mexican woman, who was holding a cob of corn in one hand and a burrito in the other. The salesman looked at Michelle, then pointed to himself.

"Me go, me go." He then picked up a box and followed her.

On their way to the Buick, she purchased four area rugs, six face towels, a twelve-inch knife, and a 9mm pistol for her protection. She'd already gotten rid of the gun that had jammed on her.

Once her purchases were in the car, she drove to Fifth Street and Alameda, and turned right. The streets were filled on both sides with street people pushing their life savings in shopping carts, panhandlers, and addicts trying to earn or steal to support their habits. A bum approached the Buick while she waited for the traffic to clear, and without asking, he pulled out a spray bottle and rag and began cleaning her windows. She handed him a five-dollar bill.

He might help me one day, she thought. *Hell, he may even save my life one day.*

She then made a left turn, drove about fifty yards, and parked. She smiled to herself, so sure that she was being very clever.

Those so-called undercover cops will never find me here. Yeah, I'm the one who's going undercover! she thought.

She got out of her car, found a nice spot, laid a few rugs on the ground, and began setting up her tent.

Detective Bell and Detective Ohno were still lost. Several months had gone by and they were no closer to catching

Michelle than in the beginning. Michelle was wealthy, clever, and extremely intelligent. With her contacts and money, she could be anywhere. Several of her friends, whom the detectives questioned, had expressed doubt that the police would ever catch her.

CHAPTER 33

One day soon after Melody's salon reopened, Pat and her mother were shopping at a dollar store. As Pat rolled down the aisle in her electric wheelchair, putting selected items into her basket, Tosha walked past her, did a double take, then turned around and approached her.

"Girlfriend, is that you?" Tosha asked.

Pat looked at the gay man wearing skin-tight jeans and a cut off T-shirt, which revealed his stomach and navel.

"Am I who?" she asked sarcastically.

"Ah, uh, didn't you, ah, damn. Don't you drive a Lexus and know a beautician named Melody?"

Pat, bewildered, looked at Tosha more closely.

"Yes to both of your questions. But what does that have to do with you?"

"You don't remember, do you?" Tosha shook his head back and forth in disbelief.

"Remember what?"

"The day of your accident."

Pat dropped the can of Lysol she was holding as her mind began drifting into the past. Tosha helped her remember.

"Girlfriend, am I glad to see you. Do you know that bitch turned gay while she was fooling with your husband?"

"What are you talking about?" Pat stuttered, wide-eyed.

"You mean you forgot? That big, fat detective didn't tell you? He ain't shit, girlfriend, because he said he was going to tell you about what he discovered."

"Who was going to tell me what? A detective? What are you talking about?" Pat was still stuttering. While they were talking, her mother walked up, pushing a shopping cart full of items, and stared at Tosha, then back at Pat.

"Am I interrupting something?" she finally asked.

"No, Mom, ah, not at all."

"Hi, I'm Tosha. I'm glad to meet you," Tosha said enthusiastically. "Your daughter was with me the day she had her accident. I dropped her at her car after we had witnessed her husband and Melody kissing like newlyweds. I told her that every day between two PM and six PM, her husband would always be at Melody's, so I offered to prove it to her. I drove her to Melody's at about three o'clock, and as sure as the sky is blue, they walked out hugging and kissing like they were in high school."

Her mother stood there, shocked by what she was hearing.

"Are you sure this was our Larry?" Pat's mother asked.

"I'd put my life on it, girlfriend. My man lives a couple blocks from her, and every day I drove down that street to get to my man's house. My man loves me, you know, and he says a day without this," Tosha pointed to his butt, "is like a day without water or food. So I make it a habit to be there to please him every day of the week."

Tears began flowing down Pat's face as memories of the day she was with Tosha returned.

"And, girlfriend," Tosha continued, "I'll bet you were so messed up in the head after you saw your husband kissing that bitch who had been doing your hair for years, you flipped out. You probably ran a light, or just weren't paying attention to what you were doing. But it's good to see you're doing well. Ask the detective about it. He knows everything."

Tosha's words felt like a machete tearing though Pat's flesh. He then voluntarily left his name and number with them, smiled, and left. Pat's mother knelt down and embraced her daughter.

"It's gonna be OK, baby, I promise. We're going to see what lie he's going to tell." Her mother was very upset by what she'd heard.

Forgetting the items she stored in the basket of the wheelchair, Pat turned her wheelchair around and headed out of the store. Her mother left the basket full of items in the middle of the aisle and followed her outside.

During the last several months, Pat occasionally pulled Detective Bell's card from her purse and stared at it, not remembering why she had it. But now, accompanied by her mother, she was headed to his office seeking information that should've been brought to her attention before now. She'd already called him, so he was expecting her.

When Pat and her mother approached the front desk of the police station, an officer escorted them to Detective Bell's office. Once entering, he stood up and greeted them, but Pat refused his handshake and immediately began stating her case.

"You've got nerve, Detective! You've got some fucking nerve!" The detective closed his door and sat behind his desk.

"How may I help you, Mrs. Myers?" he asked.

"Don't try to be nice to me, Detective! I should've known you were full of shit when I first laid eyes on you!" She was very angry.

"Why, Detective?" Pat's mother interjected. "Do you know that we've been helping Melody with her business and other situations? Apparently not. Do you know that every two weeks my daughter, or one of my granddaughters is sitting in Melody's chair, paying her our money? She's probably laughing at us like we're some damn fools." Detective Bell adjusted himself in his high back leather chair.

"What are you ladies talking about?" he asked.

"You know what we're talking about, Detective. We stumbled across Tosha, a gay beautician you questioned during your investigation into Melody's shooting. Why didn't you tell me my husband was fucking my beautician? Why didn't you tell me, Mr. Detective, that my accident occurred after I witnessed my husband and Melody kissing in front of her home? Why? When you came to my house that day, you already knew. But what I want to know is, why didn't you tell me?" Pat was forceful and direct.

Detective Bell sighed.

"You knew! You fucking knew!" Pat attempted to continue to speak, but she began crying instead. Her mother embraced her.

"It's going to be all right, baby. Don't worry. Both of them will get what's coming to them. You can't do wrong for too long and get away with it."

"How do you plan to handle this situation, Mrs. Myers?" the detective asked Pat. Regaining her composure, she wiped the tears from her face.

"What I didn't know wouldn't hurt me, right, Detective?"

"It wasn't my job to tell you, Mrs. Myers. There are many things we discovered that I wanted to bring to people's attention, but I would've been out of line. The truth hurts, Mrs. Myers, and right now, the truth has caused you a lot of pain."

"Yeah, you're right, Detective. You are absolutely right." Pat now had an attitude.

"Now back to my question, Mrs. Myers. How are you planning to handle this?"

"I'll let you know, Detective. Believe me, I'll let you know." Tears fell from her eyes again as she turned her wheelchair, waited for her mother to open the door, and left the office.

"So what are you going to do, baby?" Pat's mother asked during their ride home.

Pat had been in a daze and had not spoken since they left

the police station. There were so many things running through her mind that she couldn't concentrate on any one thing. She was confused and had no idea how to proceed.

"I don't know, Mom," Pat finally answered while continuing to stare out the window.

"Are you going to tell Melody you know about her and Larry?"

"I don't know."

"I hope you don't plan on doing anything stupid," Pat's mother said as she pulled into the driveway. "If I were you, I wouldn't tell either of the girls, because both of them would probably be ready to kill her." She then got out, opened the sliding door, and let down the wheelchair ramp. "Are you going to be all right, baby?"

"Yeah, Mama, I'll be OK."

"Now don't you go in there and do anything crazy. You don't need more problems than you already have. Call me if you need me, you hear?"

"Yeah, Mom, I hear you." Pat then wheeled herself into the house.

It was five PM and Larry hadn't yet made it home.

So, Melody has been fucking my husband for four years, Pat thought. She then wheeled herself to the den and fixed a stiff drink. It had been years since she had a drink. She picked up the remote to the stereo and played a song by Mary Wells entitled "Two Lovers." The lyrics went, "Well, I got two lovers and I ain't ashamed. Two lovers and I love them both the same." She tried switching songs, but it seemed like everything she put on was about someone cheating.

She then sat back, staring out the window, drinking and talking out loud.

"And that bitch called herself my friend. My mama warned me about bringing bitches to my house around my husband. She's been fucking my husband for years and I was too damn blind to see it. No wonder he comes home at the same damn time every goddamn evening. And no wonder he doesn't want to fuck me anymore. It takes two dirty muthafuckas to do some shit like that. Not one, but two. A man is gonna be a man, I guess, and a whore is gonna be a whore, whether she has a job or not. I feel like killing both of them. Both of them." She then finished her drink and fixed herself another one.

Angrily, she started a song by the Spinners entitled "Love Don't Love Nobody." The lyrics were, "It takes a fool to learn, yes sir, that love don't love nobody . . . It takes a fool, to learn, yes it does, girl, that love don't love no one."

"Twenty-nine fucking years I been married to him," Pat suddenly yelled. "And he does me like this! For years this bitch has been doing my hair every two fucking weeks, and she does this to me! So they just said, 'Fuck me! Fuck ole handicapped Pat!' Ain't that a bitch! But you know what? You know what? They belong together, both of them! Together in hell!" She then turned her glass up and finished her second drink. Larry still hadn't made it home.

Larry made it home a little later than his usual time. Pat had gotten rid of the strong odor of alcohol on her breath by brushing her teeth, gargling with mouthwash, and letting a couple of garlic cloves settle on her tongue. She didn't want him to know she'd been drinking. After thinking of a plan, she fell asleep in her wheelchair.

Most days when Larry came home, she would already be comfortably lying in bed. But not tonight. He wondered why Selma hadn't tucked her away like she usually did before she got off. He quickly dismissed the thought and awakened her with a kiss.

"Daddy's home, Mama. Wake up." After laying her comfortably in her adjustable bed, he said, "You can go back to sleep now. I'll see you in the morning." He then left the bedroom, fixed himself a drink, went to the den, and relaxed in his recliner, sipping vodka on the rocks. He felt pretty good about himself. After a long swallow, he began thinking.

I've sent two of my kids to college. I operate and maintain my own business. I married a beautiful woman who is now a paraplegic, but has a fixed, steady income of nearly a thousand dollars a month. I've got a beautiful mistress who gives me sex whenever I want it. I drive a brand new truck and live in a new home. I feel like a king on a throne. I got the whole, wide world in my hands. Some guys have all the luck, and get all the breaks. I've got it all. Every man chooses his path, and I've chosen mine.

Larry grabbed his cell phone, planning to call Melody, but noticed on his caller ID that there had been a call from the Riverside Police Department.

What the fuck! It must be that goddamn detective! I wonder what the hell he wants? He'll probably tell me to stop fucking Melody, or he'll want to know if I fucked Michelle yet. What a fucking asshole, he thought, then dialed Melody's number.

CHAPTER 34

Big Steve

Big Steve had written Melody several more letters, begging her to write him, but he still hadn't received any letters from her. His preaching continued and his faith, wisdom, knowledge, and understanding increased as time passed. He'd gotten to a point where he could easily draw large crowds with just his presence.

On Sundays, Big Steve and his associates arranged for microphones and large speakers to be set up on the field for church services. All races attended. Everyone enjoyed listening to him preach, mainly because they could relate to what he was talking about. One of his favorite phrases as he preached was, "Been there, done that." Even though he'd never been a hardcore career criminal, he could relate to what inmates had been through. One way or another, their convictions were always drug related. They had either stolen something to try to get drugs, sold drugs, or they were drugs users and murderers.

Steve's parents wrote him at least three times a month. They told him that when he was released they had a surprise waiting for him. They were very proud of their only son for giving his life to God and making a plan to live right. Steve figured they probably bought him another car or arranged for him to move into his own apartment.

Chaplain Acres was so proud of him that he tried everything in his power to get him an early release. The chaplain went as far as contacting several churches in the Moreno Valley area in order for Steve to continue ministering the word of God once he was released. Even though he'd been employed as chaplain by the prison for over thirty years, Chaplain Acres's request for Steve's early release was denied.

CHAPTER 35

Pat and her mother were the only ones aware of the fact that Pat had been taking physical therapy classes for the past year. It was supposed to be a surprise to her family. The reality was that Pat was never actually paralyzed at all, but in the beginning she was diagnosed with a slight concussion, which had only lasted about a week. She had paid her doctor extremely well to falsify her medical records to reflect that she had amnesia. Thank God Angela had moved back home during the time Larry began giving her overdoses of medication, which were actually nothing more than mild painkillers, but with her being not fully recovered, she had no choice but to go along with it. Larry thought the pills were mind altering drugs, which were used to calm the brain, and in some cases have been known to lock the brain.

Pat had faked her illness for two years. When she and her mother had the encounter with Tosha, in the dollar store, she was already aware of Larry's affair with Melody, but she pretended like she didn't know. She could've won an Oscar for her acting.

She remembered the day of the accident clearly. Even though her body had gotten banged up pretty badly, her mind was always intact. Actually, she was testing her husband's love for her. Unfortunately, he had failed the test.

It was 8:30 when Selma awakened Pat with breakfast the next morning.

"Good morning, my dearest one. How are you feeling on this beautiful Friday morning?" Selma asked. Pat wiped the sleep from her eyes.

"I'm fine, Selma. Just fine. How's your family?"

"Everyone's OK, Pat. I'll be glad when the kids are done with college, you know? Things aren't getting any cheaper these days," Selma replied, smiling.

Suddenly thoughts of Melody and Larry appeared in Pat's mind, causing her to go into a trance.

"Are you OK?" Selma asked, noticing the sudden change in Pat.

"I'm fine, Selma. Thanks," Pat answered, regaining her awareness.

"Your husband is already eating, honey. I'll let him know that you're about to do the same."

"Thanks, Selma. Will you please do me a favor? Remind him that today is Friday and I have an eleven o'clock appointment with my beautician."

"No problem," Selma replied. Then she disappeared.

Detective Bell had been unsuccessfully trying to contact Larry. Even though he would be out of line to inform Larry of Pat's knowledge about his relationship with Melody, for some reason, he felt obligated to do so. After calling Larry and Pat's home and discovering that they had gone to Melody's salon, the detective smelled trouble. Hurriedly, he climbed into his car and sped to the salon.

As Larry wheeled Pat into the salon, the smooth sound of Marvin Gaye's "Sexual Healing" filled the building. The pedicure, manicure, and hair styling sections were filled with customers. Business was booming for Melody, and had been since the reopening of the salon after it was seized and Melody was able to buy it back. As Larry stood alongside the wall waiting for a seat, Pat wheeled herself to Melody's booth.

"Hey, girlfriend," Melody greeted enthusiastically.

"Hi," Pat replied dryly. "I'm just here for my biweekly appointment. I should've called you, but—"

"It's OK, girl, you're fine. As soon as I'm done with Shirley, I'll fit you in, OK?"

"Thanks," Pat answered without looking up. She then wheeled herself away.

As Melody put the finishing touch on Pat's hair, Pat began making conversation.

"You and I have been friends for a long time, Melody, and you know, I really feel comfortable talking to you about certain things—basically about anything." She was appraising herself in the mirror.

"Thanks for the compliment, Pat. You make me feel very important and needed, too." Melody was smiling like always.

"I've got a little situation and I need some advice," Pat said while holding a straight face.

"I'm always willing to help and advise people, especially friends of mine. Everyone needs a little counseling every now and then," Melody responded cheerfully.

"Good," Pat answered. "My cousin is having problems with her marriage. She's caught her husband on numerous occasions cheating with friends of hers. Anyway, to make a long story short, her friends are still fucking her husband. I feel that since you've always given good advice, you can tell me how to advise my cousin."

"She should leave the muthafucka," Melody advised instantly. "You see, Pat, most men are dogs from birth. They pass the stage of being cute, harmless little puppies and somehow become full-grown dogs with a capital D. That's the very reason I'm single. Trust no man," she replied humorously.

Suddenly, without holding onto anything for support, Pat stood up and took steps toward a disbelieving, wide-eyed Melody. Pat then reached into her purse.

"How much do I owe you, Melody?" she asked.

Bewildered, Larry jumped up from his seat at what he was witnessing and stood with his mouth agape.

"Trust no man, huh?" Pat said angrily, pulling out a .38 from her purse. "Trust no man, huh?" she yelled, now aiming at Melody's head. "No, Melody, I say, trust no bitch who calls herself your friend! But like a damn fool, I trusted you! You backstabbed me! You've been fucking my husband and you call yourself my friend! How could you? How could you?" Larry rushed toward her.

"Pat, put up that gun!" Larry shouted. "Please, put up the—"

Pat fired two shots at his head. Then she turned and emptied the chamber into Melody, killing her instantly. The customers ran outside when they first saw the gun. Calmly Pat laid the gun on the counter, grabbed her purse, took out Detective Bell's card, and proceeded to dial his number, but before she could finish, he stormed into the salon at the same time. Pat smiled at her daughter, then at the detective.

"I saved you the work of conducting an investigation, Detective. Now, you don't have to waste your time looking for evidence or suspects. I had to do what I had to do to confirm my suspicions. Actually, I have no regrets about what I did. I hope that both those muthafuckas rot in hell."

Bell didn't bother cuffing Pat. Instead, he read her her rights and took her down to the station.

The medical examiner pronounced Melody and Larry dead a few seconds after checking the bodies.

Six months later, Pat pled temporary insanity and convinced a jury that she didn't know what she was doing at the time of the shooting. She was sentenced to only four years in a mental health facility. Fortunately, she'd only serve two years.

Epilogue

Once Big Steve served his prison sentence and was released, the surprise his parents had waiting for him was his own church. They'd bought an old building, had it completely remodeled, and converted it into an attractive church. It had the capacity to seat three hundred people.

A week prior to his release, his parents had gotten over a thousand fliers printed, advertising the grand opening of The Church of God in Christ of Moreno Valley.

On the first Sunday of service, Steve preached and testified in front of a full congregation. Among the listeners sat Detective Bell. Steve's parents sat hand in hand, proudly admiring their son as he walked the floor, preaching the word of God.

"Praise the Lord, praise the good Lord," Steve said thankfully. Every seat in the church was occupied. There were four huge speakers mounted on each wall, which allowed his voice to be heard clearly throughout the church. There was an additional speaker placed on the front porch so that passersby could also hear the word being preached. To Steve's surprise there were three senior citizens alongside the porch, sitting comfortably in their wheelchairs with open Bibles. He began preaching.

"Like the prodigal son, I have returned. You see, I've always considered myself a Christian, but due to Satan's clutches, I failed to please the Lord. It's easy for someone to say, 'I'm saved and I'm a Christian and I belong to Church such and such,' but the question is whether that person is just talking the talk, or are they walking the walk. You see, there are a lot of us in here who just talk the talk, but haven't walked the walk in their so-called Christian life. The book of James teaches us, my people, that we as Christians can't just be hearers and talkers of the word, but instead, we have to be doers of the word in order to please God. You see, I was once lost, but thank God, now I'm found," Big Steve preached. He then suddenly became more emotional.

"I was blinded by darkness once upon a time! Everything looked good to me! The illegal money, the fancy cars, the prostitutes, the drugs, stealing, lying, cheating, it all looked good to me, because that's how Satan wanted it to look! Satan had me blinded by his tricks and tools! He had me thinking that what was right, was wrong, and what was wrong, was right! Oh yes, people, he had his clutches on me! I was a man who was raised by loving parents with morality, respect, and kindness! I was raised not to lie, and not to steal, but the devil had me doing his dirty work! I was totally blinded to God's word! Praise the Lord, I say praise the Lord because now I can see! When I was thirsty, he gave me a drink of his precious blood. When I was hungry, he fed me his precious word! I say glory halleluja! Halleluja! Praise the Lord! Praise his holy name! Praise him! He's worthy to be praised! Praise him!" Big Steve shouted while walking the length of the stage, sweating and sparked and energized with the word of God. He was fueled with energy from above and loving every minute of it.

"Though I walk through the valley of the shadow of death, I will fear no evil! For he is with me! His rod and his staff shall comfort me! Brothers and sisters, I tell you, the devil is a liar! He told me to lie down and stay down! But the holy spirit told me to get up and walk boldly! Walk boldly in Jesus Christ! Not just today, but for the rest of my life! Can I get a witness? You see, a righteous man will fall down seven times and still manage to get back up! I said he will what?" Steve yelled, holding the mic toward the congregation, who all shouted, "Get back up!" Steve then continued.

"But for the wicked man, it isn't possible! For he who digs a pit shall fall into it! And he who rolls a stone will have the same stone rolled back at him! Amen?"

"Amen," the congregation sounded. After taking a few sips of water, he continued.

"Brothers and sisters, it's time to stop living lies, and it's time to quit being led, or should I say, misled by the blind and the ungodly. Can the blind lead the blind? Open your minds and your hearts to the Lord, my people! Take heed to the Lord's words! Having your own husband should keep you from doing something immoral.

"Husbands and wives should be fair with each other about having sex. A wife belongs to her husband instead of to herself, and a husband belongs to his wife instead of to himself. So don't refuse sex to each other, unless you agree not to have sex for a while in order to spend time in prayer. Here is my advice for people who've never been married and for widows. You should stay single, just as I am. If you don't have enough self-control, then go ahead and get married. After all, it's better to be married than to burn with desire. God bless the child that has his own. Don't be messing around in someone else's puddin'," Steve preached.

After services were over, just about every male member of the newly formed congregation approached Steve with a handshake. The women greeted him with holy kisses. He felt better than he'd ever felt in his life. His parents stood proudly, watching and admiring the child they'd raised.

As Detective Bell stood in front of the church after services, Steve approached him with a smile, offered a handshake, welcomed him, and then invited him to come back. The detective made small talk without revealing his identity. He then complimented Steve on his sermon.

A street person, pushing a shopping cart full of cans and bottles, along with other unidentifiable junk, approached Steve and the detective.

"I enjoyed your sermon, Mr. Preacher Man. You're good, and I'll be right here on your steps next Sunday listening to your words," the redheaded woman said as she smiled and then continued pushing her cart slowly down the street. After she'd taken a few steps, Steve and the detective trotted toward her.

"Thank you, ma'am," Steve said once they caught up to her. "I'm glad to hear you enjoyed hearing the Lord's words. I'd be delighted, and so will the Lord, for you to come back on Sunday, but not standing on the steps, ma'am. Please sit in the church among the other members of the congregation." Steve was very earnest.

"God bless you, ma'am, and please come back," Detective Bell said as he reached into his pocket, pulled out a five-dollar bill, and handed it to the woman.

"Thank you, sonny, and God bless you, too," the woman replied, and then continued her journey.

As she walked away, Detective Bell stared hard at her, then took another look at her, wondering if he knew her from somewhere. He quickly dismissed the thought and continued conversing with Big Steve.

As Michelle pushed her shopping cart down the street, she smiled to herself.

Stupid ass detective. They're nothing but a bunch of overpaid, brainless assholes.

About the Author

Samuel was born in Indianola, Mississippi, but raised in Compton, CA. Unexpectedly, Samuel discovered his writing talent in the third grade one day while sitting in class visualizing characters making conversation and gestures while doing various things. Samuel immediately set aside his class-work and began putting his visions into words. Afterwards, while class was still in session, Samuel approached his teacher and handed her what he'd written. His teacher was so amazed by Samuel's creativity that she turned it into the principal. The principal was bewildered, but at the same time, proud to have a third grade student of his school write something so attention-grabbing and perfectly worded. The principal had his secretary run off over 500 copies of Samuel's short story, and then proudly distributed the copies to students as well as staff members.

Samuel enjoys making the big bucks driving big rigs cross-country while dispatching 25 other company drivers. He plans to soon retire from truck driving and become a social worker. That will give him more opportunity to write more books and spend more time at home. Samuel is currently working on his second book, *Marriage Mayhem*, due out in late 2007.

Excerpt of
Marriage Mayhem
by Samuel L. Hair
coming in December 2007

Prologue

"When I first met your sorry-ass, you didn't own a car, didn't have a place of your own to live, and you didn't even have a goddamn plan! Now all of a sudden you know every damn thing!"

"Fuck you, Jermaine! You think you're big shit because you drive a BMW, got a book published, own a few houses, and make lots of money driving trucks, but you ain't nothing but a piece of dog shit! All you do is floss around town in your fancy cars and talk about people who's less fortunate than you! What really pisses me off is that you're always trying to belittle me one way or another. If you knew how to talk to me maybe you could get anything you wanted out of me whenever you want it. I had tricks that treated me better than you. At least they talked to me nice and treated me special. There were times that I drove over a hundred miles just to give a man some head who had talked to me nice over the phone."

"The only reason they talked to you so nice is because they wanted a good, satisfying headjob, but you were too stupid to recognize it. And secondly it's not my fault that you're a welfare recipient and didn't have a car or a job when I met you! Hell, don't hate me for my accomplishments, Karen. If your thinking was right, you can accomplish what you set forth to do, and have nice things, but that's your problem, Karen. Your thinking pattern is all fucked up. All you want out of life is a goddamn welfare check and a place for you and your kids to sleep. Your own sister told me that you've been on welfare, on crack, and a ho for as long as she can remember." He smiled, and then continued.

She tried hard to maintain composure, but his words were about to set her off at any given moment.

"Jewell told me the reason you're always saying or thinking unusual things and carry on like an uncivilized nut is just because you're on some kind of psych meds." He paused to smirk.

"She also told me that you have never, out of all the worthless men you've been with, had a good, responsible, successful man. She said that's the reason you don't know how to treat me. She told me that all the men of your past were either one of your tricks, a crackhead who called himself trying to make money, but y'all were too busy smoking up the product, or a wanna-be thug!" He nodded in disgust.

"That a goddamn shame, Karen. It's unbelievable, but of course, drugs cause people to do disgusting things that a woman would have losers in the presence of her children. What that really tells me, though, is that you have no self-respect, no respect for your kids, and your self-esteem is gutter level." He had wanted to say those things to her a long time ago.

Karen stared at him angrily but silently for a few moments. She then composed herself and approached him, smiling.

"The bed that you bought and sleep in when you're home, I just want you to know that I've been fucking Tyrone, Lester, and big dick Danny in it while you're so goddamn busy making money driving trucks across country. At least I'm being honest about it." Then she smiled and added. "Ump, as big as their dicks are, I'm surprised you couldn't tell when you called yourself fucking me last night." Then she walked away feeling somewhat compensated for the verbal beating he had given her.

"What! I'll kill you, bitch! You had another muthafucka in my house and in my bed while I was working! I'll kill you, Karen!" he yelled, and then stormed toward her.

The kids witnessed the entire episode.

LOOK FOR MORE HOT TITLES FROM
Q-BORO
B O O K S

TALK TO THE HAND - OCTOBER 2006
$14.95
ISBN 0977624765

Nedra Harris, a twenty-three year old business executive, has experienced her share of heartache in her quest to find a soul mate. Just when she's about to give up on love, she runs into Simeon Mathews, a gentleman she met in college years earlier. She remembers his warm smile and charming nature, but soon finds out that Simeon possesses a dark side that will eventually make her life a living hell.

SOMEONE ELSE'S PUDDIN' - DECEMBER 2006
$14.95
ISBN 0977624706

While hairstylist Melody Pullman has no problem keeping clients in her chair, she can't keep her bills paid once her crack-addicted husband Big Steve steps through a revolving door leading in and out of prison. She soon finds what seems to be a sexual and financial solution when she becomes involved with her long-time client's husband, Larry.

THE AFTERMATH
$14.95
ISBN 0977624749

If you thought having a threesome could wreak havoc on a relationship, Monica from My Woman His Wife is back to show you why even the mere thought of a ménage a trios with your spouse and an outsider should never enter your imagination.

THE LAST TEMPTATION - APRIL 2007
$6.99
ISBN 0977733599

The Last Temptation is a multi-layered joy ride through explorations of relationships with Traci Johnson leading the way. She has found the new man of her dreams, the handsome and charming Jordan Styles, and they are anxious to move their relationship to the next level. But unbeknownst to Jordan, someone else is planning Traci's next move: her irresistible ex-boyfriend, Solomon Jackson, who thugged his way back into her heart.

LOOK FOR MORE HOT TITLES FROM
Q-BORO
BOOKS

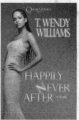